DEVIANT HACKER

MAFIA WARS - BOOK NINE

MAGGIE COLE

PULSE PRESS

PROLOGUE

Declan O'Malley

THERE'S NO HIDING FROM THE TRUTH. IT'S SOMETHING I'VE believed my entire life and still do. Yet, the day I stepped into who I really was and embraced my true O'Malley roots, I learned a hard lesson.

My entire life, my moral compass had been a lie. I was a killer and not just any kind. I could extend a man's life until he was begging me to steal his last breath. Every second of torturing him, I got off on. All I could see is the wrong he had done. I became the judge, jury, and executioner.

There was no going back. Once I started, I couldn't stop. The same holds true now. If a man harms my family, there's no limit to what I will do to avenge his wrongdoing.

Rules and boundaries no longer exist. The deeper I sink into my family's issues, the more I only care about making sure our clan is protected. Any enemy we have, we're clear on, and I'm prepared at all times to take them down.

I never lose sleep over it, except for now. For the first time, I don't know who our enemy is.

Several months have passed since an anonymous reporter has been publishing stories about Jack Christian's company. It went public, and we've been implementing the plan Liam and Finn concocted in prison to bankrupt it. We shorted the stock, so we'll make money when the price drops, but whoever this reporter is, they're intentionally trying to destroy everything we've orchestrated.

I've hacked into every server I can to find out who this guy is that's derailing the billions we planned on making. It leads me nowhere. He's a ghost, and night after night he stays hidden.

I'm tracking every financial news outlet he posts his articles on. The wall of my office is covered in computer screens with real-time data coming in. All I keep doing is digging, trying to find something to lead me to him.

It always led me to more dead ends—until tonight.

It's around three in the morning. One of the screens on the wall beeps, indicating a new article has been uploaded. I trace the location of the guy's IP address.

"Got you!"

I practically run to the wall and peer closer. The location is an apartment building sixteen blocks away. I snap a photo of the location with my phone, and the location disappears.

I have to give this bastard some credit. He knows what he's doing and is a master at covering his tracks. But not this time. I've found him, and he's going to pay for harming my family.

I grab my bag from the garage shelf and get in my SUV.

My heart races the entire time I'm driving. It's dark, pouring down rain, and there's barely any traffic. When I get to the apartment, I switch my tracker on my phone. It'll pinpoint exactly where this guy is from his IP address that I now have.

Blood slams into my skull, and adrenaline pumps harder, racing through my veins. I open my bag and put chloroform on a rag then shove it in my coat pocket. Whoever this guy is, he's going to die by my hands, but not until I torture every last piece of information he has, out of him. I slide my black gloves on and get out of the car.

The apartment complex is in a rough and dangerous neighborhood. The lock to the front door of the building is busted, and I walk right in. There are no security cameras, which only makes my job easier.

I climb three flights of stairs. When I get to the unit, I pick the lock. It's cheap and only takes a few seconds. I slowly turn the knob and creep through the apartment.

It's cold, as if the heat isn't on. Everything is dark like outside, except for one room that has a green glow. I make sure I don't make a noise and peek past the doorframe.

Several computer screens sit on a table. The guy wears a black hoodie. He types quickly. Even from the back of him, I can tell he's smaller than me. I'm not going to have any issue carrying him out of here. I grip the chloroform rag and slide it out of my pocket, along with the cloth bag I brought.

I sneak behind him, put the bag over his head, and cover his mouth with the chloroform.

He attempts to struggle but quickly passes out. His laptop is connected to the screens, so I yank the cords and shove it in my backpack. Then I remove the dark blanket out of my backpack, wrap it around him, and toss his limp body over my shoulder. I leave the building the same way I came, feeling fortunate it's raining so hard and this guy doesn't weigh a ton.

I leave him wrapped in the blanket, put him in my back seat, and am back in my garage within a few minutes.

I've never taken anyone I kidnapped to my house before. But I've stewed over this for months.

My assumption is this isn't our typical enemy. Whoever this guy is, he's smart. He knows things about us, or he wouldn't be doing this. Or, someone is paying him, and that's an entire other scenario that may require just as much interrogation. Plus, he might have some skills I don't. If so, he's going to show me before I kill him.

Night after night, I've obsessed over this guy, wanting to know who he is, why he's messing with my family, and who else may be behind this. He's screwed with the wrong person. And I've prepared for this dickhead. I turned a small part of my basement into a cell. I'll keep him alive for months and torture him daily if needed.

I sling him over my shoulder once again and enter my house. I go down the steps and into the cell. There's a cheap mattress on the ground and a toilet. I installed restraints in the cement block wall. Nothing else exists in this small, dark corner of my basement.

My pulse continues to increase. I lay him on the mattress, unwrap the blanket, and clasp the cuffs around his thin wrists.

Jesus, does this guy eat?

Maybe he's only a teenager?

My stomach flips at the thought, but then I remind myself he's screwing with my family. I take a deep breath, ready to see who this man is who has the balls to try and fuck over the O'Malleys.

I slide the hood off his face and freeze.

Am I seeing things?

My heart beats so fast I clutch it, staring down at a young woman.

Not just any woman.

A lass with the face of an angel. A coed who has been in the pub, sat on my lap, and flirted with me.

She never came back. All these months, I've looked for her, but she never reappeared.

She's innocent.

She can't be. She's intentionally been sabotaging our family.

She stirs, and a small whimper fills the air. I continue to stare, in a trance, fixated on whoever this creature is in front of me, chained to my wall.

Her blue eyes flutter open. When she fully comes to, she recognizes me, and fear registers all over her face. She tries to move her arms and realizes she's trapped. In a desperate move, she tries to kick me in the balls.

My instincts take over. I lunge on top of her, pinning her to the mattress and stopping her from having any ability to move her legs.

It's the wrong move. Heat creeps into her porcelain cheeks, the same way it did when I flirted with her in the pub. A lock of her dark hair falls on her face, and I force myself not to tuck it behind her ear. Her hot breath merges with mine, and I curse myself for getting a hard-on. She glances at my lips then pins her frightened gaze on me once more.

I jump off her, slam the cell door closed, race upstairs, and pour three fingers of whiskey, downing it in three mouthfuls.

Jesus. How can it be her?

I should take her to Liam and have him deal with her.

No. She sought me out at the pub. She's not going anywhere until I find out every single thing about her.

I sit down at the computer. For the rest of the night, I watch her through the cameras I installed earlier this week. It may be dark in the cell, but the system I installed makes it look like the lights are on. I see every move she makes. I wonder who she is and why she came into my pub. If Finn hadn't killed a man and Liam hadn't come to get Killian and me that night, there's no doubt I would have asked her out. I would have refrained from taking her home that evening until I took her on a nice date first.

Did she even tell me her real name?

Several minutes pass, and she looks directly at the camera. Those same damn eyes that got me at the pub register on my screen. I peer closer, mesmerized by her and wondering how I'm going to get the information I need.

She's a woman. I've never hurt any female before.

She's the enemy, I remind myself. But then I think about all the ways I'd get information out of a man. Everything makes me cringe when I consider doing it to her.

By the time morning comes, I'm no less conflicted and there aren't any solutions. My only hope is she'll break easily from the mere suggestion of pain. I avoid thinking about what I'll do if she doesn't.

I'm in over my head. I should call my brothers, Liam, or Finn and have them weigh in on what to do about this situation.

Yet I don't. All I do is continue to stare at my angel-faced enemy.

1

Simona Carter

Simona Carter

THE COLD ISN'T SOMETHING FOREIGN TO ME. MY COLLEGE tuition is so expensive, I cut corners wherever I can. It includes the heat in my run-down apartment. The old windows are so thin, they don't keep the warmth inside, so I learned a long time ago to wear lots of layers and leave the furnace off. Turning it on only results in throwing money in the trash. And I'm barely surviving.

Yet, I can't seem to stop shivering. Wherever I am, it's dark. The chill from the cement floor seems to seep through the mattress I'm lying on, digging right into my spine. I'd hide my freezing fingers in my sweatshirt, but I can't move them.

The only light in the room is a tiny green glow from a corner of the ceiling.

He's watching me.

It's him.

Why did he kidnap me?

Has he been stalking me since that night in the pub?

How else would he know where I live?

What does he want from me?

Months ago, my friend from college, Tonya, made me take a study break and go out. Before we left, we had a few shots. By the time I got to the pub, the alcohol had hit me, giving me a nice buzz.

The moment I walked in, Declan and I locked eyes. It was the most magnetic moment of my life. He didn't hesitate, and within seconds, he asked me my name and bought Tonya and me drinks.

Since I need to get through school and don't have anyone to rely on but me, I don't date. It's not from a lack of offers. I stay away from anything that can deter me from my goals. My time is more valuable working my waitress and cafeteria jobs and studying than getting distracted.

Something about Declan made me lose my inhibitions though. Danger swirled in his blue eyes. He was a stunning specimen of a bad boy. The rolled-up cuffs of his button-down shirt displayed intricate tattoos of red and black ink. Petals and leaves from a red rose weaved through a wheel and peeked out of the top of his shirt. I even dared to move it aside and trace it. They were a work of art, showcasing his ripped flesh.

His face wasn't just gorgeous. It was chiseled perfection with one imperfection that made him human and even more interesting to me. A vein ran from the side of his hair to his eyebrow then curved, stopping at the corner of his blue orbs. Tiny specks of gray mixed into his brown hair, and while I knew he was much older than me and I should stay away, I couldn't.

I had never come across a man like him. I may have done one too many shots and been inebriated, but something about him made me lose any resolve I had.

Earlier in the week, I had gotten my belly button pierced. It was the one thing I did for myself in over three years. The only reason I did it was Tonya got a job doing piercings and offered to do it for free. Since I always wanted one, I let her. Somehow, the topic morphed from his tattoos to my piercing. I was sitting on his lap, about to show it to him, when he got a text and left. He promised he'd be back and told me not to go anywhere, but he never returned.

It was a total buzzkill. When closing time came, I wasn't just drunk. I was hurt and pissed.

I guess I didn't have a right to be, but something about him not returning made me think he probably had a girlfriend or wife at home, and I was just someone to pass the time with. Not that I frequent the bars often, but I promised myself I'd never go into that pub again.

What made it worse is I never forgot him or his woody, spicy scent that was all over my shirt. I couldn't bring myself to wash it. From time to time, I'd smell it just to torture myself. Then I'd reprimand myself for even thinking about him.

Now I'm chained to the wall, lying on a mattress that's so thin, I feel the hard cement on my spine. And I curse myself. Before I realized he had me chained and his prisoner, I knew it was him. The crackling of my skin almost made me dizzy. Then the fuzziness of him and whatever he drugged me with wore off, and my reality became clear.

That was before he pounced on me, caging his hard, warm flesh on top of my body and assaulting me with his delicious scent. The vein near his eye pulsed, flaunting a bittersweet memory of how much I obsessed over his features that were etched in my mind. My mouth watered when his hot breath hit mine, just like in the pub.

Thinking about our brief encounter before he left me alone, makes me wonder what is wrong with me. I curse myself for my loins throbbing for a man who drugged and kidnapped me.

That had to be what happened. If it wasn't, how did I get here, and why can't I remember it?

For hours, my brain spins, trying to figure out why I'm here and how I'm going to escape. I'm still groggy from whatever drug he gave me. My mouth is dry, and I've never craved water so badly. A new shiver digs into my bones. I attempt to pull at my restraints again, but it only hurts my wrists. I whimper in pain, and the situation I'm in claws its way into my emotions.

I don't want to cry, but I can't help it. At some point, it's too exhausting to keep my eyes open any longer. My mind tells me to stay awake so he doesn't hurt me, but I succumb to my heavy lids.

When I wake up, my body is stiff. The cold only seems to have grown worse, and the green light continues to mock me. It could be the same night or the next day. Everything looks the same as when I fell asleep—a deep, seemingly endless blackness.

The longer I'm alone, the more I contemplate if days have passed. My fingers are so cold, I'm scared I might have frost-bite. My teeth chatter. Panic takes hold. I need to figure out a way to make him release me from the restraints if I stand any chance of escaping. I manage to find my voice and yell, "Stop being a coward and come face me!"

Anxiety builds in my chest. He's probably going to hurt me, but I keep screaming the same thing as well as, "Help!"

My voice turns hoarse. I kick my legs, but it only results in pain shooting through my feet. My fear gets the best of me, and I sob so hard, I struggle to breathe.

The darkness continues to surround me, broken only by the green light of the camera. Once again, I fall asleep, but it isn't restful. When I wake up, my neck, shoulders, and arms hurt. My butt and spine feel like there's nothing between me and the concrete. Tingles painfully poke my limbs.

Why am I here?

Why hasn't he come back?

How could I have been so dumb to give a psycho any attention?

"I need to go to the bathroom," I try to yell, but my voice is nearly gone. I repeat it several times, but it's as low as if I were in a conversation with someone.

I cross my legs, trying to hold it, not wanting to lie in a pool of my bodily fluids.

The door opens, and a dull light floods the room. I blink as my eyes adjust to it. Declan steps through the doorway, and new chills consume me.

His frame looks more prominent than I remember. His T-shirt is fitted, showcasing every hard inch of his muscular frame. It frightens me further. He could overpower and break me without even trying.

"I'm going to unchain you so you can use the bathroom. If you try anything, it'll be the last time I let you use the toilet," his deep, commanding voice warns.

He's going to release me.

How do I get away from him?

He steps closer, and his spicy, woody scent fills the damp air. He puts his warm hand over mine, and I start crying.

It's the nicest thing I've ever felt, yet mentally, I'm aware it's not.

He freezes, takes a deep breath, then unlocks the cuff. Instead of letting my hand go, he encloses it with both palms, then blows hot air between them.

I close my eyes, telling myself to make him stop but wanting him to keep warming me up. When he releases my hand, I hate myself. I want to beg him to hold it again.

He straddles me then uncuffs my other wrist, doing the same thing with his palms and breath. His body heat penetrates me, ironically sending more chills coursing through my veins.

"Please," I whisper, unsure what I'm saying or even asking him. If I don't use the toilet, I'm going to have an accident. Yet, the thought of him taking his warm body off mine is torture.

He slides off me, tugs me off the bed, then guides me to the corner of the room, next to the mattress.

"Please. I need the toilet," I beg.

"Right there." He motions.

I glance behind me and see the faint outline of a toilet. He's not letting me out of this room. Am I going to be stuck here forever?

I think it can't get any worse, but he crosses his arms. "Well, do you have to go or not?"

"I...yes."

"What are you waiting for?"

"I-I...aren't you going to leave?"

His face hardens. "No."

"Why?" I ask in a shaky voice.

He reaches for me. I jump back, running into the toilet and falling on the seat. He crouches in front of me and fists my hair.

Adrenaline spikes in my cells. I gasp, and he leans so close, I can taste his breath. "You haven't earned the right."

I swallow hard, unsure what that means or if I want to know. My bladder reminds me I'm two seconds shy of needing a diaper. "I-I have to go!"

He releases me and steps back. I slide my pants to my ankles, making it just in time. I stare at the ground, trying to avoid his gaze, but I can't escape the feeling of his eyes on me.

Embarrassed, I find the toilet paper, finish, then flush. I rise. Determined not to show him any weakness, I hold my chin high. "Where is the sink?"

"Hold your hands out."

"Why?"

He lunges toward me, and I step back until I'm against the wall. My pulse races so fast, I get dizzy. His heart beats hard into my shoulder, and he forces my chin up.

I place my hands on his chest.

His mouth moves inches in front of mine. "Let's get something straight. When I order you to do something, you don't ask questions."

My lips tremble harder. His chiseled face becomes blurry from my tears. I've never felt like I had a home. I bounced around from one foster home to the next, and nowhere has ever felt safe. My apartment is full of cockroaches, many undesirable tenants who scare me, and thin walls. I suddenly miss it and would do anything to be inside it. I choke out, "Please let me go home."

He drags his finger down my cheek. Tingles burst on my skin from his touch. I detest myself for reacting to him and remind myself he's my captor, not the man I assumed he was the night we met. Yet, I close my eyes and lean into his touch.

He places his forearms against the wall. His lips hit my ear. "Is your name even Simona?"

Stunned, I stay silent. Why is he questioning my name, or how does he not know it's real if he's been stalking me?

He doesn't move, staying pinned against my shuddering body. His chest pushes into mine, and his erection twitches against my stomach, sending a zing straight to my core.

His tongue swipes my lobe before he speaks. "Answer me. And if you lie, there will be consequences."

My body quivers from the contrast of his warm frame and the cold chill in my bones. It mixes with the desire I can't seem to shake for him, along with my fear. I answer, "My name is Simona."

He inhales deeply, as if smelling me. His nose brushes against the back of my ear. "What's your last name?"

"Carter."

His knuckles travel down the side of my body, and I squirm. "Tell me, Simona Carter. What did you think you would accomplish by coming into my pub? Hmm?"

I blurt out, "It was a night out. I'm-I'm sorry. I won't ever go again. Please let me go home."

He slowly enunciates, "Who sent you?"

Why is he asking me this?

"No one," I quickly respond.

He draws his face away from my ear and lifts his head so he's staring at the wall above me. I glance up, and the vein around his eye pulses. He sniffs hard and pins his scowl on me. In a rough voice, he interrogates, "So you came to the pub on your own. No one forced you?"

In confusion, I ask, "Forced me?"

"Paid you to go? Offered you anything in exchange? Held a gun to your head?"

"No. Of course not!"

He swallows hard and more anger builds in his face. "What did you think you would accomplish that night?"

I gape at him, no words coming to my mind about how to answer his strange question.

Blue flames burn so hot in his eyes, they could ignite me on fire, and I cringe. He seethes, "What was the plan, Simona? Did you think you would sleep with me and get in my head?"

I inhale sharply.

He misinterprets my reaction. Disgust and betrayal fill his expression. "That's what I thought." Before I can deny anything, he grabs my hands, squirts sanitizer on them, and orders, "Rub until it's gone."

I obey and admit, "I don't understand why you have me."

"Lie back down." He points to the mattress.

The notion of being left alone in this dark, damp room again makes my heart squeeze. "No! Please!"

He picks me up then sets me on the thin bed, lunging over me and quickly securing my wrists. I grasp his fingers, and he freezes.

"Don't leave me in here. Please! I-I-I'm so confused!" I cry out.

For a split second, I think he'll let me go. What appears to be guilt and sympathy cross his face. But it's gone as fast as it arrives. "If you want out, you're going to have to earn your way out."

My voice cracks. "How?"

He studies my face, glancing at my lips, then back to my orbs.

"Tell me! I'll do whatever you want. Please! Don't leave me in here!" I plead.

He pauses then pushes back, but I weave my legs around his thighs and hold them as tight as I can, trying to stop him from leaving.

"Don't go!"

It makes no sense. He captured me. I'm convinced he wants to hurt me, but I'd rather have him physically create pain than be left alone in this room.

His chest rises and falls faster. He scoops his arms under my body, and things I shouldn't be feeling assault me. I mold against him. His erection pushes on my pussy, hardening and competing with the concrete I might as well be lying directly on. His intoxicating lips brush mine as he says, "Let's get something straight, Simona Carter. You won't ever play games with me again. And I'm going to break you, inch by inch, until you tell me every detail about how you know what you do and why you decided to come after my family."

"What? I don't—"

He puts his hand over my mouth. "Listen to me closely. There won't be another warning. The next time you attempt to use your body to trick me into getting what you want, I won't stop you. But know this, you won't be getting what you want after I'm through with you."

My insides quiver harder. I blink hard, but tears soak his hand.

"Tears won't save you. I suggest you come to terms with the fact that this is your new life. It's you and me. When I ask a question, you answer. Honestly. If you lie, there will be consequences. You can either earn your way out of this cell and into somewhere more comfortable, or you can rot here." He removes his hand.

"Tell me what you want to know. I'll tell you! Please! Just don't leave me here."

He tilts his head and slowly opens and closes his eyes, sighing. He strokes my hair. "Now, what fun would that be if you didn't have time to think about what you've done?"

"I don't know what I've done!" I admit.

"Wrong answer!" he barks.

I jerk my head back, but there's nowhere to go. My body trembles underneath him, but I pretzel my legs around his thighs tighter, desperate for him to not leave me here.

He seethes, "Release your legs from me now, unless you want me to take this a step further."

I must be as crazy as he is. Nothing seems worse than staying in this cell on my own. And he's so warm compared to the chill I can't escape. Without thinking, I beg again, "Don't go."

In a stern voice, he snaps, "Last warning."

I pick my head up and claim, "No! I'm not staying here—"

His mouth covers my lips. It's hot and aggressive, and his tongue ravishes mine, destroying my ability to reason or do anything but kiss him back. It's nothing like any other kiss I've ever had. It's savage, as if he could destroy me with his tongue alone. His arms tighten around me, encasing me with his flesh, killing the chill in my bones and replacing it with a bubbling heat.

I shift my hips against his erection and whimper in his mouth. He pulls away with crazed eyes, out of breath, and the vein near his eye pulsing.

I freeze, hating myself for enjoying his mouth and body on mine while wanting more.

He pushes off me, reaches for something, and holds a bottle of water to my mouth. "Drink."

I obey, swallowing fast to get as much as I can, happy to have a distraction from what just happened.

He caps the bottle and pushes out of my legs, still wrapped around his thighs. He rises and glares down at me. "When I come back, you better be ready to answer my questions."

The door shuts and darkness envelops me again. I scream for him to return, but he doesn't. The only thing that calms me is taking deep breaths of his lingering scent. As soon as I regulate my heartbeat, the chills take over again. I wonder what he thinks I know or why he believes I'm out to hurt his family. Before the pub, I never met him. I didn't even know he existed. The only other person I am aware of who is related to him is his brother, Killian. He was there that night, and Declan introduced us. I don't even know their last name.

Time passes, and I pull on my restraints only to create agony in my arm. Anxiety builds in my chest so much, I get heart pains. The loneliness and fear set in. I focus on the green light, screaming, "Declan!" over and over, thrashing on the mattress and hurting my legs, but he never comes.

Before I fall asleep, the hysteria dies slightly. Shame fills my soul. He kidnapped me, and I'm desperately begging for him. I took every morsel of what he gave me in his kiss and responded with more enthusiasm than to any other one I've ever had. I contemplate if wanting him is worse than if I die in this room, and decide it is. I resolve not to let him touch me ever again.

I only wish I could kill the itch I have for him to come back into the room and do it all over again.

2

Declan

Why did I kiss her?

What was I thinking?

It's been almost a day since I was in the basement and her lips were on mine. Mesmerized, I stare at the screen and listen to her scream my name, thrashing around the mattress. She does it every few hours when she's awake.

She was so cold.

Why's a young woman like her trying to mess with the O'Malleys?

I'm so engrossed with studying her, I don't hear Nolan come in the room until he barks, "Who is that?"

My gut does a nosedive, and I spin in my chair. "I found our problem."

He points at the screen. "Why is she chained to a wall? And tell me that isn't your basement."

I lick my lips and stare at him.

"Declan! What the fuck are you doing?"

"Finding out everything I can. She knew about what we were doing. I want to know how and why she targeted us," I claim.

He grinds his molars. "She needs to go to the warehouse."

"She isn't leaving my house. And you're going to shut your mouth about this."

He furrows his eyebrows and huffs. "You think I'm going to broadcast it?"

"It was my job to find out who was behind the articles. Now that I have, it's my business to interrogate her. This stays between you and me."

His face hardens. "Since when do we keep things from Killian?"

"He's going on his honeymoon. Tell him after," I say, trying to buy some time before Killian comes over, too.

Nolan points in my face. "If Liam and Finn find out you've got this girl and didn't tell them—"

"But they aren't going to find out until I tell them, are they?" I arch my eyebrows and slap his finger out of the way.

Nolan takes a slow, controlled breath. "This isn't—"

"Finn has enough on his plate trying to locate Brenna. And Liam is dealing with all the other O'Malley issues. This stays between us for now," I reiterate.

"Declan!" Simona cries out and thrashes her lower body on the mattress again before sobbing.

I wince inside then remind myself she's the enemy.

Nolan steps closer to the screen. "Who is she?"

My gut takes another dive. How could she have come into the pub and I had no clue she was using me? And then I looked for her over the last few months whenever I went back there. How big of a sucker am I?

And now I kissed her and fell right into her seduction again. She knows I'm into her and didn't even seem upset by my kiss.

Jesus. I need to get a grip.

"Declan! Who is she?" Nolan repeats.

As much as I don't want to admit it, I do. "She came into the pub a few months ago. It was the night Finn killed Eric Baskin."

"Is she connected to him?" Nolan frets.

"No. Yes. I don't know." Eric was a hedge fund trader who set up dozens of our offshore accounts and positioned us to profit from the fall of Jack's company. The night he killed him, Finn found out Eric put our accounts in his name.

Nolan runs his hand through his hair, never taking his eyes off the screen. "What do you know about her?"

"Her name's Simona Carter. The night I met her, she told me she was a student at the Illinois Institute of Technology. Last night, I traced her IP address when she uploaded a new article to several financial sites. I picked her up in a shitty apartment building on the South side."

"She posted another one?" Nolan asks.

"Don't worry, I took the article down before it got posted."

Nolan studies her further. "She's gotta be pretty smart if she got into the Illinois Institute of Technology."

More intelligent than any man or woman I've ever met.

Too sexy for her own good.

And once again, I need to remember she's the enemy.

I keep my thoughts to myself and reply, "If it's true. I just found out her last name. I'll hack into the school and see if she's registered. Regardless, she's one of the most brilliant hackers I've ever come across."

Nolan assesses me then the screen. He turns and leaves the room, moving toward the basement door.

I quickly circumvent him and stand against the wood. "What are you doing?"

"She looks pretty desperate on that screen. Let's talk to her, find out whatever it is we can, then you're getting her out of your house," he orders.

I cross my arms. "No. I'll handle the interrogation. And she's staying here."

He gives me a knowing look. "What happened at the pub?"

I tell a half-truth. "Nothing. I left to help clean up Finn's mess."

"Jesus. You fucked her, didn't you?"

"No. But if I did, it wouldn't matter," I claim.

"Bullshit."

"What does that mean?" I bark.

Nolan grunts. "You can't screw a woman without making her breakfast the next day and going into the friend zone when you're finished with her."

I huff. "Just because I know how to treat a woman whether they're in or out of my bed doesn't mean I wouldn't be able to step away from a situation. Especially if the woman I had sex with revealed she was my enemy."

He gives me a look as if he doesn't believe me.

"It doesn't matter what you think. I didn't sleep with her," I reiterate. I don't add that I kissed her and did the impossible when I ripped myself away from her.

"You're making a bad judgment call," Nolan warns.

"No. I'm putting her in a position where she has no other option but to tell me the full truth. Now, is there a reason you came over?" I inquire.

He sighs. "Have you talked to Finn?"

"It's been a week or so. Why?"

He shifts on his feet. "Maksim thinks he's spinning out."

The hairs on my arms rise. Finn stayed with me for about a week after he murdered Eric. One day I came home, and he was gone. He returned to living in hotels, refusing to stay with any of us. Before prison, he and I were the closest.

Maksim was his best friend. Now, I'd say he and Liam are closer from spending fifteen years together in prison. I ask, "Why does Maksim think that?"

"Finn got back from Philly and met Maksim for a drink. It was more dead ends. He told Maksim he's starting to think he'll never find Brenna. Then he started a bar fight with a man who looked at him the wrong way."

"That's not like him."

"No, it's not. Maksim said if he weren't there, Finn would have killed the guy."

I scrub my hands over my face. "I'll talk to him. See what I can find out. Does Liam know?"

Nolan shakes his head. "Not yet."

"Okay. Keep it between us for now. Let me feel him out."

"All right. Now, why don't you step aside and we can find out what we need from this woman? She can't stay here, and you know it," Nolan claims.

I grunt. "She's not going anywhere. I appreciate your concern, but I have this under control. I'll let you know what she tells me."

Nolan sniffs hard. "You're making a horrible mistake."

"Thanks for your concern, little brother. If there's nothing else you need to discuss, feel free to show yourself to the door. And forget she's here until I'm ready to tell the others."

He scowls. "This is going to bite you in the ass."

I point in the direction of the front door. "Time to leave."

He grumbles as he exits, "Never pegged you for the stupid one."

I sigh in relief, lock my doors, and put on the alarm so no one can enter without me knowing. Liam, Finn, Nora, and my brothers all have keys to my house. I return to the screen. Simona's tear-filled eyes stare at me as if she can see me. Her lips tremble harder than they have been.

She's going to be frozen again.

She hasn't eaten, either.

Guilt eats at me, but starving and freezing her are part of breaking her. I go into the kitchen, make a bowl of tomato soup and a grilled cheese sandwich. I put it on a tray with a spoon, napkin, and hot tea. On my way to the basement, the blanket on the back of my couch catches my eye. I debate for a moment then drape it over my forearm.

As I'm climbing down the steps, the damp, musty basement hits me like a brick wall. More guilt floods me about what I'm doing to her.

She's not innocent, I remind myself for the millionth time.

When I get to her cell, I take a few deep breaths and tell my dick to behave. I open the door and turn on the light.

She gasps and blinks her eyes hard a few times while adjusting to the fluorescent lights. I hate everything about those kinds of bulbs, but it's another way I decided to make her feel desperate enough not to withhold any information from me.

Abhorrence resurfaces when I see her purple lips. It's the first time I've seen her in the light since the pub. Her body is shaking and her teeth are chattering. Her blue eyes pop against her black hair just like the night I met her, except now there's only anxiety, fear, and a sense of desperation in them. The warmth and laughter from the pub are mere memories.

What am I doing?

Stay the course.

I set the tray and blanket on the ground and look down at her. "Are you ready to be a good girl?"

To my surprise, she glares at me. I'm unsure why I expected anything else, but it cuts me like a knife. I dismiss it and taunt, "Ah. I see you're in the pissed-off phase."

She looks toward the other wall, and a tear falls down her cheek.

Oh, my little angel. I'm going to break you and make you mine.

What the fuck am I thinking? She can't be mine. She's an enemy.

I kneel on the mattress and move her chin so she's facing me. It's cold like it's been in the freezer. I demand, "When I'm in the room, you look at me."

"I hate you," she whispers.

I lean closer so I'm an inch from her mouth. I glance at her purple, trembling lips. "That's funny. The way you kissed, wrapped your legs around me, then pushed your hot little pussy against my cock, I'd say it's anything but hate, angel. More like desperate need."

Her porcelain cheeks flush, and my dick reactivates. She tries to avoid me again, but I hold her so she can't.

Unable to stop myself, I take my knuckles and brush them against her cheeks. "Yeah. That's what you want, isn't it? My body inside yours?"

Her blush turns crimson. She takes a shaky breath. Heat erupts in her blue orbs.

It's all I need to continue. Her reaction to me is a domino falling, and now I can't stop myself. It's a chain reaction and goes against any moral code I have left. I stroke my thumb over her shivering lips. She inhales sharply and writhes next to me. "Maybe you want my cock in your mouth, lass? Hmm?"

The devil already has his place in hell for me, but if I haven't already solidified it, I have now.

I expect her to throw daggers with a look. Hell, I want her to hate me so I stop myself from falling into this trap I can see but can't seem to stop from entering. Instead, her eyes grow heavy, and she licks her lips, softly swiping the pad of my thumb with her tongue.

It takes away all my resolve not to have her. Regardless of how we got here, there's no denying we have chemistry.

Testosterone races in my veins, and I make a new decision. I'm going to have her. She's going to beg me, and when she does, I'm going to enjoy every minute of what her young, barely used body can do with mine. She wanted to fuck with me and mess with my head. So I'm going to do the same to her. It's vigilante justice, I tell myself.

First, I need to break her.

To remind her what I can offer her, I lean into her ear and tease her lobe with my tongue. It's cold, like the rest of her body. She whimpers, and I keep my eyes on her face, murmuring, "I'm going to unlock your cuffs. Unless you want me to keep you restrained while I lick and suck that throbbing pussy of yours?"

Her eyes close, and her breath labors.

"Is that what you want, angel?"

She doesn't reply, but her struggle is all over her expression. Her breasts rise and fall faster, as if to tease me further. And she wants to hate me and tell me she doesn't want me.

But she does.

She can't.

Blood rushes into my head, making me feel off-balance. I straddle her, unlock the cuffs, and look down at her. "Time to eat. If you're a good girl, I'll leave the blanket with you."

Confusion takes over her face and she glances at the floor. It's like watching Pavlov's dogs hear the bell. Hope floods her expression, and she swallows hard, trying to stop more tears.

I slide off her and sit on the mattress, which might as well be a piece of paper. The cold from the concrete penetrates my ass. I swoop her up and place her on my lap.

She attempts to push herself off me, but I tighten my arms around her and hold her wrists with one of my hands. I command, "Stop moving."

She tries harder, but I overpower her. She's not as strong as I am, and the cold and lack of food have weakened her.

I reach for the blanket and hold it in front of her. "If you stop moving, I'll wrap this around you."

She glances at it, fighting her ego that's telling her not to let me help her and the promise of warmth the blanket holds.

"Promise to stay still, and I'll put this around you while you eat."

Her eyes dart between the tray and the blanket.

I brush my lips against her cheek. I lower my voice. "It's warm. Don't you want to warm up?"

She shuts her eyes and scrunches her face. Her body relaxes, so I release her wrists.

I push her head into my chest. "Be a good girl and promise."

Her body continues to shiver, and I wait. She stays silent.

I could put the blanket on her, and I'm pretty sure she won't fight me, but she's going to understand I'm in charge. "If you don't promise me, I'm taking the food and blanket out of here. Then I'm chaining you to the wall, turning the lights off, and not coming back for at least another day. Is that what you want?"

Hot tears soak my T-shirt. I fight with myself to just put the blanket over her, but my inner demon won't allow me to.

"Three. Two. One." I fist her hair and make her look at me. "You've made your choice."

Her face crumples. "No. Please! I promise!"

Since it took her so long to behave, I reiterate I'm in charge. "Say it again."

She squeezes her eyes shut and whispers, "I promise."

"Open your eyes."

She slowly obeys, and my heart cracks. There's so much pain in them.

"Good girls get rewarded. Bad, disobedient girls get punished. Decide which one you want to be."

She swallows hard then blurts out, "Are you going to kill me?"

It's a question I should answer yes to. She has screwed with my family. The fact I can't confirm is the exact reason I should turn her over to Liam. Then everyone else can decide her fate. Before I have time to analyze the best response, my answer rolls out of my mouth. "No. I'm going to keep you."

A tepid breath flies past her lips. I'm unsure if she's relieved or not. I unfold the blanket and secure it around her, binding her hands inside it. I turn her on my lap then pick up the tray and set it on the mattress. I circle my arm tightly around her, hold the cup of soup, and place a spoonful near her mouth.

She keeps her lips sealed and turns away.

I brush the hair off her neck with my nose and murmur, "You need to eat."

Her voice cracks. "I can feed myself."

I lick the back of her ear, and she squirms on my lap, making my erection twitch. I heckle her again. "I haven't heard you tell me to stop or not to touch you. Why is that?"

She avoids my question and, in a firmer tone, says, "I can feed myself."

"That isn't happening."

"Why?"

I put the cup and spoon down then turn her into me. "I've already told you not to question me. Now, I'm going to pick the spoon up, and you're going to open your mouth."

Defiance fills her eyes. "I'm not hungry."

"You *will* eat."

"No. I won't," she claims.

Anger flares through my bones. It's been way too long since she had food, and she shouldn't be defying me. I threaten, "You eat now, or I'll put you in a straitjacket and force-feed you. Choose."

She lifts her chin. Her eyes, full of betrayal, drill into mine. In a hurt voice, she admits, "I knew you were dangerous, but I didn't peg you as someone who would be cruel to me."

My heart almost splits in two. I ignore the burning in my chest and reply, "Is that why you thought you could use me?"

"I don't know why you keep saying that! I never thought about using you! I-I liked you." Her face turns red again, and she looks away.

She sounds so convincing. I almost believe her. But it's because I want to, so I force myself to remember who she is and why she's here.

"You should never underestimate me. This is your last warning." I pick up the grilled cheese and hold it next to her mouth. "Eat."

She turns as if she's going to obey then glares at me. Right as her stomach growls, she seethes, "You eat it."

The rage in my chest builds. If she were a man, I'd hold her mouth open and shove it down her throat. But she isn't. It's another warning bell ringing in my head about why I shouldn't have her here. She's my prisoner. I'm the one calling the shots, not her. Hesitating for even a second shows her my weakness.

Instead of acting out my threat, I create a new reality. I slide the tray on the floor, tear the blanket off her, then spin her on her back. The moment she hits the mattress, I lunge over her and cuff her one wrist. I snarl, "You want to feed yourself? Fine. Feed yourself."

Her eyes widen.

I toss the blanket on the ground so she can see it but can't reach it. I push the tray an inch past where her unrestrained arm will reach. I pull out my pocket knife.

"Wh-what are you doing?" she sobs.

I straddle her. "Don't move, or you'll get cut." In an upward movement, I slice through her three sweatshirts and then the long sleeve T-shirt, tearing them off her restrained arm then pulling them off her other. I throw them past the blanket, then remove her pants, shoes, and socks.

"Stop! I'll freeze!" she cries out.

After she's in only her panties and bra, I rise. "You should learn to be grateful. There are only two options here. Good girl or bad girl. Reward or punishment. I told you earlier, take your pick."

3

Simona

GNAWING HUNGER EATS AT MY GUT. I'VE NEVER FELT SO COLD or helpless. The tray is so close, yet I can't reach it. I attempted to get it with my foot, but the tea spilled all over the grilled cheese and only pushed it farther away.

Why didn't I let him feed me?

Why did he say I wanted to use him?

Exhaustion sets in, but the fluorescent lights are on, buzzing in my ears. My entire body hurts from the inside out. I finally give up trying to get the food.

The green light is on. As much as I hated the dark, I'm starting to wish Declan would have turned the lights off. The buzzing only seems to get louder. My throat feels dry and raw, which I assume is from all the screaming I did earlier.

I'm out of tears. I curl up on my side, trying to get some warmth, but I'm just too cold. I drift in and out of sleep, never knowing how many hours have passed. My body won't stop convulsing. Every time I wake up, confusion about where I am and why sets in. When the door finally opens, I'm so cold, my body feels numb, and I think I might die. I hear sounds, but I don't move to look.

Declan sits next to me, my back to him. His large, warm palm presses against my spine. It should feel good, but it doesn't. A stinging sensation erupts on my skin under his hand, and a low wail escapes my mouth.

"Are you ready to be a good girl?" Declan asks, but it seems like he's screaming through a tunnel.

I try to put words together. "Gooo... gooood..." I take a few breaths and blink, refocusing on the wall, but it's blurry.

Declan turns me over and my eyes roll. He growls, "Shit!"

He unlocks my cuff, picks me up, and everything becomes blurrier. He carries me somewhere, but I'm not sure where we're going. My body continues to shiver, and I move between moments of consciousness and blacking out.

When I finally wake up and can focus, I'm in a bathroom. There's a soft light, and it takes me a few minutes to realize I'm in the bathtub. Declan's arms and legs are pretzeled around me.

I should push him away, but I don't. The cold has escaped. He's warm and feels safe even though I know he's not, but there's no more fight left in me.

"You okay?" he asks.

I take several deep breaths then slowly glance behind me. The hatred in his eyes is gone, replaced by concern and protectiveness. His vein pulses.

Don't fall for it, I tell myself. He's out to hurt me. He has crazy ideas that I don't even understand. I need to erase whatever attraction I felt for him and figure out how to get out of here alive.

He tucks a lock of my hair behind my ear. When I don't answer, he states, "You aren't shaking anymore."

Anger fills me. "I guess that's what happens when you leave a naked woman in a damp, cold basement. But you got what you wanted. Did you enjoy punishing me?"

Guilt flickers across his face but quickly leaves. His expression hardens. "I told you to choose, Simona."

Tears prick my eyes, and I turn away from him, sarcastically laughing, then wiggle out of his grasp to wipe my face.

He tugs me back into him. I'm too weak to fight. I sink into his warm flesh, wishing he was normal and not a complete psychopath who will probably kill me.

His lips brush against my cheek. "It doesn't have to be like this."

I shut my eyes and whisper, "What do you want from me?"

"Not tonight. You need food and rest."

My lips tremble again. I beg, "Please give me clothes. I-I can't take the cold any longer."

"If you're a good girl, I promise you won't be cold tonight."

Relief fills me, though it shouldn't. He could be lying, and I'm just going to return to freezing again. Yet, I hold on to his promise, willing to do anything he wants not to have the chills eat at my bones. I rest my head against his chest and close my eyes, pretending for a brief few moments I'm not his prisoner and I'm here willingly.

How could I have thought about him for all these months and not known he was out to hurt me?

Why does it feel so good to lie against his naked flesh?

My eyelids fly open, and panic beats hard in my chest. How did I not realize we're both naked? I attempt to move my hands, but he continues embracing me. The oxygen becomes stale in my lungs, and my breathing turns ragged.

"What's wrong?" he asks.

What a loaded question. Where would I even begin? I could have died in that basement cell. And I promised myself the next time he touched me, I wouldn't allow my physical reaction to him to cloud my judgment. I manage to choke out, "Let me out."

"Be a good girl and relax a few more minutes. You had all the signs of hypothermia and only stopped trembling a moment ago," he orders.

I cringe, fighting my instinct to give him a piece of my mind and not wanting to disobey him and return to the horror of freezing to death. I mumble, "Whose fault is that?"

He drags his finger across my forehead, and tingles flare under his touch. He tucks a lock of my hair behind my ear and mutters so low, I barely hear him, "I wish things were different between us."

"The feeling is mutual," I blurt out in a whisper. Never in my life have I ever wanted anything so badly. New tears well, and I melt further into his hard frame, loathing my inability to stop finding comfort in him.

For years, I kept my focus on my goals and just surviving. One night of letting loose, and now I'm paying for it. Disgust fills me that I was stupid enough to think about him all these months. On several occasions, I had to stop myself from going back into the pub to see if I had it wrong. I kept thinking maybe something happened and he didn't have a girlfriend or wife at home.

I was playing with fire just by fantasizing about him. Yes, he was a couple decades older than me and would be a distraction. But the itch wouldn't go away, and I still refrained from attempting to find him. Now, I'm at his mercy.

He seems to hate me, and I can't figure out why. Every time he accuses me of something, it only perplexes me more.

"What's your favorite food?" he asks, surprising me again. His demeanor and tone are like the night at the pub. I'm starting to wonder if he's a real-life Jekyll and Hyde. I remind myself not to fall for his nice act and stay silent.

His chest fills with air, pushing into my spine. "Honest answers get you a reward. Let me guess. Sushi?"

Not wanting to appear too eager but also preferring a reward over a punishment, I admit, "I've never had it."

Shock fills his voice. "Really? Don't all college students regularly dine on sushi?"

I snort. "Yeah, the ones with money."

"Ah. So is it ramen noodles and peanut butter sandwiches for you?"

I turn my head and glare at him. In an angry tone, I confess, "I'm allergic to peanuts. Try not to force it down my throat when you put me in a straitjacket, unless you want to kill me."

His lips twitch.

"Glad you find this funny," I snap.

His face falls. "Actually, I don't. And stop fighting me when I tell you to do something. It'll make life for both of us a lot easier."

I shake my head and focus on the ceiling. His life? He's holding me prisoner and is worried about his life not being hard?

"Are you allergic to anything else?"

I sigh. "No. Only peanuts."

His hot breath hits my ear, and I curse myself when I involuntarily shiver from the delicious zing running down my spine. He murmurs, "I promise I won't feed you any peanuts."

And we're back to him acting like we're dating and gives a crap about me.

I close my eyes, staying silent, wishing again he were my boyfriend and not my captor. There's never been anyone, boy or man, who I've immersed myself in, but my gut tells me if he was like this all the time, I could with him.

If only he weren't a raving lunatic.

His hand drops to the side of my thigh. He caresses it with his thumb, and a buzz rushes straight to my pussy. I do everything in my power not to turn over and kiss him. I should push his hand off me, but I don't. I can't seem to move. He questions, "So if it isn't sushi, what is it?"

The image of him taking me right here in this tub makes my insides quiver. I don't doubt if I turned over, he'd make me his in an instant. His erection digging into my lower back isn't helping matters. In order to not do anything that could develop into that, I answer, "Spaghetti with marinara sauce."

"What about meatballs?"

I huff. "Once again, you seem to think I have money to buy expensive food."

His hand turns into a fist on my thigh and he strokes me with his knuckles. The sensations that hit me are so intense, I get dizzy and am grateful I'm resting against him.

He asks, "But you like meatballs?"

I shrug. "Sure. Who doesn't?"

"What about garlic bread?"

My stomach growls, and the gnawing hunger from earlier returns. I've gone without food for extended periods of time, but I assume it's never been this long. I turn my head and inquire, "How long have I been with you?"

Hardness swirls into kindness. It's the most polar thing I've ever seen. "Long enough you need to eat." He glances at my lips, and heat flushes my cheeks. I quickly turn away.

He moves me forward, gets out of the tub, then takes a few steps to remove a towel off the rack and wrap it around his body. My heart stammers. The back of his body is perfectly sculpted flesh. His full arm sleeve tattoo of roses, a compass, and abstract art is stunning. His other arm is only half covered, with similar details. He spins, revealing a skeleton on the side of his torso.

I gape at him, and shame fills me when I realize I'm staring. His arrogant expression tells me he's fully aware of my attraction to him. It's another blow to my already-fragile ego.

He holds a towel out.

"Just set it on the ledge. I'll get out when you leave," I state.

His blue eyes drill into mine. "No." He sets the towel down, reaches into the water, and pulls me to my feet. He lifts me out of the tub and sets me next to him.

I gasp. My insides quiver so hard, I reach for his arm to steady myself.

He takes the towel and diligently dries every inch of my body. Paralyzed, I hold my breath. When he finishes, he secures it around me.

"Do you want to brush your teeth?"

I nod.

He motions to the sink. There's a new toothbrush and mouthwash. A hairbrush sits next to it. I stare in the mirror for a moment in horror at my messy locks then reprimand myself. It doesn't matter what I look like. He's not my boyfriend.

Declan doesn't leave, watching my every move as I swish with mouthwash and brush my teeth and hair. When I finish, he spins me into him.

I stare at his chest, only inches away, wishing he would return to being an ass. His attention toward me is distracting me from the truth. My desire for this man I thought was someone else needs to wither and die. Quickly.

He swoops down, picks me up, and a combination of feelings I don't want to feel toward him, along with panic, besieges every atom I have. Before I can figure out what is happening, he carries me out of the bathroom, lifts the covers on his bed, and sets me on my knees. He removes my towel, and his eyes trail over my body. Blue fire blazes from his orbs when he finally pins his smoldering gaze on mine. "Get under the covers."

Bare of anything I have left, I open my mouth to speak, but nothing comes out. The bed is the most luxurious thing I've ever knelt on. The sheets are soft, the blankets are warm, and it confuses me.

He's not taking me to my cell?

Is this to torment me before he makes me go back down there?

My pulse pounds in my veins. Unable to make my limbs budge, he gently slides me under the blankets until my head is on a pillow. It smells like him, and I sink into it. He strokes my cheek as if I'm his. "Get some rest. I'll wake you up when dinner is ready."

I don't reply, still not understanding why he's not taking me back to my cell. Part of me is too scared to talk. I want to thank him for letting me stay in his bed, but my brain screams not to. I shouldn't show gratitude for anything when he kidnapped me.

He hesitates then spins and walks into his closet. When he comes out, he's in shorts and a T-shirt. He glances at me then turns out the lights and shuts the door.

I take deep breaths, attempting to calm my pulsing body and racing heart while snuggling deeper into the warm cocoon. My mind races about everything—the kidnapping I don't remember, the cold cell I want to forget, except for Declan's hot kiss, which only makes me feel more guilty, and his body pretzeled around mine while he acted like he cared about me. And now I'm in his bed, smelling him, wishing he were next to me, and detesting everything about myself.

As much as I want to sleep, I don't. I can't turn my thoughts off or eliminate the throbbing between my legs. When the door opens, Declan turns on a soft light. I don't move, afraid he's going to make me leave. I pretend to sleep, but he sits on the side of the bed and caresses my cheek.

His sexy voice fills my ears. "Simona, wake up, angel."

It's something else I don't understand. Why does he call me an angel? He made it clear he hates me.

I open my eyes, and a small smile appears on his face. "Time to eat. Put this on." He holds out a T-shirt.

At least he's not making me eat naked.

My stomach growls again, and I obey. He leads me out of the bedroom, down a hall, and the smell of spaghetti and garlic bread hits my nostrils. I turn the corner, and there's a kitchen, dining area, and family room. The table only has one plate. A glass each of red wine and water are next to it. My mouth salivates, looking at the food and smelling the aroma.

He pulls out the chair and sits then tugs me onto his lap. My chest rises and falls faster. His spicy, woody scent mixes with the food, intoxicating me. The thought that he's going to torture me further by making me watch him eat almost destroys everything I have left.

He spins the noodles on a fork until they wrap around the tines perfectly then brings it to my mouth.

Unable to stop myself, I allow him to feed me. Nothing has ever tasted so good. The robust tomato sauce and garlic flavors burst on my tongue. After several bites, including part of a meatball and garlic bread, he holds the glass of wine to my lips.

I'm not a fan of wine. I've only drunk it a few times when the other kids in my last foster home dared me. Something tells me not to reject his offering. When it hits my tongue, I'm surprised. It's delicious, and I softly moan.

He chuckles. "That good?"

I take a deep breath and face him. I gingerly ask, "Aren't you eating?"

"No. I already did. It's late."

"Oh?" I arch my eyebrow. Something about knowing what time it is excites me.

"Yeah. It's midnight."

I bite my lip, waiting for him to make the next move, unsure what I'm supposed to do.

He takes a sip of the wine while intensely studying me.

I nervously blurt out, "Do you always kidnap women and feed them wine?"

The vein above his eye twitches. He replies, "No. I've never kidnapped a woman before."

Something about that statement lights me up. I officially become more messed up than I worried about earlier. The fact I'm the only one fills me with satisfaction.

He holds another forkful of food to my lips.

I open my mouth and allow him to feed me until everything is gone, including the wine. My head buzzes from the alcohol, being close to him for so long, and the crazy idea that if the situation wasn't what it was, this could actually be a pretty sexy date.

It's not, I repeat in my head for the thousandth time.

What makes it worse is when he slowly swipes the corner of my lips then puts his finger in his mouth.

My cheeks heat so rapidly, I almost break out in a sweat. I squirm on his lap, and an arrogant expression fills his face.

"Do you want anything else?" he asks.

You. Me. To return to the night we met, before everything changed between us.

"No, thank you," I reply, trying not to stare at his lips but failing.

I need to stop this.

He's not a good guy.

His words snap me back into reality. He mumbles, "I think it's time for bed."

He rises with me and walks to his bedroom.

Suddenly, I need it all to stop. There's no room to be fuzzy on what we are to each other. I'm not falling for his charm. Nor am I here on my own accord. The last thing I need to do is give myself to him. I attempt to get out of his grasp. "Let me go!"

He puts me on the bed, and his eyes turn to slits. "Get under the covers."

"No!" I reply and try to get off the bed, but he pins me down.

"Simona, what are you doing?" he seethes.

"I'm not staying here."

"Yes, you are. Now, I'm going to release you. Be a good girl and get under the covers."

"No! Take me back to my cell if you aren't going to let me go home!" I might have gone crazy, or maybe it's the wine making me choose the cell over his warm bed. All I can think is if I stay next to him all night, I might lose my resolve to see him for who he is.

His eyes widen, and he breathes hard, staring at me. "You'll freeze to death if I take you back to your cell."

"Then let me die! It'll be better than staying with you!" I shout.

Hurt appears in his face. It makes me feel bad and happy at the same time. He stays silent.

"I'm not staying with you!" I claim.

He growls, "You'll do what I say."

"No, I won't!" I writhe under him.

The vein around his eye pulses, and he reaches into the drawer, grabs my wrists, and restrains them to the headboard.

I tug at the cuffs, but just like the cell, I can't go anywhere.

He jumps up, pulls the covers over me, and shakes his head. "You were doing so well, angel."

4

Declan

I THOUGHT SHE UNDERSTOOD. WHY DID SHE HAVE TO MISBEHAVE?

She looks like she hates me.

Of course she does. I kidnapped her, and she almost died of hypothermia.

Jesus. What the hell am I doing?

It's been three days, and I haven't gotten any information out of Simona. I've spent all my time researching anything I could about her, but besides her college record, there's not much to find. She's barely on social media. Most of her time is spent waitressing or at her job in the school cafeteria. She also frequents the school library based on the number of times she's scanned her identification to enter.

When I hacked into the grade reporting system, I wasn't surprised she had an A+ in every class. Still, a feeling of pride swept through me. Then I reprimanded myself. She's using her skills to try and destroy my family's future.

My mistake could have killed her.

The guilt over her hypothermia eats at me. She's never going back in that cell again. I curse myself for hurting her like that. It's another reason I should turn her over to Liam and the others. I'm too close to the situation. All I still see is my angel's body going into shock. Yet, I can't give her to them.

After dinner, I thought we were getting somewhere. I figured if I fed her favorite dinner to her then allowed her to get some good rest in a warm bed, we could talk tomorrow. She'd have a clear head, be over the shock of her kidnapping and willing to tell me all the things I want to know.

Instead, she would rather go back to her cell and risk death than stay next to me. We didn't move forward. We only went backward. And it's cutting me in so many unexpected ways.

I can't stop asking myself why it has to be her who's screwing with my family. My radar must be off. All I keep thinking about is how good we could be together. I've questioned several times if I could ever get past this and forgive her. Then I remind myself not to get soft. She's the enemy, and I need to find out why.

When I leave the bedroom, she's screaming for me to release her and turn on the light. It takes all my resolve not to do what she wants, beg for her forgiveness, and make her mine.

If I don't get out of here, I'm going to crack. I can't put her back in the basement, and I can't listen to her. But I also don't need any of the O'Malleys who watch over my house to hear her. So I go back into the room, open my dresser drawer, and take out a ball gag. I've never used it before. It was a gag gift I planned to give Arianna at Killian's wedding, but her father stopped me mid-speech. I tossed it in the drawer and forgot about it. I hold it up. "You can either stop yelling or wear this. Make your choice."

Anger and more defiance flare in her expression. She takes her leg, attempts to kick me in the balls, and yells, "Help! Someone help me!"

I shake my head, yanking the covers off. I grab the cuffed chains I keep under my bed, attached to the posts at the bed's foot.

She screams louder. "Let me go!" Her body writhes, but I secure each restraint on her.

I sit on the bed, and she turns her head away from me. It doesn't stop me. I lean over, slide the ball in her mouth, and put the band over her head.

Her eyes widen, and she attempts to scream, but it's muffled. No one from the outside would ever hear it. Her orbs fill with tears.

I run my knuckles down her cheek. "You made this choice, not me, lass."

She shuts her eyes and tears fall. My heart splinters in two, but no one can know I have her. I warned her, and she disobeyed.

"Look at me," I demand.

She refuses to open her eyes.

My pulse shoots to the sky. I don't want to punish her, but she has to learn who's in charge. I repeat my command then threaten, "Last warning."

She still doesn't obey.

I sigh inside. "Three. Two. One." Unable to help myself, I drag my finger down her neck, through her cleavage, and stop before I hit her pussy. I figure she'll open her eyes, but she doesn't.

I grip the collar of my T-shirt she's wearing and rip it down the center.

Her eyes pop open.

I rip both sleeves and pull them out from underneath her. I fight my desire to stare at her and lean an inch from her mouth. "Clothes and the ability to speak are rewards. Lying in my bed, with covers, is a privilege as well as being unrestrained. Next time you want to defy me, remember this." I wipe the tears off her cheek then kiss it. "Enjoy your time alone, angel."

Anxiety plagues her face. More guilt annihilates me. But I can't give in to it. I step to the end of the bed then study her body, chained and sprawled out, so damn tempting, my head spins. Her nipples pucker into hard nubs, rising and falling faster above her perfectly pert breasts. A silver hoop in her belly button creates a flashback of the night I met her. The youthful pink color peeking out from her pussy teases me to stay and convince her to beg me to take her. The only thing I don't like is the ball gag.

A necessary evil, I convince myself.

The longer I stare, the harder I get. And maybe it's my eyes and wishful thinking, but I swear the room begins to smell like her arousal.

Her blue eyes stare at me, full of so much emotion, but I don't miss the lust and confusion growing within them or the way her cheeks flush. She glances at my crotch and swallows hard.

I reach for her foot. "Ah. I see. You've never been chained to a bed before, and you don't understand why that sexy pussy of yours is throbbing so hard, do you?" I rub the erogenous zones in her foot.

A soft whimper fills the air, and my pants become so tight, it hurts. Her cheeks burn brighter, and I continue to stimulate her senses.

I don't take my eyes off her face, watching her every reaction. When her lower body writhes and a louder moan fills the room, I release her. "I told you, this can go one of two ways. While I'm gone, think about if you want to be a good girl or a bad one. The choice is yours."

I spin to leave, and she frantically makes more noises, but I force myself not to look back. I turn off the light, shut the door, then turn the thermostat down a few notches. It won't be as cold as the basement, but it'll assure she remembers how bad it is in the cell. She won't be telling me to take her there anymore.

I find my keys and get in my SUV. No one has ever tested me as much as Simona. The innocent vibe I got the night I met her hasn't gone away. It's hard to remember she caused my family to lose millions by her actions. If I hadn't found her, she'd have driven everything to the ground.

It doesn't take long to get to the pub. It's a weeknight, near closing time, and none of my brothers or Liam are there. Finn sits at the end of the bar, nursing a whiskey.

I pat his back and take the stool next to him. I nod at Molly to bring me the same. "I haven't seen you in a while."

He turns, scowling. "I was in Philly."

I proceed with caution. "I heard. Dead end?"

He glances at the wall, angrily shakes his head, and downs the rest of his drink. "I knew that bastard was lying. Even in death, he got one over on me."

"Why didn't you tell me you were going? I would have gone with you."

Molly sets my drink down, and Finn nods for another. She refills it then sets the fifth on the counter.

When she's far enough away, Finn replies, "It was a dead end. No use taking you away from our other issues. Where are we at on that? Did you find the prick who's been trying to fuck us?"

My chest tightens. I take a large mouthful of whiskey, and it burns my throat all the way to my stomach. I probably should lie to Finn. I'm taking a huge risk, but I don't have the heart to lie to him after all he's been through. This issue is also stressing him out, so I need to take that off his plate. "Yeah."

He spins. "Who is it?"

"No one you know."

His green eyes are slits that pierce mine. "Is he at the warehouse?"

I take another mouthful. "No."

"You haven't picked him up yet?"

I tap my fingers on the bar. I shouldn't have come here. There was no way I would have avoided this. "It's not a he."

Finn freezes.

Blood pounds hard between my ears.

He lowers his voice. "A woman's trying to screw us over?"

"Yeah."

"Is she a Bailey?"

I down the rest of my drink and refill my glass. "I don't know who she's with yet."

"If she's not at the warehouse, where is she?" he asks.

I consume more alcohol. The vein around my eye pulses. It's something I hate. It happens whenever I get really angry or nervous. And Finn sees it. I answer, "She's tied to my bed right now."

His eyes widen. "You're joking."

I toss back more whiskey than I believe I've ever gotten inside my mouth for one gulp. I wince from the burn. "Nope. Afraid not. It's a step up from the cell I created in my basement."

Finn rises. "Let's go."

Oh shit. I bark, "Sit back down."

"Are you out of your mind?" he growls.

I sigh and motion to his stool. "Keep your voice quiet and take your seat."

He glances behind him and returns to his position. "You need to take her to the warehouse. Tonight."

"Not happening."

"Why?"

"I was assigned to fix this issue. I have. And I'm going to make sure I get every morsel of information out of her I can."

He glares at me. "In your bed?"

"Just semantics." I downplay the situation.

"Bullshit."

I consider another glass, but I remember I drove. "It's not. We have to do things differently. She's not a man."

"Who is she?"

"A student at the tech school."

Finn sniffs hard. "A student. How old is she?"

"Twenty-one."

"Jesus. She's a child!"

I groan. "Get off your high horse. She's a legal adult, smarter than all of us put together, and fucking us."

Finn scrubs his face. "Liam know about this?"

"Not yet."

He pulls his phone out. "Call him. Now."

I yank it away from him and slam it on the counter. "I told you this in confidence. I'll tell Liam when I'm good and ready. He's handling enough issues with our territory threats. I stopped our problem. The stock will go back in our favor. Plus, I'm going to find out what we need to know."

He jabs me in the chest. "You're playing with fire."

"I know what I'm doing."

He growls, "You tell Liam, or I will."

"I said, I'll tell Liam when I'm good and ready. Until then, keep your mouth shut. I'm leaving. Do you need a ride?"

He picks up the bottle and fills his tumbler. "No."

I sigh. "Where are you staying?"

"Michigan Ave."

"I wish you wouldn't have moved out," I admit.

He glowers at me. "If I had known you were going to do this, I wouldn't have."

"Listen to me. I have this under control."

His nostrils flare. "There's a reason we have the warehouse. This girl, whoever she is, better not get under your skin."

"She won't." It's a lie. Simona already is. I add, "I've gotta go. I'll keep you posted. And let me know what I can do to help find Brenna. You don't have to keep going about this on your own."

His face hardens. He spins in his chair, and I know the conversation is over.

I pat him on the back and leave. When I get home, I open a new bottle of whiskey. What I had at the pub should have taken the edge off, but being in the same vicinity as Simona has my blood pumping again. The vision of her chained to my bed, naked, is like a slow-motion film.

I curse myself for not having a security camera in my room. Not being able to see what she's doing is driving me crazy. It hasn't been long enough. She needs to learn her lesson that I'm in charge. She's going to listen and obey me.

I debate about sleeping on the couch, but my curiosity and the itch to see her win. Plus, she doesn't want me in the room. So it can be another form of punishment for her, I decide.

I open the door and flip the switch to the fireplace. The room erupts in a warm orange glow. My angel is still spread out, wide awake, her blue orbs spinning with emotions.

The blankets are on the floor where I left them. I step over them, strip out of my clothes, and slide in next to her. I slip my hand under her head and drag my knuckles down the side of her torso. Her skin isn't warm, but it's not cold like it was earlier.

She whimpers, and her eyes flutter.

"Have you thought about whether you're going to be a good girl or a bad girl?" I ask.

She turns and defeat fills her eyes. I see it all the time when I'm torturing men. Something about seeing it in Simona tears at my heart.

I stroke her cheek. "Nod if you're going to be a good girl, and I'll remove the gag." I hate it. If she hadn't screamed, I wouldn't have used it on her.

She furrows her eyebrows and closes her eyes.

I give her a few moments, but each second makes my skin heat. Being next to her, seeing her young, unused body, and all the things I want to do to her begin to drive me crazy. I decide as soon as I get her put to bed, I'm sleeping on the couch. I don't trust myself around her. She's at a breaking point, but something within me doesn't want to push her over the edge quite yet.

I lean into her ear. "This doesn't have to be like this. You chose this. I warned you. Now, show me you're going to be a good girl. I'll remove your gag, put on the covers, and you can get a good night's rest."

She slowly opens her lids and nods.

"Good girl," I praise then slip the band over her head and pull the ball away from her.

A big breath of air comes out of her lips.

I reach for the bottle of water and hold it to her mouth. "Take a sip."

She drinks half the bottle.

"Do you want more?"

She shakes her head and clears her throat. "No. That's enough."

I stroke her silky hair then wrap it around my fist, unable to stop. "I'll put your blankets on and let you sleep."

"Where are you going?" she says, her voice laced with panic.

My gut drops. I hate seeing her like this, and I wish for the hundredth time she wasn't here under these circumstances. "You made it clear you don't want me sleeping with you. I'll let you stay on your own tonight."

"No! Please don't leave me again!" she frets, and tears fall down her cheeks.

I study her, not expecting her outburst, my heart cracking from how scared she sounds.

"Nothing will happen to you. I'll be in the other room."

"Declan! Please!" she cries out again.

Her pleas don't make sense to me. She was clear she didn't want to be anywhere near me.

I swipe my thumb under her eye and bring my face close to hers. "One thing you should know about me is I know my limits. Right now, I can't stay here."

"Why? You can!"

I sigh and debate about lying to her. But I don't. To torture myself further, I cage my body over hers, and she gasps. Her hot breath merges with mine, and I stroke her hair. "I want you too badly, angel. And you're not ready for it."

She moves her face so her lips touch mine. "I-I can't take this anymore."

"Take what?"

Tears leak down her face. "Everything."

I quickly slide my arms under her body. "You've had a rough day, but you're strong. Tomorrow can be better. It's up to you. In time, you'll see that everything is up to you."

"Please. Don't leave me! If you do, I'll never forgive you!"

Her threat cuts me to the core. It shouldn't. Yet, since I took the bag off her head, nothing I feel around her is anything for a typical O'Malley enemy. I sniff hard. "Angel, if I stay, I'm going to tear into your pussy so many times tonight, you won't be able to walk tomorrow. And I told you, I won't be doing anything until the time comes where you're begging me to make you mine."

She inhales hard and pins her heavy gaze on me. In a firm voice, she orders, "Don't go."

5

Simona

Time seems to stretch on forever. I don't know how long he's been gone. From time to time, I heard men's voices from outside. I don't know why I would. I believe I'm toward the back of the house, but why would men be near his home, even if I'm in the front?

The darkness engulfed me, just like when I was in the cell. I've never liked not controlling the light. When I was a child, several of my foster homes were violent. It wasn't the adults but the other children in the home. I'd try not to fall asleep in fear of something happening to me. Sometimes I wouldn't be able to keep my eyes open. Those were the nights I usually got attacked.

In my apartment, I would keep things dark because of the cost of electricity. But I always had my laptop or something to give me some light. Plus, I had the flashlight on my phone. It made me feel in control.

Everything is quickly spinning now. It's been too many days of being in the dark, unable to make any decisions, and fighting my fears.

Ironically, Declan makes me feel safe when I'm around him. The times he acts out of control, I still don't feel as horrible as being on my own. Whether the gag is on or off me, something about him in my presence eliminates my long-term demons. It makes my body feel things I'm not sure how to stop, but it's better than the anxiety from him leaving me on my own in the dark.

"Tell me again," Declan orders, his eyes erupting in blue flames.

"Don't go. Please!" I desperately beg, my lips trembling at the thought of him leaving but also him staying. I told myself not to give in to him, but feeling safe and protected is what I need right now.

His voice hardens. "Did you not hear what I said? A few hours ago, you begged me to put you in your cell. This isn't what you want. You aren't ready for me."

Afraid he'll leave, unable to stop the throbbing in my body whenever I'm around him, and too confused about everything, I succumb to my deepest desire and push the self-hatred to the back of my mind. I can't stop wanting him. I have since I first laid eyes on him. For months, I dreamed of him. The rational voice screaming he's a psychopath and not to let him touch me loses.

Too scared whatever I say will make him leave, I lift my head the extra inch and press my lips to his.

The moment I do, his arms tighten around me. One hand fists my hair, tugging my head back slightly. His tongue fills my mouth, dominating, torturing, creating a need so hot in my veins, I think I might melt into his body. A sweet flavor, I'm guessing whiskey, erupts on my taste buds.

I tug on the handcuffs, attempting to reach for him, but there's no slack.

He keeps my head positioned so I can only see the ceiling and top of the headboard. His hot mouth travels down my neck, then, in the same manner as our kiss, he consumes my breasts, as if he's fucking them.

The carnal moans filling the air, coming from me, I've never heard before. I've only had sex twice. The first time was with a boy in my high school. I wasn't in love with him, nor was he my boyfriend. I got drunk at a party and didn't even remember most of it.

The second was my first year of college. The teacher assigned me a male study partner, and we grew close. He kept wanting more. Every time we got together, he tried to convince me I was scared of my feelings, and if we were together, I'd realize them. One lonely night, I gave in. It didn't change my feelings for him. There wasn't any chemistry on my side. Things grew awkward after I told him we had to go back to the friend zone. He stopped talking to me. After that, I stayed away from most people and especially boys.

But Declan isn't a boy. He's a man. Every move he makes, he does with confidence and ease, as if he knows exactly what I need.

"Jesus, you're flawless, angel," he mutters and moves to my other breast. More intense zings explode in my body.

"Declan," I whimper and try to reach for him again, but the cuffs stop me.

He doesn't take his mouth off me, reaches for the headboard, and does something. His fingers wrap around my wrists, and he brings them to his head.

The cuffs are still on. Somehow, he released the tension but only enough to touch him. And I don't know why, but the thought goes through my head that I'm glad he didn't remove them.

I grasp his hair, as if I could somehow get him closer to me, digging my nails into his scalp. A feral groan ricochets out of his chest, reminding me again that he's a man who could crush me or protect me and may possibly do both.

I don't dwell on the thought. It leaves as quickly as it appears because he shimmies down my body, running his knuckles down the sides of my torso. I shudder as his tongue flicks at my belly button ring, sending a shock of electricity to my loins.

I battle the restraints again, but I can't move them past my breasts.

His eyes meet mine, glowing like the devil. Arrogance reignites in them, and he grabs my hips, tugging my body toward the end of the bed. My arms once again have no slack, but my legs now do, although it's not a lot. He gracefully glides between my thighs and lifts them over his shoulders. The excess slack disappears.

"Fuck, you're a good girl. So wet for Daddy," he mumbles, drags his middle finger through my wet heat, and slides it in my hole.

"Oh God!" I cry out, writhing and arching my back, finding it hot he called himself Daddy and wanting to hear it again. I push into his finger, relishing how it alone fills me, then suddenly worrying about how the rest of him will ever fit.

"Relax, angel. Your night is just starting." His tongue swipes from his finger to my clit then lazily rolls around it before he picks up the pace and aggressively flicks it while inching his digit in and out of me.

"Oh...oh...Declan! Oh!" I scream while hyperventilating, yanking on the chains but not getting anywhere.

His mouth becomes lightning inside a cave, explosive, bright, so full of energy, my head spins. He's a machine rotating between low and high power, and every time my endorphins almost bubble over, he stops them from overflowing.

Sweat pops out on my skin, dripping down my body. He reaches for my breast and pinches my hard nipple. My thighs squeeze his cheeks, and another deep groan fills the air.

"Please!" I whimper.

He continues to torture me, and when he begins to take me back down, my body caves. A violent tremor racks through me. My inner walls spasm on his finger. Like a surfer riding a wave, he speeds back up and extends my orgasm past the point I could ever believe possible.

"Don't stop! Declan! Please don't stop!" I plead, seeing white light, grinding my lower body against him.

He works me harder, keeping the adrenaline coursing through my veins, adding another finger, then curling and twisting them inside me.

"Oh God!" I whimper, and my body convulses harder, squirting so much juice, the sheets become soaked under my ass. A collision of stars explodes in my eyes, and I grip the chain as hard as I can.

He pulls his fingers out and drags his tongue up my torso, playing with my belly button ring, paying more homage to my sensitive nipples, then assaulting my mouth with his tongue.

My orgasm is all over his face. I've never tasted it before. It's filthy and surprises me how much I desperately want more.

"Greedy lass," he mumbles then his hands reach down and grab my ankles, holding them as close to my body as possible. In one thrust, his cock penetrates me.

"Oh fuck!" I moan into his mouth. All my fantasies about Declan were tame compared to this. My lack of experience had me thinking it would be better than my previous times, but nothing comes close to the way he fills my body or how every touch creates a new fire.

His hard flesh against mine is beautiful chaos. It slides against my breasts, sending a constant stream of tingles down my spine. He palms my head with one hand, and his biceps tighten under me, holding me so close, there's no room between us.

He begins to thrust, and something rolls back and forth over my clit.

"Oh," I moan into his mouth, not sure what it is but loving everything about it.

He dives to my lobe, sucking it, then mumbling, "So tight for Daddy."

Endorphins slaughter me again, keeping me in a sustained state of mayhem. I've never felt so much heat or adrenaline. My entire being quivers with bubbling lava raging, burning hotter and hotter until I'm ambushed with sweat.

"Declan," I cry out, gripping the chains so tight, my fingers hurt.

He speeds up his thrusts, and whatever is moving over my clit only intensifies my orgasms. His fist tugs my hair so my head shifts back as far as possible. He moves his face over mine. "Did you think about me after you met me?"

I don't analyze the question, I only whimper, "Yes."

"How often?" he demands, the vein near his eye pulsing.

I admit, "Daily...oh God!" My eyes roll from another surge of pleasant torture.

He groans, pounding into me harder, drags his teeth down my neck, then licks upward to my mouth. His fist relaxes, and his fingers glide through my hair, holding my head firmly to his lips. Our predatory tongues collide, both of us attempting to consume the other whole, never getting enough.

Declan's spicy, woody scent mixes with that of the whiskey and my arousal. Our sweat creates an intoxicating aroma so powerful, I'd smell it all day long if I could. The sweet friction of his cock, sliding against my walls, pushing deeper than I ever thought possible, shatters me to pieces. My body convulses harder, spasming on him more intensely than before.

"Fuck, you make it hard for me to keep going, lass," he growls and then grunts as if restraining himself.

"I need to feel you," I breathe.

He skims his hand up my arm and weaves his fingers through mine and orders, "Don't let go."

"Yes. Oh God, yes!" I yell, gripping his hand with every bit of strength I have.

His blue flames reconnect with mine, pulling me into a bottomless pit of everything that's him. A bead of sweat rolls over his vein then drips down his chin. I lick it before it falls, wanting to taste every part of him.

He lowers his mouth and sucks hard on the curve of my neck. It's more divine torture. Every touch he gives is expertly delivered and deliciously received.

"Do it again," I beg.

He sucks harder and then bites into the sensitive spot. I arch my back as much as possible, but there's nowhere to go except into his hard torso of muscle.

"Lass, I need to come in your hot, tight cunt," he warns.

The boys I was with never talked dirty to me. They stayed quiet while we had sex and so did I. Something about Declan's filthy mouth turns me on even more. Before I know what I'm saying, I demand, "Yes! Oh God! Keep talking!"

A breath of hot air assaults the spot he just bit, sprinkling tingles deep within my core. He brings his lips to mine and drills his gaze into my orbs, challenging me. "You want me to pound your pussy harder?"

"Please! Oh God!"

His lips curve and he obeys, assaulting me with his body in a perfect, graceful manner. My mouth freezes in an O, my body spasming and out of control. He clenches his jaw, the blues in his eyes fire off more determined arrogance, then he states, "Your pussy juice is my heroin. Until I get more out of you, your daddy's not giving in to your wishes."

I'm unsure why I love him calling himself my daddy. But I blurt out, "Please come in me, Daddy. Please. I-I...oh fuck!" His cock hits something so deep inside me, a tidal wave of endorphins confiscates all my cells. My body spurts more fluids, and I squeeze his hand so hard, I think it might break.

"Jesus, angel," he roars in my ear, and his cock ferociously pumps inside me, stretching me farther, keeping me buzzing in my high.

"Declan!" I breathe into the curve of his neck, my voice hoarse and body on fire.

His flesh vibrates against me, pressing into my torso. He sucks on the same spot on my neck, and a new wave of buzzing ignites in my body.

We start to come down, our chests pushing into the other, our perspiration merging together. He lifts his head, and a wicked twinkle forms in his eyes. "Are you ready to see how good girls get rewarded?"

I swallow hard, still trying to catch my breath, unsure there's anything else he could do that would ever feel anywhere close to how good he just made me feel.

I'm wrong. Completely ignorant.

He releases my hand, flips his over, and drags the backs of his nails down my arm. I shudder, and his cocky expression returns. His flesh floats down my body, and he begins lapping up my juice. It's slow, mercilessly creating a new type of pleasant sensation all over my still-quivering region.

I thought there was nothing left for my body to give or any other way I could feel. The truth slowly burns through me.

I tilt my head toward the ceiling and take deep, controlled breaths.

"Such a good lass," he murmurs then returns to feasting on my most intimate parts.

I'm on a never-ending roller coaster of highs. These are different than the ones I felt before. They're calmer, almost sleepy. It's as if my pussy is spent and getting a massage.

"How do you know what to do so well?" I inquire in a whisper, staring at the headboard, my wrists restrained in the cuffs, breathing through my teeth.

He grunts. "I'm a man, not one of those boys I'm sure you're used to." He rubs his nose on my clit then takes a long, drawn-out sniff, followed by a similar exhale, which hits right on my entrance.

I whimper, not understanding how everything he does can feel so different or how he can pay so much attention to me when we've already had sex. When his tongue strikes me again, I cry out, "There! Oh God! Right there!"

He chuckles, continues to play with me on that spot, and my head spins again. I squeeze my thighs so hard on his cheeks, I wonder if I'll crack them. New drops of sweat roll down my thighs. It goes on and on, and after I can't see straight, he removes my ankle cuffs.

I assume he might take my wrist ones off, but he flips me over on my knees like I'm a piece of paper that doesn't weigh anything.

His thighs move between my legs. He gathers all my hair, tugs my head back, and puts his cheek next to mine. The smell of my orgasms wafts in my nostrils. "Daddy's not done with you."

I don't know how much more I can take. I'm already feeling like a rag doll from all the adrenaline.

"You're going to ride me. Use the chains if you need to. And for the rest of the night, you only call me Daddy." He yanks my hips over him, and his cock once again fills me.

"Oh God, Daddy!" I cry out.

"Fair warning. I go longer the second time around."

6

Declan

EVERYTHING ABOUT SIMONA EXCEEDS MY EXPECTATIONS. SHE surprises me in too many ways. The way our bodies form to each other is chocolate melting with butter. Her dirty words and pleas flying out of her lush mouth are cocaine for my ears. Every time she calls me Daddy, my ego expands. I'm unsure why. I've never had a woman call me that, but something about her doing it creates mayhem in my veins.

I tend to have sex with younger women, but Simona is the youngest one I've ever touched. I'm two years past double her age. Finn said she's a child, but in my eyes, she's an adult, capable of making decisions on who she wants.

If she hadn't kissed me, I would have left the room. She's pleaded for me all night, just like I promised her she would. But I'm not finished with her. Her throbbing pussy on my mouth only made me hard again, and she may be a rag doll in my arms, but she's going to learn to use the chains to her advantage and mine.

The moment I enter her, her walls sheathe my cock in a hot, wet blanket. I've never made a woman squirt twice in one night before. I don't know if it's because she's so young or if it's our bodies together, but her tight channel is pleasant torture, squeezing my dick so violently at times, I have to work hard not to give in to the temptation of spiraling too soon.

No one has ever tasted as good as her. I'd drink her for breakfast every morning, just to start my day off right, if I could. Her breasts are natural and perky, not too big and not too small. When her pink nipples harden, they become the largest I've seen on a woman. Every time I touch them, she moans like an animal in ecstasy. It fascinates me. I decide I need my hands free to further manipulate them and her matching pink clit.

Her black locks stick to her face, covered in sweat, making her lust-filled blue eyes pop more than usual. She's an angel, ready to be desecrated by sin, and I'm the one who's going to do it.

I lick her cheek and demand, "Ride me. I want that tight cunt of yours working me hard."

Like the good lass she is, she grips the chains so tight, her knuckles turn white. Instead of lifting her pussy straight off me, she circles it.

I almost blow my wad. She's young and seems so inexperienced. No matter what she was planning with those articles she published, I fight the inner voice telling me she's innocent. It makes me want to protect her against all enemies, including myself. But is it even possible? She came into the pub, targeting me. Plus, she's now riding me, owning my cock, knowing exactly how to make me even harder.

"Fuuuuck," I growl then bite her ear and twist her nipple.

"Daddy," she moans, injecting my ego with more satisfaction.

She obeys my commands so well. If only she'd do it all the time out of the bedroom, too. Ready to play some mind games with her, I ask, "Should I rub that sexy, throbbing clit of yours, my greedy little lass?"

"Please," she breathes, her voice hoarse and lower body already trembling.

I move all her hair over one shoulder and trace her other nipple. I drag my teeth over the spot on her neck I sucked on. It's red and turning purple.

She gloriously shudders in my arms.

"Please what?" I taunt.

"Please, Daddy."

I hold in my groan. "What do you want Daddy to do?"

"Touch me. Please."

I lick over the mark. A salacious sound vibrates out of her mouth. I study her face and threaten, "Maybe I should put you back in the cell. Give you what you asked me for earlier and leave you hot and wet."

She furrows her eyebrows. Panic creeps into her eyes.

"Isn't that what you wanted?" I remind her.

Confusion fills her expression.

Part of me feels guilty for doing this, but I'm going to get it through to her she's not going to try and hide from me ever again. "Answer me."

She freezes and closes her eyes.

"I didn't give you permission to stop fucking me." I grab her hip and move it until she resumes circling at the speed I want. I taunt, "Is that what you really wanted? To be back in the cell?"

She swallows hard. The flush in her cheeks deepens to crimson. "No."

"Why did you demand it?" I put my hand on her mound but don't touch her where she wants me to.

A breathy sigh comes out of her. "Yes. Please touch me there."

I pinch her clit, her walls clench my cock harder, and her body writhes against mine. She cries out, "Oh God!"

I slide my hand over her mound. "No more until you answer my question. Why did you tell me to put you back in the cell?"

"I-I don't know."

"Don't lie to me, lass. I'll have to punish you," I remind her.

She tries to move her hips faster on me, whimpering.

I grab one and slow her down. "Your pussy doesn't get rewarded until I say so." My arm around her chest tightens, pulling her so close to me, her head rests on my shoulder.

Her voice cracks. "What will my punishment be, Daddy? Will you chain me in the cell then come fuck me?"

Jesus. She's a naughty vixen and might become the death of me. My cock twitches inside her. I reply, "Is that what you thought of when I left you down there?"

She exhales breathily. Her lids fall, and she whispers, "I'm so close. Please let me come."

"Answer me, or this is over. I'll have you suck me off and leave you on edge," I threaten.

She swallows hard. "Why does it matter?"

"You know why."

She shakes her head. "I don't. Nothing you say makes sense to me."

I almost call her a liar again but decide I'll deal with her disobedience tomorrow. "Yeah? It seems like you have a selective comprehension of what I say. Or does it only make sense when it has to do with your pussy?"

Her heavy eyes drill into mine.

Since she isn't answering my question, I decide to make her admit something else. "Did I get it wrong? You didn't want this or me?"

She doesn't flinch. "I've wanted you since I met you."

Her answer is perfect. I press my lips to her ear and bring my hand to her clit, rotating between pinching and stroking it. "See. It wasn't so hard to be honest, now was it?"

"Oh-oh...no!" An orgasm rips through her body. Her eyes roll, and I refrain from ejaculating inside her.

I keep her high going and murmur, "It's better to be a good girl. I prefer rewarding you, angel."

She rides me faster, and I let her, continuing to show her how good behavior gets rewarded, enjoying every second of her greedy body desperate for mine.

I get her to the edge of coming again and order, "Now, tell me why you demanded to go to your cell."

She begins to tremble, and I pull my hand off her and hold her against my thighs so she can't ride me. Her eyes widen in need. She begs, "Please, don't stop."

"Answer me," I bark.

"Please," her raspy voice pleads in desperation.

"Tell me now!" I roar.

She blurts out, "I didn't want to give in to the temptation! You-you kidnapped me and want to hurt me!" Shame fills her expression, tears appear in her eyes, and she turns away.

I clutch her chin so she can't avoid me. "Am I hurting you right now?"

"No."

"This is what I want to do to you. I already told you, I don't like punishing you. I have no desire to hurt you."

Her lips tremble, and a tear leaks down her chin.

I swipe it with my thumb and reveal more than I should. "I don't want a response right now. We'll discuss this tomorrow. But I'm trying to understand how a lass like you got involved in this."

"I-I don't—"

I quiet her with a kiss, inching my tongue in and out of her mouth until she's moaning, breathless, and riding me hard again. I decide there's been enough talk about our issues. Then I shut up the voice in my head telling me this isn't for the long term. At some point, she's going to tell me the truth, and I already know there's no way I'll be able to forgive her. Once you screw with the O'Malleys, there's no going back. Now that Nolan and Finn know, it's only a matter of time before Liam comes making demands to make me take her to the warehouse. My time with her is limited. The notion of keeping her forever isn't realistic.

I don't release my hold on her, keeping her as close to me as possible, wishing our circumstances were different. I slide my nose along the bruise forming on her neck.

"Oh God!"

I murmur, "Who am I to you, angel?"

She doesn't miss a beat. "My daddy."

"That's right. Your daddy is going to take care of your sweet pussy all night. You know why?"

"No, but please don't stop. I-I... Oh God!" she cries out, and her body violently convulses against me.

I reiterate, "I told you. Good girls get rewarded. Now say thank you." I press my thumb against her clit and rub it fast.

"Th-th-thank you, Daddy!" she screams then her mouth becomes an O.

The groan that flies out of my mouth starts in my chest and echoes in the air. She's so perfect. If only she didn't decide to come after my family.

I push the thought to the back of my mind and refocus on her, using every trick I know not to erupt inside her piece of heaven.

It has to be. There's no way anything on or off this Earth would feel better.

She turns her head and presses her lips to mine, trembling in my mouth and no longer able to control herself by gripping the chain. She's a rag doll in my arms, and I grasp her hips and slam her over and over on me until my tormented dick can't handle it anymore.

"Fuuuuck," I growl when my cock savagely pumps inside her and dizziness overpowers me.

She trembles longer than I do, collapsing against my body. I bury my face into the curve of her neck and inhale her scent, calming my heart rate.

Simona finally glances at me. Hope fills her orbs. She quietly asks, "Will you remove my restraints?"

My chest tightens. My heart wants to give her everything she asks for, yet I also don't want her to play me for a fool.

"Please. I promise I'll only stay in bed. With you," she adds.

I debate, going through all the scenarios of things that could happen. I finally come to a conclusion I'm comfortable with and reply, "You've been a good girl. I'll put a cuff around one of your ankles and release all the tension."

She blinks hard and looks away.

My heart sinks, but I remind myself not to be a sucker. I position her face in front of mine. "This is a first step. If you continue to show me you can obey, we'll get to the point where I won't make you sleep in them."

She takes a deep breath, swallows hard, then states, "I-I need to know something for my mental health."

Her mental health. More guilt swarms me. I can only imagine what I'm doing for her mental health. "What is it?"

Anxiety riddles her face. "You speak like I'm never leaving this house for the rest of my life. Is that my fate?"

Another knife slashes my heart. Unprepared, I stroke her cheek and ponder her question. Unable to deal with the painful expression I'm sure will erupt on her face, I avoid telling her the truth and lie. "No, angel. If you're a good girl, I'll eventually give you outdoor privileges."

The relief in her expression creates more remorse and also satisfaction within me. She seems appeased.

"Do you need to use the bathroom?" I ask.

"Yeah."

I grab the key out of my drawer and unlock her cuffs. I check her wrists to make sure there aren't any bruises and then rub them. "Are they okay? Do you have pain anywhere?"

She smiles. "No. I'm okay. Umm, can I ask one more thing?"

"Sure. What is it?"

Shyness fills her face. "Can I use the toilet without you watching?"

My bathroom has a separate room with a door, so I agree. "Yes."

Her smile grows. "Thank you."

I help her off the bed, lead her to the bathroom, then allow her to shut the door to the toilet. I rest against the sink and decide to test her further. If she attempts to flee, I have so many men outside my house, they'll pick her up within minutes. No one knows about her, but they wouldn't let a woman leave my house naked and in the dark without stopping her. When she comes out, she washes her hands and spins into me.

"Let's try something, shall we?"

"What?" More nerves appear in her gaze.

My stomach flips, but I need to see if I can trust her a little. "I'm going to go to the bathroom, and you're going to stand here and wait."

She arches her eyebrow. "You are?"

"Yes. Unless I can't trust you?"

Silence fills the room for a moment. She doesn't answer and props herself up on my counter then crosses her legs.

Amused and turned on by her sexy, naked body, I step in front of her. I put my hands on the counter next to her hips. "I'm suddenly having visions of you putting your feet on my chest and playing with yourself."

Her cheeks heat with flames. She licks her plump lips and asks, "Is that what you want, Daddy?"

My dick twitches like I haven't already come twice tonight. "Oh, you naughty lass."

She smirks.

"I'm going to the bathroom. Don't make me regret this. Remember, I prefer to reward you."

She takes a deep breath. "I won't go anywhere. I promise."

I take a step backward then go into the toilet room. I don't shut the door, pee as quickly as possible, and find her sitting exactly where I left her. Pride fills me that she obeyed. I wash my hands then slide them through her hair, tilting her head toward me.

Why does she have to be so utterly gorgeous?

She smiles, and apprehension fills her expression.

"What's wrong?"

"Why did you leave the night we met?"

My gut twists. I can't exactly tell her I had to clean up a dead body. It also makes me realize I left her, promised her I'd come back, and didn't.

She was only there to get in my head.

Why does she look so hurt?

"Something came up I couldn't get out of."

She scrunches her face. "With your girlfriend?"

Surprised, I stroke her cheek. "No. I don't play the field when I have a girlfriend."

"I'm assuming you don't have a wife since you're keeping me a prisoner in your house?"

More shock fills me. *Did she believe I never came back due to a girlfriend or wife?*

She could be trying to mess with my head.

Deciding it's best if she doesn't ask any more questions tonight, I reply, "You assume right. Let's go to bed." I pick her up and carry her to the bed then keep my word. I only chain one of her ankles and release all the tension.

She curls into the pillow and yawns.

I face her and tuck a lock of her hair behind her ear. "Are you comfortable?"

She blinks a few times. "Yes."

"Better than the cell?" I tease.

A tiny smile curves on her lips. "Yeah."

"What's your favorite breakfast?"

She shrugs. "I rarely eat it. It's cheaper if I skip it."

Anger attacks me. It's not the first time she's mentioned she doesn't have money. She goes to an expensive private college, but I also know her apartment is one step away from rundown government housing. The thought of her not being able to afford to eat makes me feel sick. I ask, "But if you could eat anything, what would it be?"

She doesn't hesitate. "Pancakes." She yawns again.

I kiss her forehead. "Turn over."

She obeys.

I tug her into me, spooning her. I gently kiss the mark on her neck then order, "Go to sleep, angel."

She sleepily replies, but I don't miss the worry in her voice. "Please don't leave me."

"I won't," I promise. If she only knew how much it would take to drag me away from her.

7

Simona

When I wake up, I'm alone. The sun is shining, and the smell of pancakes wafts in the air. My stomach growls, but I sink into the pillow and stare at where Declan slept. My cheeks begin to hurt from my smile. I replay last night, including the time I woke up, still half asleep, and slid on top of him.

I sit up quickly, in a panic, then cover my face with both hands, taking deep breaths. *What was I thinking? The man has me chained to his bed.*

I lift the covers to look at the restraint on my ankle, but it's gone. Confusion once again becomes a halo around me. More anxiety floods me.

Am I allowed to get out of bed?

Why did he take the cuff off?

I had the chance to run last night when he went to the bathroom, and I didn't. I let my fear of being naked in the dark stop me.

I'm such a liar. I was too exhausted from the hours he spent ravishing my body.

Did I seriously talk dirty and call him Daddy?

Why did he have to be so good?

What is wrong with me?

Groaning, I start to get up but stop. He said if I obeyed, he'd give me outside privileges. I don't know if it only means I can go in his yard or if he'd take me somewhere, but whatever it looks like, I want it.

I make a judgment call and several times yell out, "Declan?"

He opens the door, and his eyes drift down.

I pull the sheet over my naked breasts.

I need to pull it together.

Arrogance appears on his face. I want to slap him and kiss him at the same time. His deep, sexy voice sends a delicious chill down my spine. "What's wrong, angel?"

Angel. Lass. Both of his pet names send heat straight to my pussy.

I swallow hard and try to figure out what to say. He arches his eyebrows and patiently waits for me to speak. I manage, "Thank you for uncuffing my ankle."

His eyes sear into mine. "You're welcome. It's your reward for staying in the bathroom last night."

More throbs consume my body, and I hate myself even more. I'm never getting out of here if I don't use my head and stop whatever this is that went on between us. He may be the best lover on earth, but he's still a complete psychopath. "Umm...am I able to get out of bed?"

His lips twitch and approval appears on his handsome face. "Yes. Whenever the cuffs are off, you may roam freely around the house. Assuming you don't do something to lose your privileges."

I blurt out, "You mean try to run."

His face hardens. "Yes. Or lie."

My stomach flips. No matter what I try to tell him, he keeps assuming I did something to him. He said we would talk today about how I got tied up in whatever he keeps referring to, but I don't have any idea what he thinks I've done. "I'm not a liar. I don't have any desire to tell you anything untrue."

"That's good." He studies me, and I try not to squirm. His intensity makes my blood heat.

When I can't take it anymore, I ask, "Can I go to the bathroom and shower?"

He motions to the door. "Of course. Don't take too long. I'm making pancakes."

I tilt my head. "Do you have a T-shirt or something I can wear?"

He licks his lips and cockily says, "Lass, I've seen you in every position, several times, and ate your pussy while you screamed my name too many times to count. And now I'm looking at you, in my bed, which still has your juice all over it. The room smells like sex and sweat. So I'll give you a T-shirt to wear around the house, but right now, I'm going to watch your sexy little body hightail it to the bathroom."

Fire blazes into my cheeks. I glance at the bed and take a few deep breaths. He's wearing gray joggers and a fitted white T-shirt that displays every sculpted part of his torso. I say, "But you're clothed. Isn't it fair for me to be, too?"

He cocks an eyebrow. "You want me to get naked?"

Yes, please. Then do what you did to me last night all over again.

I'm officially insane. A few orgasms, and I act like my captor is my boyfriend.

It was way more than a few.

Doesn't matter!

I clear my throat and avoid answering his question. I trot to the bathroom, then close the door. I shower, enjoying the hot water, realizing I hadn't bathed in several days. When I finish, I brush my teeth and swish with mouthwash. Since my hair is a mess, I brush that, too.

There's a knock on the door. I inch it open.

"Little bit more, lass, and then the T-shirt can get to you," he teases.

I stick my hand through and grab the shirt.

"Come out to the kitchen when you're ready. Breakfast is waiting," he orders.

My heart skips a beat. I reprimand myself again. Just because he fed me my favorite dinner and now made breakfast doesn't make him a good guy.

I need to figure out how to escape.

I throw the shirt over my head and meet him in the kitchen. A platter of pancakes sits in the middle of the table. One plate has three stacked on it. A bottle of syrup and a stick of butter are next to it. A glass of orange juice and a cup of coffee are full and ready for me.

My stomach drops. I don't know why I thought last night changed anything. I ask, "You aren't eating?"

"Already did. It's almost eleven."

"Oh."

He curls his finger and motions for me to step forward. I obey, and he sits and pulls me onto his lap. He glances at my lips and inquires, "Butter, syrup, or both?"

My flutters go crazy, and zings race up and down my spine. It's too much touching him after everything that happened last night. His spicy, woody scent creates havoc in my veins. His large palm cups my ass as if I'm his and this is just an ordinary, sexy breakfast between two people who aren't captor and captive.

Attempting to calm my quivering insides, I stare at the pancakes, watching him butter, cut, then pour syrup over them. I question, "Why do you make me sit on your lap and feed me?"

His body stiffens. He finishes doctoring my food, puts a forkful to my lips, and softly orders, "Eat your pancakes, angel."

I sigh, open my mouth, and try not to groan from the sugary goodness bursting on my tongue.

"Good?" he asks, with a hopeful look in his eye.

It only adds more perplexity to this situation. Why does he appear to care? If he's my captor, shouldn't he just use me for sex, then be a nasty ass the rest of the time?

I swallow and nod. "Yeah. Thanks."

He tucks a lock of my hair behind my ear then drags his finger over my jaw. His other thumb strokes the top of my ass.

Tingles erupt under his touch. I close my eyes and reach for his shoulder to steady myself. When I open my lids, he moves both hands to my cheeks and slides his tongue in my mouth.

There's no way to escape him or his possessive hold on me. I don't stand a chance against him. He's too dominant and electric. The crackling of my skin intensifies. I fall into him and his warm body, turning in the chair until I'm straddling him and returning every ounce of affection he gives me.

I wish I could stop. He's like an addiction I never knew I had. Every flick of his tongue against mine is a metal rod stoking a fire. His palm bunches my T-shirt. He drags one finger over my spine, and I shudder.

"You don't like sitting on my lap?" he mumbles into my mouth then sucks on the pulse beating hard in my neck.

"Oh God!" I moan.

He moves his arm under my shirt and fists my hair. His hot breath hits my ear. "Answer me, angel." His hand moves between us, and he slides two fingers up me, then strokes my clit with his thumb.

"I-I...oh God!" I tug at his hair.

He grunts. "I think there are a lot of advantages to sitting on my lap, don't you?" He moves my face back in front of his and returns to kissing me like I'm his possession.

I am his possession. The thought hits me like a brick to the face.

This isn't right.

Maybe I could stop it if everything about him didn't feel so damn good. My head spins, and I grind on his hand, not able to control myself.

"Fuck this. You need more, don't you, lass?" he taunts.

"Yes," I reply into his mouth, back in his trance, wanting him to possess me and not allowing my guilt to tell him to stop.

He assaults me with his tongue then asks between kisses, "What do you want from me, angel?"

For you to control me.

For you to dominate me.

For you to make me yours forever.

Before I can contemplate the message I'm sending him, I whisper, "Please fuck me, Daddy."

He groans, lifts his hips, and drops his joggers. "Jesus, you're perfect."

I'm more screwed up than I assumed. My ego shoots to the sky at the knowledge that a man like him thinks I'm anywhere in his league. I disregard the fact he's a complete psychopath and I have no idea what he'll really do to me.

I slide over his erection, moaning and trembling, still sore from all he did to me last night, but not able to stop myself from doing it again. It's so wrong. I know it is. I still don't even understand what he thinks I did. But I push all the guilt to the back of my mind about who he is and why I shouldn't be voluntarily allowing him to have me.

He sits straighter, holds me so close to him there's no air between us, and removes my T-shirt. His palm on my back holds me tight to him, and when he thrusts, the same sensation I had the night before ignites. Something, I don't know what it is, rolls on my clit. Every time he thrusts, it creates mind-boggling friction between us.

"Doesn't Daddy make you feel good, angel?" he murmurs then nibbles on my nipple.

"Oh shit!" I scream out.

"Answer me," he orders.

"So good, Daddy," I breathe out and grind my body against whatever it is that's rolling on my clit, while sinking deeper onto him.

His tongue swipes my ear, and I whimper. He demands, "You like me taking care of you. Don't you?"

I close my eyes, fighting my rational voice ordering me to tell him taking care of someone doesn't involve kidnapping.

"Admit it. You love sitting on my lap and driving me insane."

My ego does another victory pump. I don't know how I'm driving him mad when he's got my body humming whenever I'm near him.

His phone buzzes, and he kisses my neck, grabs it, then freezes.

"What's wrong?" I ask.

He tosses his phone down. His tone turns rough. "And you love it when I put my hands all over you." He pinches my nipple and starts thrusting again.

"Yes!" I cry out, not able to deny any of it.

His lips brush my ear. "When you thought of me over these past few months, what did you want from me?"

Heat burns in my body. There are too many sensations and emotions tugging at me. I shouldn't be doing this, but I can't seem to say no.

"Tell me. What did you want from me?" he forcefully interrogates.

"You! I wanted you!" I breathe. "This! Oh God!" My clit hits whatever is between us, and my body erupts in tremors. My eyes roll, and I grip his shoulders.

He tugs my chin in front of his face. I blink, trying to bring him into focus. He growls, "Don't lie to me, lass."

"I'm not!"

His face hardens.

I don't know what's happening or why he doesn't believe me. I slide my hands to his cheeks and firmly say, "Only you."

Agonizing betrayal fills his expression, and he freezes. My heart races, unsure what I've done. He lifts me off him, rises, then maneuvers me into his bedroom.

"Declan. I don't understand what's happening right now," I admit.

He barks, "Bad girls get punished. I told you not to lie to me."

"I-I didn't!"

He shakes his head, clenching his jaw. It's as if he's holding back his temper and disgusted with me. I'm lost why he thinks I'm lying.

The vein near his eye pulses, matching his angry glare. It scares me. I realize I don't know him. He's back to Hyde, and I'm afraid he's going to hurt me.

"Knees on the headboard."

"Wh-what?"

"Do what I say and stop asking questions," he orders.

Trembling, I put my knees against the headboard.

He gets behind me, and I think he might take me, but he grabs the cuffs and demands, "Clasp your hands together and put them above your head."

I do what he says.

He secures one cuff around both my wrists then stands on the mattress and attaches the other restraint near the top of the headboard so I'm practically rising off my knees.

My breathing turns short.

The sound of the chains moving on the ground fills my ears, and more fear hits me. He attaches them to my ankles, and I have no ability to move.

"Declan, please. I don't know—"

He fists my hair and tugs my head back so my cheek is against his. "I won't allow you to lie to me. You're going to stay here and think about your bad behavior. When I get back, I want the truth."

"The truth to what?" I cry out.

"Stop trying to play me," he seethes.

Tears stream down my face. Frustrated, hurt, and bewildered by everything he thinks I've done that I'm clueless about, I scream, "I don't know why I'm here! Tell me!"

"Stop lying! You targeted my family and me. Whatever I have to do to get the truth out of you, I will. So you better be prepared to talk when I return."

I sob, "I don't know your family! I only met you once!"

"Liar! Who are you working for?" he growls.

"What? I'm not working for anyone!"

"Don't push me, Simona," he warns then releases me and gets off the bed.

A new fear fills me. I'm stretched out and naked. If he's leaving, how long am I going to be like this? What if he keeps me here forever?

"Declan!" I shout.

"Stop talking! While I'm gone, you don't say a word."

"Don't go! Please! Declan!" I scream as loud as I can, feeling like my lungs are caving in on me.

"I said be quiet."

"Declan! Let me go!" I scream, turning my head to look at him.

He goes to his drawer, pulls out the gag, and pushes the ball in my mouth. My pulse shoots to the sky as he secures it over my head. He murmurs in my ear, "I didn't want this. You chose it by not obeying. I hope for your sake you make the right decision when I return." He leaves, and I hear the garage door rise and an engine start.

I work on calming my racing heart, but all I can do is think about what he's going to do to me when he returns. I don't know what he believes I did. And I curse myself for not escaping last night when I had the chance. But I won't make that mistake again. If I survive his wrath, I'm going to run the first chance I get.

8

Declan

A BLOCK AWAY FROM MY HOUSE, I PULL OVER. MY SKIN'S crawling, and the twitch in my vein is only getting worse. I take a few deep breaths and reread the text I received.

Nolan: *A new article is out. The stock price is moving up. Who is she working for?*

"Dammit!" I shout, hitting the steering wheel. The quick rush of pain does nothing to take my mind off the sting I can't escape. I've spent too many hours trying to get Simona to a point where she'll tell me the truth. I assumed after last night she would confess, and then I could make some decisions about what to do with her. Once again, she tempted me. Instead of interrogating her like I should have been, I fell prey to her big blue eyes, pouty red lips, and naivety.

I need to stop thinking she's innocent. She's not. She's screwed with my family's future. I'll be damned if I spend the rest of my days living off drug and gambling money. When my brothers and I committed to the clan, Liam's father made us close our construction business. My paycheck now comes from others' addiction, and I don't like it. If I don't get to the root of who's masterminding these articles, all the work we've done to make this deal happen is about to go up in flames.

Four days have passed. I'm no closer than I was before. The only thing I can rule out is that Simona's acting alone. Someone is in charge, but it can't be her if she doesn't have access to any technology. I wish there were a possibility she's not involved in this, but that isn't reality. It burns me deeper than I thought possible that she's lying to me.

I click on the link Nolan sent and read the article. My gut does a nosedive. The same article I destroyed is now all over the financial sites, claiming Jack Christian's company will have record quarterly earnings. A quote from Jack says, "I've never felt as optimistic about where the business is heading. The new patents rolling out will redefine the cybersecurity industry."

It's all fabricated. Jack is ashes, distributed all over Lake Michigan by Obrecht and me. And Judge Peterson shared his fate.

Another text pops up.

Liam: *Meeting at my house. No excuses. Now.*

Shit, shit, shit!

I toss my phone in the cupholder and continue to Liam's house. When I pull in, Nolan gets out of his Jeep. He waits for me and crosses his arms, scowling.

"I don't want to hear it," I bark when I get out.

"Who's she working for?" he seethes.

My chest tightens. "I haven't found out yet."

"You've had her for four days!"

I ignore his exasperated look and stomp toward the front door. Liam opens it before I climb up the last step. His glower matches Nolan's.

Great. There's no getting out of it. I'm going to have to come clean about Simona.

When I enter the house, Finn's eyes are slits throwing me daggers.

He better not have told Liam. It needs to come from me, or Liam is going to go ape shit. I trust Nolan to keep his mouth shut. I never pinned Finn for a rat, but he and Liam are too close. And he's too off-kilter right now from not finding Brenna.

As soon as the door closes, Liam barks, "We need to uncover whoever is putting these articles out. If the stock price rises much more, we're going to have to put more money into our accounts or bail. This entire plan will fail. Where are we at, Declan?"

The oxygen in my lungs turns stale. I wish Killian weren't on his second honeymoon. He's better at calming Liam down when Finn isn't around. From my discussion with Finn last night at the pub, I don't expect him to come to my rescue.

Admitting to Liam I've kept Simona a secret isn't going to go over very well, either. I choose my words carefully. "I picked up a hacker who was posting articles. I'm interrogating and will find out who's behind it. The article that got posted today is the same one I deleted from the financial sites the other night."

Liam's face turns red. He moves closer to me and drops his voice. "You picked someone up and kept it from me?"

"I'm doing my job. You've got enough to deal with."

"This is the most important thing we have going on. You know this," he accuses.

I fire back, "Yes, and when I get the details we need from her, I'll make sure you're informed."

Liam's eyes widen. "Her?"

My heart races so fast it hurts. "Yeah."

"I was at the warehouse this morning. Where is she?" he growls.

My gut somersaults. No matter what, I need to leave here keeping Simona with me. After this morning, I should turn her over, but I can't seem to give her up. I tell a half-truth. "At my house. I have her chained up, and she's about to break."

Finn sniffs hard, but I avoid looking at him. I'm grateful he didn't tell Liam before I did, but I'm wondering what he'll say. I'm clear how he feels.

Rage continues to bloom in Liam's expression. "What in God's name were you thinking, taking her to your house?"

"She's a woman. It's not a typical situation. The warehouse isn't the right environment to get her to talk."

Liam points in my face. "She's an enemy. We learned all about female enemies from dealing with Dasha and Orla."

Dasha is Adrian Ivanov's ex-wife, who had the Polish mob put a bullet in him. He almost died. Orla was the Bailey princess who stalked, threatened, and attempted to kill Nolan's wife, Gemma.

I slap his finger away from me, cross my arms, and declare, "This isn't the same thing. I have her contained. She isn't running all over town plotting to kill anyone."

"You should never have an enemy at your house. It's why we have the warehouse," Liam explodes.

Nolan interjects, "Can we take a breather for a minute?"

"Did you know about this?" Liam seethes.

I lie again. "No. I didn't tell any of my brothers."

Liam turns to Finn. "And you?"

Finn's hardened expression never changes. To my surprise, he replies, "No." It surprises me. Not once have I known him to ever lie to Liam.

"If Declan is about to break her, it's not in our best interest to move her right now. We need to focus on finding out who else is posting these articles," Nolan states.

Liam takes a deep breath and stares at Finn.

Finn nods. "Nolan's right."

Liam spins. "You have a week. And I want to see who this girl is."

"No. I don't need you coming in and destroying the progress I made." I can't take any risks of Liam finding out I'm no closer to knowing the truth than the night I picked her up. Since I cut up her clothes, if he sees her chained to my bed, naked or even with a T-shirt on, he's going to know I'm in over my head.

"Where in your house do you have her chained?"

Blood pounds hard, slamming into my skull. I can't lie about this one. I already admitted to Finn she's in my room. I firmly state, as if it's not a big deal, "My bed. The cell I created in my basement and had her chained in almost gave her hypothermia." I omit telling them I stripped her naked and intentionally kept the heat off.

Nolan shifts on his feet, and I realize he didn't know I moved her from the cell. I'm sure I'll get an earful when we leave.

Liam's green eyes flare so hot, I think he might reach for my neck and attempt to strangle me. "You made a cell in your house? What the fuck, Declan? You've been planning this all this time?"

The more I talk, the deeper I seem to bury myself. "I knew I was picking up a hacker and possibly one with more skills than me. Before you all took a turn at interrogating, I wanted to assess whatever talent the hacker had that I don't so I can further my abilities. It makes sense for me to have twenty-four-seven access."

"Who is she?" he demands.

"Her name is Simona Carter. She's a student at the tech school. I've not come across a hacker with her skills. It's to our advantage you let me learn whatever I can from her," I reiterate and curse myself again for spending four days without even attempting to have Simona show me what I don't know.

Liam steps closer. "How old is she?"

"Twenty-one. Almost twenty-two," I add, as if that will make the situation any better.

"You have a twenty-one-year-old chained to your bed. Did you fuck her?"

I avoid his question. "She's the enemy. I know what I'm doing. And you're wasting my time keeping me here. I need to return and find out who else is posting these articles."

"Jesus. You are screwing her, aren't you?" he asks incredulously.

"Did you not hear me say I need to get back so we can figure this mess out?"

"Bring her to the warehouse. You're not keeping a woman who's half your age in your house when you're also fucking her. Goddammit, Declan! I expect more from you," Liam curses.

"No. She stays at my house."

"She goes to the warehouse. Today. Now."

"We're already short on time. Do you want to lose all the progress I've made? If you put her in the warehouse, you will," I threaten, my stomach flipping at the thought of Simona going there.

"Progress you've made? By servicing your dick?" Liam rants.

Nolan steps between us. "Okay, enough! This situation is what it is. If Declan thinks we'll waste time on this by moving her, then we need to trust his judgment. Let's not lose focus."

Liam continues giving me a look of death.

"Nolan is right. You gave him a week. If he doesn't get anywhere by then, we move her to the warehouse," Finn adds.

Liam takes several calculated breaths. "If my father were alive, he'd bring you in front of the council."

My stomach twists, and I swallow the bile rising in my throat. "Well, he's not. You're in charge. If that's what you need to do to make yourself feel better, then do it." It's a stupid thing to say on my part. The council will interrogate me for days on end, and Simona will immediately go in front of them. They will decide her fate. As angry as I am that she's lying to me, I don't even want to think what might happen to her if the council gets involved.

Liam's jaw clenches and he looks at the ceiling. Darragh's death hasn't been easy on him. Liam got out of prison and barely got any time with him before Darragh passed.

"That's not the right solution," Finn quietly states.

"I'm leaving. Unless you have anything else to say?" I announce.

Liam snarls, "You have one week. Use it wisely. After that, she goes to the warehouse."

I leave without responding. Nolan follows me out of the house. When I get to the car, he growls, "Your bedroom?"

I spin. "I'm past this conversation. Unless you have something to say to help me figure this out, mind your own business."

"This is my business. It's all of our business."

"Shut up and let me do my job." I open the door, but he slams it shut.

"Declan, you're in over your head."

"No, I'm not. And get your hand off my door."

He shakes his head. "If Gemma finds out about this, she's going to have issues with me. And she'll never forgive you."

I love Gemma. She's become a sister to me. But I say, "That's her issue, not mine. And the only way she's finding out is if you tell her."

"Never thought your dick was more important than family," he accuses.

I jab his chest with my finger. "You better watch your mouth, little brother."

"She needs to go to the warehouse."

"Keep your opinion to yourself." I get in my car, quickly reverse out of the driveway, and within a few minutes, I'm in my garage. My blood is still boiling, so I take several moments to breathe.

When the vein near my eye stops throbbing, I get out and enter the house. It's been a half hour since I left Simona. If she were a male, I'd leave her alone and restrained longer, but the guilt eats at me. Her muscles are probably shaking by now, but she won't have any long-term damage. If I wait much longer, it's going to take days for her muscles to repair. Plus, the plate of pancakes sitting on the table adds another layer to my already-conflicted resolve.

I grab a bottle of water, open the bedroom door, and study the perfect vision in front of me, minus that damn ball gag I hate.

She chose it, I remind myself again.

Her black hair hangs to the middle of her back. The way her arms stretch toward the ceiling gives me a perfect view of the side of her breast.

Those pink nipples are going to ruin me for all other women's breasts. They're as hard as last night, on full display, and one look makes my erection begin to grow.

Her creamy skin and heart-shaped ass make me want to keep her like that and take her from behind. Something about Simona in chains, with her fate in my hands, is majestic. She's a unicorn.

She's my enemy.

Her arms tremble, and she grips the chains like she did last night when she rode me backward. My cock aches, dying to resume what I didn't finish with her earlier this morning.

I need to make progress, or Liam will come here and demand I take her to the warehouse. I reprimand myself for my attraction toward her, approach the bed, and set the water bottle on the table.

She turns to look at me, gagged, with her big blue orbs glistening.

Unable to resist, I run my knuckles down her frame, starting at her wrists, moving slowly over the side of her breast, the curve of her waist, hips, and thigh.

She shudders and closes her eyes. Her chest rises and falls faster, and my blood heats.

"Are you ready to talk, angel?" I softly ask.

A tear drips down her cheek.

I wipe it away and outline the gag. "I hate putting this on you."

Confusion fills her expression.

"Nod if you're ready to talk," I order.

She pins her eyebrows together and gives me another look that breaks my heart.

"Nod, angel," I repeat and palm her ass.

She blinks hard and nods.

"Good girl." I rub her ass then remove the gag. I pick up the water bottle and remove the cap. I hold it to her lips. "Drink, lass."

She obeys, thirsty, drinking almost the entire thing. I make a mental note to keep her hydrated better. The last thing I need is another incident like the hypothermia one.

I drag my knuckles up her body this time until I reach the restraint. Not able to keep my thoughts to myself, I admit, "You've made me so hard, angel."

She takes a shaky breath.

I press my forehead to her cheek and kiss her neck, murmuring, "No one has ever looked sexier in chains than you."

A tiny whimper flies out of her mouth.

I groan then slide my hand on the inside of her thigh, stroking her higher and higher until I reach the edge of her pussy. My testosterone builds in my cells. I convince myself if she's relaxed, she'll tell me more. "You're wet, just like a good girl should be. Do you want Daddy to make you feel better before we talk?"

She inhales through her nose, not responding, but her legs shake. Her throat pops forward when she swallows hard. I tilt my head and see defiance and lust swirling in her eyes, and it only makes my erection throb.

"If you don't answer, I'll make an assumption," I add and wish I could eliminate the guilt about how things went down between us this morning.

The fight continues in her expression. To test the waters, I pull her chin toward mine and kiss her, parting the seam of her lips with my tongue.

She gasps, and I flick inside her mouth a few times, then retreat, staring at her. Blue, heavy flames erupt in her eyes. I return to her lips, and she begins kissing me back. I retreat, assess her some more, and when I move toward her, she meets me halfway, greedily exploring my mouth.

Her response to my kiss tells me all I need to know, but I break it and hold her head near mine. "Are you ready for Daddy to make you feel better?"

Her perplexity reappears.

Since she doesn't voice her choice, I decide for her. I release the tension in the ankle chains. "Time to stand up." I put my hands on her hips, move her on her feet, and spin her so her back is against the headboard. I adjust the chain so her arms stay above her head, and there is barely any slack.

I kneel in front of her and take her pink nipple into my mouth. Then I slide both hands up her arms and lock my hands between hers.

She moans, arching her back into the headboard and gripping my hands hard. I release them, and grasp her wrists with only one hand. Pinching the nipple my mouth was on, I lightly bite her other one.

"Oh!" she softly cries out.

I spend several minutes enjoying her breasts then let go of her wrists. Moving down her body, I work her belly button hoop with my tongue, slipping a finger through her wet heat.

"Oh God," she whispers.

My finger circles her clit, and I put my face in front of hers. "Who am I to you, angel?"

In a raspy voice, she declares, "My Daddy."

"Yeah, lass. That's right. Now tell Daddy you want him to make you feel good." I rub her so fast, heat flies to her cheeks. She almost orgasms, but I slow her down.

She doesn't answer me, so I do it several more times until she begs, "Please."

"Tell me," I demand.

She loses her resolve. Her desperate voice shakes, "Please, Daddy. Make me come."

She's fucking perfection.

My tongue automatically flies out of my mouth and into hers. I push her over the edge, and she moans like a wild animal.

I say against her lips, "Good girl. Daddy loves the taste of your pussy. Grip your chains, angel."

Lightning bursts in her eyes. Her arms shake, and she clutches the chains.

I sit back on my knees for a moment, looking up at my brilliant, lust-filled, restrained, and going-to-tear-me-apart-when-this-ends woman. There's never been a more beautiful sight.

Her gaze meets mine as her entire body quivers.

I slide my palms up her dewy thighs and bring my nose to her sex, inhaling the luxurious scent I'll never get enough of, then kiss her pussy.

"Oh," she breathes.

Debating on where to start, I decide to nibble on her clit.

"Oh God!"

"No more God, lass. If you yell his name one more time, I'm stopping. Is that what you want?" I threaten, glancing up.

"No! Please don't stop!"

"Please who?"

"Please, Daddy!"

My cock aches so badly, I almost abandon my mission and sink it into her. But then I'd be cheating my mouth out of its meal. I throw her thighs over my shoulders and slowly explore her pussy. Her salty-sweet flavor bursts in my mouth, making me need more. I shove my tongue inside her tight channel, inching in and out in circles until she's writhing against the headboard.

Her voice gets louder. "Oh...oh...."

It's so angelic, I need to hear more. I order, "I better hear what you want, or I'm going to stop." I blow on her pussy then wait.

It doesn't take long before my threat works. Every word rolling out of her mouth is a firecracker lighting me up. She grinds her lower body into my face. "Please, Daddy."

"Please what?"

"Lick me. Please."

I groan and obey, reaching up and playing with her nipples while slowly lapping at her sex.

"Faster," she demands.

I increase my speed but not much.

"More," she orders and continues riding my face.

Nothing on Earth has ever given me this much pleasure. Every desire she voices drives my ego higher.

"Suck me, Daddy," she whimpers.

I stop moving my tongue and drag her clit into my mouth with my lips, applying a little bit of pressure.

"Add your tongue!"

I hold in my chuckle, knowing exactly what she wants, and slowly flick to drive her crazy.

"More! Daddy... I'm-I'm...oh God, Daddy!" she cries out.

I ignore the God since she added the Daddy and increase it a little more, then slow it down, keeping a rotation to hold her off from flying over the edge.

"Please!" she begs, over and over. Sweat pops out all over her skin. Her thighs squeeze my cheeks so hard, it becomes hard to breathe.

The chains creak above me. I pin her body tighter between my face and the headboard and latch on to her pussy like my life depends on it.

She screams obscenities and violently convulses.

No longer able to control myself, I shimmy up her body, drop my joggers, and thrust into her.

Her mouth forms an O, and her eyes blink several times. I move my knees so they hit the headboard and my barbell piercings will massage her clit. They run from the base of my penis to my hip. Each ball sits next to the other, positioned in a straight line with my cock.

She moans, and her eyes flutter.

I reach up, wrapping my hand around both her wrists. My other hand fists her hair. Like a needy animal, I mercilessly thrust inside her, trying to find the sweet relief from the torture she's put me through today. Every move I make, I press into her, making sure her clit stays stimulated.

Her sounds become incoherent. The blue in her eyes gets lost several times from rolling. Our tongues battle, as if in war, trying to own the other.

"We're good together, angel. Tell me the truth, and we'll figure this out," I blurt out, surprising myself with what I'm advocating. It's not a ploy. I want her. I don't know how I'm going to give her up. Yet, I know this can't end well.

"I-I-oh!" she whimpers, her fingers tightening around the chains and inner walls collapsing on my cock.

It's like I opened Pandora's box. I do everything in my power not to end this moment, needing her to trust me so we can figure out how to move forward.

I pin my gaze on hers. Against her lips, I reveal too many of my cards. "I want you, angel. Not as my prisoner but because you want to be mine. Give me the truth so we can move on."

She never stops moaning, and her eyes never focus. She's too far gone into her orgasms. When her body spasms harder, I lose the fight, releasing into her like a bomb shooting out of a cannon.

In my aftermath, I stay frozen, except for my lungs fighting to find air.

Still trembling, she slowly opens her eyes. Emotion swirls in them, and I don't know what to make of it.

Unable to pull myself out of the hole I'm creating, I release her cuffs and guide her arms around my shoulders. I stroke her cheek. "I meant what I said. I only need the truth from you."

Her words could be a knife slashing me. The tear dripping down her cheek looks real, making me believe she's an outstanding actress. Her lips tremble and her voice shakes. "I keep telling you, I don't know what you're talking about."

9

Simona

The vein around Declan's eye pulses. Hurt fills his face. Then rage replaces it.

It makes no sense why he believes I'm capable of doing anything to him or his family. He's a dangerous man. His brother Killian looks like one, too. *Who am I compared to them and their power?*

He grinds his molars and focuses on the space above my head.

I rarely get to touch him since most of the time he keeps me restrained. I slide my hands on his cheeks and force him to look at me. Trying to keep it together and not become a sobbing mess again, I beg, "Please. Tell me what you think I did. I-I don't understand why you're accusing me of hurting you."

A brief moment passes where I think he believes me, but then his eyes turn to slits. His rough voice probes, "Are you going to tell me that you aren't a hacker next?"

How does he know I'm a hacker?

My silence infuriates him more. He shakes his head in disgust, pulls out of me, then releases my legs from his waist.

"Wait!" I grab his arm, but he shrugs me off him.

"Don't tell me any more lies!" he bellows.

"I'm not! You caught me off guard. How do you know I'm a hacker?"

His face darkens. "Do you really want to go down this path?"

"What path?"

More hatred fills his face. "Where you pretend not to know anything and I guide you through it step-by-step."

Fed up with his accusations that I don't understand, I put my hand on my hip and assert, "Yes. If that's going to help me understand why you hate me so much and think I'm out to harm you, then walk me through it. I have nothing to hide!"

He scrubs his hands on his face, pulls up his pants, then jumps off the bed. He steps toward the door.

I panic he's going to leave me again or that I'll never find out what he thinks I've done. I yell, "Where are you going? Don't be a hypocrite! If you want to accuse me of something, then have the balls to tell me what it is!"

He freezes, then spins, his eyes shooting blue flames.

"I'll tell you whatever I know. Just be honest with me," I beg.

He sarcastically laughs. "You have a lot of nerve talking about honesty."

"I'm not a liar," I sternly say.

"Fine." He goes into the closet, comes out with a T-shirt, and tosses it to me. He unlocks the restraints around my ankles and says, "Talk."

"I'm taking a shower first."

"No, you aren't," he growls.

Anger bubbles so fast in me, I hold my ground. "Yeah, I am. You're dripping down my legs. And thanks for protecting me by using a condom when you fuck me."

A look of guilt flies onto his face.

"Hopefully, you don't have any STDs. And God forbid I get pregnant and have to raise a child while chained to your bed," I hurl at him, worrying for the first time about having sex with him multiple times without any protection.

His eyes widen.

To hurt him, since he thinks that's all I'm capable of, in a snotty voice, I add, "Oh, sorry. That would mean you give two shits about me and not just yourself. Way to take care of me. *Daddy*." I push past him, the most pissed I've been since arriving here. When I get to the bathroom, I slam the door and stay under the hot shower for a long time, unable to stop the tears from escaping.

When I get out, I dry my face and find the determination not to feel sorry for myself anymore. I won't waste anymore of my tears on him. I brush my teeth again then comb through all the knots in my hair, cursing him for not having conditioner.

Still upset that I could get pregnant and bring a baby into this environment, when I promised myself I would never subject a child to any situation like what my parents put me in, I toss on the T-shirt. I study my reflection in the mirror and tell myself to calm down and pull it together. I need to find out what he thinks I've done and somehow make him see I haven't harmed him.

I go out to the main room. The table has a platter with ham and cheese sandwiches. A bowl filled with berries is next to it. There are two place settings with glasses of water, napkins, and plates. Two laptops, including mine, are off to the side.

The hairs on my arms rise. *Why does he have it?*

He pulls out a chair and motions for me to sit.

I snap, "What? You aren't going to feed me?"

He glowers. "If you want to get lippy, I'll happily sit you on my lap and do just that."

"Yeah, I'm sure you would," I fire back and sit down. "And next time you kidnap a woman, add some conditioner to your shower."

He ignores my comments, sits next to me, and nods to the food. "Eat."

"Why? Do you want to make sure our baby isn't malnourished?" I challenge.

He sniffs hard, and his vein twitches. "I said to eat."

"Whatever." I pick up a sandwich and add some berries to my plate since I'm starving. Once I take a few bites, I can't stop, and eat in blissful silence, trying to ignore the weight of Declan's stare on me. I finish all my food and my water then stare at the kitchen, my insides starting to quiver again. I don't know what to say or do. Looking at him is only going to cause me more pain.

He quietly says, "Why aren't you on birth control?"

The question angers me. I hurl out, "Why don't you have a vasectomy?"

"How do you know I didn't?"

"Did you?" I ask in surprise.

His lips twitch. "No. I'm Catholic."

I snap, "Which would mean you shouldn't expect me to be on the pill!"

"Aren't all women these days?" he asks, as if he really believes that.

"You're such a dick."

He ignores my insult and lowers his voice. "I'm clean, so you have nothing to worry about. I always protect myself."

Rage torpedoes me. It's not only at him. I never told him to put a condom on. I kissed him when he was going to leave the bedroom last night. I'm the one who begged him only an hour ago to fuck me again. I spout, "Except with me? Why is that?"

He takes a deep breath, grinding his molars while the vein near his eye twitches. Genuine shame covers his face, but I remind myself he's my captor and not to be trusted. Relief consumes me when he avoids my question and states, "We need to talk, angel."

"Stop calling me angel. Don't say I'm your lass or anything else but my name. Let's not confuse this situation. All I am to you is someone you see as an enemy."

Surprise fills his face.

I huff. "Do you think I'm stupid?"

In a deadpan voice, he states, "No. I think you're the most intelligent woman I've ever met."

My heart skips a beat, and I reprimand myself. "You know nothing about me."

"I know you're acing your classes at one of the toughest private technical schools in the state, possibly the country. And you're a better hacker than I am."

I hold my breath. *How does he know my grades?*

"You aren't the only one who can hack," he winks.

"You broke into the school's records?" I fret.

"Yeah."

"I could get kicked out for that!" As soon as I say it, I realize I shouldn't be worried. He's already told me he plans on keeping me here forever. If I'm able to escape, I can't stay in Chicago.

"I looked at other students' besides yours. But it's untraceable since I erased my footprint."

"How long have you been stalking me?" I demand.

His head jerks back. "Stalking you? After I met you at the pub, I didn't know where you went. I only knew it was you when I lifted the hood off your face in the cell."

So many things about that statement irritate me. "Where I went? I stayed like a moron until closing time. I waited for you since you promised you were coming back." It's another admission I wish I didn't make.

Remorse fills his face, but I'm not falling for it. He seems to know way too much about me. He claims, "I told you I had an issue to take care of. I meant to come back."

I ignore his statement. "And maybe before you throw a hood over someone's face, you should make sure they're the right person first. Since you've mistaken me for whoever this person is who's harming your family. Unless you're another level of psycho than what I have you pegged for and it's all in your mind!"

His eyes turn to slits. "Let's cut the sarcasm. Who are you working for?"

"Are you referring to my school cafeteria or waitress job?"

"Don't play dumb, angel."

"I'm not your angel. Stop acting like I mean something to you!" I turn my head and breathe through my quivering emotions. Why did I let him touch me again? I played right into his hand. All he wanted to do was butter me up so I admit to whatever this crazy notion is in his head.

Silence cuts through the air. My beating heart is so loud, I wonder if he can hear it. Repulsion fills me. I hate the fact my body is still buzzing from being next to him. I don't know why I can't turn off wanting him. The sexual energy between us never dims and only seems to consume me to a point I feel as if I might combust if he doesn't touch me, even after he's shown his cards. He's a textbook psychopath. Everything I fought to escape from my childhood, he represents. I'm not safe here. And I'm fooling myself that I am when I'm in his arms; it isn't helping me escape my predicament. No matter how good it feels to be with him, I'll never truly be protected. It breaks my heart that the one person I need to shield myself from is the only man I've ever craved.

He gets up, goes to the minibar, and pours himself two fingers of whiskey. Looking out the window, he sternly asks, "Did you not hear what I said to you earlier?" He downs the alcohol in two mouthfuls.

My insides quiver. I blink back tears. "You seem to like calling me a liar but are okay with being one yourself."

He spins, and I avoid looking at him. "It wasn't a lie. I want to get past this with you."

I wipe my face. "I don't believe you."

"Why?"

"You can't get past something when the other person is a raving lunatic who doesn't listen."

"I'm listening. All I've wanted to do was hear what you have to say. Yet, all you do is deny everything," he states, so full of conviction and hurt, I question if I have lied to him then reprimand myself.

He's the one misinformed, not me.

"For the last time, I haven't done anything. I don't know what you're even referring to!" I shout for what feels like the millionth time.

He takes three steps, slams the tumbler down on the table so hard, it cracks. His hands wave in the air, and he growls, "Who hired you for the articles, Simona?"

Flashbacks of my last foster home, before I ran away, erupt in my mind. I hold my hands over my face in fear, cowering and shaking.

Time seems to freeze. He reaches for me, and I jump back so fast, the chair I'm seated in topples. I fall to the ground and shriek when my back slams into the edge of the wooden frame.

He leans down, but I coil into a ball, covering my face again. My chest tightens. Pain streaks through my heart. I wince from the throbbing in my back and cry out, "Don't touch me!"

Declan crouches at eye level. He holds his hands out like I'm a wounded animal. "I'm not going to hurt you."

I let out a teary laugh and admit, "You already have." Everything crashes down on me. My tears fall freely. The entire situation with Declan and what I want him to be, but he never will, blinks like a neon sign taunting me. The tremendous pain shooting through my back hurts worse than anything I've felt in years.

It feels like forever passes before Declan softly says, "Let me look at your back."

The pulsing hasn't stopped. I don't know what else to do, so I don't fight him.

"Before I move you, I think it's best if I pull the chair away and you roll onto your stomach."

"Okay," I sob in agreement.

He carefully takes the chair away from me. I roll over, wincing. He strokes my cheek and pulls the T-shirt up to my neck. He studies my back and mutters, "Jesus."

"What?" I panic.

"You already have a large bruise forming."

I close my eyes and try to breathe through the throbs like I used to when I was a child. Maybe it's the situation, but it only makes me feel suffocated.

"It looks like it's the top of your right shoulder area." He presses his palms into my lower back. "Does this hurt?"

"No."

"I think it's your delt and lat muscles. I'm going to slide my arms under your stomach and thighs then lift you on your feet. Let's see how you feel standing."

I nod.

He wipes more tears off me then slides his arms under my body. "Count of three, okay, angel?"

"Okay." I sniffle.

"One. Two. Three." He gracefully lifts me then tilts my body so I'm on my feet. He moves his hands under my armpits. Worry fills his eyes. "Any different pain?"

I swallow hard. "No. Just below my shoulder area."

He dips down and kisses me. It's sweet and gentle. It makes everything so much worse.

More tears fall, and he wipes them away.

"Let me get you to the bedroom. You need to lie down and take an anti-inflammatory. I'll rub some arnica on your back." He moves me toward the bedroom before I can object.

When I get there, the wrist cuffs are hanging from the headboard. The ankle chains drape over the bed from when he released me. Our reality gets shoved in my face once more. My love-hate relationship with the restraints only makes my emotions spin out of control until I'm ready to lose every bit of pride I have left. I scrunch my face and choke out, "Are you putting those on me?" The damn breaks, and I sob again.

Declan surprises me. He tugs me into his chest, holding me tightly to him by palming my ass with one hand and my head with the other. He presses his lips into my hair. "Shh."

"Why do you have to hate me?" I cry out, loathing myself further for still caring and showing him my raw feelings.

He tightens his hold on me. "Shh. I don't hate you. I want to, but I can't."

His admission cuts me deeper.

"I don't know what you think I did. All I do is go to school and work. I-I never even go out, except the night I met you," I hysterically confess.

"Shh. I need you to calm down, angel. We'll talk about it later. Right now, we have to take care of your back," he states.

Pain keeps me from pleading my innocence anymore. I keep crying, unable to stop for a long time. When I pull away from Declan, my tears stain his shirt. He wipes my face, gives me a chaste kiss, then says, "Hold on."

He slides all the chains and cuffs under the bed. He pulls back the covers and pats the mattress. "Take off your T-shirt and lie down on your stomach, lass."

I step forward, and he moves my arms above my head, then tugs the T-shirt off me. I get into the bed, and he covers me, then kneels on the floor.

He strokes my hair. "I'm sorry this happened."

"I'd never hurt you. And I don't know who your family is, except for Killian. You introduced me to him," I claim, crying again.

Something passes in his eyes. I can't figure it out. I'm too distraught.

He inhales deeply and brings his lips to mine. "We'll talk about this later. I'm going to get the first aid kit and some water."

I say nothing. He studies me but finally rises and leaves the room. He returns and gives me a prescription-grade anti-inflammatory, rubs the muscle relaxer on my bruise, and slides next to me. "You're probably going to fall asleep from the pill I gave you."

He's right. I keep mumbling that I don't know what I did and wouldn't hurt him or his family. I eventually fall asleep, unchained, inhaling his skin and wishing things were different.

10

Declan

Something happened to Simona. I don't know what, but she cowered when I got angry. She thought I was going to hit her. Granted, I kidnapped her, but not once has she recoiled in fear of me physically hurting her.

It takes all the control I have not to interrogate her until she tells me what happened and who hurt her. But I vow when she's feeling better, I'm going to find out.

She finally falls asleep. The nagging feeling I'm missing something isn't going away. My angel was seriously hurt, but she cried herself to sleep, repeatedly claiming her innocence.

Her bruise only gets more prominent, filling the entire side of her upper back. She slammed hard into the wood. I'm grateful it wasn't on her spine or vertebrae and she didn't break something. The pain has to be excruciating. A normal person would only be crying over their injury. She's maintained her innocence even when I was trying to get her to forget about it. Her distraught behavior leads me to believe she's either the best actress in the world, or I'm missing something.

When I'm confident she's passed out, I go into my office. I need to get to the bottom of Simona's involvement before a week is up and Liam demands I take her to the warehouse. The thought eats at my heart, and I fight the urge to take her out of Chicago and hide her forever.

Not once in my life have I ever been in this predicament. I'm losing time and need to gain ground. Sighing, I text Nolan. He created an algorithm to track any information that appears on Jack Christian's company.

Me: *Has anything new popped up?*

Nolan: *Besides your dick in the coed?*

Me: *Knock it off.*

Nolan: *Nothing. Have you found out anything yet?*

Me: *Not yet.*

Nolan: *Why are you risking this? You should follow Liam's advice on this one.*

My blood pounds harder. There's no way anyone is getting their hands on my angel. Not now or ever. For the first time in my life, I might have it in me to kill an O'Malley. It officially makes me know I'm in over my head.

Me: *Drop it. If anything pops up, let me know.*

I return to the dining area and grab both our laptops off the table. I go into the bedroom, study her sleeping, then open up both computers.

I hacked into Simona's laptop the other day. It took me longer than usual, but the security level didn't surprise me since she's so talented. I scroll through her social media again, looking for anyone who I may have overlooked, but the account is so bare of personal contacts, it's pointless. All she follows is fashion brands or influencers who flaunt products. And it strikes me that she has good taste. The brands she follows are a mix of high and low end, but everything screams sexy sophistication. Besides her fashion following, she only has a few connections with other students or co-workers. It's glaringly obvious she doesn't seem to have much of a life besides her two jobs and school.

That's what she claimed.

Maybe she's telling the truth? I attempt to shut the voice up in my head for several hours, but it's only getting louder.

I reread her email messages, including the new ones, but everything is school related. Guilt crashes through me when I read a new one from her professor.

Simona,

You haven't been in class this week. Is everything okay? You've never missed, and the hands-on work we're doing is 40% of your grade.

Please let me know if something personal has popped up. You've worked so hard for your degree, and as you know, this class is a requirement for graduation.

Sincerely,

Professor Milliken

I CLOSE MY EYES AND SIGH. HER PERFECT GPA AND YEARS OF hard work are going down the drain. It makes me detest myself.

I reread the rest of the emails, trying to find something, anything I missed. There isn't anything.

A new email arrives. The subject line reads, Lease Termination. It's from her landlord.

MS. CARTER,

Thank you for getting caught up on your late rent payments. I no longer wish to keep you as a tenant since you struggle to pay on time each month. Per our lease agreement, I'm not renewing your terms. As of today, you are no longer entitled to stay in your unit. Please move out by the end of the week to avoid eviction, which will result in court costs. Also, as stated in the lease agreement, you are responsible for those costs, should I have to start the eviction process.

Sincerely,

Mark Smith

I PULL UP THE ATTACHED AGREEMENT AND CRINGE. IT'S TILTED toward the landlord, which doesn't surprise me. The end of the week is in two days. I debate about what to do then text my cousin, who owns a moving company.

Me: *I need a job done tomorrow. It's on the South side and shouldn't take long.*

Cathal: *Send me the address. Where do you want the items taken to?*

Me: *My house. You'll have to pick the lock. It's an easy one.*

Cathal: *Done.*

I send him the address to Simona's.

I exit the email account and am about to close her laptop when a notification pops up from a site called College-TechMoney.

I've not heard of it, and I click on the notification.

BusyCEO: *I have another job for you.*

The hairs on my arms rise. I glance at my sleeping angel. Betrayal and anger fill me. She swore she only had two jobs. She never mentioned this.

I decide to reply.

TechStudent001: *What is it?*

BusyCEO: *Same as before.*

My pulse climbs faster. I take a risk.

TechStudent001: *Another article?*

BusyCEO: *Yes. But you bailed last time. What happened?*

TechStudent001: *Did you not get my message?*

BusyCEO: *No.*

TechStudent001: *Oh! I'm sorry! My computer crashed. I had to get it fixed, but everything is working fine now.*

BusyCEO: *That's good to hear. Not everyone on this site is as competent as you.*

TechStudent001: *LOL. Thanks.*

BusyCEO: *I'm sending it now. Same drill as before. Middle of the night. And delete your footprint.*

TechStudent001: *No worries.*

My gut drops. There's a ding, and another box pops up. I click on it, and a new positive article about Jack Christian's company is on it.

A third notification box pops up.

CollegeTechMoney Money Center: *You've got a pending payment due upon job completion. Check this box when you've finished your task. We'll notify BusyCEO and release your funds. To view your account, click here.*

I click the link, and bile rises in my throat. A trail of all the jobs Simona has taken is listed. For every job, she gets ten dollars. All the articles posted online, she did.

There are no other jobs, except from BusyCEO.

My angel is screwing us over for ten dollars an article?

I stare at her, peacefully sleeping with tear-stained, porcelain cheeks. All I hear is her trying to convince me she doesn't know what she did to hurt me.

Is it possible she didn't know what she was doing, and I've been wrong this entire time?

A horrible feeling claws at me, sinking deep into my soul. If I've been wrong, how will I ever make this right with her?

Panic spreads throughout me, but I force myself to turn my attention back to CollegeTechMoney. I research whatever I can on the company, but there's no info other than the main website. I attempt to hack into the server, but my initial attempts fail.

I text Nolan.

Me: *I need you to come to my house.*

Nolan: *Now?*

Me: *Yes.*

Nolan: *Gemma and I are on our way to dinner.*

Me: *Stop by. Leave Gemma in the car while we talk.*

I shut the bedroom door and pace my living room. There's only a slim chance Simona knows the real identity of Busy-CEO. That means we're probably no closer to ending this.

Cringing, I close my eyes again, replaying all the shit I've done to her over the last few days.

She's never going to forgive me if she's innocent. Simona's angelic face pops up in my mind, and I hate myself more. *How did I not see there was a possibility she couldn't be part of this?*

Ten dollars.

Jesus. She didn't even get paid fairly.

Nolan walks in and says, "Make it fast. I'm not ruining my night with Gemma over your crazy shit."

"It's not her."

"For crying out loud! Get your dick out of your head!"

"Listen to me! There's a site called CollegeTechMoney. Have you heard of it?"

His eyes turn to slits. "No. What is it?"

"There isn't a lot of information on it, just a website. People pay college students to fix their tech issues. Simona did post those articles and erase her footprint. But someone named BusyCEO paid her."

He scrubs his face. "You just admitted she got paid to fuck us over. Get your head out of your ass."

"I don't think she knew," I insist.

"Is that what she claims? How convenient—"

"She doesn't even know I'm aware. She fell and got hurt. She's sleeping. I was on her computer, and a job came in. I pretended to be her. He wants her to post another positive article."

Nolan steps closer. "She's getting rich off—"

"It's ten dollars an article."

Silence fills the room. Nolan doesn't take his steely gaze off mine.

I firmly state, "I don't think she knew what she was doing. We need to find who BusyCEO is, and in the meantime, we better start releasing negative articles to counteract the positive ones."

He glances around the room and lowers his voice. "Whoever is behind this wants to take us down. You know how our enemies cover things up. Stop thinking with your dick. If she's part of them—"

"When you thought Gemma wasn't part of the Baileys, but still didn't fully trust her, did I have your back?" I hurl at him.

Nolan takes a deep breath. "Yes."

My heart races. "I don't think Simona is part of this. And I can't leave tonight. She's injured. I need you to stop at Liam's. Until we find out who's trying to take us down, I think we keep her account and pretend to be her. I'll accept the jobs and do what's required. Then we know what's coming, so we can counteract it with a negative article. I'll have her show me what she was doing to erase her footprint so fast so we can do the same with our articles."

He clenches his jaw. "So we buy time until we can track this guy down."

"Yeah."

He shifts on his feet. "I'll stop at Liam's. But he's going to want more answers."

"Not tonight. He needs to stay away tonight," I insist.

"Until you're positive she's not involved in this, you need to keep your head clear," he warns.

"I am."

He doesn't look convinced, but his voice softens. "How badly is she injured?"

"Her back has a horrible bruise from the edge of the chair. I gave her an anti-inflammatory prescription pill. She's been sleeping for a few hours," I inform him.

"Does she need to get an X-ray?"

"I believe it's muscular, but I'm going to keep an eye on it."

He pauses then lowers his voice. "What are you going to do with her? If she didn't know what she's doing and is innocent in this, what if she goes to the police once you release her?"

My gut twists. She would have every right to try and take me down after what I've done to her. Instead, I reply, "Isn't that why Liam has the police captain in his pocket?"

Nolan sniffs hard. "Highly doubt Liam will want to owe the captain a favor over this one. That prick is going to require a big one to put kidnapping a college student under the rug."

I sigh. "Yeah, I know."

"Keep me posted." Nolan throws me another suspicious glance then leaves.

I pace for another few hours, trying to figure out how to approach this with Simona. I need to know the truth. My gut is screaming there's no way she knows what she's involved in —not for ten dollars an article.

The bedroom door opens and Simona walks out in my T-shirt. More guilt eats at me that I cut up all her clothes. I step toward her and cup her cheeks. "How are you feeling, angel?"

She puts on a brave face. "It's throbbing still. I'm sure it'll go away soon."

"I'm sorry you got hurt."

She nods. "I know. You already told me that."

I caress her jawline with my thumb. "Are you hungry? You should eat before you take more medication. I can cook, or we can order in."

She smiles. "Yeah. I'm starving, actually."

"What do you like besides spaghetti?"

She shrugs. "Anything without peanuts."

"No peanuts. Got it." I wink.

A tiny laugh escapes her lips, and my heart stammers. I find myself praying she didn't do it and somehow, I'll be able to make this up to her.

She bites on her lip. Her big blue eyes are slightly foggy from the medication and sleep. She's so beautiful, and for the first time since I kidnapped her, I wonder how I couldn't see her innocence.

I don't know that yet.

She has to be. It was ten dollars. She's struggling to pay her rent.

Why didn't she tell me about the job?

My ongoing wish that things could be different between us changes.

It's no longer a wish. It's a need deep within me, burning through my soul.

My animalistic craving for her only expands until I have to act on it. Palming her ass, I tug her close to me, fist her hair, and part the seam of her lips with my tongue. She gasps then hesitates, as if struggling to return my affection. It happens whenever I initially kiss her. I retreat and study her, watching the blue flames ignite in her eyes, then slide my tongue back into her mouth. This time, she succumbs, kissing me hot and hungry like she always does. Her body molds to mine. Unlike when she's chained, her hands lace into my hair, and she massages my temples with her thumbs.

Tingles race down my spine. I groan and remember she's injured. If I don't stop, I'm going to take this too far. I break our kiss, murmuring, "Why don't we order from the pub. One of the guys can deliver it."

She opens her mouth then shuts it.

"What is it, lass?"

She pauses then asks, "You said the pub is yours? Is that what you do for a living?"

A tidal wave of remorse hits me. I didn't just accuse her of destroying my family. I believed it deep within my core. Does she really know nothing about us? Has she not lied?

I drag my finger over her forehead and tuck her hair behind her ear. "It was my nana's. When she passed, my sister Nora inherited it. My brothers and I watch over it. We call it ours, but it's Nora's."

Her question-filled expression never changes. "So, you're Irish then?"

"Yeah."

"Is your last name O'Malley, or was that your nana's maiden name?"

She doesn't know my last name? I question again if she's playing me. My gut says she isn't, which only increases my anxiety. "Yes. It's O'Malley. What's your heritage, angel?"

Darkness fills her face. "I-I don't know."

My chest tightens. "Why not?"

She shifts uncomfortably. Pain fills her blue orbs. "I grew up in foster homes. I never met my father and barely remember my mother. She overdosed when I was fifteen."

Images of her as a child with her black hair and big blue eyes, being shuffled between houses, makes me want to kill someone. I lost my parents, but I was an adult. I can't imagine not having a stable home, my brothers, or Nora. I tighten my arms around her. "I'm sorry. That must have been difficult."

She bites on her lip, saying nothing.

"Do you have siblings?" I ask.

"No. At least, none that I know of. Can we change the subject?"

I want to ask her more, but I refrain. "Sure. Let me pull up the pub menu, and you can tell me what you want."

"Fish and chips," she blurts out.

My lips twitch. "Good choice. People come from all over for it."

She nods. "I heard people raving about it after you left me that night. It looked and smelled delicious."

That night. What I wouldn't give to have a redo on that night.

Without analyzing it, I tell her, "When you feel better, I'll buy you a dress and take you somewhere nice. You can pick what kind of new food you want to try."

She freezes. Then she pins her eyebrows together. Her lips tremble. She finally speaks. "I'm...umm... I'm confused. You're going to let me leave the house?"

My heart races. I have questions for her, but she's injured. I don't want to create any more stress for her this evening. Everything I've learned in the last few hours tells me she's an innocent pawn in this mess. And all I've wanted to do since the night I met her is take her out on a nice date. I'm not immune to the fact this is a fucked-up proposition from me to her. I'm probably crazier than I thought to expect her to even want to go, much less look at me. "Yeah. If you want to go to dinner with me?"

Her bewilderment grows. "I have a choice?"

Anxiety attacks my chest. This is what I've done. Taken away her choices. If I've done this mistakenly, how do I turn it around?

I struggle to find the right answer. If she did do this and is still playing me, I need to stay in control. If she didn't, I'm going to regret this for the rest of my life. With my heart pounding into my chest cavity, I reply, "Yeah, angel. You've been a good girl. You get to choose if you want me to take you out to dinner."

Please say yes, I repeat during the deafening silence.

She hesitates so long, I feel like I'm going to break out in a sweat. I think she's going to say no. She finally, cautiously, says, "Okay."

Happy and relieved, I peck her on the lips and place two orders for fish and chips. I text one of my cousins who guards my house to pick it up for me.

The entire time, she doesn't move, as if unsure what she should be doing.

I finish then command, "Spin, and let me see your back."

She obeys, and I lift the T-shirt. The bruise is black-and-blue. "I think I should put some more cream on it."

She doesn't argue, and we return to the bedroom. I remove her shirt then have her lie on her stomach. I rub the muscle relaxer over her wound and kiss the nape of her neck.

Her soft inhale puts my cock back into a state of chaos. I lie next to her and prop my head on my elbow then drag my knuckles down her spine.

A flush creeps into her cheeks as she shudders. The heavy look in her eyes that appears whenever I touch her returns.

Chaos reigns in my veins, buzzing so fast, I almost get dizzy. Placing my palm on her ass, I refrain from making any other moves on her. "After dinner, you need another anti-inflammatory."

Something passes in her expression. It reminds me of a wounded animal and tears at my heart. The longer she stares at me, the glassier her eyes become.

I slide my arm under her head and scoot closer. "What's wrong, angel?"

She takes a shaky breath, as if she's about to lose all control over her emotions. A tear gracefully glides down her cheek.

Her voice shakes, tearing at me further. "I wish I wouldn't have met you the night I was at the pub."

My heart almost stops. "Why?"

She closes her eyes, and a dam breaks within her. She barely gets out, "I'm too confused. I need to stop thinking I'm anything more to you than your prisoner."

11

Simona

DECLAN'S WARM BODY PRESSES CLOSER TO MINE. HIS BLUE EYES widen as if he's panicking. It's another sign I'm reading too far into everything that's happened between us. All the notions I have about us somehow making it past this crazy situation need to stop.

I'm his prisoner. He gets to control, possess, and decide my fate. Whenever I disobey, he'll determine the consequences. And the more I deny trying to hurt him and his family, the angrier he's going to get.

He claimed he doesn't hate me, but he does. I've seen it too many times in his expression. So I need to remember when he's acting like the man I want him to be, that it's not who he is. His affection is purely physical and will never go past that into anything more profound.

Why did it sound like he was asking me on a date?

It's not. It can't be when I'm his prisoner.

He acted like I had a choice to say yes or no.

Is he going to take me out on the town like his trophy to display? How would I even act in public with him? Will others know I'm his prisoner, or will they think I'm a woman at dinner with him of my own free will?

I would have done anything to go on a date with him when I first met him, and all those months I obsessed over him, I dreamed about it. Now, it only adds more perplexity to our warped situation.

His warm hand caresses my bare ass. Zings fly straight to my pussy. I wish I could turn off my reaction to him. It clouds everything. No matter how much I tell myself I won't let him have me, the moment he touches me, I lose my resolve to tell him no and not fall into who we are physically.

He brings his face right next to mine. In a gravelly voice, he firmly states, "You are more to me than just my prisoner."

The statement only keeps my tears flowing. I've never met any man I felt drawn to, fantasized about, or wanted. What he's done to me should make all of that go away. He should repulse me. Yet, all our time together has done is make my craving dig deeper into my soul.

The last few days have shown me that I'm a screwed-up human being. I want to believe I mean more to him. It's as if I *need* to be more, but his version of meaning more and mine must be two different things.

As messed up as our situation is, I want him to tell me I'll always be his. I want him to keep me, not because he hates me and is scared of whatever it is he thinks I'm capable of doing to him and his family, but because he needs me as badly as I feel I need him.

It will never happen though. The mounting disdain I have for myself only grows. I'm addicted to his touch, obsessed with how he's the only man who's ever lit me up and seems to know how to do it over and over again. Desperation for him to crave me as a woman he sees as special, and not because I'm his captive and sleeping in his bed, consumes me.

None of my wishes will ever come true. The longer I keep allowing myself to want these things, the more damage I'll do to myself.

"Shh." He keeps stroking my cheek and wiping my tears.

It's painful to look at him. When I do, I see the lie of a future I keep telling myself we could someday have if we could figure out how to get past our current situation.

Like every time Declan is near me, he uses his body as a weapon. This time, his lips and tongue are his way of stealing so much of my breath, I can't continue crying. It doesn't matter how many times I tell myself not to give in to him; there's no way I'm able to resist. He's a sinkhole of every good feeling you could ever experience. Once you step in, there's no way to pull yourself out.

I know better than to wish for things, especially for people to stay. It's only a prescription for disappointment. I need to untangle myself from this never-ending cobweb of sexual tension so I can think straight.

"I told myself not to take you home the night I met you," he mumbles.

I freeze. *Does that mean he didn't like me as much as I perceived? Is that why he never came back?*

His fingers lightly massage my scalp. He keeps his lips against mine while he speaks, and his large palm never stops stroking my ass. "It's true. All I thought about was bringing you back here. I've never wanted to get anyone in my bed as much as I did you. But I knew you were special. If I hadn't gotten that text, I would have asked you out. It would have been for the next night because there was no way I would have been able to stay away from you for any longer."

My heart is a chaotic blend of skipping a beat and rupturing in two. I stare at him, craving to be those two people from that night.

"Since then, every time I walked into the pub, I looked for you. All night long, I'd watch who stepped through the door, hoping it was you."

New tears fall. I choke out, "Why are you telling me this?"

His face hardens, and I don't know what to make of it. The longer his silence lasts, the more anxiety grows in my chest. He deeply inhales and curls my hair around his fist. He speaks slowly, as if wanting me to soak up every word of his reply. "I've never looked forward to kissing anyone as much as I do you. I don't get off fucking them the same way I do when I'm with you. And I don't drive myself insane obsessing over anyone else the way I obsess about you. So this may not be an ideal situation, and I'm a selfish bastard, but there isn't any other woman in the world who I care about more than you."

My heart stammers. It's the most beautiful thing he could have said to me and equally just as painful. His statement mirrors my feelings. It makes me question if being his prisoner is wrong if I get him as a byproduct. I refrain from saying it's worth giving up my freedom for him, but it almost slips from my lips. I'm aware of how erroneous my thinking is, yet I could happily drown in him for admitting to me what he just did.

The doorbell rings. He gives me a chaste kiss. "That's dinner. Stay here, and I'll bring it in." He gets up.

"I can come to the table," I offer.

He gently smiles and drags his finger over my jawline. His eyes twinkle. "No, angel. Let me serve you in bed." He leans into my ear. "Daddy wants to keep you naked. Not because you're my prisoner, but because your sexy little body is giving me another hard-on. And after I feed you, I'm going to make you see how obsessed I am with you."

I laugh through my tears and heat fills my face.

"Lass, when your cheeks flush like that, you don't know how many dirty thoughts race through my mind." He kisses my cheek, pats my ass, and winks. "Don't go anywhere. Remember, good girls get rewarded." He puts a blanket over me and walks away.

When he's near the door, I become a stupid girl again, seductively replying, "I'll be a good girl, Daddy." The voice in my head reprimands me while my loins burn at the thought of being rewarded.

Shit. I've become like Pavlov's dogs, salivating over the slightest suggestion of sex.

He groans, dramatically places his hand over his heart, and steps out of the room.

He's cute when he's being funny.

I'm his captive, for crying out loud! I shouldn't be thinking like this.

Ugh!

I wipe my face and think about what he said while biting my smile. I shouldn't keep allowing myself to feel anything toward him or let myself sink into any happy thoughts about us together. There is no us, just him and his captive, yet I don't know how to stop.

A few minutes pass, and he comes into the bedroom with a tray. A heaping plate of fish and chips, two bottles of water, silverware, napkins, and a bowl of condiments are on it. He sets it down, fluffs the pillows against the headboard, and I sit up. The blanket falls and he glances at my breasts, licks his lips, then meets my gaze. "Do I have to put a T-shirt on you?"

My heart beats faster, and I arch my eyebrows. "Are you giving me a choice again?"

"Yeah, angel. Whatever you want is okay."

"I think it's only fair if I'm naked, you should be."

What am I doing?

Since when do I let my loins rule my rationale?

Surprise takes over his expression, but arrogance quickly replaces it. He rises, reaches behind him, and pulls his T-shirt off, displaying his inked, chiseled flesh. He keeps his eyes on me and drops his pants.

He's so damn sexy, I don't stand a chance. I linger over his body parts, working my way down, then freeze.

"Like what you see, lass?"

My face heats again. His long, thick cock is hard, but the metal, marble-sized balls pierced in a perfect vertical row from the base of his penis to his hip bone make me clench my insides. I swallow hard. "You have piercings. I wondered what it was."

He smirks then swaggers to the bed. "All for your pleasure, angel. Scoot up."

I obey, and he slides behind me. I lean into him and glance up. "Is this another way of me sitting on your lap so you can feed me?"

His hand slides over my pussy, gliding back and forth in a lazy rhythm. He kisses my ear. "Admit you like sitting on my lap and letting me feed you while my cock suffers in pain, thinking about all the things I want to do to you."

My skin crackles, and the buzzing in my veins intensifies. Closing my eyes, I squirm from his dexterous touch, trying to forget about all the worries I have about what this is between us, if it's okay for me to like sitting on his lap while he feeds me, and all the other taboo things we seem to do.

He sucks on my lobe, and his other hand circles my nipple. "So many benefits, my angel. Did I tell you how sexy these pink nipples of yours are, or how much they turn me on?"

I whimper and turn my head, meeting his filthy gaze.

His lips press against mine. His tongue slowly flicks at the speed of his fingers. He mumbles, "This is what I meant, angel. See why I look forward to your lips?"

I moan, turning to Jell-O, sliding my tongue back in his mouth and wanting more.

He retreats. "I'm not hurting your shoulder, am I?"

"No. You make me forget about it," I admit.

"That's good." He brings his finger to my lips and commands, "Be a good girl and lick."

I obey, moving my tongue from the base of his finger to the tip, then starting all over again. The salty-sweet taste of my arousal fills my mouth.

His cock twitches against my spine. "You're such a good girl, lass." He moves his hand to his mouth, and he sucks his finger, his blue flames studying me.

In a trance, I whisper, "You're so dirty, Daddy."

He kisses my collarbone, and tingles erupt from the spot his lips touched. "Time to eat, angel. You have more medicine to take tonight." He reaches for a fork, uses the side to cut a piece of the fish, then holds it to my mouth.

I take a bite and groan. It's crispy on the outside, flakey on the inside, and seasoned to perfection.

He gets another forkful, says, "Good, isn't it?" then shoves it in his mouth.

I finish chewing, swallow, and nod. "Delicious."

He holds another bite to my lips, and I accept it.

"It's my nana's recipe."

"That's nice. Do you have a lot of family traditions?" I ask.

"I suppose so." He offers me a fry, and I bite half of it. He pops the other half in his mouth.

I finish it and am unsure why but admit, "I always wished I had some—even just one. Sometimes on holidays, I feel out of place. Maybe it's because everyone is getting ready to celebrate with their families or going to parties. I never have anything to do."

His arm tightens around my waist. The beat of his heart pounds faster into my back. "What about other family members? Do you have any cousins or aunts and uncles?"

"Not that I know about." I snag another french fry and take a bite then hold it to Declan's mouth.

He chews it, opens a bottle of water, then holds it to my lips. I take several sips, and he takes one, then puts the cap back on it. "You said you were in several foster homes. How many?"

The clawing in my gut I always feel when I think of my childhood awakens. "Eight."

His body stiffens. He quietly asks, "Why so many?"

My voice drops as I admit things I've never spoken about to anyone. "They tried to put me back with my mother a few times. It never lasted more than a week. One of the kids I lived with set fire to the house. My fifth foster mother died of cancer. In the last place I was at, two boys would beat on me at night. The social worker was coming to visit the next day, and I knew if she saw my bruises, she'd move me to a different house again. I didn't want to go anywhere new. I'd had enough. So I ran away."

Deafening silence fills the room. I stare at the food, wishing I didn't say anything. *Why did I blab my past so easily?*

Declan's hot breath continues to hit my neck. He asks, "Is that why you thought I was going to hit you when you fell?"

My stomach lurches. I had forgotten about my reaction. Shame crawls into my cheeks. Everything that happened to me in my foster homes, I've tried to forget. It was years ago. It's embarrassing that I still let it affect me.

His voice softens. "Angel?"

"Yes." I close my eyes, wishing I never opened my mouth. The confusion I always feel around Declan returns. He's my captor, not my boyfriend. The last thing I should be doing is confiding in him about anything regarding my life.

"How old were you when you ran away?"

"I need to go to the bathroom," I lie and push at his arms. He releases me. I avoid looking at him and leave the bedroom, shutting the bathroom door and locking it.

For several moments, I stand with my palms on the counter, staring at myself in the mirror. Every day I'm with Declan, I do more things that surprise me. All it does is add more perplexity around our situation.

These intimate moments, where we talk like a couple, need to stop. Sex with Declan, no matter how good it feels, needs to end. At all times, I can't forget he doesn't care about me. The only thoughts I should concentrate on are how to get away from him.

As time passes, my determination grows to keep things between Declan and me nonsexual and our boundaries clear.

I need to escape. I did it at fifteen. I can do it now.

Tonight. I'll convince him to keep the chains off me if he attempts to use them and leave while he's asleep.

I review the layout of the house. Declan's house is four times the size of my apartment, but it's doable. Right as my confidence becomes unbreakable, another blow hits me. Men's voices reach my ears. I freeze and listen closer.

The first voice heckles, "It's just a cat, you pussy."

"Shut up!" another man orders.

Their voices trail off, and dread fills me. *Why are there men around his house?*

He's a dangerous man and probably into other bad things.

I can get past them. I'll grab a knife and run as fast as I can.

My heart and blood pump harder. *Could I really stab someone?*

If that's what it takes, I need to do it. I've worked too hard for my freedom to stay Declan's prisoner.

Resolved to leave tonight, I take a deep breath and leave the bathroom. Declan's on the phone, sitting on the edge of the bed with his back toward me.

I freeze, listening.

"He's taking him to your place and not ours?" He rubs his hand through his hair and sighs. "Jesus. I'll meet you there." He hangs up and looks at the ceiling, shaking his head.

He's leaving.

I can't let him restrain me.

I step forward and crawl on the bed then wrap my arms around him. It feels normal, as if I should be comforting him. He reaches behind me and slides his hands on my thighs, and my zings go out of control again. "Is everything okay?"

He turns his head. "I have to go out."

"Right now?"

"Yes."

"When will you be back?"

His face hardens. "I'm unsure. It might be a few days."

"A few days?" I ask in a panicked tone, but it's not all false. For some reason, the thought creates anxiety in my chest.

He rises and pulls the covers back. "You need to rest. I'm going to leave you the anti-inflammatory pills. Take one after you finish eating, one tomorrow after breakfast, and then every six hours after. Help yourself to anything in my kitchen."

I reach for his cheek. I wish I could admit this was all an act, but something about him leaving like this worries me. "Will you be okay?"

Something passes in his expression. I don't know what to make of it. It looks loving, but I remind myself he's a psychopath and not anyone I should have feelings for, or I should think has real ones for me.

"I'll be fine," he replies then hesitates but finally says, "I'll have my brother Nolan check on you tomorrow."

"That's not necessary. I'll be fine."

He wraps his arm around me, palming my ass, and strokes my cheek. "No, angel. You're hurt, and I hate that I have to leave you right now. I can't be away for days and not make sure you're okay."

"I just need rest," I proclaim.

"I'm still sending him over."

I nod. I'd rather him not know I'm gone until he gets back in a few days, but it is what it is. Tonight is the perfect opportunity to escape.

"I have to go, angel."

As much as I'd like to convince myself I'm acting, my heart spikes with pain. This is the last time I'll see him. Never again will I feel his body against mine or meet anyone who lights me on fire the way he does. I'm not so naive to know what Declan physically gives me isn't normal.

I slide my fingers through his hair and pull his face toward mine, desperately kissing him, wanting to savor every moment of what it's like to have a man make me feel as if I'm the only woman on earth who he needs and wants.

Like every time we kiss, my skin buzzes. Adrenaline heats all my cells. I mold into his muscular frame as he possessively owns my body.

It's bittersweet and hits me harder than I anticipated. My eyes tear up, and I hate myself for being emotional. He's my kidnapper, not someone who cares about me. At any moment, he'll turn from Jekyll back into Hyde.

He ends our kiss, his blue flames smoldering, and holds my face close to his. "I'll try to return as soon as possible."

I nod. "Okay. Ummm...be safe."

He gives me another hot kiss then has me sit, covers me up, and puts the tray of food over my thighs. "Make sure you eat before you take the medicine, and drink lots of water." He puts the pill bottle on the table, kisses my forehead, then goes into his closet.

I eat, not sure when I'll have my next meal. I can't return to my apartment. I have no wallet, phone, or anything.

My laptop catches my eye on the table next to his side of the bed. *I'll find a backpack and take it.*

He steps out of the closet dressed in all black. After another hot kiss, he leaves. The sound of the garage door hits my ears then the start of a vehicle's engine. The door closes, and my mind spins with what to do.

I need clothes.

I look in his closet, but my shoes and pants aren't there. My washed undergarments are on a shelf. I put them on then go into the basement.

The musty smell and cold hits me as soon as I open the door. I turn on the light. My chest tightens as I make my way down the stairs and into the cell. I slide on my pants, socks, and shoes. I'm grateful he kidnapped me in my sneakers. I grab my shredded tops and go back into the bedroom.

My sweatshirts and shirt are useless. I'm unsure what I thought I could do with them. I toss them on the bed and go into his closet. I put several layers on. Everything is too large for me, but it's better than nothing.

There's a small duffle bag. I dump out the contents, which looks like workout clothes. I put my laptop in it. Since we both have Mac computers, I test his charger. It works on mine, so I keep it plugged in while I look around the rest of the house.

I've never been a thief. But the lessons of the street I learned when I fled my foster home stuck with me. I find a few hundred dollars of cash and pull his couch apart to find any coins that might have fallen through the cushions. There are several dollars' worth, and I toss them in the bag.

I study the knives in the kitchen and put two in my bag and keep one out to hold in my hand in case I run into his men.

I need to take food and water.

The fridge has water, so I throw six bottles into the bag. I ransack the pantry and find several boxes of energy bars. Every one of them gets thrown into the bag.

There's a hallway closet near the front door. I find a black wool hat, gloves, scarf, and a coat. I put all of them on, tucking my hair into the cap, then putting the hood of his sweatshirt over it. I wrap the scarf around my face so only my eyes peek out.

I sweep the house one more time, looking for more money and anything I should take that could help me. There's a small plastic container in the laundry room I missed the first time around. It's filled with more coins and bills. I dump it all in my bag.

My stomach somersaults. The backpack digs into my injured shoulder, and I wince and grit my teeth at the pain. Gripping the steak knife, I open the door. An alarm blares, making me jump.

Shit!

I fly out of the house and halfway down the sidewalk, I run into a man's chest.

"Lass, where's the fire?" the voice I heard earlier asks.

I don't answer or look up. With as much power as possible, I jab the knife into him.

"What the fuck!" he screams and releases his hold on me.

I leave the knife jammed into his side and run past him. I get halfway down the driveway when another man tackles me.

A blood-curdling wail flies out of my mouth from the pain of my body hitting the pavement. The man's strong body smashes into my bruised back, knocking the wind out of me.

Another voice I've never heard fills my ears. "Nolan, we've got a problem."

12

Declan

DARKNESS SURROUNDS THE OUTSIDE OF THE IVANOV GARAGE. Snowflakes started to fall, and the pavement was slippery, so it took more time to get here than usual. It's only the end of October. We don't usually get snow this thick before November.

Finn's SUV is parked and covered in snow, but there's no sign of Maksim's car. I'm sure he had his driver drop him off.

I text Maksim I'm here. He called to say Finn picked up Judge Peterson's son Matt. Instead of taking him to our warehouse, he opted to take him to the Ivanov garage. I'm unsure why Finn would do that. Now that Obrecht had his day with Jack Christian and Finn killed the judge during that same event, he should be executing things on O'Malley ground. Maksim and Finn seem to have gotten close again, but it doesn't make sense. I want to know his reasoning for this.

I told the guards outside my house if anything happened to call Nolan, and I might be gone for several days. I didn't let my brother or Liam know where I was going. Something tells me if Finn wanted them to know, he would have taken Matt to the warehouse.

Maksim lets me inside.

Finn scowls, "What are you doing here?"

I cross my arms. "Why aren't you at the warehouse?"

Finn's eyes turn to slits. "Thought Matt would enjoy seeing Maksim and me in action. Plus, none of you stopped me from killing the judge too soon last time."

I sigh. Finn was so enraged, he snapped the judge's head backward and broke his neck earlier than he should have. Maybe he's right to have called Maksim in on this.

Maksim sits on top of the desk and sharpens his knife. "We should set some ground rules."

"What's that?" I ask.

"I'm in charge."

"Excuse me?" Finn barks.

Maksim remains calm and arches his eyebrows, continuing to scrape the blade on the stone. "You're too close to this. It's why you killed his father earlier than you should have. You called me for a reason. Don't let your ego take charge of this."

"Fine," Finn grumbles.

"He's a pussy like his father. If he knows anything about Brenna's location, I expect him to sing within five minutes," I state.

Finn crosses his arms and snarls, "He knows. There's no way the judge kept that from him. Those two were thick as thieves."

I take my knife out and hold my hand out to Maksim for the stone. He gives it to me, and I sharpen my blade. "What accessories do you want to use?"

Maksim's eyes darken. "Liam gave us some of your acid wands. That sounds fun."

"I'm kind of partial to your staple gun."

Maksim nods in approval. "Grab it."

Finn paces the small space. I study him while moving the steel over the flint. He's agitated, similar to the night we tortured and killed Jack Christian and the judge.

"Finn," I call out.

He spins, his expression bathed in hatred.

"I think—"

A loud pound on the front door fills the room and Nolan's voice booms, "Declan!"

Due to having to concentrate on driving through the snow, I forgot to call Nolan to check on Simona. I glance at Maksim. "Did you tell my brother I was here?"

"No."

I open the door, and Nolan's red-cheeked scowl makes the hairs on my arms rise. I blurt out, "What's wrong?"

He shakes his head. "Got a call from your guys. You need to go home."

"What happened?" I ask, stepping toward the door.

Nolan follows me outside and spins me toward him. I almost slip and fall, but I grab his arm.

"What the fuck!" I shout.

"She tried to escape! Did you leave her roaming your house freely?"

The knife I just sharpened could be slicing through my heart. *She wanted to leave me?*

I ignore his question, regain my composure, and attempt to leave, but Nolan follows me. He barks, "Declan!"

A new panic fills me. I spin toward him. "Tell me she didn't get hurt."

"She stabbed Tiernan with a steak knife."

I freeze. There's no way my angel has it in her. "What are you talking about?"

"They moved him to Liam's house, and the doctor is stitching him up."

I should care more about Tiernan, but I'm so angry and hurt that Simona would break my trust. "You still haven't told me she isn't hurt."

Nolan shakes his head. "What the fuck is wrong with you? I just told you she stabbed our blood. Why are you worried about her?"

Enraged like him but for different reasons, I grab the top of his coat. "Answer my question!"

He pushes me back. "Get your hands off me."

"Tell me!"

His glare intensifies, but his voice drops. "Yeah. She's hurt."

Bile rises in my throat. I swallow it down. "How?"

"I don't know."

"Did they take her to Liam's so the doctor can examine her?"

"No. She's still at your house. That's all I know. I came straight here once Liam confirmed you weren't at the garage."

"Those idiots!" I stomp to my SUV, grab the snow brush, and frantically clear my windshield.

"Did you forget she stabbed Tiernan?" Nolan accuses.

I ignore him then get in my vehicle and turn on the engine. I reverse and drive as fast as possible, but the snow is so thick, I can barely see.

Too many thoughts spin through my mind as I grip the wheel, attempting to calm my racing heart.

My angel is injured. She was already hurt earlier today. What did they do to her?

She wanted to escape from me.

It takes way too long to get home. My rage and panic mix into an all-time high. When I enter the house, I growl, "Where is she?"

My anger boils and overflows when I step into my family room. My angel is sitting in a dining room chair with a rope around her. Tears stain her cheeks, and so much agony is in her blue eyes, I want to kill my cousin Callum.

I grab his collar and yank him toward my face. "What the hell are you doing?"

His eyes widen in confusion. "What do you—"

"Get the fuck out of my house before I tear you apart," I threaten then push him away from me. I take my knife out of my pocket and tear through the rope then crouch in front of Simona.

Her entire body is trembling. She has on several of my shirts and her pants and shoes I kidnapped her in. They're damp and dirty. I pull her into my arms, and she buries her face into my chest and sobs.

I put my hand over her head and turn my head. "Callum!"

He spins; his gaze throws darts at mine.

"What happened to her?"

He swallows hard. "She stabbed Tiernan and ran. I stopped her."

Simona shakes harder.

"How?" I seethe.

Callum shifts on his feet. "I tackled her at the end of your driveway."

The quivering wrath in my body intensifies. In an attempt not to scare Simona further, I keep my voice low. "You tackled her?"

"She stabbed Tiernan!"

"Get out of my house!"

His scorn blazes hotter than I've ever seen it. He spins and slams the door behind him.

For several minutes, I debate on how to handle this situation. I prioritize her injuries. I murmur, "Let's get these clothes off so I can examine you. You might need a doctor."

She slowly meets my gaze and says nothing as more tears fall from her eyes.

I wipe my thumbs on her cheeks. "Where does it hurt, angel?"

She scrunches her face and takes several shaky inhales.

"Lass? I need to know."

Her lids open. "Everywhere."

I'm going to kill Callum.

I fist the bottom of her shirts and order, "Raise your arms."

Her arms move several inches, her breathing picks up, and her face contorts.

"Stop."

She freezes.

"Where does it hurt when you move your arms?"

"Under my right breast."

Shit. "Don't move." I take my knife and slit through the several layers of shirts then remove her bra, pants, shoes, and socks. Bruises cover her breasts, stomach, knees, and thighs. I could be wrong due to the swelling, but it looks like at least one rib, possibly more, is sticking out of place.

The vein near my eye pulses. I remind myself to stay calm and instruct, "Spin."

She turns.

Black-and-blue marks cover her back but worse than when I left her. Her heart-shaped ass matches.

I pull my phone out of my pocket and dial Liam.

He answers after one ring, growling, "Declan!"

"Send the doctor to my house."

"He's stitching Tiernan."

"How long will it be?"

"Do you have nothing else to say about this?"

"Forget I called. I'm taking her to the hospital."

Liam demands, "You'll do no such thing."

"Fuck you and your orders." I hang up and step in front of Simona. "Let me help you get your clothes on. You need X-rays."

"Wh-what are you going to do to punish me?" she frets, and another round of tears fall.

I sigh and embrace her. I mumble into her hair, "Angel, you're hurt. I think you broke your rib. I need you to calm down."

"But I-I...oh God!"

"Shhh," I repeat, attempting to calm her. "We'll talk about this later. Right now, I need to get you to the hospital."

She pulls her head back, wincing, and cries out, "Why are you acting nice right now?"

My heart tears over and over until it feels like nothing is left. And maybe I don't have a heart after what I've put her through.

I don't know the entire story about her involvement yet.

She could be playing me and tried to run to hurt me.

The ten dollars could be a cover-up.

Jesus, why am I thinking this?

I need to find out the truth.

I tilt her chin, lean down, and give her a chaste kiss. Something about her makes me blab too much of the truth. "All I care about is you. I thought I was going to have a heart attack when Nolan told me what happened. The most important thing is finding out what your injuries are so we can take care of them."

Her lips continue to tremble. The confusion and pain never leave her expression.

I help her into her pants. "Stay here. I'm going to get some towels to wrap around you."

She sniffles and stares at the ground.

The anger toward Callum only grows, along with the nagging sensation I've felt most of the evening. What if she's innocent and I've caused all this? I take a handful of bath towels out of the closet and return to her. I wrap one around her and tuck the corner under her armpit. "I'll get a—"

"Declan!" Liam's voice bellows through the house, and Simona jumps. I protectively circle my arm around her.

Liam freezes when he steps into the room. His green eyes look like a wild animal ready to pounce on its enemy.

"You aren't stopping me. She needs medical attention. I think Callum broke at least one of her ribs. Let's go." I pick a blanket off the couch, wrap it around Simona's shoulders, and lead her toward the door.

Liam steps in front of me. "You can't take her to the hospital."

"Did you not hear me? Now get out of my way," I explode.

Simona whimpers, and I curse myself for scaring her.

Liam glances at Simona and briefly shuts his eyes. He refocuses on me but lowers his voice. "You know why you can't take her there."

"Let them take me to jail," I say angrily then calm my delivery. "Come on, angel."

"I'll send Doc to his clinic. You can't go to the hospital," Liam reiterates.

I freeze, debating if he can give Simona the medical attention she needs.

"I'm sure he has all the equipment the hospital will use to assess her injuries," Liam states.

I meet his eyes. "If there's anything he can't do that she needs, my next stop is the emergency room."

"Don't do something stupid, Declan," Liam warns.

I ignore him and guide Simona to the garage then help her into my SUV. She winces, and I tighten the blanket around her, then tuck her hair behind her ears. "I'm sorry, angel. Try to relax."

I close her door, turn on the engine, and scrape the ice off the windshield better than when I left the Ivanovs' garage. She's with me, and I'm not risking an accident due to my carelessness. When I finish, I get in and reverse out of the driveway. I refrain from driving faster than I should due to the weather, reminding myself Simona's safety comes first.

We're almost to the clinic when she speaks so quietly, I barely hear her. "What if the doctor asks me questions?"

More guilt eats me. This is my fault. No matter if she's innocent or not, I caused this. I should have told her there were bodyguards outside my house. Then she wouldn't have tried to escape.

The stabbing pain resurfaces about her wanting to leave me. I know it's irrational since I kidnapped her. But it guts me. I briefly glance at her but need to focus on the snowy road. I reply, "You can be honest with Doc. He knows who I am and all about my family."

"Who are you?" she asks in such a perplexed voice, I cringe inside. We're a notorious crime family in Chicago. She didn't know I was an O'Malley. Once she learned, did she not put two and two together?

I grip the steering wheel tighter. "Angel, have you not heard of the O'Malleys?"

She sniffles. "No. Should I have?"

My chest tightens. "Let's talk about this another time. Whatever Doc asks you, tell him the truth."

More silence fills the small space. Blood pounds in my ears, and snow falls so thick, my wipers can barely keep the windshield clear enough to see. I pull into the parking lot for the clinic as Doc is unlocking the building. I shut off the vehicle and gently turn Simona's chin toward me. "I mean it. Whatever he asks, don't lie."

Her face crumbles. She whispers, "Why are you being nice to me? I-I'm so confused again."

I swipe at her tears, but there are too many. The truth is the only thing I can convey. "This is my fault, not yours. I hate myself for hurting you."

"But I went outside. I-I—"

I put my fingers over her lips and firmly reiterate, "This is my fault, not yours."

Agony riddles her face. I gently kiss her then get out and help her into the clinic.

Doc waits for us and, without saying a word, leads us to an exam room. He steps outside while I carefully help Simona undress.

I forgo the paper sheet and cover her with the blanket. "Do you want to sit or stand?"

"Stand. It hurts to sit."

The bruise on her ass fills my mind. I detest myself even more as I give her another chaste kiss then repeat, "Remember, no lies, angel."

I open the door for Doc to come back in. He's been our family doctor for years. Darragh put him on payroll years ago, and Liam kept him on it. Since he's close to retirement, I'm sure we'll need to replace him soon. He smiles at Simona and asks, "What happened, dear?"

Anxiety fills her face, so I hold her hand and answer, "She tried to leave my house when I was gone. Callum tackled her on the driveway. She has bruises everywhere, and I'm worried about her ribs. Her upper shoulder injury is from earlier today when she fell backward on a chair. The corner did a number on her."

Doc's facial expression never changes. He says, "I'm going to lift this to examine you. Do you want Declan to stay or wait outside?"

Panic erupts across her face, and she grips my hand. "Stay. Please."

Doc nods, steps closer, then removes the blanket.

Bile once again rises in my throat. The bruises are getting worse.

Doc focuses on her ribs. "Take a deep breath."

She struggles and grimaces in pain.

"Try to cough."

She does, but it creates more agony for her.

My pulse pounds harder. *Why was I so stupid to leave her and not warn her my cousins would be outside?*

Doc gingerly touches her ribs and a few other places on her front and back. "Let's take some X-rays. I'm pretty sure your rib is only bruised, but let's make sure." He leads us to the X-ray room.

I wait next to him, staring at my bruised angel, feeling like the worst person on earth. I struggle to remind myself Tiernan and Callum didn't know what was going on, so it's not entirely Callum's fault he hurt her, but I still want to kill him.

Simona barely speaks during the entire process and the rest of the exam. The X-rays show no signs of spinal or vertebrae damage and no fractures or breaks on her ribs.

"I can give you an MRI to confirm the bruise on your rib, or I can treat you for it," Doc informs us.

Simona shakes her head. "I don't want an MRI."

"Are you sure it isn't in her best interest?" I ask Doc, concerned he might miss something.

He shakes his head. "It won't change my instructions. You also have a lot of swelling. Some ice baths would be good for your entire body. I'll write you a prescription painkiller and anti-inflammatory. I have some samples to get you through tonight."

Simona stays quiet. He gives her a glass of water and two pills then hands me the prescription and samples. We both thank him. I wrap Simona back in the blanket then help her into the SUV. When I get in, I start on the engine and grab her hand while I let the vehicle defrost. "Are you doing okay?"

"Just tired and hurting."

"I'm sorry, angel. As soon as we get home, I'm going to run an ice bath. After, you can rest."

Exhaustion cripples her face. She opens her mouth then shuts it. Her lids fall heavy, but a tear leaks down her cheek. Her voice shakes, "Did I kill that man?"

13

Simona

DECLAN ASSURES ME THE MAN I STABBED WILL RECOVER. I still can't believe I did it. I could have killed him, and the reality scares me. Is that who I've become? A murderer? Does my freedom warrant another person's life?

As soon as we get inside, Declan has me soak in a cold bath. It makes my teeth chatter. A deep chill seeps into my bones within seconds, reminding me of the hypothermia I had only a short time ago.

How long has it been? I rack my brain, trying to count the days or weeks I've been here, but nothing is registering. My entire body throbs in pain, and every move I make adds to it.

"Sorry, angel. A few more minutes," Declan soothes, caressing my hair.

I can't look at him. His expression and mannerisms only bring me right back to a state of bewilderment. Besides yelling at the men, every move since he rushed into the house and untied me has been one hundred percent focused on taking care of me. Several times, he claimed everything is his fault. He should be angry with me for attempting to escape, but he only seems worried about my injuries. It doesn't make sense, but the prescription the doctor gave me has my mind too foggy to ask more questions.

When my body is numb from the cold, he helps me out of the tub, dries me off, and guides me to his bed. I carefully lie down but wince. No matter how I move or position my frame, everything feels worse.

He pulls the covers over me until they're under my chin then sits on the bed, caressing my cheek. "Are you hungry?"

"No."

He holds a bottle of water to my lips. "Okay. I need you to drink some of this."

I pick my head up and swallow several sips.

He sets the bottle on the table and studies me with the same worried expression he's had since since we got home. I tear up again, and he leans closer so his face is inches from mine. His voice is soft, not resembling anything close to what he sounded like earlier when he accused me of hurting him and his family. "Why are you crying, angel?"

"Why aren't you mad at me?" I ask, even though I already have several times. My lids feel heavy, and I blink fast, trying to stay awake.

He sniffs hard and lowers his voice. "I'm mad at myself. But if I'm honest, it kills me you wanted to leave me."

It's a bomb exploding around us. My emotions hit me harder. I want to say I didn't want to leave him. If he hadn't kidnapped me, I'd never think twice about running from him. If we could take all the good parts of us together and somehow eliminate how we got here, I would. Yet, I know we can't. I'm not sure where it leaves us. If he has men outside the house, I'm never going to be able to escape. And if I'm his prisoner, how can we ever be anything real?

It's all too much for me to try and figure out, and I'm losing the battle to stay awake.

He leans forward and kisses me. "Go to sleep, angel. You need rest."

The medicine hits me harder. I close my eyes and mumble, "Chains."

"No more chains, lass."

"Hmm. Part of me loves them," I admit, succumbing more to the darkness.

His lips brush mine again. The last thing I hear is, "Yeah. You're a goddess in them."

Against all rationale, I feel safe with Declan watching over me. Maybe tomorrow he'll show his wrath about my failed attempt to flee. Right now, I'm not worrying about it any longer. I can't. My body begins to warm, and I fall into a deep sleep.

In the middle of the night, Declan wakes me up and makes me take more medicine. I swallow it, drink some more water, then snuggle into his warm body. I wince but groggily confess, "I like you when you're Jekyll. It's how you were the night we met, when I thought I could make an exception and date you."

He strokes my hair. "An exception?"

"Mmhmm. I always say no when I get asked out." I yawn.

"Why is that, lass?"

"I don't need any distractions," I confess.

He kisses my forehead. "What don't you want to be distracted from?"

"School. Survival." I yawn again, run my fingers down his biceps, and murmur, "You're so warm."

He lightly caresses my ass. Tingles erupt under my bruise, but it doesn't hurt. He mumbles into my hair, "Get some more rest, angel."

I rotate between sleep and Declan waking me up. He gives me my medication, makes me eat, and keeps me hydrated. During these times, the throbbing of my body reminds me of what happened, and I don't fight the urge to sleep more.

At one point, I wake up on my own. The room is dark, and Declan isn't with me. I go to the restroom, wash my hands, then stare at my body in horror. The bruises are a mix of yellow and black. I decide to take a shower and wince when the water hits my skin. I reach for the shampoo and freeze. My brand and conditioner are next to Declan's. Even my body soap and loofa are here.

Blood rushes through my veins. I wash my hair and let soap run over my skin then carefully dry off.

Another shock hits me when I step into his closet to find a T-shirt.

I must be seeing things, or I'm still asleep.

My clothes are hanging next to his. I touch them and then open the top drawer. My underwear, bras, and socks are in it. Lined up on the floor next to his are the few pairs of shoes I own.

My pulse increases. *How did these get here? Where is he?*

I reach for his T-shirt then pause. My only nightgown and robe are hanging next to it. I take them off the hanger and put them on.

For several moments, I stare at the closet, not sure what to make of it. He cleaned a drawer out for me. Most women would be thrilled. Our clothes all fit together, as if we do. I almost believe it. Yet, we can't be a couple. I'm his prisoner, not someone he could ever have genuine feelings for, even if he claims I'm all he cares about. Or can he?

All the ways Declan has taken care of me, when I had hypothermia and now, make me want to believe it proves he does. Then I remind myself he's the reason I got hypothermia in the first place, and afterward, he still chained me to his bed.

The chains. I close my eyes, and delicious throbs compete with the agonizing ones. I'm unsure why I love the restraints when I also hate them.

If only he would have used them on me just for sex.

I wonder again where he is, so I stumble through the house, still a bit groggy from the drugs. I have no clue what time it is or how long I've been asleep. The main part of the house is empty, so I venture down the hallway and into the office, pausing at the door.

Declan stands in front of a wall with a dozen monitors. His desk is raised so he can type. Information flies across the screens. He types fast and mutters, "Come on."

I step closer, reading the information, and my heart pounds harder. CollegeTechMoney's interface is on the middle screen, and Declan is attempting to hack into it. I blurt out, "What are you doing?"

He jerks his head toward me and then freezes, as if caught with his hand in the cookie jar. I suppose in some ways he is, but it doesn't last long. He rises and lurches in front of me.

My skin sizzles from the mere act of him standing a few inches away. When he slides his hands through my hair then gently guides my head up, I hold my breath. The spicy, woody scent of him bursts into the air, as if it could suffocate me in pleasure.

"How are you feeling, angel?" His blue eyes drill into mine, full of nothing but worry and concern. It feels so genuine, as if he could be mine and I could be his.

I want it to be our truth. More than anything I've ever wished for, this is the one thing I would give anything to turn into reality. Yet, I know too well from life that hoping for the impossible is pointless.

Falling into the false security of us is something I need to avoid, so I don't answer his question. "Why are you trying to hack into CollegeTechMoney?"

His expression hardens. He steps closer so his hard flesh is against me. The zings intensify, creating a small earthquake in my belly. His fingers hold my head firmer. Instead of answering my question, he states, "I'm weaning you off your pain meds. Doc thinks it's time."

"How many days have I been sleeping?"

"Four."

I gape at him. "How is that possible?"

"Doc said your body needed the rest. I've been icing you on and off, but you were so out of it, you never woke," he claims.

I've never been able to sleep longer than a few hours. I figure it's a residual effect of living in the foster home and trying not to get beat up in the middle of the night. My lack of ability to sleep for extended periods is how I developed my hacker skills. It started as a hobby and then I learned more in my college courses.

"Angel, you haven't answered me. How are you feeling?" Declan asks.

"Better than I was but still sore," I admit.

He nods. "Doc said you'll feel a bit more pain as the meds wear off. You can still take over-the-counter pain pills. Let's go back to bed."

I don't move. "Declan, how did my clothes get in your closet?"

He takes a deep breath. "Your landlord sent an email. He isn't renewing your lease and gave you a few days to vacate. I had the movers bring your stuff here."

It's another bomb blowing up. I barely breathe, trying to process it all. It shouldn't matter I no longer have my apartment since I'm Declan's prisoner, but it does. Even if I figure out how to escape him someday, I'm officially homeless. I finally blurt out, "You read my emails?"

Something in his expression eats at me. It's a cross between guilt and entitlement, as if he has a right to invade all my privacy. "Yeah. I've searched your entire computer."

My insides quiver. "Why?"

He shifts on his feet, not releasing me. "We'll talk about this when you feel better."

"No! I want to know right now why you did that, as well as why you kidnapped me. And don't give me an answer that doesn't fill in the blanks."

"Simona—"

I push on his chest, and my voice rises. "I can't take this anymore! I don't even know how long I've been with you. All I think about is why you believe I'm out to get you. Then you play with every ounce of emotion I have, trying to convince me you care about me. So stop this sham and tell me!"

He leans closer to me, his blue orbs firing a concoction of surprise and fear, making my desire to be his tear me apart further. He speaks so close to my lips, his hot breath merges with mine. "One thing I won't ever do is lie to you about what you mean to me. We may have gotten together in an unusual way, but if you're innocent as you claim, then fate wanted us together."

Rage churns through the butterflies flaring in my gut. I cry out, "*If* I'm innocent? How many times do I have to tell you I don't know why I'm even here?"

"Let's go to the bedroom. I'll give you your medication and then we can talk."

"No. I'm not taking anything until I get answers," I declare.

"Your pain is going to get worse," he warns.

"Worse than what you're doing to my heart?" I accuse, revealing more than I should.

The vein near his eye twitches. He stares above my head and grinds his molars.

"Declan—"

He meets my gaze with a mix between a scowl and hurt. His voice is eerily calm. "Okay. Why did you lie about your jobs?"

I jerk my head backward and out of his grasp. "I never lied! I waitress and work in the cafeteria. Well, I did, but I'm sure I've been fired by now. Plus, all the years of my hard work are down the drain since I'm sure I've flunked out of school by missing all my classes and project due dates."

Remorse bursts on his face. "I'll figure out how to fix that. I promise."

"How? Did you become the dean of the college, and I'm unaware of it? Or are you going to kidnap her and my bosses until you get your way?" I snap.

Silence hangs between us. It's thick and ugly, filled with reality. The longer it stays put, the more everything overpowers me. I blink back tears, willing myself not to cry and to be strong.

He finally says, "You didn't tell me about CollegeTechMoney."

Every time I think I have my fill of confusion, it only expands. "What about it?"

"I asked you who you were working for. You didn't tell me about BusyCEO."

"It's just something I've done a few times for extra cash. It's not a permanent job," I retort.

He cups my cheeks before I can move away. "Listen to me. I need to know everything about your conversations with him and how you started working for him. The former chats all disappeared off your account."

Anxiety pounds into my chest. "You kidnapped me for posting a few articles?"

His face darkens, and he blurts out, "Those articles lost millions of dollars for my family. They have the potential to bankrupt us."

My pulse skyrockets to the moon. "I-I…you ripped me away from my life for money?"

He shakes his head. "There's more to this than money."

"Such as?"

He steps forward and I retreat, attempting to take all this information in. I'm dumbfounded about why he abducted me, but I never considered it was about money. Something about that fact makes this all worse. He follows me as I retreat, wincing when my back hits the wall.

He presses his body against mine. In a firm voice, he orders, "It's time to take your medicine."

"No. Answer my question."

The vein near his eye pulses. "I can't. No matter what, I'll never tell you. It'll put you in danger, and I won't do that."

A sarcastic laugh flies out of my mouth. "Danger? You snatched me in the middle of the night from my home, kept me in a cell until I had hypothermia, then chained me to your bed. Your thug outside slammed his big body over mine and against the concrete. Nothing you can say will ever put me in more peril than you already have!"

Shame takes over his expression until my heart tears into tiny pieces. Even at this moment, I can't stop my feelings for him. He presses even closer to me and holds my face again. "I'm not excusing what I've done. However, you don't have any idea what real danger is, and I don't ever want you to know. No matter what, I'll make sure it never reaches you. If I have to, I'll destroy anyone who attempts to show you a glimpse of the evil I've faced too many times."

My entire body trembles against his. Physical and emotional pain strive to break all the strength I have left.

He orders, "Tell me everything about BusyCEO and College-TechMoney, like how you got on their site and the conversations you've had. I also need you to show me how you were able to delete your footprint so quickly."

Tears win, and a river flows, dripping over his fingers. The sting that hits me when I ask my next question almost cripples me. It shouldn't. It should be the only thing I want, yet it feels like a death sentence. "Then are you going to let me go?"

He closes his eyes, the vein continues to twitch, and the pulse in his neck beats so hard, I can see it. He slowly lifts his lids, and his tormented blue orbs meet mine. "I don't want to let you go."

My gut dives at the same time relief spins like an out-of-control windmill. I put my hand between us on my stomach. My voice shakes. "So I'll always be your prisoner, even if I tell you what you want and it's clear I don't know anything about whatever it is you think I did?"

His thumbs stroke my cheekbones. I refrain from closing my eyes and telling him to just keep me as his. Instead of answering my question, he states, "Don't throw what we have away. It doesn't just show up on your doorstep. Trust me on this. I'm forty-four, and not once have I ever had what we have."

I swallow hard, squeezing my eyes shut, wanting what he said to be true but fighting it with rationale. "So, I'll always be your captive?"

His lips brush against mine. "No. I'm saying we have to figure out how to get past this because I'm not letting you go, angel."

I force myself to look at him while more tears tumble. My destroyed heart shatters into a million more pieces, and I don't think I'll ever get it back. "I have nothing to hide. I'll tell you everything I know. Then I'm leaving today."

14

Declan

TREPIDATION WASHES OVER ME LIKE A SURFER GETTING CAUGHT in a wave's undertow. I'm drowning in it, searching for all the ways to pull myself out and stay afloat, but it continues to drag me to a cruel death. For too many minutes, I stare at my angel as her tears soak my fingers. The oxygen in my lungs turns thick and stale.

Crazy notions about how to keep her here grow roots in my brain. Chaining her to my bed or just holding her prisoner in my locked bedroom while I'm gone all seem like solutions. It wasn't insane when I thought she hurt my family and me, but I can't convince myself it wouldn't be now. Not once did I ever want her to be guilty of trying to harm me, but suddenly, I do. It would be better than the consequences of her leaving because she's innocent.

There's no more question about it. Simona didn't know what she was doing. Deep down, I can't deny this, and she doesn't need to utter another syllable. Somehow, my angel naively got wrapped into this.

The lump in my throat inflates like a balloon ready to pop. I swallow, but it goes nowhere. "You're injured. I won't let you go anywhere until you're no longer wounded."

She glares at me, and she might as well grip my heart and squeeze all the blood out of it. The defiance in her eyes is crippling. "I'm either your prisoner, or I'm not. Make up your mind."

I do what I feel is more potent than words to show her how serious I am about what we have together. I kiss her.

She freezes at first. Her breath pounds against my lips, and her tongue remains paralyzed from returning my affection.

I retreat, pleading with her with my stare, then attacking her mouth once more until she slowly begins to respond.

Heaven and hell are wrapped into our kisses, exploding in a violent battle of right and wrong, truth and lies, innocence and guilt.

"Don't destroy us," I murmur and return to her lips.

She turns her face, driving a stake into my heart.

I kiss under her ear and proclaim, "Whatever I have to do to make things up to you, I will."

Her breath penetrates my skin, taunting the fire I'm trying to contain. She whispers, "Are you releasing me after we talk or not?"

The twitch in my vein near my eye intensifies so much, I think it might blind me. I slide my hand under her jaw and force her to look at me. "You *are* free, but I won't allow you to go anywhere while you're injured. No matter what I've done, I won't risk harming you further."

The mixed emotions in her eyes will haunt me forever. Her face slowly crumples and she begins to sob.

I tug her as close to me as possible, trying to be cautious of her bruises and hating myself for everything I've done to her. If I could sell my soul to erase all the bad stuff I've done and return to the night we met so she only experiences the man I want her to know me as, I would. There's no plan on how to make this right, yet I stroke her head repeating, "I vow I'll put us back together."

She pushes out of my arms and wipes her face. Lifting her chin high, she asserts, "I can't do this with you. If you mean what you say, and you care about me, then you'll leave me alone. I'll tell you everything I know. Then I want you to release me."

Bile makes its way up my throat. I swallow it down. "I told you—"

"I'll take care of myself. I've done it my entire life," she proclaims.

It only makes my gut churn faster. She shouldn't have had to ever go through life on her own. Since I met her, I've wanted to be the man to take care of her. I blurt out the first thing that pops into my head. "You don't have an apartment anymore."

Her lips tremble harder. Shame erupts inside me, and she turns her head. I reach for her cheek, and she cries out, "It won't be the first time I had nowhere else to go. Ask me what you want to know so I can leave."

"Simona—"

"Do you not understand I can't be near you? You've torn me to shreds, and now you're unraveling all the thread until nothing remains!"

Silence pierces the air, creating more distance between us. A level of panic I've never experienced before slices through my veins.

"Fine. I'll go now," she states and spins, moving toward the door.

"Wait!"

She turns back toward me, and darts of agony stab my eyes. "I can tell you everything while I pack. There isn't much to tell anyway. If you had asked, I would have told you."

"Simona—"

"I needed money. I posted some articles, erased the footprint as directed, and got paid ten dollars. I don't know who BusyCEO is, nor have I ever cared. It took four minutes. If I could have done it all day, I would have. It's the only time in my life I didn't have to fight for a dollar. For once, it was nice to do something easy. I'm sorry it resulted in you losing money. So now you know." She leaves the room.

I follow her to the bedroom. "Simona, wait."

Her voice continues to tremble. "Please stop doing this. I can't stay here. All of this between us isn't real. Once I'm gone, you'll see."

"That's not true!" I insist, but I'm losing the battle. It's the same feeling I used to get when I boxed; my opponent took me down, and I was unable to get up. It was rare, yet when it happened, nothing ever felt so horrible.

She goes into the closet and pulls her clothes off the hangers.

"You can't drag all your things around. Just take a breather for a minute."

"I've done it before," she fires back and continues ripping items into her hands.

It hits me there's no getting around this. I can't keep my angel here against her will now that I know the truth. The pit in my stomach hurts. She's lived on the streets in the past. I assume it was when she fled her foster home, but I may never learn all those details due to what I've done.

Only one solution pops into my mind to make sure she's okay. "Stop, so I can find you a safe place to stay."

She freezes then stares at me.

I take a few deep breaths, but she misinterprets me trying to calm myself down and think.

Hatred flares in her glare. "I'm not going to be under your thumb."

I hold my hand out. "It's freezing. You're injured. I caused this, so I will make this right." I pull my cell out of my pocket, and even though it kills me, I call Maksim.

His Russian accent hits my ear. "Declan, what's going on?"

"Do you have any apartment or condo units available right now? Preferably furnished," I ask.

Simona's expression turns into a questioning one.

"Three. One's in Boris's building. Are you moving?" he teases.

"No. I need one today and no more questions."

The line turns silent for a moment, but then he replies, "I'll text you the addresses. Take your pick and send me the names of whoever you want to have security clearance."

"I'll take the one in Boris's." I'm familiar with the building, and the security is airtight. I hang up, and nausea hits me. There's no getting out of this. Simona's leaving, and the only thing I can do is make sure she doesn't make any decisions that could harm her further. I take a suitcase off my shelf and offer it to her. "My friend Maksim has a place you can stay. I won't have you roaming the streets. It's either there or here."

For several moments, she focuses on the suitcase as her tears hit the handle. She finally drops her clothes on the ground and sits next to them. She winces then unzips the bag.

I swallow my pride. "What can I do to help you?"

She closes her eyes and replies, "Can you get my things from the bathroom? And my computer. Or did you still need to steal my information?"

I contemplate lying, but she's smart, and I've already done enough harm. "I already copied your hard drive."

She glances up, and her betrayed eyes claw at my heart.

"Did you want me to lie?" I ask.

"Do you expect me to give you points for that?"

"No, lass. I don't have any expectations right now, with the exception that I figure out a way to win you back," I confess.

"You can't win something back that was never yours," she fires at me, but her voice breaks, and she turns away, crying again.

I kneel next to her and wrap my arms around her. "Don't say that."

"It's true. Y-you can't care about someone you kidnap!"

"I made a mistake, angel, a horrible one. I'll regret it until I die. And you can get space from me, but what's between us isn't going to fade."

She pins her eyebrows together and reaches for my face. Her palm shakes against my cheek. I put my hand over hers, briefly closing my eyes. She whispers, "I wish we could go back to the night we met, but we can't."

Self-loathing claws at my bones. Before I can respond, she rips her hand away from me and returns to packing. "Please get my things."

I debate about pleading my case but decide to do what she asks. I gather her items in the bathroom, her laptop, and her cell. When I return to the closet, she's dressed, and my gut flips. I hand her things to her.

She asks, "Did you go through my phone, too?"

"Yes."

She takes a deep breath. "So you have my number?"

"Yes." I text her a message.

ME: *It's me. I already miss you.*

"And now you have mine. Don't ask me not to contact you," I warn.

She wipes her face, zips the bag, and grimaces as she gets up, hissing through her teeth.

"Please stay here. I'll leave you alone, except to help you," I promise.

She blinks hard. I think she might agree, but then she takes the knife and digs it deeper into my heart. "Can you tell me where I'm going so I can leave?"

I'm unsure how she thinks she'll get there. She has no money for a cab. A notification popped up on her phone saying her bank account was overdrawn from her electric bill. I scoured her online statement, and she was living penny to penny, barely scraping by. It doesn't surprise me with what she gets paid and her tuition bill. I have no idea how she's managed everything on her own.

I grab the suitcase handle. "I'll drive you."

"Where's the rest of my stuff?"

Her only other items are in three boxes. It's a few things from her kitchen, bath towels, and bedding. Her monitor screens are in the other. The lease said all the furniture was the landlord's. I reply, "In my garage. I'll bring them with us if you want."

"Please."

I nod, motion for her to go first and lead her to the SUV. I help her into the front seat, cringing inside from the apparent pain she's in, then put the suitcase and boxes inside the rear end of the vehicle. When I shut the trunk, I take several deep breaths, resisting the urge to order her back into the house and keep her with me.

Her eyes are closed when I finally get in the vehicle. I run my knuckles over her cheek, and she shudders. It only solidifies my determination to do whatever it takes to make her mine again.

"Angel," I murmur.

She rolls her head against the headrest and opens her glistening eyes.

I try one last time. "Please stay until you're better."

Sorrow and determination saturate her eyes. "I can't." She turns away, squeezing her lids shut.

Those two words annihilate me. I tell myself to be a man and do what she wants so I don't make it worse for her. I start the car and drive to the building Boris and Nora live in. I already have security clearance, but I text Maksim Simona's name. I pull up to the valet, have them take the boxes and her suitcase inside, and hand them my keys. I help Simona out and lead her to the security station. It only takes a few moments, and we're soon standing inside the unit.

The bellhop brings her items inside. Simona stands in front of the window, looking out at the Chicago skyline. It's a windy day, and white caps cover Lake Michigan. The lake hasn't frozen over yet, but snow is on the ground.

I tip the bellhop, and he leaves. I go to Simona and slide my hand around her waist.

She looks up. Her lips quiver and she nervously admits, "I-I can't afford this place."

"Don't worry about money. You don't have to pay anything."

"Why?"

"My brother-in-law owns this building. He and my sister live in the penthouse. There's nothing to fret about."

She swallows hard. "Do-do they know about me?"

Shame fills me. If my sister Nora knew what I did, she'd hate me. "No. No one except my brother, Nolan, and cousins Liam and Finn know about you."

She spins into me. "Who came to the house the night I was injured?"

"Liam."

She scrunches her face. "So three people knew you kidnapped me?"

My gut dives. "Yeah. They weren't happy about it." I fail to add they wanted me to turn her over to them.

She straightens her back. "What are you involved in that three men would allow you to keep me as your prisoner?"

The vein near my eye throbs as I try to figure out how to respond to her question.

She reaches up and swipes her thumb over it. "Please tell me."

I don't know where to begin or what to say. All I'm confident about is that I want to be with her. If she's eventually going to let me back into her life, she can't be entirely in the dark.

I cup her cheek. "You're a smart woman. Research the O'Malleys. When you're ready, I'll answer any questions you have."

She hesitates but then replies, "You will? No matter what I ask?"

"Yes." I release her and pull out her medicine. "I'm going to unpack the boxes and your clothes. You should take this and rest. Every six to eight hours, you can have one. Let me get you a glass of water." I don't wait for her to reply and lead her to the kitchen. I fill a glass and hand it to her, along with a pill.

She takes it then says, "I can unpack."

"No. I will. You can point to where you want things or lie down and trust me to do it. Take your pick."

She tilts her head. Her lips twitch. "Trust you to put away my one suitcase of clothes and my box of secondhand dishes when the kitchen is already full?"

"What's so funny about that?"

She shrugs. "My trust level for you isn't that low."

Hope rises inside me. "It's not?"

A tiny smile erupts on her lips. She shakes her head. "No."

"Okay. Why don't I tuck you into bed, and you can let me take care of these things?"

She glances at the boxes. "I don't think I need anything in there, except my monitors. Will you set them up and put the other stuff in the front closet?"

"Sure." I obey her orders then roll her suitcase toward the bedroom, stopping near her. "Come on. You need to rest, angel."

Hesitating, she takes a calculated breath.

"What's wrong?"

She confesses, "This feels confusing to me again."

"There's nothing to be baffled over. I told you I'm going to right the wrongs I've done. Nothing has changed regarding my intentions or feelings for you, and it isn't going to."

She bites on her lip as if pondering my words.

I move her chin up. "You want me to fight for you? I will. I'm not going to back down about this."

She sighs. "I... I need to think. I can't right now."

The somersaults in my gut increase. I lean down and kiss her. I shouldn't, but I can't help it. It's only a chaste peck on the lips. It makes my craving for her intensify, and I keep my lips on hers and declare, "I'm putting you to bed. Then I'm unpacking your suitcase and ordering you groceries. When they arrive, I'll put them away. If you're asleep, I'll lock up when I leave."

A war rages in her head. I can see it in her eyes. She finally succumbs and replies, "Okay. Thank you."

I kiss her forehead, lead her into the bedroom, then pull her nightgown out of her suitcase. She goes into the bathroom and changes then comes out. I tuck her into bed and kiss her again. "My number is in your cell. The building security is top-notch. If you need anything, I'm only minutes away."

She opens her mouth then shuts it. I wait until she softly says, "Thank you."

"For what?"

She nervously takes a breath, and her words crack my heart all over again. "Letting me go."

15

Simona

Two Weeks Later

EVERY NIGHT, I FALL ASLEEP TO THE VISION OF DECLAN'S alarmed gaze and insistent words. "I haven't let you go. You're here because you insisted you need this right now. Don't confuse it with the truth. We *will* be together again, angel."

Like every issue surrounding Declan and me, the polarity of my thoughts could be pinballs slapping against my brain, flying fast and furious. Whenever I wake up, it's dark. The curtains don't allow any light in, but if I keep them open, the blinking city lights make it impossible to get any rest. The clawing in my chest that occurs when I can't see anything begins. I wish I had a nightlight. I had one in my apartment. At Declan's, I only felt panicked when he wasn't sleeping next to me, but it rears its ugly head every time it's dark now that I'm alone.

My brain is a soundtrack that never stops replaying.

Calm down. You're in a condo with security.

Why did I tell him to go?

Stop being a baby.

I miss him so much.

After several deep breaths, my racing heart begins to calm. I keep my eyes shut and try to return to sleeping, but it's always pointless.

The same torturous thoughts I had before I fell asleep still perturb me. Declan's voice and eyes never disappear. I try to convince myself I don't wish he were here, but it's useless. I do wish he were here. Nothing has ever felt as good as the safety of his arms, or the way our bodies seem to fit perfectly together, or how he dotes on me. I even miss the intimate way he likes to feed me.

Jesus. I need to get a grip on reality.

I shouldn't find comfort in the last statement he made before he left. But I hold on to his declaration to keep me and the possibility to once again be his, as if my life depends on it.

The more time that passes, nothing becomes clearer. I assumed it would, and if I could be alone, my clear, rational thinking would take over.

It hasn't. My craving for Declan only deepens, creating a hole in my heart I can't figure out how to climb out of. Day after day, I ask myself the same question.

How can I still want him?

He's made choices that screwed up my life, and I don't have room for anything to be off-kilter. My professors flunked me. The emails I received from them warning me about not missing any more classes paralyze me. I want to reply and beg them to give me a pass and allow me to make up any work, but I don't know what to say.

My managers all texted me when I missed my shifts, and after several attempts where I didn't respond, they fired me. The restaurant I work at reminded me to return my uniform, or they would deduct the cost from my last paycheck. The deadline passed, so now, I have no source of income and my final check went up in flames.

Granted, the luxury condo I'm in is better than being on the streets. My landlord not renewing my lease puts me in a bad position. He emailed yesterday claiming there were issues with the apartment and he wasn't returning my security deposit. It's a lie. I took good care of the place, but it's his word over mine. I don't have money for another deposit or the first and last month's rent on another place. I lived in a shelter for half a year and saved up to afford the shitty apartment I had. In some ways, I should be grateful for Declan's interference. I would have been on the street with a trash bag full of my clothes and my three boxes.

I promised myself I would never be homeless again, yet here I am, full of anxiety, unsure how to not end up in the same situation I crawled my way out of.

How long can I stay here?

Where will I go when it's time to leave?

I need to get new jobs.

Will I be able to retake my courses and graduate?

The sting of that question digs deep. It's supposed to be my final year. Every course I take is expensive, and I've worked hard not to waste a penny. I attend every session and study hard. Having to repay for a class I was acing burns me.

It's another reason I should tell Declan to stay far away. He's taken the only things I had in my life and crumpled them into tiny balls then thrown them so far out of my reach, I wonder how I'll ever retrieve them.

My phone vibrates, and I turn, wincing from the pain. It's hooked into my charger on the nightstand. I pick it up, and Declan appears on the screen.

I swipe it then curse myself when my flutters take off. He texts me every day, all throughout the day. It always leads to the same conversation.

There's a string of messages, and everything feels more intense than the previous ones. The first message must have arrived when I was asleep.

Declan: *I miss you. When can I see you?*

An hour ago, he sent another one.

Declan: *I hated leaving you. Not seeing you is driving me crazy.*

My heart beats faster, and I read the message he just texted.

Declan: *Are you awake?*

Another message pops up.

Declan: *Can I come over and make you dinner?*

I begin to text yes then freeze.

What am I doing?

I need him.

No, I don't. I've gotten this far in life without him.

That's because I didn't know what it was like to have him.

I've seriously lost my marbles. He kidnapped me and assumed I did things to hurt him. Why am I even debating this?

I need to stay away from him. Distance will give me closure.

I text him what I always do.

Me: *Not tonight. I need space.*

Several moments pass. Dots appear on the screen like he's typing but then disappear.

Guilt and heartache are a hammer pounding into me so hard, I don't think and reply.

Me: *I miss you, too.*

Declan: *Thank you for telling me that, angel. I'll do anything you want to make this right.*

Blood slams between my ears. My fingers move, in a trance, furiously typing.

Me: *I wish I knew what to tell you. I don't believe in staying in the past, but I don't know how to move forward with you.*

For five minutes, I fixate on the screen. My heart bleeds. It doesn't make sense how Declan could care about me when I was his captive, yet deep down, I know my admission hurt him. That wasn't my intention when I sent it, but my heart won't let me lie. I'm aware my text tore him to shreds.

Declan: *Staying away from me isn't going to solve this. It's been several weeks. I've respected your wishes. Now, please let me come over.*

The temptation is higher than ever to tell him to hop in his SUV and speed over to my condo. My inner demons fight, having the same dialogue they always do.

Declan: *Whatever I have to do to figure this out, I will.*

Unaware I was holding my breath, I exhale in relief, then curse myself again. Clinging to the notion Declan and I will find a way to be together isn't intelligent.

Declan: *If you don't want me to come over, let me take you to dinner.*

It's not the first time he's asked. My bruises faded and are barely there anymore. I've been off medications for a week. I've even gone for some brisk walks outside, dealing with the cold air and wind slapping my face. I've always said no to dinner, but my resolve is quickly vanishing.

A public restaurant will be safe.

Will it?

I could go to dinner, we could talk, and I could come home by myself.

Declan: *You said you researched my family. Don't you want your questions answered?*

All my nerves vibrate. I did research the O'Malleys. It's clear they're one of the most prominent crime families in Chicago, and I must have been living under a rock.

It's another reason I should stay away from Declan. The new facts should make me afraid of him.

I'm not though.

When I texted him that I looked the O'Malleys up online, he said it wasn't something we could discuss over the phone. I didn't have to ask why. He wanted to come right over, but I stopped him. That was a few days after I arrived here. Oddly enough, I don't have a lot of questions about the O'Malleys. What I want answers about surrounds the articles I placed online that led to him kidnapping me.

Declan: *I'm making a reservation. I'll pick you up at seven.*

Me: *Don't take my choices away again.*

Declan: *This isn't the same thing. You're avoiding me.*

I close my eyes. He's right. My cell vibrates from another text, and I read it.

Declan: *You said you miss me. Was that a lie?*

Me: *No.*

Declan: *It's dinner tomorrow night, or I'm coming over right now. What do you prefer?*

My mind spins. At some point, I need to put on my big girl panties and deal with him. The problem is, I still don't know how to let him go. I want to tell him to come over tonight and stay, but I don't. I finally decide dinner is safer.

Me: *What time tomorrow?*

Declan: *I'll pick you up at seven.*

I don't send him any more messages. I leave my phone on the table, go out to the kitchen, then eat yogurt and berries. I spend the rest of the evening catching up on assignments I should have already turned in. Then I study for my end of the semester exams. I'm unsure why I do it since I've already failed the classes, but something won't let me not finish my work.

When it's past midnight, I return to the bedroom. Loneliness hits me harder than usual. As if Declan can sense it, he texts.

Declan: *Are you awake?*

Me: *Yes.*

Declan: *This is killing me, angel. I need you back in my bed. I can still smell you on my pillows.*

I smile at his admission. I'd do anything to have something of his so I could inhale his scent. For the first time since leaving him, I do something stupid. I've avoided it for the last few weeks, throwing him into voicemail whenever he attempted to contact me, but I dial his number.

He picks up on the first ring. His deep and sexy voice is just how I remember it. "Angel."

My chest rises and falls faster. I suddenly feel shy and I'm not sure what to say. "Hi."

"Hold on."

My phone beeps, and a notification to accept or decline a video chat pops up.

Somersaults flip fast in my gut. I hit the green button, and he appears.

Jesus, help me.

He's not wearing a shirt. His hard, inked flesh almost makes me groan. Every chiseled inch of his face, along with his intense expression, lights me up, and my skin hums.

"Turn the light on," he commands.

I obey.

He studies me and swallows hard. "God, I've missed your beautiful face."

His comment shoots straight to my loins, waking up all the parts of me that were dormant before him. The last few weeks, I tried to forget about them, but there's no more hiding. If anything, they're pissed. I attempted to wash them away, and now they scream at me to deal with them. And Declan leaning against the headboard, with memories of how he restrained me to it, aren't helping.

Heat flushes my cheeks. I admit, "I miss you, too."

"You should let me come over," he states.

Yes, yes, yes! Come over now!

No, no, no!

I refrain but go somewhere else I shouldn't. "What would you do if you came over?"

Blue flames burst in his eyes. He doesn't hesitate and orders, "Put the phone on the dresser across from the bed. Then take off your nightgown."

My pulse skyrockets, and my voice cracks. I tease, "Have you been thinking about my dresser?"

"I've been thinking about everything, lass. Now do what I say. Remember, good girls get rewarded."

All the reasons I should end this disappear. I can't think. It's been too long since he touched me or ordered me around. I submit to him and fall right back into my role. I position the phone on the wood and stand back. Slowly, I remove my nightgown and stand bare before the phone screen. "What about you, Daddy?"

He groans, and tingles run down my spine. Nothing sounds sexier than the feral noises Declan makes. He rises, balances his phone on the headboard slat, and kneels toward the end of the bed. Fisting his cock, he asks, "This what you want to see, angel?"

The metal piercings running from the base of his erection to his hip make my clit throb. I nod, lost in the visual of him, unable to stop staring.

"Zoom the camera on you then get on the bed. Put your ass on the mattress and your feet on the edge of the trunk at the foot of the bed," he instructs.

I don't hesitate then sit on the end of the bed and spread my legs as wide as possible.

"What now, Daddy?"

"Show me how wet you are."

My hand slightly shakes from the anticipation. The weeks of missing him reach a peak. I want him here, touching me, yet I can't seem to allow myself to tell him to come over. Seeing and hearing him is a torturous pleasure. "Like this, Daddy?" I swipe my fingers over my sex, dipping inside a few times, then circling my clit, moaning from the sensations.

Red creeps into his face. He never stops fisting his cock. His voice turns rougher. "Rub your juice on your gorgeous pink tits."

I glide my hand up my torso then roll my fingers over my nipples until they're rock hard.

"So sexy, angel," he mumbles.

"If I were with you, what would you do to me?" I breathe.

"Clasp your hands behind your back."

I lace my fingers together and squeeze them tight.

He licks his lips. "If you were here, I'd wrap the chain around your torso, then cuff you to the headboard right like that. No slack. Then I'd kneel in front of you and control that pretty mouth of yours while you suck my cock."

Excitement buzzes in my blood. Declan's never let me have him in my mouth before. Something about being chained, with my hands restrained behind my back, and him fisting my hair turns me on in a way I haven't been before.

"Move one of your hands back on your pussy," he demands.

I unlock my hands and slide one back over my clit.

His blue flames get hotter. "While your mouth is all over me, I'd reach down and stroke you."

I circle my hips in conjunction with my hand.

"Slow down," he orders.

Heat floods my cheeks, and my skin boils. Everything I've held myself back from doing in my attempt to forget about him, I now allow myself to feel. The adrenaline builds in my cells, and I whimper.

"Close your eyes, lass."

My eyelids shut. I breathe harder.

"Can you taste my pre-cum on your tongue?"

"Yes," I whisper, pretending he's in my mouth, sliding me on and off him.

He murmurs, "Daddy's so hard for you, angel. I'm going to fuck your clit faster now, but you need to ask me first."

"Please, Daddy! Oh God! Please!" I beg, circling my fingers quicker.

"Can you smell me? I can smell your sweet pussy."

That spicy, woody scent I love washes over me. My hand behind my back twitches, and I tighten my fist, pretending I'm clutching my other hand. I admit in a raspy voice, "I love how you smell."

"Daddy's about to come in your mouth. What do you want, angel?"

"Make me come with you, Daddy. Please," I plead, on the cusp of coming unhinged and move my hand faster.

His voice sounds like he's gritting his teeth. "Open your eyes."

My lids fling open, right as I lose all control. My eyes roll, and my body violently convulses. I cry out, "Oh God!"

"Fuuuuuck!" he growls.

When I can focus again, I stare at the screen, watching Declan's chest rise and fall, until he grabs the phone.

My legs wobble when I stand. I go to the dresser and pick up my cell. I slide under the covers.

His voice softens. "God, I miss you."

Suddenly emotional, I blink hard.

"Please let me come over."

I open my mouth and almost tell him yes but then shut it. All the reasons I've analyzed for too many days reappear.

"Simona, I'm sorry. You have to forgive me," he states, his eyes full of regret and fear.

"I-I..." Through this entire ordeal, I've not once thought about forgiveness. Is this only about me giving him absolution?

"Why do I get the feeling you can't forgive me?" he says in a voice so full of panic, it cuts into my soul.

I trace the screen over the vein near his eye. It's twitching, and all I want to do is be in his arms. I admit, "I'm figuring things out."

Disappointment and hope swirl in his expression. He deeply inhales. "Will you promise me something?"

"What?"

"No matter what, you won't cancel our date tomorrow night."

There are a million reasons I shouldn't agree to that. Yet, I need to see him as much as he needs to see me, maybe more. I vow, "I promise I won't cancel our date."

16

Declan

I WOULDN'T CLAIM TO BE A NERVOUS MAN, BUT THE FIRST thing I think about when I wake up is that I have a date with Simona. It excites me while also making me feel like I'm sitting on pins and needles. Besides our video chat last night, I haven't seen her in a few weeks. It's driving me mad. I've done everything she's asked, trying my best to give her the space and time she needs, but I'm dying. I've never craved anyone before or felt this pain in my heart. If I don't see her soon, I'm going to explode into millions of pieces.

Her physical absence hasn't stopped me from monitoring her. I check in with the Ivanov's security team several times a day. Any movement she makes outside her unit, they track. A guard follows her whenever she leaves the building. She doesn't know it, but there's no way I'm leaving her unprotected.

I still don't know how she got on CollegeTechMoney's website. There are still questions I need to ask her, but I can't do it over the phone. Every day, I wake up determined she'll let me see her, but it's always a no. Even when she researched my family, she still didn't let me come over.

Liam's patience is wearing thin. The pressure he's putting on me to question Simona is higher than ever. I'm one step away from going in front of the council. I can't say I'd blame him if he pulled that card, but Simona made it clear she isn't ready to see me. I'm trying my best not to do anything to push her further away, but if Liam does tell the council, they'll bring her in for questioning. Since she's innocent, they won't harm her, but it'll scare her. And I don't want to put her in that position.

Since she left, the only things I focus on are righting the wrongs I did to her and trying to stop BusyCEO from ruining the future of the O'Malleys. He's sent two articles since Simona left. Each one, Nolan and I counteracted with a negative one the day after. The only thing that worries me is I'm not as quick as Simona at erasing my footprint. The comment BusyCEO sent to Simona stating not everyone on the site was as competent as her sticks with me. It makes me wonder if he's somehow watching her activity or if he knows her identity.

It doesn't help I still can't figure out how to hack into CollegeTechMoney's server. It's more secure than anything I've seen. When I tried to register as a student or employer, messages popped up saying they weren't accepting applications at this time. It raises every red flag I have.

As frustrated as I am about not being able to hack into the site, not knowing how to fix the harm I've done to Simona eats at me more. It's not right, but I still have access to her email. She didn't change her password. The only messages are from her professors telling her she's failed the classes for not attending and turning in assignments. It makes me ill. I've racked my brain over it, and today I'm paying her dean a visit.

It's early when I wake up. I send Simona a text.

Me: *I can't wait to see you tonight.*

I go to the O'Malley gym and meet my brothers and cousins for a workout. Killian's back from his second honeymoon. When he found out what happened, he wasn't too happy with me. Nolan told him before he left. When he got back from Hawaii, he came storming into my house, but Simona was already gone.

As soon as I get to the weight area, Liam crosses his arms. "Did you talk to her?"

I refrain from telling him I had a video chat and jacked off faster than ever just by talking dirty and watching her come. "No. But I'm taking her out tonight."

"Like a date?" Killian asks.

"You got a problem with that?" I bark.

He pins his eyebrows together. "Aren't you pushing it? You're lucky she hasn't called the police. I know she's a smoking-hot lass and all, but—"

"Shut up and mind your own business." I push past him and rack the bench press.

Liam follows me, scowling. "Doc sent me a bill."

"He was supposed to send it to me. What's the damage?"

Liam sniffs hard. "Since Doc's on payroll, what the fuck could you possibly need from him for ten grand?"

"None of your business."

Liam slams his water bottle on the floor. "Goddammit, Declan! Enough of this sudden desire to hide things from us!"

Rage builds so much, I can hardly see straight. "My business with my woman is just that—my business."

"Your woman? The one you chained in your basement but then conveniently moved to your bedroom?" Finn sneers.

I spin. "Got anything else you want to say?"

His eyes turn to slits. "You're destroying every ounce of trust we have for you."

My anger multiplies. All the years of holding in shit I never said comes barreling out. I push him against the wall and jab his chest. "That so? Interesting coming from you. You sat in prison for how many years, not telling us a fucking thing about the night that got you there. You're on a never-ending mission to find Brenna, but no one has seen the woman since Maksim dropped her off the night of the murder. You're as tight-lipped as a priest in confession. So, what are you hiding?"

His jaw clenches. Hatred fills his eyes. He reaches for my neck, and I grasp his.

The gym erupts in shouting. Nolan and Killian pull me back; Liam steps between Finn and me. Our uncle Patrick comes running up. "What the hell is wrong with you?"

Liam shrugs past him and points in my face. "I want to know right now what the ten grand is for."

My nostrils flare, and the vein near my eye pulses. "I said I'll pay it. And it's not your business, so stay out of it," I say through clenched teeth.

Liam shakes his head, his green eyes glowing like a crazed animal. "I want to know how she got on that site and what her conversations were with whoever hired her. You bring her to me tomorrow, or I'll have you *and* her go in front of the council."

"You mother—" I lunge at him, but Killian and Nolan hold me back.

"Declan, calm down," Nolan shouts.

I spin on him. "You two are the biggest hypocrites I've ever met."

Nolan jerks his head back. "What the hell did I do?"

"Don't tell me to calm down. You married Baileys. Not once did you take them in front of the council."

"He's got a point. Both of you were sticking it in a Bailey. That is hypocritical," Killian chimes in.

"Shut up!" Liam growls.

Killian holds his hands in the air. "Chill out a bit. Jesus. You can't get pissed at Declan for getting serviced by a hot coed while you were both slipping it in our archenemy."

Uncle Patrick slaps Killian hard across the face.

"What the fuck, Paddy!" Killian grumbles, holding his cheek.

Patrick points to him. "Shut your mouth. That's their wives you're talking about. You should know better now that you're married."

"My wife's an alliance, not an enemy," Killian blurts out.

Patrick goes to slap him again, but he ducks.

"Killian, you're such a dick," Liam bellows.

Patrick spins and motions to the rest of us. "All of you. Either work out, or get out of my gym. Take your female problems elsewhere." He stomps away.

"Fuck all of you. I'm out of here," I bark then take off to the locker room.

"Tomorrow! Take your pick, Declan," Liam warns.

"Fuck you, Liam!" I shout back then push into the locker room and grab my bag.

"Declan, hold up," Killian calls out.

"I don't want to hear it. I'm done with all of you."

Killian holds his hands out. "Cool it. Just stop for a minute."

"The council? All the shit I've done for this family, and he threatens my woman with the council?"

"You, too," Killian adds.

"Thanks for reminding me."

He smirks. "Chill out. I'll talk to him. But you need to find out whatever you can."

I release a frustrated breath. "No shit. You think I don't know this? It's a little challenging when I can't even get her to take my calls."

"But she agreed to see you for dinner, right?" he asks.

"I'm not pressuring her to talk to me about any of this tonight. I did a lot of stupid shit I need to make right," I forcefully admit.

He sighs. "Penance. I know. But at least it's fun while doing it."

"Penance? What are you talking about? You think I went to confession? And what the hell is fun about penance?"

"Disregard what I said. It's between me and the big guy. Just...look. You seem super caught up on this lass. I'm worried about you."

"She has a name. It's Simona," I bark.

His eyes widen. "Calm down before you have a heart attack, old man."

"Is there a point to this conversation? I'm about to do more damage to you than what Uncle Patrick did."

Arrogance crosses his expression. "You know I'll kick your ass."

"I'm done." I sling my bag over my shoulder.

"Wait."

I cross my arms. "Spit it out."

"You're serious about her?"

"No. I'm just trying to win her back for fun and games. What a stupid question." I glower at him.

He shifts on his feet, looking annoyed as much by me as I am with him. "Okay. Has Nora met her?"

I scrub my face in frustration. "Nora? You think I told Nora I kidnapped a woman, chained her to my basement wall until she got hypothermia, then kept her restrained in my bed?"

"Not the details. But they live in the same building. Nora's female. Simona's female."

"What are you getting at?"

He shrugs. "I think it helped Arianna to be friends with the women. They can talk you up."

I sigh. "I know you're trying to help right now, but I kidnapped her. I didn't just piss her off the night before our wedding. This is a bit more complicated than you and Arianna."

"You should introduce her to Nora. She's right there," he insists.

"Nora won't ever talk to me again if she finds out what I did."

"Is Simona going to tell her?"

I push past him. "Thanks for trying to help. I have to go." I leave the gym as fast as possible. It's not even seven. Snow covers the ground, irritating me further. I need to work out, so I go to the Ivanov's and get past Leo, who's always at the front door. I jog up the stairs.

Maksim and his three brothers, plus Adrian and Obrecht, are all there.

"Declan. What's going on?" Maksim asks.

"Need a gym. I was going to kill all the O'Malleys if I stayed at ours. Mind if I work out?"

He studies me. "Nope. Everything okay?"

"Yeah. Thanks." I brush past him, toss my bag in the locker room, then jump on a treadmill next to Sergey.

He arches his eyebrows. "Was it Killian or Liam's mouth who ran you out of the place?"

I grunt. "Add Finn and Nolan to it with a mix of my uncle Patrick. Although the slap he gave Killian was a bit amusing."

Sergey chuckles. "Looks like I missed all the fun. Warm up. Then I'll spot you."

My anger starts to dissipate. "Thanks." I spend an hour and a half with the Ivanovs, shower, then drive to Simona's school campus.

My gut somersaults. I have one shot at making this right, and I need a win before my date with Simona tonight. I pull into the parking garage, find the building my meeting is in, and follow the signs to the dean's office.

A younger woman with a thick, blonde braid sits behind the desk. Her nameplate reads Suzie. She looks up. "Can I help you?"

"Declan O'Malley. I have a meeting with the dean."

She furrows her brows and mumbles my name. More nerves flutter in my belly. I hacked into the system and added myself to the calendar. She looks up. "Ah. There you are. Why don't you have a seat, and I'll let the dean know you're here."

"Thank you." I don't sit. I read the different plaques on the wall, barely comprehending what they say. It seems like a long time, but Suzie finally leads me back to the dean's office.

An older woman, closer to retirement age, with dark hair and gray streaks running through it, pink cat-eyed glasses, and a matching suit, rises from her seat.

Suzie announces, "Declan O'Malley."

"Dean Whitehouse. Nice to meet you." She holds her hand out.

I shake it. "Declan O'Malley. Thank you for seeing me."

"Please sit." She motions across her desk.

I take a seat and put a thick yellow envelope on my lap.

"Mr. O'Malley, what can I do for you? I'm afraid I don't have any notes regarding this meeting." She smiles.

I return her smile and open the envelope. "There's a student in her last year whose situation I need to discuss with you. Until about a month ago, she was in line to be the valedictorian. Her name is Simona Carter."

Dean Whitehouse's eyes turn to slits. "Yes. It's come to my attention Ms. Carter seems to have dropped out without giving us any notice. I hope everything is okay?"

"She's getting better."

Dean Whitehouse leans closer. Concern fills her expression. "What happened to her?"

"Unfortunately, we don't know for sure. We believe Ms. Carter's apartment got broken into, but she lives in a building with no security on a rather rough side of town. I hadn't heard from her, and when I checked on her, she was severely injured and left for dead. For several weeks, she was in a coma."

"Oh my God!" Dean Whitehouse puts her hand over her mouth and her eyes widen.

I nod. "These are her medical records, signed by her doctor, along with a letter stating she should be okay to return to school and normal activities within a week or so. He wants to make sure she doesn't add any extra stress right now."

"But she's going to be okay?" Dean Whitehouse asks.

"Yes. She doesn't remember what happened to her, but the doctors said she has almost fully recovered from her injuries. As I'm sure you can understand, Simona is very concerned about flunking her classes. I wanted to discuss with you what options she has. She is confident she can take her finals and make up her missed work."

"Oh dear. Yes. Let me speak with her professors and see what we can do."

"Great." I smile bigger and lean forward, ready to seal the deal. "I saw the school is raising funds for the library wing in your name?"

Her face slightly flushes, and pride lights it up. "Yes. We're close to having all the funds needed."

"You need fifty thousand, correct?"

"Yes."

"Great." I take an envelope out of my pocket and slide it across the desk. "As soon as I receive confirmation that Simona's grades won't be affected and she can make up any missed work without any penalties, I'll tell my bank to release the funds in this envelope."

The dean gapes at me then sits up straighter. "Well, that's umm..."

"Very generous of me since you were going to take care of this anyway?"

She nervously laughs. "Yes. Well said."

I rise. "Great. So we have an understanding?"

She rises. "Yes."

"Perfect. There are two checks in there. One's for twenty. If it's past noon when I get confirmation, you can cash that one. If I receive the guarantee before noon, you get to deposit both. The second one is for thirty. My card is on the envelope with my email. Make sure you cc Simona as well."

A large grin forms on her face. "I guess I'm clearing my schedule for the rest of the morning to speak with her professors."

"Sounds wise." I hold out my hand and shake hers. "It was nice meeting you. I look forward to receiving your email." I leave, feeling like I should be skipping through the parking lot but not wanting to push my luck until everything is a done deal.

I drive into the city and pull up to Skylar Ivanov's design boutique. I'm in the middle of picking out a dress to send to Simona to wear on our date, when my email buzzes.

I read it, sigh in relief, and pump my fist in the air. Then I text Simona.

Me: *Read your email, Ms. Future Valedictorian.*

17

Simona

It's as if he made the impossible happen. I reread the email from Dean Whitehouse several times. It's an email to Declan, and I'm cc'd.

Dear Mr. O'Malley,

Based on the circumstances, all of Simona Carter's professors will allow her to make up her classwork and turn in any late assignments. The only stipulation is she must get caught up before the end of the semester.

We wish her a speedy recovery and look forward to seeing her back on campus.

Sincerely,

Dean Whitehouse

. . .

HOW DID HE DO IT?

What does she think I'm recovering from?

Surely, he didn't tell her what happened?

My curiosity wins. I dial Declan.

"Angel," he answers, with a renewed pep in his voice.

"How did you do it?"

"I'll tell you on our date."

My flutters reignite. I've had them all morning from thinking about seeing Declan. Then I went into my closet and looked at my pathetic wardrobe of jeans and T-shirts. I never have any reason to dress up, so I have nothing fancy. I blurt out, "Can we go somewhere casual?" My face burns as soon as it escapes my lips.

Why don't I have at least one fancy article of clothing?

The line turns silent. Declan's heavy breathing only increases my anxiety. He finally replies, "I want to take you somewhere nice, Simona. That's what you deserve. Is this your way of trying to end our dinner sooner?"

"No. I just..." I squeeze my eyes shut. This is so embarrassing. I've never had to worry about my clothes before.

"Just what?" he pushes.

"You've seen my wardrobe." My heart pounds harder.

"A delivery is on its way to you as we speak. You don't need to stress over this."

I sharply inhale. My insides quiver in relief and also more nerves. "What is it?"

"You'll see. And a car will pick you up in an hour."

"Why?"

"Because Daddy is always going to take care of you, angel. So enjoy your day. I'll see you at seven." He hangs up before I can reply.

The doorbell rings, and I set my phone down, then answer it. One of the security guys says in a thick, Russian accent, "Ms. Carter. This is for you." He holds out a garment bag with a Skylar Ivanov logo on it and two plastic bags.

"Thank you."

"Have a good day, ma'am." He leaves.

I shut the door and take the items to my bedroom. My hands slightly shake as I unzip the garment bag and remove a teal-blue, satin, split-thigh dress. Buttons run down one side, stopping at the thigh-high split. It has spaghetti straps and is the most glamorous item I've ever held in my hand.

There's also a long, black leather trench coat. It's soft and I run my hands over it several times.

Then I open a bag and pull out a shoebox. I freeze, staring at the Jimmy Choo logo.

He didn't.

I may not have nice clothes, but I look at fashion online. I'm actually obsessed with it. But everything I see has always been a fantasy. I have too many bills to pay to buy anything extravagant.

I slowly lift the lid and gape at the silver-toned metallic sandals. The open toe, high stiletto heel, and ankle strap with a side buckle create an elegant and stunning piece.

I inspect them closely then set them on the bed next to the dress. I open the last bag, and I squirm on the mattress. There's only one item—a crotchless black leather thong with flat, studded accents. It's another thing I've never worn. My underwear all come from Walmart, and while I try to pick out the sexiest ones, they don't carry anything like this.

I peek in the bag, looking for a bra, but there isn't one. I pick the dress up again and feel the material. It's thicker than I assumed. I pull my T-shirt up, play with my nipple until it's hard, then press the luxury satin against it.

No matter how I move it, I can't see my nipple. I release a breath and place the dress back on the bed, staring at everything.

My phone vibrates. I pick it up and read the text.

Declan: *The boutique forgot to send over your evening bag. It'll get there after you leave. Pick it up at security when you get back, okay?*

Me: *This is...*

I take a deep breath, overwhelmed by the contents on my bed.

Declan: *You don't like it?*

Me: *No, I love it. Thank you.*

Declan: *I can't wait to see you in it.*

Me: *I'm not sure if I'll be able to walk in the shoes.*

Declan: *Don't worry, angel. You'll be on my arm.*

I smile, thinking about inhaling Declan's intoxicating scent while being escorted wherever we're going.

Declan: *I have to go, angel. Enjoy the rest of your day. I'll see you at seven.*

Me: *Wait!*

Declan: *What's up?*

Me: *What do I wear? Right now?*

Declan: *Whatever you have on is fine. Enjoy.*

My head spins, wondering where he's taking me. I go into the bathroom, brush my hair, then stare at my reflection. My makeup consists of mascara and lip gloss. It's from the clearance section of the grocery store. I cringe thinking about the fancy dress and shoes. For once in my life, I wish I knew how to put on makeup and do my hair, besides throwing it in a ponytail, messy bun, or wearing it naturally straight. The night I met Declan, my friend Tonya fixed me up. I almost call her, but then I'd have to explain my luxury condo and where I've been the last month. Plus, she hasn't spoken to me since I refused to go out with her again.

I groan, and the buzzer goes off. I press the button and security tells me that my driver is here. I shove my ID and phone in my pocket then go downstairs and get into the car.

It's another thing I'm not used to. My transportation consists of a bus, aside from the night Tonya and I went out and she hired an Uber. This is nothing like that. It's a black sedan with tinted windows, leather seats, and a divider window, giving me privacy from the driver. I text Declan.

Me: *I'm getting anxious. Can you tell me where this driver is taking me?*

Declan: *To relax.*

Me: *You know I don't speak Morse code, correct?*

Declan: *Are you sure about that? You're a much better hacker than I am, and even I know it.*

Me: *Really?*

Declan: *Yep.*

Me: *Why do you know that? Were you in the military?*

Declan: *Nope. But my daideo was. Every O'Malley man learns it.*

Me: *Interesting... If I ever need to send a secret message, I know who to call. Now, where am I going?*

Declan: *So demanding. Maybe I should go inside with you, put you over my knee, and spank you?*

I bite my lip, unsure if he's joking or serious, or if I would like it or not.

Declan: *That hot little pussy of yours would go nuts. I'm not sure if you'd be able to adhere to the rules.*

My insides pulse, and I decide I'm willing to let him spank me.

Focus!

Me: *What rules?*

Declan: *Of the place you're going to. They like it quiet.*

Me: And this would be?

Declan: *Look out the window.*

The car parks on the curb, and I glance outside. A sign on the window reads, Lush Tranquility: A Day Spa.

Me: *How did you know I was here? Do you have a camera on me?*

Declan: *Daddy protects his angel at all costs. It includes knowing where you are at all times.*

Me: *Did you put a tracker on my phone?*

Declan: *What do you think?*

Me: *Of course you did.*

My insides quiver with rage and something else. It's once again the polar opposite. A part of me is happy he's watching me.

I'm so fucked up.

Declan: *Be a good girl, get out of the car, and go enjoy your present.*

I take a deep breath and look back at the sign. I've never been to a spa before.

Me: *I don't know what to do here.*

Declan: *Walk inside, give the girl your name, and she'll explain all the things I booked for you. If there is something else you see on the list and want, add it.*

I focus some more on the spa. My anxiety multiplies. This is something rich people do. I'm going to be a fish out of water.

Declan calls me.

I answer. "Hey."

"Why is your gorgeous ass still in the car?"

"Umm..." How do I even explain this? I finally say, "This seems a bit out of my league."

The line turns silent. I cringe at what I admitted and wonder why I'm still sitting here. I've always imagined what it would be like to go to a spa.

The door flies open and Declan orders, "Scoot over, angel."

I gape at him but obey. He gets in and yanks me onto his lap. I gasp, and my insides melt. His spicy, woody scent fills the air. My body melts into his warm flesh just as it always does. His chiseled face fills with arrogance. He cocks an eyebrow, and it seems sexier than usual.

I ask, "What are you doing here?"

"It's been too long. I couldn't wait until tonight to see you," he confesses.

My insides do a wild happy dance. All the nervous anticipation I've felt about going out with him reignites. "You were going to join me?"

He fists my hair, gently tugs my head, and brings his lips in front of mine. He mumbles, "No. I was going to watch you stroll inside and torture myself some more." His erection grows against my thigh.

I shudder. My skin crackles with electricity.

He grunts. "Fuck. I thought I could control myself around you, but I still can't."

A grin I can't contain explodes on my lips. I admit, "I missed you."

His eyes turn hungrier, morphing into blue flames. "I'd kiss you, but I won't stop. You're going to be late for your appointment.

The worry reappears. "I-I...this is sweet of you, but I'm not sure I'm a spa girl."

What am I saying?

"Sure you are. You've just never done it before."

"It's way too much. You already bought me Jimmy Choos and the perfect dress!"

His expression is one of stern heat, making me feel like I might break out in a sweat.

Jesus. How can a man be so sexy?

He firmly states, "Daddy's going to spoil you, angel. All these things in life you haven't done aren't going to be reasons to stop you."

I stay silent, not used to the concept of anyone spoiling me or entirely sure what it means. I'm used to surviving, not bathing in luxuries.

We still haven't worked out all our issues.

He fixed my school problems.

Doesn't mean it corrects what he did.

Why am I still fighting him?

"Do I need to escort you inside and wait in the lobby until you finish all your treatments?"

"No."

"That's right. You go to a rich, private school and are excelling. You're kicking all those kids' asses. So hold your pretty head high and walk in there like you own the freaking place."

A small laugh escapes me.

"Or we can go back to my place, and I'll give you my version of a massage."

My pulse races faster. There's so much temptation to tell him yes. His eyes taunt me, but I know a part of him wants me to as well. I'm not sure if I'm ready for him yet. As much as I want to move forward and forgive him, there are still many unanswered questions. If I fall back into Declan, I'm not getting out this time.

I need answers first before I make up my mind about us.

I slowly nod. "Okay. Ummm...thank you for the generous gift."

He smiles and tucks a lock of my hair behind my ear. It tugs on my heart and amplifies all my feelings for him I tell myself I want to disappear but deep down know I don't. "You're welcome." He opens the door, slides me off his lap, then gets out. He reaches in for me.

I step into him and reach for his face.

His palm possessively cups my ass, and his other hand slides into the back of my hair. He studies me, and my mouth waters. Before I can stop myself, I stand on my tiptoes to kiss him, but he pushes his forehead against mine. "Simona, I wasn't lying about not kissing you. But fair warning, I won't be restraining myself tonight."

Reality snaps me out of my trance. I blurt out, "I have questions."

He briefly closes his eyes then pecks me on the lips. He might as well have given me a bite of chocolate cake then set it in front of me and told me not to eat anymore. "We'll talk tonight." He spins and guides me toward the door then opens it.

I walk inside.

He says, "Enjoy yourself, angel," then shuts the door before I can reply.

I watch him saunter to his SUV and just barely resist running after him.

"Hi! Welcome to Lush Tranquility. Can I help you?" a chipper woman's voice calls out.

I spin and force myself to smile, just like I did when I first got on campus and felt like I didn't belong. I step toward the desk. "Hi. I'm Simona Carter. My umm..." I freeze, stopping myself from calling Declan my boyfriend. I exhale and start again. "I'm here for some services, and it was a gift. I'm not sure what I'm getting."

She types in the computer, and a look of excitement takes over her face. "Ooooh! Whoever gave you this gift has excellent taste. They booked you a detoxification mud bath, bamboo massage, classic facial, pedicure, manicure, and salon services."

I gape at her then clear my throat. "Salon services?"

"Yep. Hair and makeup."

I bite my lip. My earlier anxiety about not knowing how to put on makeup or do my hair lifts.

"Are you ready to go back to the locker room?"

"Sure."

Another woman named Shelly leads me through the spa. She gives me a tour of the women's room then takes me to my locker. She demonstrates how the locker codes work then tells me to go into the relaxation area to wait after I put on the robe and sandals.

For the rest of the day, I have several therapists pamper me. By the time I get to the salon, I'm more relaxed than I've ever been. The stylist and makeup artists assess me. The stylist asks, "What are we doing with your hair?"

I take a sip of the champagne they just gave me. "I have a dinner date tonight."

"Hot date?" She wiggles her eyebrows.

My cheeks flush. I have too many unanswered questions to think about our dinner being anything but an information-gathering session. Still, all I can think about is getting Declan's lips all over my body. I admit, "Yeah. It's a date."

The makeup artist smirks. "So, you're going for super-sexy, maybe a bit dramatic, drive him wild the moment he sees you?"

Flutters annihilate me. I lift my chin. "Yes. That's exactly what I want."

18

Declan

THE CLOSER IT GETS TO MY DATE WITH SIMONA, THE clammier my hands get.

"Pull it together," I mutter.

I slide my sport coat on, grab the bouquet of red roses, and open the front door to leave. My chest tightens. I bark, "What are you doing here?"

Liam's green eyes glow hotter. "Now you're keeping new articles from me?"

My stomach plummets. "What are you talking about?"

He crosses his arms. "Don't play dumb with me, Declan."

"I'm not. And why would I keep that from you?"

He sniffs hard. "You seem to keep a lot from me lately."

"Don't turn this into something it's not. I've told you about all the articles. I haven't put one up since the last one I showed you."

"Then who did?"

"I don't know." I push past him. "I don't have time for this right now."

He grabs my shoulder and spins me.

"What the fuck, Liam!"

Red flares on his face. "You don't have time for this? Nothing is as important as this! Or did you forget everything we have on the line?"

My anger matches his but for different reasons. I grab him by the collar. "I've dedicated the last few years of my life to this. You were still in prison when I gave up everything I chose for my life to make your plan come to fruition."

He pushes my chest, and I release him. He orders, "Get back in the house and figure out who posted this. I want another article up by morning."

I shake my head. "It'll have to be later."

"Excuse me?"

"I'm taking Simona out."

He snarls, "She can wait. Your date isn't a priority."

I growl, "That's where you're wrong. Nothing is a higher priority than her."

His eyes turn to slits, and he steps closer. "You're choosing getting laid over the O'Malleys?"

I curl my hand in a fist, holding back the punch I want to connect to his face. "Don't talk about Simona like she's a piece of ass. You're a second shy of kissing the concrete."

"Yeah? Why don't you try it," he taunts.

It's tempting, but getting into a brawl with Liam isn't smart. He may be my younger cousin, but he's still head of the clan. I'm already past the point I should be in the conversation. "I'm leaving. I'll work on this later." I turn and walk toward the SUV in the driveway.

"So you do choose her over the O'Malleys?" he booms.

I spin back. "Keep your voice down. And let's get something straight. She's my woman. I don't get between you and Hailee, nor did I ever question your alliance even though you married a Bailey. So show Simona and me the same respect, or this is going to morph into something neither of us wants."

He points in my face. "Don't you dare discuss my wife and compare her to a woman you—"

"I love her!" I blurt out, surprising even myself.

Silence fills the air, as crisp as the cold wind hitting my cheek. Our breaths come out in a fog, each of us pinning our gazes on the other's.

"I have to win her back. No. I *will* win her back. And nothing is getting in the way of me doing that. So put me in front of the council, pull me from the job, whatever the fuck you want. But I'm leaving now. I'll deal with this issue after I do what I need to do for her." I get into the back seat of the SUV and say to Shay, "Boris's building." I hit the button for the divider window to shut.

For several moments, I attempt to calm down before pulling up the article on Jack's company. I read it then close my eyes and bang my head on the back of the seat. It's bad for us. Why did BusyCEO not come to Simona to post it? I double-check he didn't send her any requests, but he didn't.

As much as this burns me, I can't worry about it right now. There are too many what-ifs, along with this situation, and if I let myself analyze this, I'll drown in it. Nothing can come between Simona and me tonight. I need her back. Seeing and holding her today, while brief, only solidified how empty my life is without her. No matter what I have to do to make her mine, I'm going to do it.

Shay pulls up to the curb, and I get out. I nod to security, and my palms start to sweat again. I wipe them on my pants, shifting the roses from hand to hand. The elevator dings and my nerves increase.

I'm already a few minutes late. I hate not being on time. Tonight isn't the night for me to screw anything up. If our date doesn't go well, I doubt Simona will give me another chance.

I ring the bell, feeling like I'm eighteen again and not a forty-four-year-old man. I reprimand myself once more for being so anxious and not my usual confident self.

The door opens, and it doesn't help my nerves. My mouth turns dry and my heart races faster. I can barely muster one word. "Wow."

Simona bites on her red lip, her cheeks flush, and my dick gets so hard, it hurts. Her long, dark hair hangs in curls, with one side pinned back, showcasing her sculpted cheek. Her blue eyes pop, outlined in darker makeup. The teal, satin dress hugs her body to perfection. Her right leg peeks out, displaying her smooth skin all the way down to her silver stilettos.

She shyly asks, "Are you coming inside?"

I snap out of my daze and take a step forward, shutting the door. The energy of her aura zaps me. "Sorry, angel. You're just... Jesus. You're stunning."

Her cheeks turn beet red. Nerves fill her blue orbs. Her chest rises, and she replies, "Thanks. You look nice, too."

The air between us crackles with electricity. Holding the flowers to one side, I circle one arm around her and palm her ass while tugging her as close to me as possible.

She sharply inhales and lifts her long lashes as her blue orbs meet mine.

I murmur, "You smell better than I remember. I'm sorry I'm late."

She creases her forehead. "Are you?"

"Yeah. Few minutes."

"I didn't notice. I umm..." My cock twitches against her stomach, and she swallows hard. "I can't get my dress zipped."

It's pleasant torture, but I give her a chaste kiss. "Spin."

She obeys, and I slide the flowers to the front of her body. "These are for you. Hold them so I can zip you up before I change my mind and drop this dress to the floor."

A nervous laugh erupts from her lips. She takes the roses. "These are beautiful. You're spoiling me today."

I move her hair over one shoulder then kiss the curve of her neck. She shudders, and I reiterate against her skin while zipping up her dress, "I told you Daddy is going to spoil you, angel." I step in front of her.

She exhales slowly. "I should put these in water."

I don't think she realizes how much her nerves are calming mine. It's like it's giving me the kick I need to get past my anxiety and be the strong man she needs right now. I trace her jawline. "I'll do it."

I take the flowers, grab the vase on the end table, then go into the kitchen. I cut the stems, pour the flower food packet into the vase, then add water to it. After I stick the roses in, I return to her. "Ready?"

Her lips slightly curve. "Sure."

I help her into her coat then guide her out of the condo and into the elevator. When the doors shut, I tease, "You caught on how to walk."

She tilts her head. "I guess Jimmy makes it easy."

I cock an eyebrow. "Are you a Jimmy fan?"

"I always admired them, but now that I'm wearing a pair, I have to admit they're better than I imagined."

The door opens, and I grip her hip tighter. "Guess I'll have to buy you some other pairs." I step into the lobby and lead her toward the door.

"These are expensive. One pair's more than I ever dreamed of," she comments.

I lean into her. "Who said they're for you? Daddy has plans for you in these shoes."

Her face turns deep crimson.

I chuckle then move her toward the vehicle. Shay opens the door, and Simona gets in, then I follow.

The door shuts, and she asks, "Where are you taking me?"

"The Private Room. Have you heard of it?"

"No."

I glide my arm across her shoulders. "How did you like the spa?"

She smiles. "It was amazing. Thank you."

"You're welcome. Knew you'd rock it." I wink.

She turns into me further. "Do you butter up all your dates like this?"

"No. Just you, angel."

She stays quiet for a moment then asks, "How did you sort out my schooling?"

My stomach flips. I'm ecstatic Simona can still have the opportunity to pass her classes and make up what she missed, but I hate what I did to her and the fact she's going to have to play into my lie. "I told the dean I found you in your apartment, severely injured and left for dead after what we assume was a burglary."

Her eyes widen.

I add, "She thinks you don't remember the incident and are recovering. I gave her medical records I had Doc create and sign off on, along with a note that in a week or so, you should be able to return to school."

Her silence does nothing to calm my nerves.

I ask, "Will you be able to get caught up on what you missed?"

She nods. "Yes. I already did all my assignments besides the in-class ones."

Pride sweeps through me. I tug her closer to me. "Of course you did. It was easy for you, too, wasn't it?"

"How did you know?"

"You're the smartest woman I've ever come across. I've already told you this."

She tilts her head. "How can you say that? I haven't demonstrated much of my brain."

I drag my knuckles down her cheek then across her jaw. "I told you. You're a better hacker than I am. And your school record is impressive."

"Why do you think I'm a better hacker?"

I shift in my seat. "The night I kidnapped you, I watched you add the article and delete your footprint faster than I'd ever seen anyone. I still don't know how you accomplished that. It's like you were a ghost."

"A ghost you caught," she states.

Shay parks the vehicle in front of The Private Room. I take her hand and kiss it. "It took me months to catch you." I step out and reach in to help her out then guide her out of the winter cold and into the exclusive restaurant.

There's a bouncer and a woman named Lulu positioned behind a hostess stand. She has her dark hair in a French twist. Her lips and nails are the same shade of red. The small space is dark, lit only by a few dim canned lights and a candle flickering on the counter. She smiles and says, "Good to see you, Mr. O'Malley."

"And you."

She presses a buzzer and the door behind her opens. Another woman with blonde hair steps out. Lulu hands her two menus and motions for us to follow her.

I keep my hand tight around Simona's waist and guide her through the dark hall until we get into our room. The luxury booth is done in purple velvet, and a bottle of champagne is chilling in an ice bucket inside a floor stand. Black-and-gray textured wallpaper splashes across the walls. There are two silver wall sconces and more candles on the table. A black leather couch with two end tables and a small open area complete the space. Soft, seductive music fills the air.

The blonde picks up the bottle. "Carl will be with you in a few moments. Would you like champagne at the table or the couch?"

"The couch is fine. Thank you." I motion for Simona to sit.

She crosses her legs, and I take the seat next to her, then wait. The blonde hands us glasses and puts the menus on the table next to me then leaves.

I slide my hand on Simona's thigh and hold my flute up. "To you, my angel."

Her blue eyes sparkle, and the flush creeps back into her cheeks. She clinks my glass and takes a sip. I study her, take a drink, and set my champagne down. I slide my arm around her. "Are you hungry?"

"Yes. Is there really no one else coming in this room?"

"Nope. It's you and me."

"I haven't been to a lot of restaurants. Is this normal for nicer places?"

I drag my finger over her collarbone. "No. This is the only place in Chicago that's this exclusive."

"Do you come here a lot?"

"No."

"But you knew the hostess."

"It's her job to know who I am."

She takes another sip. "But you've had other dates here."

"No."

She furrows her eyebrows. "I'm confused."

"I had a few meetings here. No one was special enough for me to bring here," I admit.

Her smile grows, and everything seems brighter.

I lean into her ear. "I've been living in Hell without you, angel. When are you coming home?"

She freezes then slowly turns toward me. "Home?"

"Yeah. With me."

She avoids my gaze, staring straight ahead.

I turn her chin. "I hate what I did to you. I'll never be able to tell you how sorry I am."

She closes her eyes momentarily then pins her glassy, big blues on me.

"You belong in my bed, sleeping and waking up next to me every day, where I can watch over you and make sure you're taken care of."

"I can take care of myself," she claims, but it doesn't come out as strong as I think she attempted.

I take her flute and set it next to mine then pull her onto my lap. "You shouldn't have to. You should *never* have had to."

She furrows her brows, grappling with my statements.

I push her hair over her shoulder and trail my fingers over the nape of her neck while cupping her cheek with my other hand. "If what we have wasn't something that only happens once in a lifetime, I'd let you go. But it isn't something superficial that's going to wither and die. Now, admit to me you miss us, my bed, and me taking care of you."

She opens her mouth, and the waiter chooses that moment to walk into the room.

He says, "Mr. O'Malley. Ms. Carter. I'm Carl and will be your server this evening. Are you planning on letting the chef create what he wants tonight, or will you be ordering from the menu?"

Anxiety fills Simona's face, so I rub her neck and reply, "We'll have whatever the chef wants to make. Simona is allergic to peanuts, so please make sure he's aware."

"Will do, and great choice. What can I get for you to drink?"

"Double Jameson neat, please. Simona?"

"Ummm..." She swallows hard and twists a lock of her hair around her finger.

I'd let her drink champagne all night, but I don't want her to get sick. She and her friend drank cosmopolitans at the pub the night we met. She seemed to like the wine I gave her the night I fed her spaghetti, so I ask, "Do you want a glass of wine or maybe a cosmo?"

A tiny breath flies out of her mouth. "Sure. Wine sounds good."

"Good choice. Want me to choose?"

"Please."

I stroke her thigh and glance at the wine list. "Opus One 2016, please."

Carl nods. "Excellent choice. I'll be back soon with your drinks." He leaves.

"What do I need to do to win you back?" I ask Simona.

She shifts on my lap.

I run my thumb over her spine. "Please tell me. You're turning me into a desperate man."

Her voice is soft, but I hear the pain in it. "More desperate than when you drugged me and put a bag over my head?"

My heart almost stops. "That wasn't desperation."

Her eyes widen. "No? What was it?"

"Business." My pulse skyrockets, not sure what I'm about to say to her or where this conversation will lead. She knows about the O'Malleys. I try to prepare myself for her questions, but I'm not sure what she'll ask.

Her gaze drifts off mine.

"Angel—"

"Why do you care what happens to Jack Christian's company? You said I caused you to lose millions, but how?" she asks, going to the one topic I should never discuss with anyone.

She's not just anyone.

It's a lot to disclose.

I still don't know if BusyCEO knows who she is.

"Answer me," she demands.

"Okay. I will. But tell me first how you got on that site."

She slides off my lap.

I tug her back on. "Where do you think you're sneaking off to?"

She glares at me. "You aren't going to do this."

"Do what?"

Darts fly from her eyes into mine. "Avoid answering me while finding out whatever it is you still think I'm hiding from you."

"I don't think you're hiding anything from me," I insist.

She crosses her arms. "Yes, you do."

"No, I don't. Now tell me how you got on CollegeTech-Money's site."

"After everything you put me through, you don't get to call the shots on this discussion."

"Simona—"

Carl steps inside and hands me a tumbler of whiskey and Simona a glass of wine. "Is there anything else I can get for you?"

"Not now. Thank you," I reply and wait for him to leave.

Simona sets the glass on the side table.

I take a large mouthful of the alcohol, holding back a grimace as it burns my throat all the way to my stomach. "Let's get something straight, lass."

Blue flames seer into me, and in them, I see all the hatred I wanted to think she no longer felt toward me.

My chest tightens to the point my lungs seem not to work. I declare, "From now until I die, I'll do whatever it takes to make sure you're protected. When I'm deep in the ground, I'll see to it that the O'Malleys are still watching over you until you're an old woman taking her last breath."

Confusion laces with fear in her expression.

More guilt eats at me for not making this easier on her, but I continue. "If I ask you something, it's not due to any of my previous misconceptions. It's because you're mine, whether you realize it right now or not. And every detail that may or may not mean something to you could to me. Those reasons aren't things I'm always going to tell you about, and not because I don't want to but because it could harm you."

"So you aren't going to answer my questions?" Her lips tremble.

I hold her cheeks and study her. "I'm going to answer anything you ask me tonight unless it could put you in danger. But first, I asked you how you got on that site, and you're going to tell me."

19

Simona

Waves of anger crash into all the desire I have for Declan. Whether I'm away from him or close by, I never stop feeling the hunger for him. It makes me dizzy trying to figure out our situation. He's trying to right the wrongs he did. He's apologized too many times to count. Even the story he told me about how he got me back in good standing with my professors feels like there's additional information he's leaving out. My gut is telling me it can't be as easy as what he stated. Surely, he had to do more than just give the dean a bunch of false documents and tell her some sob story?

In some ways, the weeks apart haven't changed anything. Our relationship, if this is one or can ever be, isn't simple. It's a complex web of the past, present, and future strewn with lies, mistaken assumptions, and burning chemistry that only seems to grow hotter. I'm unsure how to get through all the sticky layers in front of me. His current demand to give him answers before he gives them to me isn't helping me weave my way through the maze of questions.

Once again, Declan is holding the cards. In this situation, I don't like it.

I rise and move toward the door.

He leaps toward me and spins me into him so fast, I almost fall. If it weren't for his arms holding me tight to his frame, I would.

My lower body throbs while my blood boils. He fists my hair, tugging it back, his piercing gaze swallowing me whole. I shudder from the intensity of everything I know he can give me. At this moment, I wish it weren't part of us. All it does is muddy my vision about the things I should remain focused on.

His eyes smolder, and the vein near his eye pulses. His voice is lower, calm even, but everything in his facial expression says the opposite. A storm is brewing inside him. I know it. I've seen it too many times, yet it competes with my own spinning tornado of rage. He questions, "Where are you going, angel?"

Lava bubbles in my stomach. "If you can't answer me without putting stipulations on it, then I can't consider being with you."

An expression I've never seen before leaps onto his face. It's a concoction of panic and hurt, reminding me of a wounded, caged animal. Almost as quickly as it arrives, it leaves, replaced with the confidence he wears so well. He takes two steps, moving my body with his until I'm against the door.

The click of the lock hits my ears, and his hard frame presses into mine.

"You can't be in charge of everything," I meekly state, melting between him and the door.

"You think I've been in charge since you left me? Hmm?"

I open my mouth then snap it shut. Is what he's insinuating correct? Have I been in charge?

He strokes my jaw with his thumbs. "You didn't take my calls. You wouldn't allow me to see you. Every demand you made, I obeyed. Through all that, you're still here, with me. You *chose* to come with me tonight. Do you know why?"

A lump expands in my throat. I swallow hard, but it doesn't seem to move. My voice comes out raspy, so quiet, I barely hear it. "Why?"

He studies me, burning every atom I have, singeing the layers of fight I can't seem to keep hold of. "Every ounce of what I feel for you, you feel for me. If you didn't, you wouldn't be here. You're sugar and I'm hot water. We've been stirred and shaken. There's no more you or me. It's us."

I close my eyes, unable to witness his determined stare down any longer, knowing in my heart what he claims is true but not able to get past the information he hasn't shared with me.

He runs his knuckles down my cheek. "Tell me how you got on that site, angel. Then I'm telling you everything even though I shouldn't."

I open my eyes. "Everything?"

"Yes. Now, tell me. We're dealing with all this tonight."

The resolve to stand my ground and make him tell me first bursts into flames. "My professor told me I could make some extra money because of my skills."

He pins his eyebrows together. "He announced it in class?"

"No. He pulled me aside."

His eyes turn into slits.

"What's wrong?"

"Probably nothing."

"But—"

He shuts me up with a kiss, stroking his tongue against mine slowly, as if exploring my mouth for the first time, causing my knees to buckle. His flesh presses me harder into the door, holding me up. When we're out of breath, he retreats, murmuring, "That wasn't hard, now was it?"

"No," I whisper.

The door handle moves, and he pulls me aside, then unlocks it.

Carl enters, carrying a server's tray filled with metal-covered plates. He smiles and chirps, "Appetizers."

Declan moves me to the booth, and I slide in. He grabs our drinks and sits next to me, slinging his arm around my shoulder.

Carl uncovers several plates and points to each. "For starters, we have mussels in white wine and garlic sauce, panko crusted frog legs, and vegetable pâté." He adds a basket of bread and crostinis next to the dishes then fills two water glasses. "Can I get you anything else right now?"

Declan turns to me. "Simona?"

"No, thank you. I'm good." I've never seen or tasted any of the items before. The smell of garlic and other herbs makes me realize how hungry I am.

"We're all set. Thanks." Declan nods.

Carl leaves.

Declan picks up a piece of bread then adds a mussel to it. He holds it to my mouth. "Try this."

"You're still going to tell me, right?"

Amusement creeps over his face. He leans closer to me. "After everything we've been through, do you think Daddy would lie to you?" He cocks an eyebrow.

My flutters take off. "I don't know. Do daddies lie?"

He wiggles the food. "No. A good daddy does whatever is necessary to take care of you. He protects you at all costs, but he doesn't lie. Eat before this goes bad."

I take a bite of the delectable dish and the rich flavor bursts on my tongue. "Mmm."

Declan's grin widens, and my loins somersault. Everything about his rugged features is handsome, including the little wrinkles around the corners of his eyes. I haven't seen him smile very often. Something about it creates happiness within me.

"Good?" he questions then adds a mussel to the remaining bread and shoves it in his mouth.

I finish chewing, swallow, and take a sip of wine. "Delicious."

He spends several minutes feeding me the frog legs and pâté then taking bites after me. He washes it down with his whiskey then wipes his mouth with the cloth napkin. His face falls. The dark storm returns, swirling in his expression. "Are you ready to hear what I'm involved in?"

I straighten my back. "Yes."

He makes another piece of bread with a mussel on it and holds it to my mouth. "You eat. I'll talk."

I accept the food, and he puts his arm around me. "You understand I'm part of a crime family?"

My chest tightens. I nod while chewing.

"It isn't making you run?"

I swallow then shake my head. "No."

"Why?"

I shrug. "I... I don't know. Ummm..." I turn in my seat and confess, "I hope you don't make me into a fool."

He strokes my hair and tilts his head. "How would I do that?"

"I don't think you would hurt me. I know you could, and I'm sure that's what all women who end up dead on crime shows think, but I just..."

He softly asks, "You just what, angel?"

I tap my fingers on the wineglass and lift my chin. "You had your chance to kill me and didn't. I'm pretty sure you would destroy anyone else who did."

I didn't think his eyes could darken any further, but they do. "I wouldn't just destroy them. I'd torture them for days, bestowing a hundred times the punishment of whatever they did to you. Only then would I steal their last breath."

His statement sends a chill down my spine. I shudder, yet it also makes me feel safe, which is something I've never experienced in my life. The thought that I felt safe when he kidnapped me pops up again.

I'm so fucked up.

Maybe I just need to embrace this.

Perhaps it's why I know in my heart he won't hurt me.

He tugs me closer and grazes his fingers on my biceps. "So we're past any issues about my family?"

I only feel calm surrounding his family issues. "Yes."

He pecks me on the lips. "Good, lass."

"How did I cost your family millions?" I try to shove down the guilt I feel.

He sees it. "You didn't know. It's not your fault. Hopefully, we'll make it back. But I really need you to show me some things."

I scrunch my face. "What?"

"How you erased your footprint so fast."

My lips curve up and I bite the bottom one.

"What's so funny?"

"It's easy."

Pride sweeps his features. He kisses me again, mumbling against my mouth, "I love how smart you are, angel."

My cheeks heat from the combination of his compliment and affection. I stroke the side of his head. "I'll show you. Please tell me what you're involved in that led to my abduction."

He winces. "Sounds so horrible."

I smirk, knowing it's not funny but suddenly seeing some humor in it. And maybe that's how we get past it. "Yeah. It was. Especially the hypothermia."

His grimace intensifies, plagued with painful remorse.

It hurts me to see him like this. I give him a chaste kiss. "I didn't say it to make you feel bad."

He sternly replies, "I'll die regretting what I did."

Something shifts. It's a brick crashing into me. If we're going to move forward and be together, I have to let go of the anger of our past, and he has to release all the self-reproach.

Deep down, I can't lie to myself. The only man I've ever obsessed over is him. And not only before he kidnapped me. The last few weeks, I still only thought of him. When I'm with him, I have things I've never had before.

Safety.

Someone who lights me up in ways I didn't know were possible.

A man who wants to take care of me, and even though I never craved this, now that I've gotten a taste of it, I can't extinguish the desire to maintain it.

I cup his cheek, and he briefly closes his eyes. I didn't plan on it, but I softly declare, "I forgive you. Now please tell me the rest."

He swallows hard. "You forgive me?"

I nod. "Yes. But I need to know the rest. Why are you involved in Jack Christian's company?"

His hand strokes my bare thigh. I forgot about my dress, and tingles rush straight to my core. He maneuvers his hand between my legs, planting it firmly where I have them crossed. He takes a deep breath. "You can never tell anyone."

"I won't."

His thumb caresses my thigh. "I won't get into why we chose Jack's company. It's too dangerous for you to know. But we shorted the stock, so when it goes bankrupt, we'll make so much money, the O'Malleys can get out of our current lines of work."

The articles I read about the O'Malleys online made allegations about their primary sources of income. It doesn't excite me or make me comfortable.

"What's on your mind, angel?"

"You mean drugs and gambling?"

Disgust briefly passes in his eyes. "Yeah, lass. Until a few years ago, my brothers and I stayed out of the family business. We had a construction company. When we pledged to my uncle and the clan, we had to shut it down. He put my brother Nolan and me on the tech side of this deal. I don't like the current way we make money, but I'm trying to change it. Once we get the funds from shorting the stock, we're setting up a cybersecurity company. It's all legitimate from there on out."

I stay silent, taking everything in, then ask, "Why Jack's company?"

Hatred fills his expression. "I can only tell you it has been brewing for decades. Jack was involved in some nasty things done to my family, specifically my cousin, Finn. I wish I could tell you more about it, but I can't."

I tap my fingers on my wineglass, frustrated but strangely not wanting to push him regarding this issue.

"Say something," he nervously orders.

"Maybe you can hire me," I tease, trying to wipe the anxiety off his face.

His eyes light up. "You want to work with me, angel?"

"I was joking. I didn't—"

He grasps my cheeks. "I would hire you in an instant. I'd even make you a vice president."

Shock slices through me. There's no doubt he's serious. My heart thumps harder.

He states, "We'll talk about this later, but don't accept any other job offers until you talk with me. Give me your first crack."

A cybersecurity company is the type of business I would want to be hired by. I ignore the excitement in my belly and smile, returning to the reason we're having this conversation. Declan is open with me right now, and I don't want to lose this chance to ask all my questions. He never said he wouldn't tell me later, but I want to know everything and hopefully move forward. "Okay. So every time I posted a positive article, the stock went up, and because of your short position, you lost money."

"Yes. Right now, it's all on paper, but it's getting close to where we placed our positions. I've been counteracting the articles BusyCEO sends with negative ones since you left."

The hairs on the back of my neck rise. "He's still sending them?"

"Yes."

"You've been pretending to be me?"

"Yes. Don't be pissed."

"I'm not," I insist. I don't need to think about it. "But why is this person putting these articles up?"

"I don't know. I haven't been able to figure out who this guy is."

"Or woman."

Declan groans. "You think I wouldn't make that mistake twice, huh?"

My lips twitch. "Well, if this person is super smart, my guess is it's a woman."

He chuckles then pulls me in for a steamy kiss, moving his hand farther up my thigh. Zings explode in my pussy. The sweet taste of whiskey bursts on my tongue, and I deepen our kiss.

He retreats, asking, "Do you have any more questions, angel?"

"Just one," I reply then dive back into his sinful mouth.

"Hmm?" His fingers taunt my clit, and I forgot I was wearing crotchless panties.

Adrenaline spins in my head and I force myself to pull away, needing to know this. It doesn't have to do with my abduction, but the question is nagging me. "Why did you decide to get involved in your family business if you had a successful construction company?"

Pain twists on his face. He blinks hard, and the vein near his eye twitches. "My little brother, Sean, was murdered."

The blood drains from my head all the way to my toes. I gape at him, wanting to take away all the grief I see on his face.

The door opens, and Carl comes in with an empty tray and another server who's carrying one full of more food. Carl asks, "Are you finished with your starters?"

"Simona?" Declan asks.

"Yes."

Declan turns to Carl. "We're finished."

"Great." Carl puts the appetizers on the empty tray then places more food on the table. He points to each. "Butter-poached mahi-mahi with seared shrimp, smashed potatoes with gouda and horseradish, and roasted brussels sprouts with sriracha sauce. Can I get you anything else?"

"I think we're good. Thank you," Declan says.

The servers leave, and I reach for Declan's face. "Hey."

He raises his eyebrows.

"I'm sorry about your brother."

He nods. "Thanks. Let's enjoy our dinner."

"Ummm...can we talk more about it later?"

The depth of his gaze creates more flutters. "Only if you come home with me."

My butterflies escalate. Am I ready to return to his house?

He holds my face in front of his. "Do you have more questions?"

Do I? I rack my brain, but it's too distracted by everything Declan—his intoxicating scent, the way his fingers are back on my thigh, and his energy zapping my core.

So much vulnerability lies in his face. It takes me by surprise. I'm only used to him being confident. Without any hesitation, he firmly orders, "I need you back with me, angel. Tell me you'll come home with me. We can move your things tomorrow."

"You want me to move in?"

"Why do you sound surprised?"

My heart screams for me to say yes. The logical part of me says it's too soon. As much as I want him, I almost lost everything I've struggled to obtain. My degree has to come first. I'm too close to the finish line. I've always stayed away from distractions, and Declan's the biggest one I could ever have.

"Angel—"

"I can't move in with you right now."

His jaw clenches. He sniffs hard, glancing at the ceiling.

I grasp his cheeks and force him to look at me. "I need to study and finish my degree."

"Yes. I want you to. You have no idea how proud of you I am. What does that have to do with moving in?"

I smile and run my thumb over his lips. "I don't think I'll be able to concentrate with you around."

"I'll leave you alone so you can study," he insists.

"But I won't want to," I divulge.

"Simona, I want a life with you."

I run my hand through his hair. "Did I say I don't want you in my life?"

He turns away and lets out an exasperated sigh. "That doesn't sound like the same thing."

"Declan."

His tortured eyes meet mine. "I'm trying hard to do everything you want and not fuck this up again, but it seems like I'm never getting you fully back."

I don't want him to feel like this. It's not my intention to hurt him, but I can't seem to give him what he wants. It would be so easy to let Declan take care of me and forget about everything I need to focus on. But I almost had all my freedom taken away. A part of me didn't care, and I would have been somewhat happy staying with Declan forever. I can't let that happen again. If we're going to be together, I can't lose myself. And as much as I want to believe we can be forever, I've never had anyone permanent in my life. I can't get swept so far into him I can't survive if he decides to let me go.

I say the only thing that comes to my mind to help ease the blow and make both of us happy for right now. "Ask me the right question."

"What's that?"

"Ask me to stay with you *tonight*."

Blue flames flicker so strong, I clench my insides. He orders, "Come home with me tonight."

I lean into his ear and whisper, "If that's what Daddy wants, that's what Daddy gets."

20

Declan

Carl takes our plates away, and I pull Simona out of the booth. "Let's dance."

Her cheeks flush. She admits, "I don't know how."

Wrapping my arm around her waist and lacing her hand in mine, I tug her closer to me. "Guess it's good I do then."

She melts into me, letting me lead, placing her fingers on the back of my neck, sending an onslaught of tingles down my spine. Her blue eyes twinkle, creating more chaos in my pants.

"You're really beautiful, angel," I tell her, grateful she's here in my arms.

Mine. She's never going to be anyone else's. No matter what, I'll make sure there's never again any reason for her to leave me.

I want her with me every night and morning. I'm trying not to let the sting of her rejection about moving in ruin our evening. We've made a lot of progress in the last few hours, but the ball's still in her court. As much as I don't like it, I need to deal with her calling the shots about us.

She bites her smile, and her nails graze my skin. For a moment, she studies me. Then she brings her lips to mine.

Jesus, she's heaven. Her kisses are injections of pure dopamine. It's physical pleasure I didn't know existed before her, a constant buzz of everything sensual, divine, and taboo.

The things I want to do to her make my head spin. Holding myself back from taking her straight to my house once she agreed to stay might be the biggest test I've ever faced.

One look at her hungry expression sends my heart racing. There's nothing about our chemistry that's one-sided. I didn't know two people could equally want the other, but when I glance at my angel, or she kisses me, there's no doubt.

Dancing with her only solidifies my beliefs. When she moans in my mouth, I retreat and spin her around.

Her face lights up in surprise, and she laughs. It's the expression I want to see more of, and I'm committed to bringing it out of her more often.

She beams. "You're a good dancer."

"Nah. You've just never danced before," I tease.

"Surprised I'm not stepping on your feet or falling in these heels."

I groan. "Don't remind me of your shoes."

She leans in and licks my lobe. "Are you having dirty thoughts, Daddy?"

My cock twitches against her stomach. "You're a naughty lass, and Daddy always has filthy thoughts about you."

She smirks.

I resist running out of the restaurant to show her what I can't stop thinking about. Instead, I pull her closer and keep dancing with her.

"Didn't know you were such a romantic," she states, but her happy glow burns brighter, which tells me she likes it.

"It would be a sin not to dance with you while you're wearing this dress."

"I don't think I told you how much I love it."

"That's good. My close friend is the designer. I'll introduce you, and you can see what else she has that you like."

She gapes. "You know her?"

"Yes. Do you want me to take you to her shop tomorrow?"

I think she's going to say yes, but then her face turns serious. "I need to spend the day finding some new jobs."

My chest tightens. "No. You aren't."

She jerks her head back and stops moving. "Excuse me?"

"You don't need to work. I'll give you a credit card."

She shakes her head. "I have tuition and loans to pay back."

"I paid the balance off today. I sent the university a check for your final semester. Then I declined your next loan installment and told them to close the account."

"You did what?" Her eyes turn to slits. She steps backward until she's against the wall, blinking a few times.

My gut dives. "Why do I get the impression you're mad at me?"

"You hacked into my financial information?" she asks, as if I betrayed her.

I sigh and lunge toward her. "I hacked into everything I could find out about you. You were still in the cell. You know this."

She scrunches her face. "And then you went back into my account today?"

"Why are you upset about this?"

"It's not your account. You didn't even ask me."

I press closer to her. "I told you, I'm going to take care of you."

She looks away, and I think she's going to cry but not from relief or happiness. It's the opposite of what I expected.

Fear I've screwed up my chance with her pummels into my heart. I don't understand why she's upset or how I seem to have broken us again in a matter of seconds. I force her chin toward me. "Angel, I'm confused why you're reacting this way."

"You declined my loans."

"You don't need them anymore."

"What if I do?"

"You won't. I paid it off, and if you need more, I'll give you more."

"At any point, did you think to ask me? Since this concerns my life? My education?" she snaps.

"I thought you'd be relieved."

"That I have no further access to student loans?"

"Yes. I just told you I'll pay for it."

Her entire body trembles with rage. Fury radiates off her, slamming into me. The look she gives me pierces right to my soul. She slides her hand between us and grips her stomach.

I cover her hand with my palm. I lower my voice. "I won't have you struggling, angel. This vicious circle you've been in, spending every waking moment trying to survive, is going to end."

She closes her eyes and takes deep breaths. Her voice breaks. "What happens if this doesn't work out between us? What do I do then?"

Her words slice through every ounce of emotion I have for her. I move my lips an inch from hers and firmly order, "Open your eyes."

Agony and panic leap out from under her long lashes, glistening in the flicker of the candlelight.

"Nothing is happening to us."

A tear drips down her cheek, and the cruel reality she's always experienced comes from her lips. "You don't know that. Everyone eventually leaves."

In my most confident tone, I declare, "There's nothing in this world that would make me give you up."

She chokes on her breath and manages to reply, "You can't guarantee that."

"Yes. I can. And if you wanted to leave me, I'd still pay for whatever you needed to finish your degree. So stop worrying about this."

"You should have talked to me first."

I wipe her cheeks. "Nothing would have stopped me from paying those bills. I won't have you penniless or running yourself ragged trying to make ends meet."

A cloud of shame replaces her worry.

It bites me harder, sinking its teeth into my heart. "You've done the impossible, all on your own. No one will ever take that away from you. But now I'm taking care of you. And there's nothing to analyze, angel. You're mine, and you're going to have every luxury I can offer you."

Silence thickens the air between us. She closes her eyes, and I see a war waging inside her. I study her until her tears stop flowing. When she finally pins her wet gaze on mine, she lifts her chin. "I'm not going to be dependent on you, Declan. I won't put myself in that position."

"Don't be ridiculous. You said your first priority is school. Now you can focus on it," I attempt to say calmly, but it comes out laced with my frustration.

"You don't get to make choices for me. You yanked them from me before. It almost cost me my entire future. I'm not letting you do it again," she seethes.

Jolted by her statement, I step back. "You just told me you forgave me."

"I did. It doesn't mean I'm going to return to the same situation."

Anger burrows in my gut. I say through gritted teeth, "Me taking care of you isn't the same thing, and you know it."

She pushes off the wall. "Isn't it? The way I see it, you made the choices then, and you're doing it again now."

"Me? You're the one who's running this ship. I'm sitting on pins and needles all day long, praying you'll just pick up the phone."

"Whose fault is that?" she retorts.

I cross my arms. "I've never once denied my wrongdoings."

"But you think it's okay for you to just continue making all my choices?"

"Why are you doing this?"

"What? Standing up for myself?"

"No. Trying to push me away."

She turns away and puts her hands over her face.

I step behind her and put my arms around her. I murmur in her ear, "It's not a choice for me. I love you, and I'm going to take care of any problem you have."

Her body stiffens. She lowers her hands. Her voice turns cold. "You don't love me."

My pulse accelerates, making me dizzy. I stand my ground. "Yes. I do."

She tugs at my arms. "Let me go, Declan."

I tighten my grip around her and demand, "Tell me what this is really about."

"I said let me go!" she cries out.

I lift my arms then she grabs her purse and bolts from the room.

"Shit!" I mutter, toss cash on the table, then follow her down the hallway. She goes into the women's room, and I text my driver.

I wait over fifteen minutes before she comes out. Her tear-stained cheeks are now dry. She avoids looking at me and moves toward the door.

The car pulls to the curb the moment we step outside. She gets in, and I follow. The darkness of the night weaves through the spark of the city. I watch her as she stares out the window, with her lips trembling.

She quietly says, "I shouldn't have thought this would work. I'm sorry. Please take me home."

A fist squeezes my heart so brutally, I can barely breathe. Was I ignorant to think things got patched up between us? Did I misinterpret her forgiveness in some way? Am I just damned for eternity and I'm never going to be able to make things right?

"Simona—"

"I don't want to fight. Please. I need to go home."

I swallow the bile rising in my throat and push the button for the divider window. "Shay, go to Simona's."

"Sure," he replies.

I shut the glass and reach for her hand. "Angel—"

"Please stop." She starts to cry again.

Every move I consider making seems like it's going to make things worse. The car ride to her place is too fast, and we're soon on the curb. She doesn't even wait for me to open the door. She jumps out on the side of traffic and races toward the building.

I follow her, and when we get to the elevator, I try again. "Simona, we can't end the night like this."

The doors open, and Boris and Nora appear.

Shit. Could this get any worse?

"Declan! What are you doing here?" Nora asks.

"Walking Simona to her place."

Nora smiles at Simona. "Hi. I'm Declan's sister, Nora. Do you live in the building?"

I groan inside then panic further when Simona replies, "Yes, but not for long. Excuse me for being rude, but I need to go." She steps past them.

Nora's smile falls, and she glances at me, her green eyes widening. Boris arches his eyebrows but pulls her out of the elevator.

I brush past them and get in as the doors shut.

Simona keeps her eyes on the floor, and as soon as the doors open, she bolts again.

I follow her to her unit and step inside before she can lock me out. She storms into her bedroom. I grab her elbow and spin her. "Simona!"

"Please go," she whispers, closing her eyes.

"Not until you tell me why you're so upset with me."

She squeezes her eyes.

"Angel, I don't understand why you aren't happy I paid off your loans. It wasn't malicious."

"You cut off my line of credit!"

"For more student loans which you don't need. I told you I'd take care of you."

"You didn't ask me! You took my choice away so I had to be dependent on you. Just like before."

My heart sinks. I step closer. "It's not the same thing. I did it to help you, not hurt you. Why can't you see that?"

She puts her palms over her eyes. "You don't get it."

"You're right. I don't. So fill me in."

She keeps her face covered. "I almost lost everything because of you."

I'm unsure if I'm more upset or enraged by her statement. The guilt never disappears, but I thought we were moving forward. I repeat, "You say you forgive me, but you don't."

She locks eyes with me and cries out, "I do forgive you for what you did. I don't forgive myself." She turns away as if ashamed.

Blood pounds between my ears. I swallow the lump in my throat, bewildered by her statement. I spin her so she can't avoid me. "Why do you need to forgive yourself?"

Her next admission rocks me, and tears spill down her cheeks. "I could have stayed with you, as your prisoner, and forgotten about everything I worked for. I-I would have totally submitted to you and been okay giving up my freedom."

The gravity of her words stuns me.

I'm trying to process her statement when she adds, "I could have been happy losing everything as long as I was with you. And it's not right. So we need to stop this."

Aching fear pulverizes my heart, digging so deep, it physically hurts. I can't lose her, but all this is my fault.

I tug her trembling body against mine. "Kidnapping you was wrong. I'm going to regret it for the rest of my life. But I didn't pay off your loans to recreate any of the sadistic shit I did to you. All the things you've worked toward, I'm here to help make it easier for you, not take them away."

"You took the only thing I had away."

I insist, "No. I got rid of a burden for you. And it's not all you have. You have me." My gut flips, staring at her.

Her face crumbles. "Until you tire of me."

"That isn't happening, angel."

"You say that, but you can't—"

"I love you. What part of that don't you understand?"

Pain laces her expression. Her lips quiver and she chokes out, "You just proved my point."

"How?"

"People who say they love you always leave."

21

Simona

ONLY TWO PEOPLE HAVE EVER TOLD ME THEY LOVED ME. MY mother said it once when I was three or four. I remember her slurring her words, the smell of tequila on her breath, and her glassy eyes. She leaned down, told me to be the good little girl she loved, close my eyes, and count as high as I could. She moved my hands over my eyes, and I did exactly that, proud that I could reach one hundred. When I pulled my hands away, she wasn't in the booth. I looked around the bar, but she was nowhere, and neither was the scary-looking man she had with her. That night, I went back into foster care.

The only other person who said they loved me was the one foster mother I had who actually took good care of me. I was almost ten. She died of cancer shortly after.

Hearing Declan say it creates a tunnel of grief I didn't expect. I can't seem to get out of it. Every time he professes his love for me, it evokes memories of those two instances. The pain feels new and harsher. It reminds me nothing is permanent. When I add it to the panic over not having the ability to access student loans anymore, I can't see straight. It was a paperwork nightmare to apply and my credit is worse than before. My landlord reports all my late rent payments to the credit bureaus, and I've gotten my utilities shut off and put into collections too many times to count. So everything Declan says, I'm unable to rationalize.

I promised myself I wouldn't lose my freedom to him ever again. We would be equals or nothing at all. What he did feels like I'm back in the cell, waiting for him to tell me my fate.

He backs me up until I'm against the wall, holding my face in his hands and studying me. I can barely breathe. My skin hums as it always does around him, tingling with desire, but I can't be with him if I'm going to lose myself. Not again.

His voice is firm, as if there's no room to argue. "No one has ever taken care of you, angel. You have the wrong impression of love. It's not fleeting, and neither am I. What I did today wasn't to tie you to me or take away your choices. I did it because I love you, and it's not in my blood not to do everything I can to take care of you."

My lips tremble harder, and tears track down my cheeks to fall over his fingers. His scent permeates my skin, digging into my cells, giving me a sense of safety I only feel around him.

A tidal wave of emotions is in that security. It calms me but also intensifies the zings rushing through my body. And it scares me.

The desire to curl into him and let him run every aspect of my life fights with the voice yelling for me not to give him the power. It'll be too easy for us to fall back into who we were.

I'm petrified the voice will win because, deep down, I want to return as his captive. It's a craving I can't douse, no matter how much I've tried. I whisper, "I'm two steps away from being back in your cell."

His face hardens. "No. I'm never doing that to you again. I—"

"You don't understand. I want to be!" I cry out, simultaneously ashamed at my admission and relieved I told the darkest truth I have.

He freezes, his hot breath merging into mine while his blue flames grow hotter. Our hearts pound into the other's chest. His erection grows until it's so hard against me, I whimper.

"You're confused, angel. You want us. I get it. All I want is us. And it's okay to want me to take care of you, but I'm not ever taking your freedom away again. You're going to accomplish everything you want. I'm going to be by your side, giving you everything we had before and more."

I blink hard, but I can't stop my emotions from overflowing. I choke out, "It's not possible. I-I feel like I have to choose one or the other. Either you call the shots and decide my life, or I do what I want without you."

He sternly declares, "No. You have to choose us—you and me. Then you have to trust me."

I stay silent, terrified of what else might come out of my mouth. I already trust Declan. I have since he laid eyes on me. It's me I don't trust around him, and I finally close my eyes and admit, "I'm afraid I'm going to get lost in you."

"Look at me," he orders.

I obey, sniffling.

"We will get lost. Both of us. It's what happens when we're together. It's how I know what we have is real. But I'm clear on what's important to you. Nothing is going to stop me from making sure you do what you need to do. Do you understand me?"

I nod, getting choked up again.

He kisses me. It starts soft and gentle then quickly turns into a typical Declan kiss of urgency and hunger until he's consuming all of me.

My body.

My breath.

My need for him I can't shake.

Before I know it, my dress pools at my feet. Declan moves me on my back on the mattress then cages his body over mine. He licks my lobe and murmurs, "Time to get lost, angel."

Scorching flames lick my skin. Surges of lightning speed through my cells. My hands have a life of their own, unbuttoning his shirt, desperate to feel his skin on mine.

Every point I tried to make gets proven. My head spins. I can no longer think about anything, except how I want him to make me his again. I whisper, "Tie me up."

A deep groan rumbles in his chest. His tongue pushes into my mouth, fucking me as I shove his shirt over his broad shoulders. I reach for his pants, unbuckling his belt, and he whips it off him. His hands pin mine above my head, and the leather circles several times around my wrists, then tightens around my headboard.

His warm mouth bends to my chest, licking and sucking my puckered nipple while his fingers twist the other one.

"Oh God!" I cry out.

His eyes roll to mine. "Who am I?"

"My daddy!" I breathe.

His lips curve, and he slides lower, flicking his tongue against my belly button ring. His fingers trace the outer edge of my leather panties then glide through my wet heat. He pauses, assessing me. "All day, I thought about you in these."

My lungs heave. "What did you want to do to me?"

He shimmies his knuckles over my clit, watching my face.

I moan, arching my back off the bed.

His eyes darken. "Have you been a good girl for Daddy?"

"Yes."

"What do good girls get?" He repeats his knuckle tease.

"Rewarded. Please."

He continues playing with me in the same manner as I writhe under him.

"Please!"

"If you want me, you have questions to answer, lass." He kisses my clit then inches his tongue in and out of my hole before his arrogant expression meets mine.

"What? Oh God! Please!" I plead. Pellets of sweat break out on my skin. I rock my hips toward him.

He teases me further then orders, "Tell me what being your daddy means."

"I'm yours," I blurt out, moving my leg over his shoulder.

He grabs my leg and kisses my inner thigh, mumbling, "Greedy girl."

"Yes. Please, Daddy."

He blows hot air on my thigh right next to my pussy. "What do I do for you?" He tugs at my clit with his teeth then licks me, rotating back and forth.

"Oh...oh..." My mind spins. Adrenaline pools in all my cells, waiting to explode in torturous agony.

He lunges up my frame. His face comes in front of mine, and his fingers circle the sensitive bundle of nerves. "Tell me what Daddy does, angel."

I rock on his hand. "Takes care of me."

He manipulates me at a controlled pace. "That's right. I make decisions to help you, not hurt you. Do you understand?"

"Faster! Oh, please!"

He freezes and growls, "Answer me."

"Yes."

"Tell me again what Daddy does."

"You take care of me."

"Why?"

"To help me."

His tongue swipes against my lips. I open my mouth, but he moves his head back. "I love you, angel."

Tears fill my eyes. I turn my head.

He fists my hair and tugs my head back so I can't escape him. "I'm going to keep telling you this until you believe me."

"Everyone leaves," I whisper.

He kisses a tear that escapes. "I don't." He moves his lips to my ear. "I'm addicted to you, angel. You can't get rid of me. Now, Daddy needs to give you a punishment for trying to run."

"Wha—"

He flips me onto my stomach so fast, my head spins. My elbows barely hit the pillow due to the restraints. He tugs my hips up so my ass is in the air. A loud crack fills my ears, and a sting erupts across my ass cheek.

"Fuck! Declan!"

"Not Declan! It's Daddy to you!" He rubs the spot, and tingles erupt. Two fingers slide in my pussy, and I clench around them. His thumb rubs my clit hard and fast.

My knees weaken, but his arm around me keeps me to him. I whimper, and right as I start to come, he slaps me again.

"Daddy! Oh God!" I scream, a high flying through my veins.

He slaps me four times before he rubs it out, continuing to stimulate my pussy, curling his fingers around my G-spot.

"Are you going to run from me again?" he barks.

"No!"

"No, who?" He smacks me again.

"No, Daddy!"

He pulls back, and I think he's going to slap me again, but his cock thrusts into me until his pelvis hits my ass cheeks. He groans as I cry out.

As soon as he's in me, he's pulling out, then pounding back in.

"Oh fuck!" I scream, my walls collapsing while trying to grip him.

He slaps me as he's going back in, and an earthquake of orgasms break me.

"Jesus, I love you," he roars, gliding his hand up my arm until it's laced between my fingers. His warm flesh hits my back. He licks my cheek then drags his teeth over my jaw. The tip of his erection hits my sweet spot again. "You love my cock in you, angel?"

I groan, my eyes roll, and the tremors intensify.

He grunts. "Yeah. I know you do. And I love your tight little pussy. You don't even know what you do to me."

Endorphins consume me, filling me so fast, I see white.

He flips me over to my back and pushes my thighs up, reentering me. His arms wrap under me, and he palms my head. "You're mine, angel. Forever. Understand?"

I nod, unable to speak or look at him, my insides spasming on his erection in another orgasm.

Our mouths meet in a fury. His kisses destroy every notion there's him and me. Like always, I lose myself to him.

"Fuuuuck, angel!" he growls in my mouth, his cock violently pumping, stretching me farther with more pleasure. He collapses over me, panting in the curve of my neck.

"You have to relax your hand, angel," he mutters.

"Oh. Sorry!" I release my death grip from his hand.

He chuckles and unbuckles the belt then massages my wrists. "You okay?"

"Yeah."

He pecks me on the lips then rolls over, removing a condom I didn't know he's put on. He gets out of bed, tosses it in the trash can, then gets back in, pulling me into him.

"Thanks for using that," I say, grateful one of us was being responsible.

His guilt-filled expression meets mine. "I'm sorry about the other times."

"It's okay."

"It's not."

The pounding of his heart beats into my ear. I stay quiet but curl into him more.

He strokes my hair and says, "I meant it. I love you."

The uneasy grief hits me again. I blink hard, willing myself not to push him away.

Not that it would be possible. He pretzels his limbs around my frame, tightening his hold on me, firmly stating, "Everything you're scared of, I'm going to prove to you is wrong."

I slowly glance up at him, and a loud ring echoes in the room.

He groans.

"Do you have to get that?" I ask.

Glancing at the ceiling, his jaw clenches.

"Declan?"

"It's Nolan. Ignore it."

I slide my hand on his cheek, and it rings several more times. When it stops, I ask, "What does your family think of me?"

"They don't know enough about you to have an opinion. Nora is going to want to meet you now."

I cringe, thinking about how we met in the elevator earlier. My stomach flips. I tilt my head. "But—"

His phone rings again, and he sighs. "Sorry, angel. I need to get that."

I roll off him, and he grabs his cell out of his pants pocket, sitting on the edge of the bed. He snips, "Nolan, make it fast."

I get on my knees, kiss and rub his shoulders.

"What?" His muscles tighten. "Shit."

I freeze.

He reaches behind him and palms my thigh. "I'll call you tomorrow."

Nolan's muffled, angry voice booms through the cell.

"I said tomorrow," Declan seethes then hangs up.

My pulse shoots up. I slide my hand over his chest. "Is everything okay?"

He closes his eyes and leans his head against my shoulder, taking deep breaths.

"Declan?" I quietly ask.

He spins and tugs me onto his lap. "I have to go home."

"Oh...umm—"

"Come with me. I can do my work, and you can sleep."

"What will you be doing?"

He stares at the ceiling again. "Another article went up."

My chest tightens. I rearrange my body so I'm straddling him then caress the side of his head. "Now that I know everything, can I help? I could try and track BusyCEO down."

Blue flames and ice mix in his eyes, and he pins his gaze on me. "Don't you have schoolwork to do tomorrow?"

"I'm pretty caught up. I can do tomorrow's assignment on a different day. It's not like I have to be back in class yet."

A struggle emerges in his expression. He shakes his head. "Your school is the priority. I don't want you up all night and falling behind."

"I won't. Let me help."

He pecks my lips. "Not tonight, angel. You need a good night's rest."

I lace my fingers behind his neck. "Why don't we try something?"

He arches his eyebrow.

"Since you think I'm a better hacker than you, let me at it. I'll sleep when we finish. Then I'll do my work for tomorrow and the next day at your place."

He sniffs hard. "No. The first priority—"

I put my fingers over his lips. "You don't want me to move in anymore?"

He freezes, and my heart beats faster. "Simona, are you telling me you'll move in?"

I shake my head. "No. I'm telling you, I'll do this with you, then I'll stay and see if I'm able to work at your place. If I am, then I might." I wink at him, the somersaults in my stomach increasing.

He stays quiet.

"I don't have to go back yet. You said the dean agreed I had time before I had to return. Let's take advantage of it and see if it works for us," I state.

He licks his lips. "The whole week."

"Huh?"

"You stay for the week. One day isn't a good enough trial period."

My lips twitch. "Seems like you're getting what you want."

He shifts and studies me.

"What?"

A determination erupts over his expression. "I want you with me, Simona. But I'm not going back on my word. If you can't study at my place, then I'll deal with you living here until you graduate. I won't compromise your degree."

My heart skips a beat. I know how serious Declan is about wanting me to live with him, but he's willing not to fight me on it if it's in my best interest. Guilt hits me. I kiss him until I'm out of breath then say, "Thank you."

"For what?"

"Paying off my loans. I'm sorry I freaked out. I...umm... I've never had anyone do anything nice for me before. I'm sorry for sounding ungrateful," I admit.

He nods and runs his thumb over my jaw. "I'm sorry I didn't ask."

I kiss him again.

Tingles erupt on my ass as he squeezes it. "Pack a bag, angel. I'd keep you naked all week, but I don't think it would help your studies."

I pout. "Aww. You're taking all the fun out of it."

Cockiness gleams from his blue orbs. He rises with me, and I lower my feet to the ground. "Don't worry, angel. I'll make sure you have lots of study breaks."

22

Declan

When I get in the car, my phone rings again. I'm fuming. "Jesus, Nolan. Give me a goddamn break. I'm on my way home now."

He barks, "There are four more articles. All different spins on positive things about the company. This guy is trying to take us out."

My stomach plummets. I grumble, "Fuck."

"The spread is already too thin. Gemma and I are on our way over. We need to sort this out, or we're bankrupt as soon as the opening bell rings." He hangs up.

Simona puts her hand on my thigh. "Declan, what's wrong?"

"He's ambushing us. More articles have been posted. Nolan and his wife, Gemma, are heading to my place. It's going to be a long night."

She stays quiet for several moments then says, "If they're posting, we should be able to find them."

I snort. "That's what I thought about you. It took me months."

She leans closer and bats her eyes. "But you have me working with you now."

Through all the anger, I chuckle. Sliding my arm around her, I kiss her cheek. "Thanks for helping."

She beams, and everything in me lights up again. "Of course." She sinks into me, and we stay silent until we arrive home. Nolan and Gemma are already at my house. Gemma is making coffee and Nolan's pacing.

"Don't tear your hair out," I taunt, dropping Simona's overnight bag near my door.

He spins. His eyes narrow in on Simona, his face hardening.

She freezes, and I tug her closer to me. "Simona, this is my brother, Nolan, and his wife, Gemma." I move Simona toward Gemma, avoiding Nolan until he can cool off.

Gemma's eyes widen, but then she smiles and holds her hand out. "Hi! Nice to meet you. Declan, is this why you've been hiding lately?"

So Nolan didn't tell her anything.

I decide less information is better. "Yeah."

Simona takes her hand. "Hi. Nice to meet you, too."

Gemma nervously glances at us. I realize she's trying to figure out what I've told Simona about this situation.

"Simona is the best hacker I've ever met. She knows everything and is going to try to help us," I state.

Another wave of surprise comes across Gemma's face, but she quickly recovers, smiling. She teases, "Good. We need more than your skills."

"Yep."

"Do you drink coffee?" Gemma asks Simona.

"Yes. I'll have some."

Gemma nods and grabs a third cup. Nolan won't touch coffee. "So how long have you two been dating?" she pries.

Simona shifts.

"Long enough," I state.

Nolan clears his throat. We spin, and he says, "Nice to meet you, Simona." He leans down and kisses her on the cheek.

She smiles. "You, too."

"Thanks for helping." They exchange a glance, but Nolan breaks it, addressing me. "We need to get moving on this."

We take our coffee and go into my office. I turn on my computer. Nolan, Gemma, and Simona take out their laptops.

I tap a few keys to pull up the algorithm Nolan created to alert us when articles pop up. I curse under my breath then announce, "Six articles now."

"Princess, how fast can you write?" Nolan asks.

"On it," Gemma replies.

Simona looks at me in question. I tell her, "Gemma is our CEO of Marketing. She's a guru with words. She'll create the negative articles to combat what's coming out."

"Great. What do you want me to work on first? Finding BusyCEO or where these articles are coming from?"

"Find the bastard," Nolan growls.

"Could be a woman," Simona points out.

"That's right. And it seems like this person is super smart. I put money on it being a woman," Gemma smirks.

Nolan grunts. "Whatever. I don't care what sex they are. Just find them."

"Easy," I warn, not liking his rough tone, but it doesn't seem to bother Simona.

Gemma pats him on the shoulder. "Take a chill pill, Prince Charming."

He looks at her and his expression softens. "Sorry."

She gives him a chaste kiss then bats her eyes until he lets out a little chuckle.

"Are you a hacker, too?" Simona asks Nolan while typing quickly.

"Not really. I'm more into algorithms, but I know a little."

We all get to work. I go through each article posted, attempting to find the footprint of who submitted them, but they all lead to nothing.

"Who wants the first article?" Gemma asks.

My station ties to all the screens on the wall. I have my desk raised so I can stand. I've always had a hard time sitting while working. "Send it to me. Simona, show us how you make it disappear so fast."

She obeys.

Nolan and I stand behind her.

"Where do you want it posted?" she asks.

"All the major financial outlets. Do them one at a time to cover your tracks," I instruct.

She pins her brows together. "It's best if I do them in a batch. I can cover my footprint at the same time for all of them. Then, if anyone is watching, I won't get caught on the later ones."

Shock fills me. "You can cover them all at once?"

Her lips twitch. "Yep."

Pride's a waterfall gushing over my house, drenching me until I feel giddy. I pat her ass and kiss her on the forehead. "Show us what you got, genius."

She blushes then works her magic, posting the article over dozens of sites and erasing everything in under a minute.

"Holy shit," Nolan mumbles.

I can't help but smirk at him. "Told you she has unheard-of skills."

There's a beep, and I glance at the screen. "Damn it. Another one!"

Like a madman, I pound on the keys to locate the footprint, but it's pointless. I'm only halfway through my attempt when it disappears.

"This person is good," Simona calmly states.

Nolan spins. "How quickly can you get the next one done, Gemma?"

"Give me ten minutes."

We get back to work. Things stay quiet, with only the sounds of everyone typing, until Gemma announces she has the next article done.

"Show me again what to do, Simona," I instruct.

She repeats her actions, and I memorize a few more steps.

"I think I'll have this down after the next one," I admit.

She whispers, "You can do it, Daddy." She winks then returns to her laptop.

I chuckle, and it's a welcome tension release. We're a few steps short of losing everything the O'Malleys have if we don't counteract this.

"Good job, ladies. The futures are already unsure where to go." Nolan points to the screen with the market on it. Jack's company is the only stock on it, and the overseas traders are clearly in turmoil. The price since the U.S. market closed shows a volatile chart.

"Too bad you can't create a massive scandal on this Jack guy. That would make things hairier than any article you write to counteract things," Simona states.

I freeze, staring at her. We've been sitting on photos Adrian and Obrecht took of Jack in an underground sex club. He's also with Judge Peterson. Now seems like the best time to use it.

She pins her eyebrows together. "What?"

"You're brilliant, angel." I pat her ass and glance at Nolan. "Call Liam. Tell him we need him to bring the photos of Jack."

Nolan hesitates. "That's the last ammo we have."

"We've got enough to string it along and keep it in the media for at least the next month. Hopefully we can bankrupt it before the scandal dies out and shut this other person down."

There's another beep, and my gut sinks. I read the screen and hear Nolan say, "Liam, we need you to bring what's in your safe."

"What is it?" Gemma asks.

I don't hold back. "Pictures of Jack with several prostitutes. Judge Peterson is with him. He's snorting coke off their bodies and doing other things, too. It was at an underground sex club."

Gemma gapes at me.

"Should be interesting enough for the media to take hold and override any of these articles for a while, right?" I ask.

Gemma grins. "Drugs and illegal sex with the law by his side? Oh, this is a PR nightmare."

Nolan slides his arm around her. "You look a bit ecstatic right now."

She laughs. "Well, it's going to be more fun than writing about cyber patents."

"Great idea. I forgot we had this," I tell Simona.

She tilts her head. Her lips turn up in a smirk. "And why do you have it?"

Nolan interjects, "Long story. Declan can fill you in later. Can you get back to finding out who this BusyCEO guy is?"

Gemma swats his arm. "Don't be rude."

Nolan's cheeks heat. "Sorry, Simona. Not trying to be."

"Good thing you hit him, or I would have, but it would have been across the face," I warn, not happy he just ordered my woman around.

Simona pats my chest. "Easy there, killer."

Nolan grunts and returns to his computer.

We follow suit, and a few moments later, Liam's voice booms, "Declan!"

"In the office," I shout.

He steps in and freezes. His eyes narrow in on Simona. She's focused on her screen and doesn't see it.

In three steps, I'm in front of him but so is Nolan. He steps between us and mutters, "Be nice."

Liam and I study each other, and he finally pushes the yellow envelope at my chest. I take it, and he steps away, saying, "Simona. It's nice to see you again."

She takes a deep breath, spins, and a nervous smile forms on her lips. "You, too."

He steps forward and kisses her cheek. "You helping?"

"Trying to."

"She's really talented. Makes Declan look like one of Hailee's kindergarteners touching a computer for the first time," Nolan claims.

I elbow him in the ribs, but I'm also grateful for him taking some of the tension away as well as acknowledging to Liam how talented Simona is. I confess, "She runs circles around me."

Simona blushes.

Liam nods. "Well, thanks."

Gemma rises, rubbing her hands together and chirping, "Give me the scandal!"

I toss it at her, and she puts the hard drive on the table, then lays the photos out. There are so many, she adds some to the floor.

"Wow!" Simona exclaims.

There's another beep.

"Another one? How many are they going to post?" Nolan mutters.

"They can post all they want. I'm going to bury them with these!" Gemma beams.

"Shit. The stock price is flying up again." Liam scrubs his hands over his face.

Gemma grabs a few photos and hands them to Nolan. "Find these off the drive. This is the best one to start with."

"How long can you stretch this out?" I ask.

Gemma smirks. "Oh, I can spin this so many ways, I'll be here all month. Give me a few minutes and I'll have something ready. The first piece should be short."

"I'll stock up on coffee, then," I reply.

She adds, "Any details about this club would be great, too."

Liam shakes his head. "The name of the club stays out of it."

"Why? It'll keep the story in the media longer."

"No name, Gemma. Come up with something creative if you want, but the real name stays out of the press," he insists.

She shrugs. "Okay. I'll let my brain run wild and figure something else out."

Simona turns back to her laptop and starts typing. Liam stands over her shoulder, watching her, but he has no idea what she's doing. He has zero skills when it comes to the technical side of things.

"You need anything else?" I ask. I can't hold a grudge against Liam forever, but I don't want him breathing down Simona's neck.

His eyes turn to slits.

"You can return to your warm bed, unless you suddenly picked up some hacking skills I'm not aware of?"

He grunts and takes the hint. "Nope. I'll leave you all to it."

"Let the games begin!" Gemma chirps.

"Didn't realize you were so into creating false news." Nolan grins.

"It's the first time I've ever been able to create tabloid gossip. This is going to be epic," she gushes.

"Glad I could make all your dreams come true, princess."

"Looks like you've got this down. I'll look forward to watching the news tomorrow," Liam states and leaves.

We stop talking and return to working until Simona blurts out, "I got you!"

My pulse increases, and I sit next to her. "Who is it?"

Simona hits a button. "This woman."

"Knew it was a woman!" Gemma claims.

I glance at the screen and the blood drains from my face, rushing into my toes. *They're still coming after us. After everything, they haven't stopped.*

Why did I think they would?

I've let my guard down.

A beautiful Italian Mafia princess stares back at me. Her perfectly positioned dark hair is in a French twist. High, sculpted cheekbones and brown piercing eyes are stunning yet cold and calculating.

"Jesus," Nolan mutters, and a chill crawls down my spine.

"Who is it?" Simona asks.

I swallow the lump in my throat. "Giovanni Rossi's daughter, Maria."

The room turns silent and suddenly feels cold.

Simona places her hand on my thigh. "Who is that?"

"One of our enemies," Nolan states.

"The Rossis are Italian mob. The Baileys, another Irish crime family, worked with them to kill my brother, Sean. Maria is the only heir of Giovanni and trying to prove she can run his empire instead of her uncle," I explain.

Sympathy fills Simona's expression. She made it clear she wants to know more about my brother. This isn't how I wanted to tell her.

How could we have not seen Maria coming?

Another thought pops into my mind, and my stomach curls. *Why was Simona chosen to help her?*

I kiss Simona on the lips. "Thank you." I rise and nod to Nolan. "We need to go talk to Liam."

We leave and get in my SUV. Nolan's hands are fisted on his thighs. We stay quiet, each processing our thoughts.

In under two minutes, we're in Liam's house.

Nolan blurts out, "It's Maria Rossi. We've been lax."

Liam's eyes widen.

Anger grows inside me, spiraling until my insides shake. After Adrian's ex-wife, Dasha, died, Liam discovered she had an alliance with Maria. I declare, "We should have taken her out when we found out she was in bed with Dasha."

Nolan paces. "How did she even know what we were up to? We've been so careful."

Fear stirs with my rage. My angel is somehow involved in this. I want to know why and to what extent. The Rossis are dangerous. Maria isn't someone to underestimate. I curse myself again for not pushing to take her out when we learned of her involvement with Dasha. "Simona told me tonight that she was pulled aside by her professor to join CollegeTechMoney. We need to pick him up."

Liam folds his arms over his chest. "What else did she say about him?"

"Nothing. I didn't dig into it. I was asking other questions," I claim, but instantly feel guilty for getting distracted and not staying on task. Her professor knows Simona's skills. I'm not naive to think Simona could be in danger.

"You need to find out," Liam orders.

"She needs security. More than what we have on her now. I want two bodyguards on her wherever she goes, right next to her," I state.

Liam clenches his jaw. "We're already tight."

"Goddammit! It's my woman!" I bark.

He holds his hands in the air. "I didn't say no. But I'm going to need a day or so to move people around and figure out what we can do."

"Call Maksim. Add one of his guys if needed," Nolan suggests.

"She's not going to be a sitting duck," I growl.

"Take it easy, Declan. I said I'll figure it out, and I will. Can we get back on the same team?" Liam snaps.

I glare at him, knowing he's right and we need to but not forgetting all the bitter words we've exchanged regarding my angel.

An alarm-like sound rings from Nolan's cell. He glances at it and mutters, "Great."

"What now?" Liam asks.

"Another article. We need to get back," Nolan advises.

"It's time to take Maria out. We should have destroyed the Rossis until no one was left," I point out.

Liam takes a deep breath and stares at us. "She's not going to be easy to find. She's a bit like Orla in that regard."

At the mention of Gemma's half-sister, the one who spent months harassing, threatening, and even assaulting her, Nolan's face turns almost purple. In a low voice, he seethes, "Then we burn the ground all around them until she comes out from hiding. Time to take her father out."

Giovanni is in the same prison where Liam and Finn served their sentences.

Liam shakes his head. "It's almost impossible. You don't understand how things work inside."

"Then figure it out. We got to the Zielinski boys. We can get to him," Nolan asserts. The Zielinskis were the sons of the head of the Polish mob. Our guys inside murdered them and we pinned it on Rossi.

Liam shifts on his feet. "Let me talk to Finn and see if we can work through the holes. What's the name of her professor?"

Another epic fail on my part. I need to stop being so careless when it comes to Simona.

I confess, "I don't know which one it is, but I'll find out and text it to you in code."

"I'll have him picked up as soon as you send me the info," Liam states.

"I'll deal with him," I growl, already wanting to rip his head off for putting my angel in any situation connected to Maria Rossi.

Liam sniffs hard. His green eyes glow hot. "I'll let you know when we have him and the party starts."

23

Simona

"IT'S UP AND THE FOOTPRINT IS ERASED!" I TELL GEMMA.

She stands next to me, and we stare at the stock price, holding our breath. The positive articles are coming in fast. It's almost to the level Gemma said would trigger something where the O'Malleys have to add more money to their accounts. She said if that happens, they're screwed.

Time seems to stand still. The price ticks higher then suddenly stays the same.

"Come on," Gemma mutters.

One of my hands grips the edge of Declan's desk, and I tap the fingers of the other on the desk's surface. I'm grateful he has it positioned so I can stand but also so I can steady myself. I feel a bit dizzy and even queasy.

The price suddenly moves down, and Gemma throws her hand in the air, exclaiming, "Yes!" She turns to high-five me, and I throw my hand over my mouth.

I run to the bathroom and hug the toilet, sick.

"Simona, are you okay?" Gemma frets, crouching behind me and holding my hair back.

Sweat pops out on my skin, and I throw up some more. My insides quiver, my head spins, and I close my eyes, trying to stop it. When it settles, I rotate and sit against the wall.

Gemma wets a towel, hands it to me, then feels my head. "You're clammy, but I don't think you have a fever."

The dizziness leaves, and my stomach stops flipping. I wipe my mouth then press the rag to my head.

"Have you been feeling sick?" Gemma asks.

"No. I suddenly felt dizzy and nauseous. Maybe I ate something bad at dinner tonight?"

"How long ago did you eat?"

"A while ago. I'm feeling better now."

Gemma studies me. "Maybe it's just a bug?"

Declan shouts my name, and Nolan yells for Gemma.

She rolls her eyes and calls out, "In the bathroom." She pats my hand and rises.

The men rush in, and Gemma pushes Nolan out.

Declan's face falls in worry. "Angel, what's wrong?"

I start to rise, and he helps me up. "Nothing. I'm fine now. I just got sick. I think it's something I ate earlier."

He feels my head. "Have you been feeling bad?"

"No. It snuck up on me."

"Let's get you in bed, and I'll grab you some water."

"I'm okay. There's work to be done."

He shakes his head. "No. You're resting. Plus, I don't think anything is going to combat what Gemma created. It's all over the media right now. You look tired, lass. Time to sleep."

Exhaustion is setting in, so I decide not to argue. I let him lead me to the bedroom. He pulls the covers, and my lips twitch. "Can I get my bag? I want to brush my teeth first."

He kisses my forehead. "I'll grab it, but I replaced your stuff in the bathroom after you left."

My heart skips a beat. Declan's done nothing but claim he wants me back. However, it's nice to know he replaced my things as if confident I'd return. I raise my eyebrows and tease, "Are you trying to earn brownie points?"

He ignores my question. "Get ready for bed. I'll be back in a minute."

I obey, and by the time I get to bed, Declan has returned. My suitcase is in the room. My nightgown is on the bed. He has a glass of water, a thermometer, and a small first aid kit.

I point to the items. "What's all this?"

He motions to the bed. "Get dressed and then under the covers. I'm taking your temperature and medicating you if necessary."

I huff. "I'm fine. I'm sure something I ate didn't agree with me." I strip and throw my nightgown over my head.

"Do you normally get sick from new types of food?" he asks.

"No. It's probably a touch of food poisoning."

"If it were, you'd be in the bathroom still, and it would have hit you hours ago. I'd be sick, too."

"I'm not sick. I just had a brief wave of nausea. I'm fine," I insist.

He holds out the thermometer. "Humor me." He sticks it in my ear, and it beeps.

"Normal, right?" I ask.

He reads it and nods. "Yeah."

"Okay. No medicine. Let me have some water and then I'm sleeping."

He hands me the glass. I drink half of it while he studies me. The vein near his eye pulses.

I reach up, tracing it. "You're making me nervous," I state.

He closes his eyes briefly, leaning into my touch. His lids flutter open. He puts his palm on my cheek. "I feel bad I kept you awake all night while you were sick."

"I wasn't. I told you it was a sudden thing."

He sighs.

"Declan, I'm fine." I yawn.

He gives me a chaste kiss on the lips. His face turns hard. "Okay, angel. Before I let you sleep, I need to know something."

My chest tightens. "What?"

"Which professor told you about CollegeTechMoney?"

"Professor Milliken."

His expression darkens. He rises. "I'll be back in a few moments."

My professor has always paid special attention to me. I thought it was because I'm smart and he wanted me to succeed. Now I'm worried he has an ulterior motive. "Declan, do you think he's involved in this?"

Blue ice pierces my gaze. "Chances are high. I'm going to find out." Declan gives me another chaste kiss then leaves.

I slide deeper into his bed and curl into the pillow. His intoxicating scent flares in my nostrils. Something I've never felt before washes over me. I can't put my finger on it. Being back at Declan's feels normal, as if I'm supposed to be here.

I'm almost asleep when he slides next to me. I stir. "Hey."

He tugs me into his arms, kissing me on the head. "Go to sleep, angel."

I don't argue. I'm tired and happy to be back in his arms. Within minutes, I fall into a deep sleep and don't awake until after noon. When I open my eyes, Declan isn't in bed.

Looking around the room, I smile. Being in his bed makes me feel alive. I inhale his scent from his pillow a few times until my stomach growls. So I go to the bathroom and do my business. When I finish and open the bedroom door, the delicious aroma of pancakes flares in my nostrils.

Declan's turned toward the stove, 80s music plays from his phone, and he's singing.

I bite on my smile, watching him. He looks so ordinary and happy. It's a contrast to the fierce side of him I know exists. His fitted T-shirt stretches across his back muscles in perfection. A gray pair of joggers displays his muscular ass. Staring at him gives me butterflies. Zings race in my blood. I sneak behind him and slide my arms around his waist, inhaling his scent.

He freezes then adds the last pancake on the platter and spins. He grins, and my heart melts. His hands slide over my cheeks, and he tilts my head, then kisses me. "Morning. Or should I say afternoon?"

"But you still made me pancakes!" I beam.

He chuckles. "I'll make them every morning if you wake up looking happy like right now."

I slide my arms around his neck and lightly drag my nails on his skin. "I could be persuaded for pancakes."

He palms my ass. A serious expression appears. "Show me you can study here, and consider it done, angel."

My butterflies spread their wings. *Am I really going to move in? Is it possible for me to put all my trust in him? Can this really be permanent?*

The last thought scares me. In my experience, nothing is forever. But I swallow down my fear, trying not to let it run my decisions.

He furrows his eyebrows. "How are you feeling?"

I shrug. "Fine. Hungry."

He studies me for a moment.

"Declan, I'm fine."

After a bit of hesitation, he gives me a deep kiss, flicking hungrily in my mouth until my knees buckle. The moment I drop an inch, he tugs me closer and continues kissing me.

When he finally retreats, I breathe, "What was that for?"

Heat blazes from his eyes. "I'm happy. You're back where you belong—with me."

My heart skips another beat. I push more warnings that nothing is forever to the back of my head and admit, "I like waking up here."

His smile widens, and he kisses my forehead. "Let's eat."

We sit at the table. The smell of coffee mixes in the air as he pours me a cup. I add butter and syrup to my pancakes then cut them. The rich sugary concoction melts on my tongue, and I groan.

Declan chuckles. "Good?"

"Amazing!" I shove another bite in my mouth.

"Glad you like them." He adds scrambled eggs to my plate. "You need some protein."

"Overrated."

He grunts. "Eat it so you don't have a sugar crash in an hour."

"I don't get those."

"No?"

"No, do you?"

"If I only eat a bunch of sugary carbs."

"Huh. Well, I don't."

He holds a fork of eggs to my lips. "Appease me."

"I can think of better ways to make you happy," I tease.

He arches an eyebrow, and my insides throb. I try to ignore it and take the eggs.

Declan leans into my ear. His hot breath hits my skin, and he murmurs, "Good girl. Daddy will remember to reward you later."

Tingles race down my neck. I turn my head, smirk, then sit back and continue eating.

For a while, we don't talk. I eat a few bites of the eggs to satisfy him. When I have less than half my stack left, I take a sip of coffee and turn toward Declan. "Thanks for breakfast."

His eyes twinkle. "You were hungry."

I glance at his plate. He has most of his pancakes left. His eggs are all gone. I claim, "Pancakes are my thing. Are they not yours?" I motion to his plate.

"More of a protein guy." His phone rings, and his face falls. "Sorry. I have to take this." He hits a button. "Liam?"

My stomach drops as I study him. Something about his tone and expression worry me.

He clenches his jaw, strokes my thigh, and focuses on the ceiling. "Give me an hour." He puts the phone down, inhales deeply, then releases it.

"What's wrong?" I ask.

He scoots his chair back and pats his thighs. "Come here."

I straddle him, and he circles his arm around me, then tucks my hair behind my ear. He runs his knuckles over my cheek, sending a shiver down my spine. I cup his face. "Declan, what's going on?"

"I need to go out."

"Okay."

He licks his lips. "I'm going to be gone for a few days."

My heart hammers in my chest. I swallow the lump in my throat. "A few days?"

He nods. "Yes."

"Why?"

A cold scowl appears. "I'm getting to the bottom about why they chose you to get on that site."

Confused, I blurt out, "Isn't it just because of my skills?"

He slowly exhales. "I'm hoping that's the only reason, but I need to make sure there aren't any other motives surrounding you."

Fear hits me. "What do you mean? There is nothing else I can offer them."

"Don't worry about this. I'm going to find out. I'm also adding bodyguards for your protection."

More alarm ignites. "Bodyguards?"

"I can't have you unprotected, angel. Plus, you're mine. All the O'Malley women have bodyguards. You'll be no different." He states it as if I have no choice in the matter and it's already settled.

I gape at him.

"It'll take a few days to sort them out. In the meantime, I'm sorry to do this to you, but I need you to stay in the house. I'll have Gemma, Arianna, and Hailee join you until I return."

"Who are they? I only know Gemma. And why would they all stay here?"

"Arianna is Killian's wife. Hailee is Liam's. And they'll stay here because their husbands will all be with me. It's better if you're all together so you aren't on your own. Plus, all their bodyguards will be here in addition to the men who watch this house."

My stomach flips. Guilt fills me. "I haven't asked about Tiernan. How is he doing?"

"He's fine. Don't worry, lass. You didn't kill him, but no sneaking out this time." He winks.

I don't find his humor about the incident funny. I still can't believe I stabbed a man with a steak knife. I stroke the side of Declan's head. Something I should have asked last night when we were discussing his family pops into my mind. "Are you really high up in the O'Malley clan? Is that why men guard your house? I assumed it was because of me, but you make it sound like they are always here."

His face turns neutral. "Can we make a promise to each other that whatever we discuss is always between us? Then I don't have to keep asking you every time we talk."

"Yes. Of course."

He nods. "Okay. Liam is the head of the clan. His father, Darragh, was in charge until he recently passed. My brothers, cousin Finn, and I are his advisors. So, besides Liam, if we're discussing structure, we're as high as you can get."

I stay silent, processing what he admitted.

"What's going through that brilliant mind of yours, angel?"

"Does that mean you have people coming after you?"

He tugs me closer. "There are plenty of thugs who want to destroy us. Other crime families are always after our territory. Decades of hate span directly from Ireland in some cases. As long as the O'Malleys have been in America, we've created new enemies."

My pulse beats hard in my neck.

Declan traces it, and I close my eyes. "Simona."

I look at him.

Confidence, worry, and a bit of trepidation fill his expression. "You don't have to be scared, but now you understand why I won't leave you unguarded or allow you to go somewhere unprotected?"

I assumed his agitation was about the thought of me going somewhere on my own, exposed to his enemies. I reply, "Yes."

"And does this make you feel different about me?"

My heart hurts at that thought. I bring my lips in front of his. "No. I'll have to get used to the guards, but if you think it's best, then I won't fight you. Thank you for your honesty."

Relief tumbles into his eyes. He presses his lips to mine, and I open my mouth, sliding my tongue against his, moving as close to him as I can. His warm palm slides under my panties. A buzz of adrenaline shoots straight to my core. I kiss him deeper and grind my pussy against his hardening erection. My nipples pucker and glide against his pecs, more sensitive than usual. Lightning streaks through my cells as I whimper.

He groans and murmurs, "I have to arrange some things."

"Can't Daddy multitask and have a quickie?" I taunt, not sure who this brave woman is anymore, and reach for his joggers.

"You naughty little girl." His lips travel across my jaw, and he fists my hair, tugging it back.

Heat suffuses my skin. My pussy throbs so fast, I get dizzy. I push his pants over his erection, trace the metal balls above it, feeling a need like never before to have him inside me. I lock eyes with him and whisper, "Please, Daddy."

His arrogant expression lights me up further. He lifts his hips, I slide his pants down, and he moves mine to the side. "Challenge accepted, angel." He drags me closer to him so my clit slides along his piercings, and thrusts into me in one move, not stopping until I hit his pelvis.

In a shaky breath, I cry out, "Oh God!"

He picks up his cell phone and wraps his arms around my back. A wet warmth flicks on my lobe. His deep murmur fills my ear. "Is your pussy extra greedy for Daddy's cock today? Hmm?"

My voice cracks. "Yes. Oh...oh...oh fuck!" Every slide of his girth against my walls feels like sensory overload. The metal balls rub my clit in exquisite pleasure. A low-grade earthquake already consumes me, creating a rolling tremor that picks up speed. I whisper, "You feel so good, Daddy."

He nips at my ear. His hands work quickly near my back, and he tosses his phone, then pulls on my hair again. My skin buzzes under his teeth as he scrapes them down my neck before sucking on my pulse.

It sends me over the edge. My head spins, eyes roll, and I scream, "Oh God!"

"You wicked, sexy girl. I didn't say you could come this soon, did I?" he taunts and grips my hip, thrusting harder into me, making my orgasm last longer.

"Oh!" Stars blur my vision. I blink, trying to focus, but all I can do is feel.

He pinches my nipple. "When Daddy gets home, I'm dressing you in chains as we discussed on the phone."

"Yes, please!" I beg, my mouth watering at the thought of taking his long, hard cock in it.

His thumb slides between us. He rolls it over my clit. My walls collapse, endorphins attacking me like overflowing fizz from a soda can. Violent spasms erupt. I hang on to his neck, losing my ability to do anything but tremble on Declan like a rag doll.

He grunts in my ear, pushes my head into the curve of his neck, then grips both my hips and slams me into his thrusts.

I suck on his skin, shaking, closing my eyes while white and black flashes in my vision.

The tip of his cock reaches deep within me. I scream into his body, exploding into millions of pieces from an intensity unlike anything I've ever experienced. My body convulses, and I soak us in my high.

"Fuuuuuck," he growls, his erection swelling as he pulls my hips up so his cock hits my belly. It pistons like a machine gun, shooting ribbons of warm, white cum on me.

Solid arm muscles tighten around me. His pecs press into my chest as we both struggle for air. Hot breath pummels my neck.

Several minutes pass until he lifts his head then kisses me as if he's still hungry for more, his cock twitching against my stomach.

I tighten my arms around him, deepening our kiss.

He retreats. "You're going to make me late."

I release a frustrated breath, ready for more.

His lips twitch, and he rises with me. I squeeze my legs around his waist. Mischief fills his face. "I think it's time to take a shower."

24

Declan

My brothers and Liam drop the women off at my house. It takes twenty minutes to get to the warehouse. When we go inside, Finn is waiting. His scowl is darker than usual. He's pacing, and I glance at the others.

Liam steps forward. "Finn, what's going on?"

He spins and cracks his neck. "When are we going to New York to see the kids? I can't remember."

My brother, Sean's, kids are in New York. His widow, Bridget, moved them to her father, Tully's, and refused to let us see them for years. Killian made a deal with him, and now we get to see them once a month. With everything going on, I had forgotten about it.

"Next week for Thanksgiving. Why?" Nolan questions.

Finn taps his fingers on his biceps. A deep line creases his forehead.

Liam steps in front of him. "Finn. Why are you jumpy?"

"I'm not."

"You are," Liam firmly states.

Finn takes a deep breath and stares at Liam.

"Why are you asking about the kids?" I question.

Finn stretches his neck toward the ceiling then turns to me. "I need to talk to Bridget. Once I do, I think she might attempt to keep the kids away from you again."

"Why?" Killian snaps as he, Nolan, and I step forward.

Blood boils in my veins. I haven't seen them yet, aside from a few video chats. We were supposed to visit, but the kids came down with the flu. They had school events we didn't want to interrupt, so we had to push our visit out. I'll be damned if Bridget takes them away from us again.

Finn glances behind him then refocuses on us. "I got the safe open."

"How?" I ask. The night I left the Ivanov garage, when the judge's son, Matt, was there, Finn found out about a hidden safe in his father's lake house. He managed to get it out of there, but it required an eight-digit code. Our cousin is a locksmith. He said it's the best safe money can buy and practically impossible to break into without the code. The only way was to use some explosives, and that would probably damage the contents. The possible combinations of numbers could take years to figure out.

"It's Brenna and Brad's birthdates," Finn snarls, as if saying their two names together is enough to make him sick.

"What did you find?" Liam asks.

Finn sniffs hard. "There was a picture of Brenna and Bridget."

A chill runs down my spine. Bridget has done a lot of things, but this...no, she wouldn't.

"It has to be from before she disappeared. You know they were close," Nolan insists.

Finn reaches into his pocket and pulls out a photo. "Brenna's hair is dyed." He holds the picture out, and I grab it.

My brothers swarm me while my gut sinks. Bridget has her arm around Brenna like she's consoling her. The background is blurred, but their faces are clear. Brenna's hair is black instead of her usual reddish-blonde.

"The date on the back is several years after I got locked up," Finn adds.

I flip it, and my stomach spins faster. It's not handwritten. It's part of the back, which was an option you could get on pictures years ago when you had photos printed.

"Jesus," Killian mutters.

Nolan rips it from my hand. "This has to be a mistake. Sean was still alive. Bridget may have made decisions we don't like since he died, but she loved him."

"Doesn't mean she didn't hide things from him," Finn says.

I open my mouth to defend her but shut it. When Sean was alive, I never would have thought it would be possible. Sean and Bridget were the definition of love. They had the relationship I always thought I wanted to find. My brothers, Nora, and I always considered her one of us. We were all inseparable. It's what made Bridget's decision to cut us off even more painful.

Killian orders, "You can't talk to her until after our visit. The kids are old enough to make decisions. Now that they know we didn't abandon them, Bridget can't just keep us away. But we all need to see them and remind them how much we love them before you talk to her."

"It's a week away," Finn seethes through his teeth.

"If you want to see Bridget, you're going to have to do it through Tully. She refused to see me when I saw Fiona and Sean Jr.," Killian states.

Finn scrubs his face.

Liam puts his hand on Finn's shoulder. "I'll set up a meeting with Tully directly after we visit the kids. I'll make it clear he's to have Bridget meet with us."

"What if he doesn't?" Killian inquires.

Liam's green eyes glow, hot and angry. "He will."

"You need to go prepared that he won't. He's protecting her at all costs," Killian insists.

Liam's voice turns cold. "Then he'll have a war with the O'Malleys."

His answer seems to settle Finn. "Fine. I'll wait a week. Let's take care of this other issue."

We get in the elevator, and Liam punches in the code only the five of us have. It takes us to the basement, where we torture those who have wronged us.

I ask, "Any news on Maria?"

Liam sighs. "Not yet. Our guys are tracking her."

"You should call Obrecht in on this," I advise.

"Agreed. No one's as good as Obrecht. He'll find her," Killian states.

The doors open, and Liam steps out. "He trained our men. At some point, we need to let them do their job."

"It's a Rossi. This isn't just anyone. And once our guys take out Giovanni, she's going to have even more power. Call in Obrecht," I demand.

Liam angrily spins. "I'm getting tired of you trying to order me around all the time."

"My woman is involved, so get over it. Put the best resources we have on this," I bark.

"Declan's right. Have Obrecht run the team," Nolan agrees.

Liam sniffs hard then glances at Finn. He nods, and Liam replies, "Fine. I'll talk to him when we finish."

"Are you all done now? Can we get back to fileting this prick? Arianna and I have plans tomorrow night," Killian declares, pausing outside the door to the cell.

"What's that?" Nolan asks.

"I'm taking her to a show."

"Like a movie?"

Killian rolls his eyes. "No. I snagged tickets to the opening night of *The Devil Wears Prada* musical. She loves the film. I'm surprising her, assuming this bastard is going to sing like a canary."

"Oh yeah? Hailee would probably like that. Wish you told me. I would have had you grab us tickets," Liam replies.

"I could barely get these. They sold out online. Meredith posted on social media that she got them, and I had to beg her to sell them to me."

"That girl you used to date? The one with the high screech?" Nolan asks.

"The one and only. She made me pay her four times what she got them for and get her a reservation to that new restaurant the Ivanovs made an investment in. It's a good thing Boris was with me. He strung it in front of her, and she finally buckled."

"I never understood what you saw in her. She's good looking, but that damn screech drove me insane," Nolan states.

Killian snorts. "You should have heard it when she came."

"Are you two done reminiscing about who Killian's dick was in so we can get this over with?" Finn grumbles.

Killian rolls his eyes. "Yes, Dad. Liam, did you get those other tools I told you about?"

"Still waiting on the order."

He groans. "Damn it. When we go to New York, I'm making Arianna's brothers give you a tour of their dungeon. It's way better than ours."

"Stop complaining," I say and open the door.

We step into the room. It's a small concrete room with fluorescent lighting that makes a loud buzz. We intentionally keep it that way to add to the agitation of our prisoners. A beam runs from one side to the other with hooks in it so we can restrain our enemies in different positions. A shelf full of torture tools has too many items to count and is front and center for the prisoner to view. Water drips from a pipe into a puddle. We purposely close the drain when we have anyone here. It's another sound that adds paranoia.

A man with brown hair in crew-cut style awaits. He has a five-o'clock shadow, but my guess is he's normally clean-shaven. Thin wired glasses sit partway down his nose, but he can't adjust them since his hands are restrained behind his back. His khaki pants and plaid button-down dress shirt are covered in sweat even though the room is cold. Instead of stripping him naked and chaining him like a lot of our foes would, he sits in a wooden chair. His mouth is gagged and secured by duct tape. Thick cuffs secure his ankles to the wooden legs of the chair. He stares at us, his eyes widening and breathing short and heavy.

Nolan pats Killian on the back. "Don't worry. You'll be home in time."

Everything about him screams computer geek. I assume this guy was the kid in school who got bullied in the locker room by the jocks. Based on his scrawny frame, it looks like he's probably never lifted weights a day in his life.

We're used to dealing with hard-core criminals. They know how to be on the offense and defense in a fight. But Professor Milliken might be the most scared I've ever seen anyone. I'd bet my entire bank account he'll cry from the first ounce of pain, maybe even before. Breaking him won't take long, but I remind myself not to get cocky.

He set up my woman.

He put her in front of the Rossis.

The hatred I feel whenever I think of the Rossis boils. They killed Sean and sent his ring and heart back with a video of them tearing it out of his body while he was still breathing. There is no mercy for anyone who does work for the Rossis.

To intimidate him further, I crack my knuckles. It's loud and echoes in the cell. The typical man we have in here wouldn't flinch on the outside, but Professor Milliken gasps and closes his eyes. I step closer and assess him.

He cowers in the chair, as if he can avoid me touching him. I rip the duct tape off his mouth. The first layer of his skin comes off, along with some of his facial hair. Red rushes to the surface where the adhesive sat. He screams through the gag.

I pull it out of his mouth and turn to the others. It's a genuine disappointment. "This isn't even fun. He's a pussy."

"At least I'll get my night out," Killian mutters.

"Didn't take you for a musical guy. Glad to see you're expanding your horizons," Nolan jabs.

"Shut up," Finn warns.

Liam steps next to me. "Tell us about your relationship with Maria Rossi."

"Rossi? A-a-as in Giovanni?" he stutters.

Let's get down to business. I slap him. His face turns toward the wall with the force and he screams, but it's a fraction of how hard I would normally hit someone sitting in this chair. Tears fall down his cheek, and I cringe inside. There's no fight in this guy. As much as I want to get information out of him, it's like picking on a kindergartener when you're in high school. I tug his chin so we're eye to eye. I growl, "Don't play dumb, or my fist is breaking your eye socket on my next hit."

"I've never met any Rossi!" he screams. His spit flies onto my cheek since I'm so close. A river of tears drips off his chin.

Tugging his head back, I get even closer, tasting his stale breath. "Then how did you learn about the website?"

"Wh-what website?"

"The one you gave to my woman!" I roar, my stewing rage building again from the thought of Simona being part of this. When he doesn't answer, I release his hair and raise my hand in the air.

He tries to move and tips over in the chair, landing on the concrete with a thud, then crying out in pain.

I glance at the others.

Finn shakes his head in annoyance and pulls him off the ground and back to a sitting position. He crouches in front of him. In a calm tone, the one Finn knows how to use to his advantage, he interrogates, "CollegeTechMoney. If Maria didn't tell you about the site, then who did?"

"Coll—" Milliken's face turns white. "This is about College-TechMoney?"

Killian claps loud. "Bravo! Now we're getting somewhere."

Milliken glances at Killian, but Finn turns his jaw back to him. "Forget about him and focus. What do you know about the site?"

He scrunches his face and turns toward me. "Simona is with you?"

Hearing him speak her name further agitates me. I lunge in front of him and shout, "You have a problem with that?"

Liam pushes me back. "Easy. He's probably in shock that she wanted to date an old guy like you."

"Are you trying to get your ass beat today?" I threaten.

His eyes turn to slits. "You want to go now?"

Nolan pushes us away from each other. "Knock it off."

"Tell us about the site," Finn repeats.

"I-I told her about it so she could make some extra money."

"No shit, Einstein. Why?" I bellow.

Milliken's voice shakes. "The dean told me to give it to her. She said she was scraping by and needed extra assistance."

Blood pounds between my ears. I seethe, "Dean Whitehouse?"

"Yes."

"She just strolled up to you and told you to tell Simona about the site?"

"Y-yes."

"She didn't ask who your smartest student was or who you thought might need extra money?"

"No. She instructed me to give it to Simona."

I clench my fists. Bile rises in my throat, and I swallow it down. I pick him up by his shirt so the chair lifts off the floor. "Why did she pick Simona?"

"I-I don't know!" he cries out. Another waterworks show emerges.

I drop him down, my insides shaking. Pulling my hair, I pace the small cell. If the dean is involved, she knows I'm with Simona. Surely, Maria is now aware of her involvement with me as well.

It puts my angel in further harm's way. The Rossis will do anything to destroy us. I gave the dean a substantial amount of money. Maria will know Simona is the way to hurt me.

"Declan," Killian calls out, dragging me out of my enraged trance.

"What else has the dean said about Simona?"

Milliken shakes his head. "She came in the other day and told me about Simona's assault. Said I was to allow her to make up any missed work."

"What else?"

"Nothing. I swear!"

"Liar!" I scream over him.

"I'm not! Before she gave me the site, I'd never spoken to the dean about Simona."

"You expect me to believe that?"

"It's true!"

"She's the smartest person in her class, probably the entire school," I growl.

He nods. "Yes! She is!"

"Then why wouldn't you have spoken to the dean about her?"

"I-I don't talk to the dean about any of my students. She doesn't typically care about their academic progress."

"Then what the fuck does she do?" Killian blurts out.

Milliken swallows hard. "She fundraises."

And I gave her my money to finish the wing in her name.

"What else do you know about the site?" I bark.

"Nothing. I tried to apply to do some work, but they weren't taking any more applications."

"Wow! You're a greedy fuck. Trying to apply for a job that's meant for college students when you're on a fat professor's salary with benefits." Killian tsks several times.

Milliken shakes harder, staring at Killian.

I snap my fingers in front of his face. He jerks his head and cowers again. I demand, "When did you apply?"

"The day I gave Simona the information. I was surprised when Simona told me she got a job on it. I figured she hadn't gotten in, either."

The vein near my eye throbs. I spin and look at my brothers. "There's no application. It automatically tells you it's no longer accepting new techs."

Killian gives me a *what does that mean* stare, but Nolan understands. His eyes widen. "They're tracking her computer."

I nod and turn back to Milliken. I crouch in front of him. "You're staying here. If I find out anything you told me is a lie, I'm cutting your balls off with a blunt knife."

His face turns white. "I-I'm not lying!"

I pat his cheek. "Then you'll get to keep your balls." I rise and leave the cell. Panic flies through every cell in my body.

Liam follows me. "Declan."

I turn. "They're tracking her online. I even scanned her computer, but somehow, they're in there. Every move she makes, they're watching. Why?"

His face hardens. "I don't know. I'll go meet with Obrecht and get him to work with our team to find Maria."

I nod. "Thanks."

"Can you tell Hales I'll be back in a few hours?"

"I'm not going home."

Liam's eyes turn to slits. "Where are you going?"

"I'm going to pay the dean a visit."

"You think that's a good idea right now? We have guys to do that," Liam states.

I sniff hard. "She's going to look into my eyes when she begs for her life."

"She can do that here. Go home. I'll call you when we have her," Liam orders.

Debating what to do, I lock eyes with him.

He lowers his voice. "Simona is home waiting for you. My father's number one rule was you don't put yourself at risk. If you go down, it hurts the clan. Now, go home to your woman and let our guys do their job."

It doesn't make me happy, but Darragh would roll over in his grave if I overstepped on this one. We're the brains of the clan, and no one has my skills. Darragh reiterated it too many times to me and how the future of the clan is dependent on Nolan's and my strengths. I decide he's right but say, "Tonight, Liam. I want her picked up."

He nods. "As soon as it's safe to get her, we will."

"That could take days," I snarl.

"When it's safe, we'll pick her up. You know how this works," Liam reiterates.

Killian and Nolan step into the corridor. Killian asks, "What are you two fighting about now?"

"It's getting old seeing you two arguing all the time. Time to get back on the same team," Nolan states.

"Shut up," Liam and I both growl at the same time. But Nolan's right. We do need to work together, and I'm sick of fighting with him. I've never been at odds with Liam before now.

Nolan smirks. "That's more like it."

Liam glowers. "Nolan, take Hales to your house if you would. I'll pick her up after I talk with Obrecht."

"Sure."

Nolan, Killian, and I get in the elevator and go to the main level. One of the drivers who stays stationed at the warehouse motions for us to get in.

Once we pull out, I roll down the divider. "Illinois Institute of Technology."

Nolan scowls. "What are you doing? You heard Liam."

I close the divider. "Liam told me not to pick her up. He didn't say I couldn't see what she's up to."

Killian groans. "Bad idea."

I seethe. "The bad idea was to use Simona. The dean is going to pay, along with anyone else involved in this."

25

Simona

"You really should get a job at the tabloids," Hailee teases Gemma. We're in the office, sitting around the table, reading the articles Gemma wrote and looking at the photos she's using for each.

The doorbell rings, and another woman walks in. She's gorgeous, with sun-kissed skin even though it's winter. Her eyes look kind, and her brown hair has highlights in it. A Greek accent fills the room. "Ladies, did you start the party without me?"

"Selena!" Arianna jumps up and rushes over to her.

I stay quiet, still getting to know Hailee and Arianna. Gemma, I'm already comfortable around since we spent so much time together the other night. The other women seem nice, but I'm not used to sitting around and chatting with anyone. I've never really had friends. Tonya is the only person at school I clicked with, but she showed her true colors when I refused to go out after the night I met Declan.

I rise, and Arianna introduces us. Selena pulls me into an embrace then pulls back. "So, you're the woman who's stolen Declan's heart, huh?"

Heat flies into my cheeks.

She laughs and hugs me again. "It's nice to meet you."

"You, too."

We sit down, and Selena studies the contents on the table. The women explained Jack is her ex-husband and told me the horrible things he did, including kidnapping her. I'm not sure what I expected, but she doesn't seem upset by the photos. There's no shock factor. It's almost as if she's seen them before.

Arianna's brows scrunch together as she holds up a photo of Jack Christian snorting coke off a woman's pussy. The woman is leaning against the back of a couch, and Judge Peterson is straddling her while sticking his dick in her mouth. He turned around and was grinning at Jack, his eyes glazed over, probably from drugs. The time and date stamp are on it. Gemma's article discusses how he was still married. "Are you sure this is the right thing to release? The media is going to hound you, Selena."

Gemma's face falls. She straightens up. "It's the only way to take down the company. We have to bankrupt it, and soon. If we let it survive, we're out of ammo. This is hot, and right now, we can drive it into the ground."

Arianna grabs Selena's hand. "But are you okay with this?"

Selena assesses the photos further then pins her gaze on Gemma. "Use whatever you want. Burn the company until it's nothing but ashes and no one remembers Jack for anything, except what a piece of shit he was."

"Was?" I question.

A deathly silence fills the air, and goose bumps break out over my arms. I scan all the women's faces, but they avoid my eyes, all nervously locking gazes with the others. I demand, "Why is no one answering me?"

Hailee shifts in her seat. "Simona, what has Declan told you? About the O'Malleys or Jack."

Minutes pass as I consider her question. Declan and I agreed to keep things between us. I don't want to break his trust, but these women are all married to his brothers or cousin. Well, except Selena. I'm unsure who her husband is other than Gemma said his name is Obrecht Ivanov. I turn to Selena. "Does your husband work for the O'Malleys?"

Her lips twitch. "No. My husband is an Ivanov. Our families are aligned."

Her answer only creates more questions. "What does that mean?"

Hailee interjects. "The Ivanovs and O'Malleys work together on things. We trust each other, and either family would help the other out without any strings attached."

"Oh. So..." I swallow the lump in my throat. "The Ivanovs are a crime family, too?"

Selena winces. "No. I wouldn't claim that." She glances at the others for help.

"It's complicated. Probably best if you have Declan explain it," Hailee suggests.

"Okay. I'll add it to my list of questions."

Hailee smiles. "So, you understand the O'Malleys are a crime family."

"Yes."

"And what do you know about Jack?"

I pause then reply, "I know about why they want it to go bankrupt and the new cybersecurity company."

Gemma asks, "You understand what our men are all capable of?"

"Yes," I reply without even thinking. It isn't a mystery that Declan is violent. I can also see it in his brothers and Liam.

Hailee nods. "Okay. So, you know they want it to go bankrupt, and they're a crime family. Add in the fact Jack kidnapped Selena and Obrecht rescued her, and no one has seen Jack unless you're reading the fake articles you posted. What conclusion would you draw?" Her blue eyes turn to ice as she waits for me to figure it out.

A chill runs down my spine. "They—"

"Don't say it out loud!" Gemma warns.

I snap my mouth shut, but a new fear takes hold. "Are we being recorded?"

Arianna puts her hand on mine. "You're scaring Simona. No, we aren't. It's just better not to get in the habit of saying things out loud."

I release a fearful breath. "Okay. So he's... I got it."

Holy shit. Jack Christian is dead. How did I not draw this conclusion earlier? Why didn't I ask Declan more questions?

Was Declan part of his murder?

Jesus. I'm dating a killer.

I pick up a photo and focus on it for several moments, pretending to study it, but I'm really trying to sort out my thoughts.

It isn't that I didn't put it past Declan to kill someone. Hell, I thought he was going to end my life when he first kidnapped me. But now I have a possible victim of his in my mind.

Selena quietly says, "He was a horrible man, Simona. Declan isn't."

I set the photo down and turn toward her. "I know. I'm sorry. I'm just processing this."

She smiles, and my heart tears. I can't imagine what Jack put her through. She's so sweet and seems kind.

Gemma clears her throat. "So you're okay with everything, Selena? Do you want to read all the articles and make sure before I have Simona upload them?"

Selena pushes her chin out. Her warm voice freezes over. "Ashes, Gemma. Leave nothing but ashes."

Satisfaction appears on Gemma's face. She rises, going to her computer and typing quickly on the keyboard. One of the screens beeps, and Declan's email account pops up. "Simona. I need you to do your thing. There is also video footage Nolan found on the hard drive. He cut it into pieces to go with the different pictures."

"Play it," Selena orders.

Gemma hesitates. "You sure? It's super graphic."

"Yes."

Gemma hits a button, and a monitor fills with a porn clip replicating the photo. Moans, grunts, and screams blare from the speakers. There are others in the room also having sex, but the camera stays focused on Jack and the judge.

When it ends, Selena turns toward me. "Upload it all, please."

I obey then delete the footprint.

Gemma taps a few keys, and the media outlets appear. Within minutes, breaking news fills almost all their platforms. The stock price takes a further tumble, and the room erupts in cheers.

My stomach growls loudly, and Gemma laughs. "Are you hungry?"

"Guess so."

"What should we order?"

I shrug, not used to spending money on takeout. "I'm not sure what's around here," I claim so I don't have to explain my lack of eating out.

"I'm dying for fish and chips from the pub, with pickles in tartar and mustard sauce," Selena says.

"Eww. That's disgusting!" Hailee wrinkles her nose.

"It sounds good to me," I blurt out.

"Yuck! And I thought you were normal," Gemma razzes.

"Pregnancy cravings are real," Selena states.

Surprised, I ask, "You're having a baby?"

Selena beams. "Yes. It's early though."

"Congratulations."

"Thanks."

"Okay, what do the rest of you want? I'll call it in," Hailee announces.

The others choose, and I get the same as Selena. Hailee orders, and it doesn't take long before Nora walks in, carrying bags. "Heard there was a girls' night and you didn't invite me."

"We're on lockdown. Well, besides Selena," Arianna informs her.

"Oh." She takes a deep breath then smiles, holding out the bags. "Who's hungry?"

I freeze. I haven't seen her since the other night in the elevator. My face scorches from embarrassment, so I hang back.

Her green eyes twinkle, and she gets past the other women who are diving into the bags. She cautiously approaches me, and her kind smile never falters. "Simona, correct?"

I nod. "Yes. Nora, right?"

"Yep. It's nice to see you again." She embraces me, so I hug her back.

"You, too. Ummm...sorry about the other night. I ummm..."

She laughs and waves her hand in front of my face. "No worries. What floor are you on?"

"Eight."

"Well, we're in the penthouse. I'll give you the code, and you can come up anytime. I'm home a lot more now because of Shannon."

"Is that your daughter?"

Her face brightens. "Yes. She's crawling all over the place, getting into trouble now."

"Aww. Do you have a photo?"

"I do!" She swipes her phone, and a picture of a baby with red hair and green eyes stares back at me.

"She's gorgeous! She looks just like you."

Nora laughs. "So I keep hearing. I see a lot of Boris in her as well."

"Food's going to get cold! Let Simona eat, Nora. Fish and chips aren't good unless they're hot!" Hailee shouts.

Nora rolls her eyes, and we sit at the table with the rest of the women.

"Liam said Declan was raving about how super smart you are, Simona," Hailee voices.

Embarrassment sparks in my cheeks. I shrug. "I know about tech."

"Don't be so modest. She's a genius," Gemma claims.

My face singes.

"Runs circles around Declan," Gemma adds.

"About time someone did," Nora chirps then takes a bite of a Reuben.

Hailee sets her drink down. "Liam says you're in school. When do you graduate?"

"After the spring semester."

"Are you interviewing already?"

I shake my head. "There's a VIP job fair in January at the college. You have to be invited by your professors. I was hoping to go."

"What do you want to do? And what line of work?" Arianna asks.

"Hacking is my favorite thing. I want to work for a cybersecurity firm. I've created some things I should patent, but I'm not sure where to start and don't have the money."

"You should come work with us. I'm surprised Declan hasn't offered you a job already." Gemma takes a bite of a french fry.

I shift in my seat and admit, "He sort of did."

Nora raises her eyebrows. "Sort of?"

Why did I open my mouth?

Declan seemed serious, but what if he wasn't?

I add fish to my fork and dip it in the tartar sauce mustard combination Selena made. "Yeah."

Nora licks her lips. "Declan doesn't offer anything 'sort of'. What did he say?"

I chew, swallow, then take a sip of water, underplaying our conversation. "He made me promise to talk to him first before I accepted any other jobs."

"You should just tell him what you want to do. Name your salary, benefits, and job position. He knows your skills. You can start where you want instead of at the bottom, doing some job that is way below your talent level," Gemma declares.

"Isn't that kind of cheating?" I ask.

She huffs. "No way! Careers are eighty percent who you know. And it's a male-dominated industry, so you know you'll hit a glass ceiling. If you work with us, you'll be able to go as far as you want."

Everything she says makes sense, but something about moving right into my dream job seems too easy. And what if Declan only said that because he's biased about me? What if I'm not good enough to be at the top of a new company? Am I missing essential skills I'll need if I skip ahead into the C-suite?

Nora snaps her fingers. "Oh! I forgot to ask you, Arianna. Do you want to take over planning the Christmas party? I have it at the pub for the O'Malleys and Ivanovs. Can you fit me in your schedule?"

Arianna laughs. "Since I only have three clients right now, I'm sure I can slide it in."

"Three? That's great! Who else hired you?" Selena shrieks.

Arianna's eyes light up. "Sasha called for the grand opening of the first phase of his new condo complex. He said Anna recommended me."

Selena's eyes turn to slits. "Did he try to haggle you down on your price?"

"Yes, but Anna warned me he was going to call. She told me how to handle him. When I insisted I couldn't do it for less and walked away, he called me back within five minutes."

Selena rolls her eyes. "He's so annoying. Every contractor we work with, he tries to underpay."

"I would have done it for the rate he wanted so I could get some more business and my name out there. It was nerve-racking walking away."

Selena pats her on the back. "Good for you for holding your ground."

We finish our dinner, continuing our conversation about lots of random topics. I learn a lot about the women. Everyone makes me feel comfortable, as if I'm one of them.

I've never tried to have a lot of friends. It was always easier to keep to myself since I often moved houses growing up. Since I ran away, my life has been about surviving. There wasn't time for friends. Tonight was fun. I wonder if I'll be able to have a group of girlfriends to hang out with, whatever that looks like.

Jeez. I don't even know how to do friend things.

Maybe I can learn.

Ugh. I'm such a social reject.

Nora and Selena leave after dinner. Hailee pulls out a deck of cards, and the four of us play euchre. I've never played before, which Hailee and Gemma claim is a sin. Arianna hasn't played, either, so I don't feel quite as bad. They teach us, and I get paired with Gemma, and Arianna with Hailee.

It's dark outside when I yawn. I'm suddenly exhausted. I toss my cards and claim, "Sorry, ladies. I'm going to fall asleep if I don't go to bed."

"It's only nine!" Arianna states.

I cringe. "Is it? It feels like it's past midnight."

"Yep."

I rise. "Well, I'm—"

Nausea hits me, and I throw my hand over my mouth, rushing to the bathroom.

Similar to the night before, I toss my cookies. Gemma rushes in, holding my hair and rubbing my back. When I finish, she hands me a wet towel.

"Have you been feeling sick all night?"

I close my eyes, resting my head against the wall. "No."

She places her palm on my forehead. "You're clammy again."

My stomach settles. I open my eyes. "I'm feeling fine now."

She tilts her head. "Maybe you should go to the doctor."

"I'm sure it's just stress. There's been a lot going on."

"Do you normally get sick like this from it?"

I sigh and shake my head.

"It won't hurt to go to the doctor."

I rise. "If it keeps up, I will. I'm sure it's nothing. Thanks for a fun evening. I'm going to go to bed, okay?"

She hesitates then smiles. "Sure."

I go into Declan's room, throw my hair in a messy bun, then shower. I brush my teeth and slide into bed, not bothering to put on my nightgown.

I'm tired, but it's nagging me that I got sick again. I don't know why it's happening. I typically don't have a weak stomach. Stress is a possibility, but I've been under a lot of it my entire life.

Maybe it's finally catching up.

Is this what happens when you get old?

I'm not old.

I always feel old.

"Ugh," I groan then snuggle down deeper, pressing my face to Declan's pillow and inhaling his scent.

I miss him. I wish he were here. I'm trying not to worry about where he is since he insisted there was nothing to worry about, and the girls stated the same thing. But I want his arms around me.

Inhaling his scent doesn't make me fall asleep. It stirs my craving for him. I kneel and use my flashlight to look under the bed. All the restraints he uses on me are there.

My heart beats faster. I pull them out then search his drawers, finding the key.

I pick up my cell.

Me: *I miss you.*

I'm surprised when he returns my text right away.

Declan: *I miss you, too, angel.*

Me: *I wish you were coming home tonight.*

Declan: *Things went faster than I expected. I'll be home sooner.*

A lust-filled excitement rushes through me. I wrap the chain around my arm and take a photo. I send it to him.

Declan: *Don't make Daddy hard when he's working.*

Me: *Exactly when will you be home?*

Declan: *Before daylight.*

Me: *Promise?*

Declan: *Promise.*

Me: *Okay. I'm going to sleep. Wake me up when you get home.*

Declan: *What are you wearing?*

Me: *Thought I wasn't supposed to make you hard when you're working?*

Declan: *Good girls answer questions and get rewarded.*

Me: *I think I'm going to be a bad girl tonight. See you soon. XOXO*

I plug my phone into the charger and wrap a chain around my breasts and waist. Then I hook the other chains at the end of the bed and on the headboard. I sit on the mattress then attach the cuffs to my ankles so my legs are spread as wide as possible. After a long debate, I attach the chain to the headboard and restrain one wrist but keep my other one free. If Declan doesn't come home, and I need to get myself out, the last thing I want is for the other women to discover I tied myself to the bed.

I drop the key on the table and pick up my phone. Arranging the camera from different angles, I take several photos and send them to Declan.

Me: *Night.*

Declan: *Jesus, you're a naughty girl.*

Me: *Daddy doesn't like it?*

Declan: *Daddy fucking loves it.*

Me: *Then Daddy should hurry home and punish me.*

Declan: *You better not play with that tasty pussy of yours.*

Me: *What if I do?*

Declan: *I'll know.*

Me: *And?*

Declan: *If you do, I'm torturing you all night and not letting you come when I get home. I'll keep you there all day tomorrow until you're crying and lose your voice from begging me. And then I still won't let you.*

Crap. I'm suddenly dying to get off. Declan's threat stops me from touching myself. If I have to choose how I'm getting my Os, I'm picking him.

I keep the blankets off me, trying to cool my hot skin and pulsing loins. I inhale more of his scent and eventually fall asleep.

At some point in the night, I feel his warm, bare skin over my frame, pushing into my hard, sensitive nipples. His deep voice sends heat right to my pussy. His lips brush against mine. "Lass, are you ready for your punishment?"

26

Declan

SIMONA'S EYES FLUTTER OPEN. A COMBINATION OF SLEEPINESS and growing lust burns in them. Her hot breath hitches, merging into mine, and she whimpers. She attempts to move her one hand, but I restrained it when I got here.

Her brows furrow. She rocks her wet heat into my aching cock and trembles slightly. Her lush mouth presses to mine. Our tongues collide in the eye of the hurricane with storms raging around us. Electrified blood crashes throughout our veins. Flesh thunders, flexing against the other. The promise of adrenaline rains in all our cells.

I lace my fingers with hers, sliding my erection and piercings over her clit. Sensual moans echo in my ears, vibrating in my mouth, matching her quivering frame.

"Naughty lass," I murmur and shimmy my pecs over her chest so the chains slide over her pebbled nipples.

"Are you going to punish me?" she whispers.

Jesus. She's so fucking perfect.

And wet.

My cock twitches, continuing to glide over her sensitive bundle of nerves. Simona's always wet for me, but right now, she feels extra aroused. It makes me harder.

Or maybe it's because my innocent little girl wrapped herself in chains and restrained herself, waiting for me to come home.

And she was so comfortable, she slept.

My ego high-fives me, happy she's comfortable in my bed, wanting her to make the decision to move in.

Her flushed cheeks glow in the dim light of the darkened room. Her red lips are already swelling from our kisses. Stunning blue eyes become heavy with need, turning me on even more.

"Daddy's so hard seeing you in these chains again," I murmur.

Her lips curve as she swallows hard, trying to keep her eyes open as I slide over her faster. She cries out, "Oh God!"

I move my hand between us, position the chain's link over her nipple, then rotate it around the edge. She moans louder, and her body trembles. "Please...oh...please make me come," she begs, her cheeks burning with fire.

"You've been naughty, angel."

"I-I...oh..." She blinks several times. "I didn't touch myself! Please, Daddy!"

Listening to her call me Daddy might be my new favorite thing. One of these days, I'm going to record her calling me it. Then I'm going to replay it while I'm away from her.

Before I woke her up, I sniffed her fingers. It gave me great pleasure to know she waited for me. So I decide she's due for a reward.

I reach up and adjust a chain. Her chin angles upward, and she gasps in surprise. It was another thing I did before she woke up. I added a flat piece of metal under her chin. Her eyes are now facing the restraints, and I scrape my teeth down her neck as she cries out.

Her pulse beats so hard in her neck, I can see it. I suck on it, rolling it in my mouth, then bite down and move the chain over her nipple faster as she screams out my name. A violent earthquake erupts in her body, and the chains rattle against the metal bars.

I nip at her earlobe. "That's it, angel. Daddy's going to reward you."

She continues whimpering, gripping the headboard so fiercely, her knuckles are white.

I move my mouth to her breasts, sucking on them and the chain and pressing my piercings harder against her clit.

"Jes...oh...oh...fuck!" she moans.

I remove the restraint from her chin, wanting her eyes on me while I taste her. I kiss her, and she hungrily devours me, continuing to make tiny noises.

"Did you have a good night?" I ask and lick her jaw.

"Yes."

I press my thumb on her clit and push three digits into her sex. She arches into me, and I bite her bottom lip and then ask, "But you still missed me?"

"So much."

I inch in and out of her, basking in her half-asleep whimpers.

She circles her hips into my hand, asking, "Did you miss me?"

"Every second," I confess.

She closes her eyes briefly.

I kiss her lids. "You're too beautiful, angel."

A small smile appears on her lips, but the lust in her eyes overpowers it. Her voice cracks as she says, "I need you in me, Declan."

I groan. It's the sexiest thing I've ever heard coming from the hottest pair of lips on Earth. "Not yet, lass."

"Please," she begs with a desperation in her eyes I don't remember seeing before.

"Your pussy belongs in my mouth, angel."

"After. Oh God, please! After!" she pleads.

It's all it takes. I'm a goner, unable to stop myself from removing my hand, reaching down, and releasing the tension in her ankle restraints. I already put a condom on before I woke her up, not wanting to be selfish. I lost my head and took her bare when she was my captive. It was another error on my part, and I won't do anything but protect her going forward. It was hard pulling out of her earlier today, and I shouldn't allow her to be in that position. I shove her legs up, thrusting in her as she urgently takes all of me.

"Greedy girl," I growl.

"Yes! Oh...thank you," she breathes, her walls throbbing against my erection.

I move her legs higher and prop myself up on my forearms so my face hangs over hers. "Daddy loves how wet you are for me." I thrust close to her so my piercings roll over her clit.

She frantically nods. "You feel...oh...keep doing that...ohhhhh!" She shuts her eyes, and her walls spasm on my erection, almost sending me over the edge.

I grunt, stopping myself from exploding inside her. "Your tight little cunt's making it hard for me to keep going, lass."

"Oh God!" she screams, cutting through the air. Her eyes roll, and her body convulses under mine.

I suck on the red mark over her pulse, and a feral moan fills my ears. I mumble, "God, I love you."

"Release me," she whispers so quietly, I think I didn't hear it.

I lock eyes with her.

"Please."

She's never asked before. I stop moving, grab the key, and reach up, releasing the cuffs.

Her arms wrap around my shoulders. One hand slides through my hair on the back of my head. The other digs into my shoulders. The blues in her orbs swirl, and sweat drips down her face. Breath flies out of her mouth in shallow bursts.

I drag my finger down her cheek. "Angel, what's wrong?"

She doesn't answer, only kisses me. It's slow and sweet. It grows deeper and deeper until it wrecks the vein of my existence. Emotions bounce through me like a fast game of ping-pong. I don't know why. But her kiss is so different from all others.

And then she mutters it against my lips, quiet and vulnerable, as if she thinks it may make me disappear. "I love you."

I freeze but only momentarily. Love and fear clash in her eyes. I see the little girl no one loved but should have and the woman who is brave enough to step into it.

My lips curve up as I tuck a wet lock of her hair behind her ear. "I love you, angel. Forever." I return to her mouth, savoring every ounce of her I can.

She digs her nails into my shoulders, her fingers grip my hair, and her hips return to torturing me.

The scent of our arousal and sounds of our fornication thicken in the air. I become so lost in us and her body trembling in my arms, I erupt in her. Collapsing into her neck, I groan from the adrenaline rushing to my head.

She doesn't release me. Her exhales permeate my skin. Her thumb caresses my neck. "I'm so glad you're home."

I lift my head. Dean Whitehouse was nowhere. The way she left her house makes me think she skipped town, as if she knew we were coming. I spent the hour before I came home debating with Liam and Obrecht about how we would find her and Maria.

I hate that my angel has threats looming around her, and I still don't know why. No matter what I have to do, I'll take them out. I don't care they aren't men. I'm not going to show any mercy. They put my woman in the middle of the fire, and they're going to burn in it.

"I want you here every day. Like this. Us. Together," I state.

She studies me with too many emotions swirling in her expression. I'm not sure what to make of it.

"You scare me when you look at me like that," I admit.

"Like what?"

My stomach flips. "I'm unsure if you're going to leave me for good and never come back or stay forever."

She bites on her lip.

"Simona—"

"Why don't we work this all out now."

My chest tightens as the air becomes stale in my lungs. "Work what out?"

"I'll ask you all my questions, and you answer."

I attempt to roll off her, and she pretzels her limbs around me. "I didn't say get off me."

I arch my eyebrow. "I'm still inside you."

Her lips twitch. "Yep."

"Jesus, you're filthy at times."

"You love it."

"And you." I peck her on the lips.

She nervously smiles. "Should I start?"

"Ask me whatever you want."

She tightens her legs around me. "Did you kill Jack Christian?"

My heart stops beating for a moment. I gape at her and finally question, "Why are you asking me this?"

"I only want answers, Declan."

The vein around my eye twitches. I pin my gaze on hers. "Yes. I was part of it."

Her expression stays the same. She drags her nails across my shoulders. "He's not the first man you've killed?"

My mouth turns dry. "No."

"He won't be the last?"

"No."

She nods, not even flinching. "When you offered me a job, was it part of convincing me to get back with you?"

Anger flares in my bones. "No. You're the most talented person I've ever met. You'd be a huge asset to our company."

"So it was a real offer?"

"Of course it was," I reply, insulted she thought otherwise.

"What did you do to get the dean to let me stay in good standing and make up my work?"

My pulse shoots to the sky. "I told you."

She arches her eyebrows.

I close my eyes. My woman is smart. I know this. Yet, I somehow thought she wouldn't even know.

"Declan—"

"I made a donation to her library wing so we could move it along. I didn't want to wait, but she had already agreed to talk to your professors."

"How much?"

"Fifty thousand."

Simona's eyes widen. "That's a lot of money."

"I wasn't taking any chances of not righting the wrong I caused you."

She releases a breath. "Did you have men following me before I saw you again?"

"Yes. It was for your protection."

"Are there threats against me?"

"Possibly. I won't take any chances. Your safety is my priority."

She continues caressing my head. "Will it always be this way? If I'm with you? I'll have bodyguards everywhere I go?"

"Yes."

"What if you get rid of me?"

I shake my head, angry again. "I'm never getting rid of you. I've told you this. I'm a man, and I know what I want."

"But if you did..."

I sigh. "I would still have protection on you. There will always be some possible danger whether you stay with me or leave me."

The silence becomes deafening. Bile crawls up my throat from worrying she's going to leave me. I know this is a lot for any woman, but Simona isn't just any woman. I've never told anyone the things I revealed to her. I don't know if I'm doing it right or not. It's the truth, and there doesn't seem to be any way to make it prettier.

"Simona—"

She puts her fingers over my lips. "I'll move in with you."

Everything stops moving—my lungs trying to find air, my heart, my pulse. It's not what I expected to hear after what I revealed, and it seems too easy. "You will?"

"Yes."

"Why?"

"Are you changing your mind?" Worry overtakes her expression. I hate that she doubts my commitment to her.

"No. But what I just told you..." I swallow hard.

She smiles. "You were honest with me."

"So you were testing me?"

She softly laughs. "I guess so."

My naughty little angel.

"What about my job offer? Are you going to take it?" I ask.

She bites on her lip, and her cheeks flush deeper.

I wait.

"I'm open to discussing things."

It doesn't sound like it's a done deal, so I push. "Meaning?"

She clears her throat. "I think you should tell me what you're looking for and what my duties would be. Then I can tell you if it's what I want to do."

"It's a new company. We can create whatever you want. I want you to be happy," I state.

Her eyes brighten. "Okay. But what if what I want to do, you don't have a need for?"

"Then I'll create one."

She tilts her head.

I chuckle and drag my knuckles down her hot cheeks. "Don't you want to have breaks with Daddy instead of at the coffee machine?"

She tries to look stern, but her face breaks out in a grin. "Are you hiring me for my body or brain?"

I smirk. "I'm hiring you for your brain. Your body is a bonus."

"I take it your HR department wouldn't approve."

I grunt. "Fuck HR. Besides, my cock's inside you right now."

She rolls her eyes, but she's smiling.

I put on my most serious expression. "You're smart, Simona. I'd be a fool to let you go anywhere else. Whatever you want, tell me and we'll figure it out. Money, title, duties, I don't care. Name it and I'll make it happen."

"What about your brothers?"

"What about them?"

"Won't they want a say?"

I snort. "They aren't stupid. They'll be on board."

She considers everything and I can see the wheels turning in her head.

"Don't overthink this, angel."

Her emotion-filled orbs plague me again, but she surprises me once more and says, "Okay. I'll figure out what I want and tell you."

"That's my girl!" I kiss her. Hard. Raw. Full of everything I feel for her and every ounce of love I have in my heart. It's all for her anyway. No one has ever gotten it before.

She clings to me, returning my affection until my dick twitches inside her. A raspy moan rumbles into my mouth.

I end our kiss and slide down her body. "Daddy hasn't forgotten what you need, angel."

27

Simona

A Week Later

Declan sneaks up behind me and moves my hair over my shoulder. His lips brush the curve of my neck, sending shivers down my spine. He murmurs, "I have a surprise for you."

I spin and put my arms around him. "Besides the new wardrobe you bought me?"

He wiggles his eyebrows. "My girl needs somewhere to wear all her new clothes."

My flutters take off. "You're spoiling me again."

His cocky expression lights me up before his words do. "It's Daddy's job to spoil you."

I bite on my lip, unable to help the giddy feeling I have. Since deciding to move in, Declan and I have been inseparable. Even when I study, he works next to me. He took me to his friend Skylar's shop. She was super sweet and helpful. She even gave me a dress she hadn't released yet. Afterward, we went to more stores, including La Perla, which had underwear more expensive than my monthly rent. Then he took me shoe shopping.

Every time I protested, Declan shut me up with a kiss. Several nights this week, we went to the pub and met up with his brothers and cousins. Hailee, Gemma, and Arianna were there, too. It's strange. I thought I would be uncomfortable around his brothers and cousins since they know about Declan's and my history, but they've made me feel welcome.

"So where are we going? Are you taking me to dinner?" I ask.

"Mmm...sort of. There will be food."

I tilt my head. "You're confusing me again."

His eyes twinkle. "We're going to New York for Thanksgiving."

I freeze, gaping at him. I didn't realize it was Thanksgiving. It completely slipped my mind with everything going on. Normally, I hide away this time of year and try not to fall into a depression over my loneliness. But New York?

His grin widens. "You look really cute right now."

"I... I've never even been on a plane!" I blurt out.

"It's not just any plane."

"What do you mean?"

"We're taking a private jet."

"What?" I screech.

He chuckles. "We leave in an hour. Time to pack." He guides me into the bedroom.

"Wait! I don't have a suitcase," I screech.

More arrogance blooms across his features, and he drags me into the closet. A new set of designer luggage sits next to his cases. My mouth hangs open as I run my hand across the hard leather. "How did you sneak this in?"

He doesn't answer, only kisses me. "Get packing. We can't be late."

I use the entire hour, asking him tons of questions about what we'll be doing so I know what to wear. He explains we're staying with Arianna's family and then he tells me about his niece and nephew.

"Wow. Why wouldn't Bridget let you see them?" I ask.

His face darkens. "We never figured it out. She always said it was too dangerous for her kids to be O'Malleys and associate with us. It's bullshit though. Her father, Tully, is the head of the Irish mafia in New York."

Nothing should surprise me anymore. Liam is the head of Declan's clan. Now that I know him, he's like an ordinary guy. But it makes me nervous. "Is her father scary?"

Declan shakes his head. "No. Only to thugs if he needs to be. Not to us. And he won't be to you. But you should also know Arianna's father is the head of the Italian Mafia in New York as well."

"Really?"

"Yeah. Why do you seem so shocked?"

I shrug. "She never said anything. But I guess you don't go around introducing yourself by who your father is."

"You'll like Angelo. He'll love you. Her brothers are cool, too."

"And they have room for all of us?"

Declan snorts. "Angelo has a mansion. We call it the compound. There's plenty of room."

"Wow."

Declan zips up my case and sets it on the ground. "We need to go."

One of his drivers takes us to the airport. There's a jet on the runway, and my stomach flips. I put my hand over it and swallow down bile.

"Angel, you okay?" he asks, studying me.

I force a smile. The last week, I've had little bouts of nausea. I got sick one other time, but Declan was working and didn't see me throw up. I'm sure he would have insisted I go to the doctor, but I'm convinced it's just stress from all the changes. Plus, I want to go back to class, and Declan insisted I wait another week. We fought about it, but I finally gave in, deciding it wasn't worth the argument. Any hint of me not one hundred percent well will result in another debate about me returning. I reply, "Think I'm just nervous about the thought of flying."

He kisses my hand. "Don't worry, lass. You have more of a chance of getting in a car accident than a plane crash."

I breathe through more nausea then claim, "I'm okay."

We get out of the car, and Declan leads me to the jet. I climb up the stairs, and a flight attendant greets me. When I turn the corner, Liam and Hailee, Killian and Arianna, plus Nora, Boris, and Shannon are on the plane.

I met Shannon earlier in the week. Declan needed to talk to Boris, and I visited with her and Nora. She's a gorgeous baby, and I fell in love instantly. When I walk past her, she reaches for me.

"Hey, Shannon," I coo and take the seat behind them. She shrieks, and Nora softly orders, "Hey! Calm down."

Shannon hits the back of the seat, and Boris takes her. He lifts her in the air, and she sees me and reaches for me again. When Boris puts her on his lap, she screams.

Nora gets on her knees, facing me. "I think she wants to see you, Simona."

I hold my hands out. "Give her here!"

She passes the baby to me, and the moment I hold her, Shannon stops crying.

I laugh. "Well, I'm happy to see you, too!"

Declan sits next to me, and he holds his hands out. "Give your favorite uncle a hug, cutie pie."

"Watch it," Killian threatens from the seat across from ours.

"It's true," Declan claims and kisses Shannon's head.

Killian grunts as Gemma, Nolan, and Finn rush on the plane and take the seats behind us.

The door shuts and the pilot announces to put our belts on. Declan passes Shannon back to Boris then laces his fingers with mine. "You okay?"

My stomach flutters with nerves. "Do I look nervous?"

His lips twitch. "Little bit. Just breathe. The worst part is the takeoff. Then you won't even notice we're in the air."

The jet picks up speed and then lifts. I fall back in my seat, taking deep breaths, and close my eyes. Dizziness hits me and I swallow more bile down.

Declan squeezes my hand, watching me. I feel his eyes, but I'm too paralyzed to move, gripping the armrest.

The aircraft levels out, and I keep my eyes shut until my stomach settles.

"All done, angel."

I take a final exhale, and my heart rate returns to normal.

Declan slides his arm around me. I lean into it and smile at him. Besides my dizzy spell, I'm happier than I've ever been. If this is what being in love feels like, I understand why almost every song on Earth is about it. His warm lips brush the side of my forehead, convincing me I'm the luckiest woman on the planet.

"That wasn't so bad," I state.

He chuckles. "Nope. Now I can take you anywhere you want to go."

Excitement pulses through me. "Really?"

"Sure. Name it, and I'll make it happen."

I bite on my smile. With Declan, everything is an abundance of opportunities and new adventures. He acts like nothing is impossible. As if all I have to do is mention something, and he'll make it happen.

I admit, "I've never thought of going anywhere. It didn't seem like it was in the cards for me."

"When we get home, I'm buying you a globe."

I laugh. "A globe?"

"Yep. You can create a list of where you want to vacation."

This is the first time I've gone anywhere. The notion of planning a trip for leisure is foreign to me. It sounds like a dream, which is something I don't usually allow myself to do.

"Shut her down, angel," Declan softly orders.

A few days ago, we got into a conversation I wasn't planning on having. He insisted I need to shift out of being in survival mode. He claimed those days are over for me, swearing I'll never again fight for food, clothing, or shelter. He was adamant he would provide luxuries I've never had.

But it's hard to turn off everything you've said and done your entire life in order to exist. Right now, my old self is screaming dreams aren't realistic, yet the new me fights her, suggesting maybe the life others have can finally be mine.

He drags his finger over my cheekbone. "What about a beach?"

I arch my eyebrow in question.

He leans into my ear, speaking so only I can hear him, enunciating each word. "You. Me. You in a skimpy bathing suit. Me rubbing suntan lotion all over every inch of your skin."

Zings detonate in my body at the thought. I turn my face, my lips an inch from his. Blue flames pin me to my seat, smoldering with intensity and the fun side of Declan, two things I fell in love with the night I met him. I confess, "I don't have a suit or know how to swim."

He pecks me on the lips. "Two hurdles easy to overcome."

"Yeah?"

"Yep. I'll teach you to swim. But I'm down with your sexy little body wrapped around mine, clinging to me."

I laugh, and the flight attendant informs us she's going to pass out dinner.

The rest of the journey we spend eating, drinking, and laughing with the others. When we land in New York, it's close to midnight. Arianna's father has several SUVs waiting for us, and we all split up.

Even though it's dark, the outline of the mansion is powerful, glowing under the moonlight. Armed guards are at the gate and surround the house. The driveway is long and circles in front of the main door. I gape at it, awed by the magnificence. I exclaim, "Wow!"

"It's impressive, isn't it?" Declan says.

Nodding, I glance at Arianna. "You grew up here?"

She smiles. "Yeah."

"Did you ever get lost?"

She laughs. "It was fun to play hide-and-seek when I was a child."

"I bet," I mumble, taking Declan's hand to get out. Arianna seems so normal. I always assumed people who had this much money were like many of the kids at my school. Nothing about her is arrogant, rude, or mean. She doesn't try to intimidate people or flaunt anything. It makes me respect her more.

"Papà!" She runs up the stairs, and an older man with dark hair embraces her. Four more men stand behind him, towering over her. They're also dark haired, handsome, and have the same dangerous vibe as the O'Malleys.

Declan leads me into the house, and Arianna introduces me to her father, Angelo, and her brothers. Dante and Gianni are identical twins. Her brother Massimo is the middle brother. Tristano is the youngest.

Arianna gives me a quick tour of the main areas. I try not to gape, but everything is so different from what I'm accustomed to in Chicago. The warm browns and golds mix beautifully with reds and blues, but everything is elegant and feels expensive. Art hangs all over the house, and while I know nothing about paintings, my gut tells me they are originals and possibly collector pieces. The entire tour is like going into an entirely different world.

We're almost back to the family room where the others are when I ask, "Do you miss living here?"

A tiny smile, maybe it's nostalgic, forms on Arianna's lips. "I miss my papà and brothers, but I'm happy with Killian. I love the home we've created."

I glance around. "This is an exquisite, beautiful house."

"Thanks."

We step into the room with the others, and I yawn. I'm suddenly exhausted, my adrenaline from all the excitement run dry.

"You tired, angel?" Declan asks.

I nod. "Yeah. It just hit me."

"Declan, you want to take the same room as last time?" Angelo asks.

"That would be great. If you don't mind, I think we'll call it a night," Declan replies.

"Sure."

We say goodnight. Declan guides me up the stairs and through the wing Arianna and Tristano share. He says Massimo, Gianni, and Dante all have their own wings.

"Seriously?"

He chuckles. "Yep."

"Wow."

He sets my suitcase on the luggage rack then studies me, sliding his hands over my cheeks. "You look worn out, angel."

"I am."

He gives me a chaste kiss. "Get ready for bed, then."

I brush my teeth, toss on my nightgown, and slide under the covers. Declan goes into the bathroom, and before he gets into bed, I fall into a deep sleep for the entire night.

When I wake up, he isn't next to me. I go into the bathroom and Declan is getting out of the shower. Water drips off his body, running over his sculpted muscles. His workout clothes are on the bathroom floor. He wraps a towel around his waist and teases, "Morning, sleepyhead."

I stand on my tiptoes and kiss him. "What time is it?"

"Close to nine."

"Did you work out?"

"Yep. Are you hungry? Everyone is meeting downstairs for breakfast before Tully brings the kids over."

"I'm starving." I stroke his cheek. "Are you excited to see them?"

He grins. "Can't wait."

"Let me take a quick shower, and I'll be down."

"Do you remember how to get to the dining room?"

"Yep. I'll make my way through the mansion," I chirp, still amazed and a bit intimidated by the house.

More amusement crosses his face. "Told you it was a compound."

"It's nice we all get to stay in one place."

He nods. "Especially for Thanksgiving."

The uncomfortable anxiety I have around the holidays pops up. I remind myself I'm with Declan now and things are different. Then it occurs to me I have no clue what I'm supposed to do to prepare for whatever will happen tomorrow. Is it like what you see on TV? Do people gorge on turkey and mashed potatoes all day? I try to push the dread away but can't seem to. I blurt out, "What will tomorrow be like? Do I need to do anything to prepare?"

His palm grips my ass, eliminating the distance between us. He grabs my neck, strokes my pulse with his thumb, and hovers over my face. I gasp as unexpected desire pools between my legs. His eyes roam my face, and I bite on my lip. "Daddy plans on showing you how thankful he is for you, all over this house."

My eyes widen. I press my hands against his chest, still warm from the shower. My voice comes out raspy. "Is that what people do on Thanksgiving?"

His mouth curves before he kisses me. He parts my lips with his tongue, owning me, destroying all my thoughts and worries about what I don't know about holidays. It's impossible to ponder anything besides him. My body is a puzzle piece fitting perfectly with his, locking into place. He ends our kiss and smirks. "Playing with your pussy all day is my new tradition. We'll mix the other festivities in."

A tiny laugh flies out of my mouth.

"Get ready, angel. Breakfast is ready soon." He pecks me on the lips, squeezes my ass, and leaves.

I toss my hair in a bun, wash my face and body, then get out. I spend a few minutes applying some makeup and put on leggings, an oversized cream sweater, and knee-high boots, all compliments of the shopping spree Declan spoiled me with earlier in the week.

I go to the dining room and slide onto a chair between Declan and Finn. Everyone is already seated. Silver-covered platters fill the middle of the table. I lean into him. "Please tell me they have pancakes."

His eyes twinkle. "I think you're in luck." He lifts the lid in front of us, revealing stacks of hotcakes.

I clap. "Yes!"

"Pass the butter," Killian says.

"Of course that's the first thing you want," Arianna chirps.

"Hey! It's a holiday. No food guilt this weekend. Plus, my bloodwork came back in stellar shape," he claims.

"That goes for me, too. Pass me a croissant," Angelo states.

Arianna groans. "You're both going to go overboard, aren't you?"

"Yep!" Killian grins then kisses her. "Eat your breakfast and splurge. It's Thanksgiving. Angelo, my Irish butter is going to make that the best croissant you've ever had."

Arianna elbows him.

"Ow!"

"Don't encourage my papà to eat your butter."

Killian puts a croissant full of butter up to her lips. "Eat."

She rolls her eyes but takes a bite.

"Good, isn't it?" He goes to put it in his mouth, and she grabs it out of his hand.

"Hey!"

She holds it away from him. "It's mine now."

"You'll pay later for stealing my food."

"Ha!" She blushes and takes a bite.

I'm not sure what her food issues are all about, but I make a mental note to ask her later. I glance at Declan, but he only winks in amusement.

"What time is the party tonight?" Gemma asks.

"Starts at seven," Arianna replies.

"Do you need help with anything?" I ask, my worries about not knowing what to do for the holidays perking back up.

She shakes her head. "Everything is all set, but thanks."

"Angelo, Finn and I need to speak with Tully when he comes to the party. Can we use your study?" Liam asks.

Angelo pins his dark gaze on Liam. "Of course. Everything alright?"

Finn's face hardens. His icy voice sends a chill down my spine. "I need to convince Tully to set up a meeting between Bridget and me."

Angelo puts his fork down and wipes his mouth with the gold cloth. "Bridget is attending the party tonight."

Silence fills the air.

Killian's eyes turn to slits. "Why is she volunteering to come? Why now?"

"It's our fault," Dante claims.

All eyes turn toward him.

"What did you do?" Declan questions.

"Gianni and I saw Bridget the other night. She was pretty intoxicated, and the guy giving her attention wasn't someone who should have been near her. He got too bold, and we had to rip him off her."

"Jesus. Is she okay?" Declan asks, his body stiffening and fists clenching. The concern in his voice surprises me. After all she's put their family through, he still cares for her. It makes me love him even more.

"Yeah. Our guys took care of him, and Gianni and I put her in our car to give her a ride home, but she started crying and didn't want us to take her back to Tully's. It seems the kids were giving her a hard time. She claims Sean Jr. hates her, and Fiona will barely talk to her," Dante informs us.

"What does she expect? She told them we didn't want to see them anymore," Nolan seethes.

Dante puts his hands in the air. "I'm not excusing what she did. Her actions are making things worse for her kids and all of you. We convinced her she needed to make things right between all of you or she would lose her kids."

Nolan snaps, "She was drunk. Bridget says a lot of things when she's drunk. It doesn't mean she's going to stick to her word."

Dante sighs. "Yeah. I grew up with her and know how she is. That's why I kept in contact with her and had coffee with her several times. I convinced her the party is the perfect place to make an appearance since there will be lots of people. It's a good first step."

Nolan crosses his arms. "Something else going on between you two?"

"Nolan!" Gemma reprimands.

"It's a fair question."

Dante glares at Nolan. "Don't ask questions that might get you harmed."

"Then why the interest?"

Dante shakes his head in anger. He points to Arianna. "Because my sister asked me to help."

Arianna's cheeks turn red, and she shifts in her seat.

"Arianna?" Killian quietly asks.

She twists a lock of her hair and furrows her brows. "I only want the best for everyone. Fiona and Sean Jr. are taking the brunt of this. Bridget is their mom, no matter what she's done."

Killian tugs her into him and kisses her on the forehead. "It's okay, lass. Thank you."

Dante continues scowling at Nolan. "So no, nothing is going on between Bridget and me, other than me sticking my nose in your business as a favor to Arianna."

Nolan's red cheeks turn pink. "Sorry."

Finn clears his throat. "So Bridget will be here tonight?"

Dante nods. "I texted her this morning, reinforcing this is the right thing for her kids. She already promised them she'd be here."

Finn's leg bounces next to mine. "Good. Then I'm going to need your help getting her alone."

28

Declan

THE DOORBELL RINGS, AND MY INSIDES FLIP WITH NERVES. I'VE waited years for this moment. My palms sweat, and I wipe them on my pants.

My brothers, Nora, and I all stand next to each other. The others are in the living room, waiting for us to bring Sean Jr. and Fiona in. They thought it was best so we didn't overwhelm the kids more.

Killian opens the door, and I blink hard. I've spoken numerous times on video chat with Fiona and Sean Jr., yet nothing can compare to seeing them in person. They're so much older than when Bridget ripped them away from us. Now they're on the brink of being young adults.

Fiona and Nora are both crying. Sean tries to hold back his tears, but they fall. I squeeze both of them, not wanting to let them go.

"Let me look at you." I cup Fiona's cheeks, and her glistening eyes fill more. "You're beautiful, darling." I kiss her forehead and hug her again. All I can think is how much her father would have worried about her with the boys. He would have wanted to lock her up, and so do I. She's invited her boyfriend to the party tonight. I'm taking him aside and having a little conversation with him to instill the fear of the O'Malleys in him.

"Don't hog Fiona," Nolan growls.

I release her and refocus on Sean. He has a bit of ginger stubble, and I swipe at it. "You growing this out?"

Pride sweeps his face. He puffs up his chest, reminding me of his father. Another pang of nostalgia hits me. It's something my brother would have bragged to us about over drinks in the pub. Hell, he probably would have given Sean a pint of Guinness to celebrate, as our father did for us, claiming you're a man once you get your first sign of facial hair.

Red crawls up his neck and into his cheeks. "That's the plan."

We spend a few more minutes in the entryway then lead the kids into the living room. Finn and Liam are the first to embrace them then Arianna since she's already met them. Nolan, Liam, and I introduce our women.

We spend the day in Angelo's compound, since it has everything. Fiona and Sean are staying all weekend, so we plan on doing fun things in the city after Thanksgiving.

We spend the majority of the day in the game room. When the women sweep Fiona away to get ready for the party, we take Sean into the gym, along with Arianna's brothers. His mom won't let him box anymore. He needs an outlet to get his anger out, so the plan is to show him how to lift.

Since Dante used to fight, the Marino's gym has all the equipment ours does, plus the cardio and weight machines. We do some warm-ups, show him how to lift, then naturally, we progress to the different bags. It wasn't the plan, but we're O'Malleys. It's in our blood to know how to box.

It doesn't take long before Sean is swinging like his father taught him.

"You've got a mean right hook. Let's see the left one," Killian orders, holding a punch shield.

Sean takes a swing.

"Hold up!" Dante calls out then pulls Sean aside. "Lean into it, like this." He takes several quick jabs.

Killian has to dig his heels into the floor not to move backward. He taunts, "Harder, you pussy!"

Dante grunts and hits the shield with so much force, Killian bounces back.

"Don't fuck with a Marino," Massimo shouts, patting Dante on the back.

"Maybe we should take it in the ring," Killian suggests.

Dante steps back. "Wouldn't want to kill my sister's husband. She's grown rather fond of you."

Killian snorts. "In your dreams."

I lean into Sean's ear. "You got a girl you like?"

"Yeah. She's coming tonight."

"She is?" I ask, surprised he hadn't told us when Fiona did.

The same arrogant look his father used to have fills his expression. "Yep."

I tug him closer to me and point at Killian. "Pretend you caught him hitting on her."

"Jesus. She's in high school, you sick fuck," Finn mutters.

Sean's cockiness grows. "No. She's not."

Killian cringes. "Don't tell me she's in middle school."

He huffs. "No. She's in college."

"College?" I ask. He's only sixteen. If she's Simona's age, I'm not on board with that.

"Yeah. She's super intelligent and skipped a grade. She should be a senior, but she's a freshman at the community college.

Relieved, I pat him on the back again. "That's a good lad. Pick the smart lasses."

"We need to get showered. It's getting close to seven," Nolan says.

"Hit 'em," I order.

"Keep your hands up," Dante instructs.

Sean replicates Dante's moves, and we all cheer him on. When he finishes, his face is red, and Killian tosses the shield, tugging him into him and messing up his hair. "You're still a fighter, lad."

Sean catches his breath, his eyes growing hotter. He admits, "I want to move to Chicago. I can emancipate myself from my mom—"

"Whoa! I know you're upset with her, but that's a drastic decision," I declare. Bridget may have done a lot, but Arianna is right. She's still his mother. Both my parents are dead, and I'd give anything to see them one more time.

"She's a bitch," Sean barks.

Killian slaps his head then points in his face. "Watch your mouth. That's your mother. You don't have to agree with her decisions, but you still need to show her respect. We've discussed this."

Anger fills his features. "How can you all stick up for her? What she did—"

"Was wrong. But you need to make things right with her. You only have one mother," Nolan adds.

"She destroyed our lives. And she won't even let me box," he protests.

I sigh. "Sean—"

"I'm a man. I'm not a two-year-old. She and Tully—"

"Do not disrespect your daideó," I warn.

He snorts hard and crosses his arms. Rage emanates off him, rolling down his body like a wave soaking a beach at high tide. "I'm an O'Malley, not an O'Connor."

"You have the blood of both families. Your anger doesn't change your DNA. And it makes you stronger to have both sides flowing through your veins, so don't try to deny either side," I remind him.

He snarls, "They had no problem attempting to erase my O'Malley blood."

Tense silence fills the air. Sean's intelligent. It's hard to stick up for what Bridget did. And Tully allowed it.

Dante breaks the silence. "Come workout here. I'll train you."

Sean's head snaps toward him, as do the rest of ours.

Dante steps forward. "We'll set up a schedule. As long as you stick to it, my brothers and I will teach you everything we know. If you want to fight, we'll get you registered when you turn eighteen. But until then, you stay with your mom and finish school here."

The air stills again as we all hold our breath, waiting for Sean to answer. I'm grateful for Dante's offer and praying Sean buys into it so he doesn't try to leave New York before he finishes school.

He shakes his head and looks at me. "Living with them is like being locked up in prison."

Liam grunts. "You don't know shit about prison or having your freedom taken from you. I can assure you, it's a thousand times worse than your current situation."

Sean focuses on the ceiling, grinding his molars. Crimson surges into his cheeks.

"Christ, you're a stubborn fuck, just like your dad," Nolan mutters.

Sean's rage-filled gaze cuts through the air at Nolan.

Trying to diffuse Sean's wrath, I put my arm around his shoulders. "Chill out a bit. You don't want to be all pissed off around your woman tonight."

He tilts his head at me, still scowling.

"That's true. Pissed off before a date usually means no ass," Killian adds.

"Just make sure you wrap your shit. You need us to buy you some condoms?" Finn asks.

Sean groans, scrubbing his hands over his flaming-red cheeks. "I'm good, but thanks."

"So what's it going to be? Am I going to train you or not?" Dante asks.

"If my mom finds out, she'll stop me. If Tully—"

"You mean daideó," I remind him.

He growls in frustration.

"Tell you what. You return to respecting your mom and Tully, and I'll take care of them," Dante claims.

Sean arches his eyebrows. "You will?"

"Yeah. Leave it to me. So, are we doing this or what?"

Sean hesitates then nods. "Okay. I'm in. Thanks."

My brothers and I exchange a relieved glance.

"We need to get ready for the party," Nolan reminds us, and we make our way out of the gym.

At the top of the staircase, I pull Dante aside. "Thanks for doing that. We owe you."

He shakes his head. "No, you don't. We're family, and Sean's a good kid. I'll talk to Bridget and Tully. I'll get them to agree so she and Tully aren't all over his ass."

"Thanks."

"No problem. We just need to keep him focused for a few more years so he doesn't do something stupid. Plus, it'll be fun for me."

"The worst thing he could do is not finish his schooling here. He's at one of the top private schools in the country. I can't guarantee he'll find a similar one in Chicago. Thanks again."

"Don't worry. I've got him."

I nod, and we part ways. I shower then get dressed. Simona walks into the room wearing an off-the-shoulder, raspberry cocktail dress we found at Skylar's shop earlier in the week. She has on a pair of black stilettos, showcasing her calves I want to lick. Her hair is in a sleek ponytail, begging me to tug it. She's the epitome of sexy and sophisticated. Her makeup has a bit of a dramatic flair, making her blue eyes pop.

My cock strains against my zipper. I motion for her to turn, and she smirks but obeys. The dress is backless and sits right above her ass.

I lunge forward and drag my knuckles down her spine, watching her shudder. When I reach the fabric, I slide a finger under it. I press my lips to the nape of her neck, mumbling, "Fuck me. You aren't wearing any panties, are you?"

She reaches for my thighs and grasps them. "No. I didn't want lines."

"You're the most beautiful woman in the world, angel." I circle her waist and palm her stomach, pinning her ass against my cock. I give myself a high five for insisting she got the shoes she tried to tell me were too expensive. I murmur in her ear, "Whatever I say tonight, do without questioning me."

She tilts her head back. "Why would I question you?"

I kiss her on the lips, retreating when she opens her mouth and her minty tongue grazes mine. "Because what I want to do to you during the party is indecent."

Her soft breath hits mine like a feather tickling my skin. Her eyes turn heavy, taunting my erection. The hope in her orbs almost makes me come in my pants. She whispers, "More than the normal things you do to me?"

"You'll have to wait and see. Let's go." I wink, release her, then lead her out the door and down to the ballroom. Before we step inside, she says, "You look really handsome."

I grin like an idiot and kiss her cheek. We enter the room, and my eyes dart to Fiona. She's in a little black dress, looking at least eighteen instead of fourteen. Her date has his hand around her waist and too close to her ass for my liking. He's got broad shoulders for his age. I'm guessing he's the high school jock and probably a senior, which doesn't excite me, either, since Fiona is only a freshman. Then it hits me he could also be in college, and the uncomfortable feeling grows within me. He's whispering something in her ear, and every protective vibe I have goes off.

My blood heats, but so does my brothers' because they reach her before I do. The look on their faces gives their disdain away.

"Fiona, you look beautiful." I kiss her cheek and pull her away from the cocksucker's hand that conveniently slipped to her ass.

Excitement shows on her face, and I remind myself to stay calm so I don't embarrass her. She beams. "Thanks. You both look great!"

"Who's this?" I nod to the punk next to her.

"This is Jeremy. These are my uncles Declan, Nolan, and Killian. And this is Simona," Fiona replies.

I reach for his hand and squeeze it as hard as I can, plastering a smile on my face while pinning my gaze on his. "Nice to meet you. You a senior?"

His jaw twitches. He attempts to let go of my hand, but I hold it a bit longer. As soon as I release it, Killian grabs it.

"Yeah, I'm a senior," he replies, but his voice cracks.

"Play sports?" Killian asks.

"He's the captain of the football team," Fiona gushes.

Of course he is.

How did Tully let this happen?

Killian's voice sounds chipper, but he's struggling to stay cool. "Fiona, why don't you and Simona go help Arianna with the kids' party while we talk sports with Jeremy."

She furrows her brows. "Girls can talk sports."

"Yeah, I know. But Simona said Arianna needed some help, didn't you?"

Simona puts her hand on Fiona's back. "Yep. Let's go give her a few minutes of our assistance."

That's my girl.

I'm rewarding her extra tonight.

"Okay. I'll be back," Fiona reluctantly tells Jeremy.

As soon as she's out of earshot, we circle Jeremy. Nolan asks, "How long have you been dating our niece?"

He smirks, and I curl my hands into fists, holding back from wiping it off his face. His voice is arrogant. It radiates off him and might as well be slapping me in the face. He states, "Awhile."

Killian steps closer. "What does that mean?"

Jeremy shrugs, his laser-sharp stare cutting into Killian's. "You know. Long enough."

"Long enough for what?" I snarl.

The cocksucker has some balls. I'll give him that.

He dares to respond, "You know."

Is this kid looking to be dragged down to Angelo's dungeon? I still haven't seen it yet or even know how to get there, but I'll figure it out in two minutes if needed.

I growl, "No, we don't. Why don't you fill us in?"

The server walks by with glasses of champagne. Jeremy's so bold, he reaches for one, then takes a long sip. It's no secret we all drank when we were sixteen. We grew up in a pub, but we still hid it from the adults. I'd like to believe he's just stupid, but it's not that. This kid is out to prove to us he's not intimidated by us and thinks he can do whatever the fuck he wants.

My pulse increases. I snarl, "Get out."

He arches an eyebrow. "Excuse me?"

"You heard me. Get the fuck out of this house. And stay away from my niece."

He laughs, as if we're a bunch of chumps, then downs the rest of the champagne. "I'll go when I finish spending time with Fiona." He attempts to step past us, but I grab him by the back of the neck, then drag him toward the door.

"What the fuck!" he shouts. His body flails while attempting to get out of my grasp.

"If I find out you come near my niece again, I'll hunt you down and skin you alive. You understand?" I glower.

"Is that a threat?"

I spin him in front of me, right near the entrance door. The bodyguards hover around it, watching, but don't interfere. I rip open the door then freeze, my heart pounding so violently, it might burst through my chest cavity.

Tully and Bridget's eyes widen.

"What the hell is going on, Declan?" Tully barks, his eyes roaming between Jeremy and me.

All the anger I've felt for years toward Bridget bubbles over, pulling me into a place I usually only feel before I sink my claws into our enemies.

Bridget's lips tremble and her eyes glisten. Time seems to stand still as we fixate on one another.

"Declan!" Tully exclaims.

I tear my eyes off Bridget, slightly relaxing my grip that got tighter around Jeremy's neck in the last few seconds. "Have you met this punk?"

"Yes," Tully cautiously says.

"Declan, let him go," Bridget demands.

Tornados full of wrath spin around me, whipping faster and faster until my skin is pulsing with it. I scowl at her. "You're not in a position to give orders."

"Watch it," Tully warns.

As much as I love Arianna and know Killian fell madly in love with her, I'm still pissed Tully tricked my brother into marrying her. While Killian may not deal in regrets, I don't forget so easily. Between that and his continuation of protecting Bridget when she's clearly in the wrong, my trust for him is gone. And how has he allowed this arrogant asshole whose neck I'm still squeezing to date his granddaughter?

"Fuck off," I growl. "Not only did he have his hands on Fiona's ass, but he also lipped off to my brothers and me. That was while he helped himself to a glass of Angelo's champagne."

Tully's ice-cold gaze cuts into Jeremy. The kid cringes, which only pisses me off more. He's scared of Tully but underestimates the O'Malleys. Well, the kid disrespected the wrong girl. He's an idiot not to have done his homework.

Tully's snarl is one he uses when he threatens someone before tearing them to shreds. "Are you stupid, son?"

Jeremy's face turns white. He swallows hard and clears his throat. "Sir, it was only one glass."

I shove him out the door, and he stumbles to stay on his feet. I growl, "Get the fuck out. Don't go near my niece ever again, or I'm coming for you. I guarantee you whatever fear you have of Tully will be grossly outmatched when I get my hands on you."

"Declan!" Bridget reprimands.

I spin and grab her elbow. "Finn needs to see you. Now."

"Get your hands—"

I release Bridget and spin on Tully. "You're both fucking up. We had to convince Sean not to emancipate himself from you. This all stops now, and shit gets cleared up, or you're going to lose your children. It won't be our fault."

Bridget covers her mouth, her face turning green. Tully says nothing, grinding his molars.

I motion to Angelo's study. "Now, Bridget."

She hesitates.

Years of emotions jeopardize revealing all the thoughts I've ever had regarding what Bridget has done. Yet, I hold it in, reminding myself repeatedly to do what is best for Fiona and Sean. I lean closer to her. "We're doing everything we can to stop Sean from cutting you off. Every breath we speak to him is about not hating you. I suggest you face up to what you've done and deal with us instead of what he will eventually do if this doesn't get worked out."

She blinks hard then closes her eyes. Tully steps forward and puts his palm on her back. He quietly orders, "Bridget, go into the study."

She squares her shoulders, holding her head high, avoiding looking at me as he leads her past. I turn to see my brothers scowling. Nolan has his arms folded across his chest. Killian's fists are clenched at his sides.

Dante steps out of the ballroom. His eyes dart to the three of us. "What's going on?"

"Bridget and Tully are in the study. I told her Sean's plans. Can you get Finn?"

He pauses then shakes his head. "No. Let me talk to Bridget first. Nolan, go get my father to deal with Tully."

"I'll find Finn," Killian states, and they leave.

Dante sniffs hard. "Bridget's a stubborn woman."

"No shit. She was once a part of us, unless you forgot," I snap.

He holds his hands out. "Easy."

I release a frustrated breath. "Sorry."

"It's okay. Let me talk to her first."

Seeing no other solution, I wait in the foyer, wondering how any of this will ever be right again, scared about the mistakes Sean might make.

"Calm down. She's scared." The words ring through the air, and a chill runs down my spine.

I spin, looking for my brother, Sean. It's the first time I've heard his voice since he died. Nolan and Killian admitted one night when they were drunk at the pub, they hear him at times, but I never have.

"I still love her. Always will," he says, and I spin again, goose bumps breaking out on my arms.

"Jesus. Fucking show yourself," I mutter, feeling a bit crazy.

His laugh fills my ears when Nolan arrives with Angelo at his side.

"What's wrong?" Nolan inquires, studying me.

I debate what to say without sounding like I lost all my marbles.

Angelo gazes at me then says, "I'm going to talk to Tully."

He walks away, and I pull Nolan to the side. "I just heard Sean."

He glances behind him. "Where is he?"

"No. Not Sean Jr., *Sean*." I stare at him, a lump the size of a baseball growing in my throat.

His eyes widen. "What did he say?"

I lick my lips and swallow. "He said she's scared and he still loves her. Always will."

Nolan looks at the ceiling, taking a deep breath. When his eyes meet mine, he rolls them. "He would say that."

Something about it makes me chuckle. He's right. Even in death, my brother would profess his love for Bridget.

Nolan's expression changes, as if a lightbulb went off.

"What's wrong?"

He slides his hand over his face. "Shit."

"What?"

"Maybe this entire time, we've been asking the wrong question."

"Meaning?"

"What if it isn't threats against O'Malleys Bridget is afraid of? What if it's threats against her?"

Every ounce of blood I have drains to my toes. Looking at Nolan, it's clear he's having the same reaction.

Killian comes back with Finn. "What's wrong with you two?"

Nolan and I exchange another glance. I reply, "I think we need to have a different conversation with Bridget," then I repeat everything Nolan and I just discussed.

Finn's hardened expression never changes. "This doesn't change anything for me. I need to know when and where she had the picture with Brenna taken."

"Agreed. Let us drill her first," I say.

Finn grumbles. "Fine."

We go into the study. Angelo is talking with Tully, and Dante is handing Bridget a glass of whiskey.

"It's time you told us who is coming after you, Bridget," Killian blurts out.

She flinches. It's only a second, but her attempt to hide it fails. "I don't know what you're talking about."

I step closer. "It's not threats against the O'Malleys you're scared of, is it?"

She grips the tumbler so tight, her knuckles turn white. "Of course it is."

I step closer and soften my tone. "Stop lying."

"I'm not."

"Bridget—"

"Does it have to do with Brenna?" Finn asks, surprising us all.

I snap my head toward him, wondering why he didn't say anything in the foyer if he suspected it. I sure as hell didn't.

Bridget's hand trembles. Her face scrunches. Her voice cracks, and my heart rips. No matter what she's done, she still feels like a sister to me. Sean's voice flies into my head, saying, *I love her,* at the same time she says, "Brenna?"

"Don't lie to me. I have the photo," Finn calmly states.

Her eyes widen, and she takes a step back.

"Bridget?" Tully questions.

Finn takes a deep, calculated breath. "You can all discuss the kids later. Everyone except Bridget out."

"I'm not leaving my daughter—"

"I'll stay with her," Dante says.

Finn's voice hardens. "No. Everyone out. You, too."

"Tully, let's go find the kids," Angelo states.

Tully points to Finn. "If you harm my daughter—"

"Don't threaten any of us, Tully. Get back on the same side like we used to be. Remember those days? O'Malleys and O'Connors? An alliance so strong, you allowed your daughter to marry into our family? Or did you forget about the son-in-law you claimed to love who fathered your grandchildren and would have given his last breath for them and your daughter?" Liam bellows, walking into the room, his green eyes glowing with disdain.

Angelo points to us all. "Everyone except Finn, Dante, and Bridget out. This is my house, and I make the rules. Now, out."

Finn sniffs hard but doesn't object again. I pat him on the back, about to leave, then stop.

Fuck this.

I tug Bridget into me. She's a piece of Sean and always will be. She's the mother of my niece and nephew, and whatever her reasons are for what she's done, I don't doubt for one minute she did it to protect them. I just don't know who she's protecting them, or her, from. I quietly confess, "No matter what's happened, I've missed you. We all have."

She breaks down, her body convulsing in sobs, and my heart cracks. I squeeze her tighter and shush her, but I can't stop wondering what her secrets are and how we could have missed asking the right question all of these years.

29

Simona

DECLAN SPEAKS IN A HUSHED TONE WITH HIS BROTHERS AND Liam. The back of his suit stretches across his body like a glove, accentuating his hardened flesh. I spend several minutes admiring him when a wave of nausea hits me.

I rush to the bathroom, shoving past the woman coming out and barely making it to the toilet before I toss my cookies.

"Simona!" Declan's voice hits my ears. He crouches next to me, holding my ponytail and rubbing my back.

Sweat pops out on my face, and I lean against him, closing my eyes.

Why does this keep happening?

Declan reaches around me and hands me a towel. When I take it, he presses his hand to my forehead. "Angel, how long have you felt sick?"

"Just now." I take a few breaths as the nausea leaves me. I wipe my mouth. "I'm okay. I'm sure it's the residual stress." I rise, turn on the water, and rinse with mouthwash.

Thank God for the rich. They have everything anyone needs at their disposal.

Declan's stare could be a laser cutting my skin. He declares, "I'm having Angelo call his doctor."

I spin to face him. "I'm fine. It's passed. Maybe I ate something bad."

"It's pointless arguing with me. Let's go upstairs."

"We'll miss the party!" I cry out. I don't remember the last time I went to a party. It had to have been in high school. Everything about this trip means more to me than anyone will ever know. I don't want to miss a minute of it.

"Party's over for us tonight."

"Declan—"

"I'm not looking to fight with you all night. The doctor will check you out."

I sigh and blink hard.

Declan cups my cheeks. Worry deepens the lines on his forehead. The vein above his eye pulses. "There will be other parties. Your health comes first."

I try to turn away, but he holds me firm.

"Simona—"

"I feel fine now!"

A tense moment passes. Declan's lips twitch, and his eyes twinkle. "If the doctor says you're fine, then I'll let you live it up all night."

I can't help a laugh.

He pecks me on the forehead. "Come on, angel."

There's a knock on the door, so I allow him to lead me out of the bathroom. When we get to the staircase, I say, "This really isn't necessary. I feel fine now."

"I'm having Angelo call his doctor."

"Simona, are you sick?" Nora asks, stepping in front of us.

I reply, "No," at the same time, Declan says, "She threw up."

"I'm fine!"

"You said that the last time you got sick," Declan says.

"When did you get sick last?" Nora asks.

"A long time ago."

Declan shakes his head. "No, it wasn't. It was last week."

"And I was fine then, too. I just got a little nauseous. I'm fine now. Can't we just enjoy the party?"

"After the doctor confirms you aren't sick." He pins his steely gaze on mine, but I don't back down. I feel the same as I always do, now that I got whatever bug in my system out.

Nora clears her throat.

We both glance at her.

She grabs my hand. "Simona, come with me. Declan, you stay here."

"What? Where are you taking her?" Declan asks.

"My room. Go talk to the men. We'll be back shortly."

"I'm calling the doctor."

"Just wait a minute," Nora instructs.

"No. Something is wrong—"

"I think Simona's pregnant," Nora blurts out.

Goose bumps pop out on my skin. I gape at her and put one hand on my stomach and the other one on the railing. All the times Declan and I had sex without any protection flash before me.

Oh my God.

I'm such an idiot.

Why didn't I get on the pill?

Why didn't I speak up and tell him to use a condom?

Declan's hand slides to the small of my back. He lowers his voice. "Nora, why do you think that?"

Nora chirps, "She's glowing. She went to bed first last night and was the last to wake up. Plus, she has morning sickness."

I can't look at either of them. I grasp the railing tighter, trying to steady myself.

Declan's thumb grazes my spine, and my lower body throbs.

I curse myself. I'm freaking out, might be pregnant, and thinking about sex. What the hell is wrong with me?

Declan calmly asks, "Do you have a test with you?"

"Yes. I picked an extra one up this morning when Boris and I went out."

"Nora, are you pregnant again?"

"No. I thought I was, but I'm not."

"Where's the test?" Declan asks.

"On the counter in our bathroom."

"Thanks. Let's go, angel."

With my insides shaking, I finally lock eyes with him.

I expect to see his vein twitching and some of the trepidation I'm feeling, but he's cool as a cucumber. My mouth turns so dry, the Sahara Desert has more moisture in it. He leans down and pecks me on the lips. In total control, as if he's not panicking at all, he guides me up the stairs.

Every step I take, I have to force myself to continue moving. If he weren't planted next to me, with his arm firm against my back, I'd fall down the stairs. The music from the party gradually gets quieter until we reach the wing we're staying in. Nothing except the blood pounding between my ears registers.

We go into Nora's suite, and Declan turns into me. He tucks a lock of hair that escaped my ponytail, behind my ear. "Are you okay?"

"I-I-I'm...what if...oh God!" I put my hand over my face.

Declan's arms wrap around me. "Everything will be fine, angel."

Panic seizes me. I glance up. "I'm not done with school. I-I don't even have a job. I can't support a baby. And what kind of mom would I make? I don't even know what a good one is like."

Declan tilts his head and cups my cheek. "You'll be a wonderful mom. And you're going into survival mode again. I have plenty to take care of you and a baby."

My eyes fill with tears. It's not about my school plans going up in smoke. It's about the visions of the few memories I have of my mother and all the shitty foster homes I grew up experiencing. A baby wasn't in my plans. I was supposed to go to school, get a decent job to support myself, and stop struggling.

"You're spinning out, angel," Declan softly says.

"Why are you so calm?"

He arches an eyebrow, palms my ass, and tugs me closer. "I've been careless where you're concerned. I didn't protect you. For that, I'm sorry. No woman's ever made me lose my senses the way you do. I've always worn a condom until you. If you're pregnant, it's my fault."

"I didn't stop you," I blurt out, not willing to let him take all the blame when I knew better.

He firmly states, "No. This is on me. But I'm not going to be sorry if you're pregnant. If any other woman told me she was, I would be. But you're my forever. So if you're pregnant,

I'm going downstairs, announcing it to everyone, and making a toast to the beautiful mother of my child."

I stare at him, still in shock and freaking out about how I'm capable of raising a child when I had zero good role models.

"Come on. Let's take the test and see what it says before you get sick again."

"I'm not—"

"You're pale. Take the test. You might not be."

I close my eyes and confess, "I am. I haven't had my period. I didn't think about it, but I should have gotten it the week you kidnapped me."

"As I stated, this is my fault. Let's take the test."

It's not his fault. I know this in my heart. We both played with fire, but I'm too stressed to keep arguing. I go into the bathroom, pee on the stick, and set it on the counter. I stare at it. Tears fill my eyes. I admit, "I don't want to be a bad mother."

He lifts me and sets me on the counter. His palms flatten on my thighs. "You'll be an awesome mother."

I shake my head. "I don't know how to be."

A sweet grin fills his lips. "You're amazing with Shannon. You have a knack, whether you realize it or not. You got shafted in the parent department, and that's why you'll make sure our kid doesn't."

Something about his confidence and how he says *our* kid, like it's the most natural thing on Earth, calms me a bit. Not all the way but maybe fifty percent back to not totally losing it.

His alarm beeps, and my butterflies spread their wings, fluttering a million miles a minute. He turns it off and stares at me.

"Shouldn't we look?" I ask but don't dare turn my head.

"That depends."

"On what?"

For the first time since Nora mentioned me being pregnant, nerves enter his eyes. "If you're pregnant, promise me you won't hate me."

Stunned, I reach for his face and cup his cheeks. "Why would I hate you?"

"This is my fault."

"I didn't exactly say no."

He licks his lips, guilt plaguing his expression. "I know better. I did nothing to protect you from this. I'm a grown man who should have the ability to think with his brain and not his dick."

"This took both of us," I claim.

"It's my fault."

"Did you knock me up on purpose?"

His eyes darken. "Of course not."

"Well, then it's not your fault. There are two of us, and we have equal amounts of blame."

His eyes close, and he slowly exhales, his breath heavy with culpability. When he opens his eyes, it pains me. "I chained you to my bed."

I don't need to think about my next statement. It flows out of my mouth because it's the truth. "I wanted every moment we spent together. Every touch, every kiss, every look you gave me."

He studies me, still not convinced.

I lean into his lips and kiss him, suddenly no longer flipping out. Everything will be okay. I have Declan. And he's right. I choose not to be a deadbeat mother. Whatever I don't know, I'll learn.

The moment our mouths touch, a fire blazes, spreading between us until it's burning us into nothing but ashes. We're no longer separate. Who am I kidding? We haven't been since the night we met. When I pull away, I smile. "Should we see if we're going to be parents?"

He grabs the test without taking his eyes off me. "Okay, angel. Whatever is on this stick, I'm going to be happy about it. And I'm not going anywhere."

My love for him deepens, hitting me at the core. I take a nervous breath and nod. "Okay. Me, too."

He pecks me on the lips then holds his palm up. We slowly gaze down.

Two pink lines run parallel to each other. My heart picks up speed. "Does that..."

He grins and pulls me in for another kiss. "Yeah. We're having a baby."

"Can you not make a toast?" I ask.

His eyes widen, as if I just sinned. "Why? I'm an O'Malley. This is what we do."

I laugh. "Can you save the toast until tomorrow when there aren't so many people?"

His blue eyes twinkle. "Okay."

"Can we go back to the party? I've never really been to one."

He drags his knuckles down my cheek, and I shiver. "All right, angel. But Nora's going to want to know."

"You can tell her."

"And my brothers, Liam, and Finn."

Amused, I arch my eyebrows. "You're like a kid in the candy store right now."

More happiness radiates off him, warming my heart further. He replies, "You said not to toast. You didn't say I couldn't tell anyone."

"That's true."

"Okay, angel. Let's get you to your party. I still have indecent things I'm planning."

I jump off the counter and tease, "Well, don't make me wait."

As we make our way through the house, I lean into Declan with a surprising sense of peace. The thought keeps spinning in my mind, *I'm having Declan's baby*. It's strange. I didn't plan it, but the more it repeats, the more it begins to feel like the right thing and not something to freak out or be unhappy about.

When we get into the ballroom, Liam hands Declan a crystal tumbler. He says, "Good news."

Declan tugs me closer and takes a sip of the whiskey. "News travels fast. Nora say something?"

Liam pins his eyebrows together. "Nora? How would she know about Giovanni?"

Declan freezes. "Giovanni?"

Liam nods. "It's been taken care of."

Declan's brothers circle us. Killian holds his glass in the air. "We finally did it."

"How did you find out?" Liam asks him.

Nolan answers, "I got an alert about the stock price."

Liam's eyes turn into an animal's glowing in the dark. "Stock price?"

Gemma steps next to Nolan, and he kisses her head. "You did it, princess."

"Did what?" she asks, confusion on her face.

Nolan grabs two glasses of champagne and hands one to Gemma and me. "You, too, Simona. We couldn't have done this without either of you. Thank you."

Gemma and I exchange a perplexed glance, and I inquire, "For?"

Nolan's face is the happiest I've ever seen. He glances at Killian, who also looks exceptionally joyful. Nolan sniffs hard. "I just told Gianluca to sell our short positions in Jack's company. The futures hit our price. By Friday, we'll have billions in our accounts."

30

Declan

SINCE FINDING OUT SIMONA IS PREGNANT, I CAN'T STOP grinning. I'm going to be a dad. Simona will be a great mother, and I've never felt like I had so many things to be grateful for this Thanksgiving.

The other great news was the icing on the cake. Liam's announcement that Giovanni Rossi is dead means Maria will have to surface soon. We may have taken Jack's company down, but she's still a threat we need to eliminate. She came after us. Our win doesn't negate our need to find out how she knew about our plan or stop her from trying to harm us in the future. Until I find out why the dean chose Simona to be her pawn, I won't rest easy.

New York would have been perfect if we didn't have the issues with Bridget, or Fiona didn't glare at me all weekend.

She was upset I threw her dickhead boyfriend out of the party. Bridget and Tully both forbade her to see Jeremy again, so at least I wasn't the only enemy, but it sucked having her hate me when I only just reconnected with her.

Bridget admitted to Finn she ran into Brenna a few years after he went to prison. She was visiting her family in New York. Finn drilled her for hours about where Brenna is, but she stuck to her story that she never saw her again. She claims Brenna was on the run and asked her to keep it between them that she saw her. Finn asked who took the picture, but Bridget seemed genuinely shocked there was one. She also kept saying she told Sean she saw Brenna when she returned to Chicago, but none of us bought it. Why would my brother have kept that from us? We all agree that he wouldn't have.

Bridget got tight-lipped and kept denying anyone was coming after her, stating it was our enemies she was worried about subjecting the kids to and reiterating Sean's death. Every time she mentioned my brother, grief would fill her expression. It hurt to see how much it still affected her, yet I also wasn't surprised. There's no way anyone could love as hard as Sean and Bridget did and not feel a lifetime of sorrow.

While we didn't get as much information out of her as we wanted, she did agree to let Dante train Sean in the Marino gym, as long as he didn't sign him up to compete. For now, we all took it as a win.

Well, all but Finn. He went over to Tully's after Thanksgiving dinner and had it out with Bridget again. It was pointless. She stuck to her story with more vigor than the previous night. Finn insists she's holding something back, and it's only frustrating him more.

When I left, Sean was happy. Fiona would barely hug me goodbye. After so many years of not seeing her, I hated that I had to leave with her pissed off at me. But if that kid attempts to come near her again, I will hunt his cocky ass down.

It's late when the plane lands. Our car finally pulls into my driveway a little while later. Exhaustion covers Simona's face. As soon as we get inside, we go to bed.

I tug her into my arms, stroking her back. She falls asleep quickly and doesn't wake up until after nine the following day.

I've been up for hours, worked out, and showered. I'm on my laptop when Simona walks into the room. She sneaks behind me and slides her hands over my shoulders.

I grab them and tilt my head. "Morning, angel. Did you sleep well?"

Her glowing expression lights me up further. She kisses my forehead. "Yep. I'm going to need to set the alarm from now on. Any later, and I would have missed my class."

The hairs on my arms rise. "Class?"

"Yeah. I need to go back today."

My pulse shoots toward the sky. "I don't think that's a good idea."

She furrows her eyebrows. "Why? The semester is going to be over soon. I have to return."

"We still don't know why the dean chose you to go on that site."

She sits in the chair next to me. "Declan, I have to go to class, especially now that I'm pregnant."

"What does being pregnant have to do with it?"

Red crawls into her face. "I want to finish my degree."

"Yes, I'm aware."

"I need to do it before the baby arrives."

"You will."

"Not if I don't get back in class. I need to arrange with my professors a time to make up all the hands-on assignments I missed. The email says I have to do it before the semester ends. It's not something I can do at home. If I don't schedule these, I'll miss the deadline," she says fretfully.

The vein in my eye pulses. "It's not safe—"

"You promised me I could go back. You said I needed to wait a week. It's been a week."

"I'm not comfortable with you returning. Until we find out why the dean chose you and locate Maria Rossi, it's not safe," I admit.

She shifts in her seat. "I'm going to flunk out if I don't go."

"You won't—"

"You don't know that! I only have two weeks left to make everything up," she cries out.

I scrub my beard, debating.

"Declan, what do I have bodyguards for if I can't use them?"

I sigh. "Listen to me. Your safety—our baby's safety—comes first."

Tears fill her eyes. "So I'm going to waste years of hard work?"

I run through options in my head. "Go get ready for class."

She freezes. "I can go?"

"Yeah. I'll come with you, as well as the guards. I'll make sure my brothers, Liam, or Finn are with you if I can't be. Just until we settle these other issues."

"You will?"

I kiss her. "Yes. Now stop worrying. It's not good for you or the baby."

Relief floods her face. "Thank you."

I rise. "What time is your class?"

"In an hour."

I groan. "Hurry up, then. I'll make you some food for the road."

"I'm not hungry."

"Too bad. You're eating," I tell her. "And don't fight with me on this, too."

She softly laughs. "Okay. You win, Daddy." She rises on her tiptoes and pecks me on the lips.

I pat her ass. "Go on."

She practically skips over to the bedroom. I text her bodyguards to be ready. Then I make a breakfast sandwich for her, go into the bedroom, and pull a bracelet out of my safe.

Simona walks into the closet with a towel wrapped around her.

"Hold your wrist out."

She obeys but asks, "Why?"

"For this."

Her eyes widen. "What's this for?"

I chuckle. "I could lie and say I got it for you, but it has a tracker in it."

She smirks. "Stalker."

"It's for your protection. Just in case."

"Okay. Thanks." She studies it and traces the delicate platinum. "It's pretty."

"Glad you like it. Get dressed, or you'll be late." I go to leave, but she stops me.

"Hey."

"Yeah?"

Her big blue eyes swirl with so many things. Happiness. Love. Excitement. She puts her arms around my neck. "Thanks for not fighting me anymore about this."

"I know how important it is to you."

"It is."

I squeeze her ass. "Hurry up before I change my mind."

She releases me and gets changed. I grab my gun then conceal it with my jacket. We leave and get into the car.

I pass her the sandwich I made. "Be a good girl and eat."

"Mmm. I'm glad you made this. I'm starving all of a sudden." She takes a bite.

I open a bottle of water and hand it to her.

"You're going to get me used to not doing anything."

My phone rings, and I glance at the screen. "I need to take this."

"No worries. I'll be eating."

I answer, "Liam."

"Get to the warehouse."

My chest tightens. I speak in code. "Did all of Italy fall?"

"Not yet, but the universities are about to."

Jesus. He has her.

"I need to take Simona home. I'll be there soon." I hang up.

"I'm going to class," she says before I can get a word out.

"No, you aren't." I roll the divider down. "Back home then to the warehouse." I raise the glass.

"What's the warehouse?"

Shit. "Forget you heard me say that."

"I need to go to class."

I pin my gaze on hers. "I'm sorry, but you can't go today. I wouldn't stop you if this weren't necessary."

"Why? What's going on?"

"It's not safe. I might be gone a few days. I want you to stay in the house—"

"What about my doctor's appointment?"

My heart sinks. There's nothing more important than Simona and our baby. But I have to take care of this threat hanging over her head. "You need to cancel. Reschedule it for later in the week."

Disappointment crosses her face.

I cup her cheeks. "Angel, we're going to be one step closer to eliminating the threats against you. This isn't something I can skip out on. It takes priority."

Her eyes widen. "Did you find Maria?"

"No."

"The dean?"

I stay silent.

"Does your lack of an answer mean I'm right?"

I continue to silently look at her.

She sighs. "Will you really be gone for days?"

"I don't know. Hopefully not. I'll have the other women come stay with you."

She shakes her head. "No. I'm fine. I have school work I can do. It was fun hanging with them over the weekend, but it'll just be a distraction. I can get ahead so I only have to do the missed hands-on assignments."

The car pulls up to the house. "Okay. I'm sorry about this. I'll make it up to you."

She nods. "I know. I'll see you soon. Be safe." She pecks me on the lips and hops out of the car.

I follow her, open the front door, then give her a deeper kiss. Another car pulls into the driveway and Tiernan gets out. I turn back to Simona. "Make sure you eat every few hours. Don't go anywhere. If you need anything, text Tiernan."

She wrinkles her nose. "I think he's still pissed at me for hurting him."

"No, he's not. I told you he understands why you did it."

"Is that why he's scowling?"

I glance back. He's watching us with his arms crossed.

"No, angel. He's just pissed off at the world right now. But it's not directed at you."

She doesn't look convinced.

I hug her, wait until she locks the front door, and go to Tiernan. "I'm going to the warehouse. It might be a few days. Make sure Simona has whatever she needs."

"Did you take away the steak knives?" he smirks.

I slap the back of his head. "Don't get smart. We've discussed why she stabbed you."

He rolls his eyes. "Whatever."

"Hey! Am I able to trust you while I'm gone?"

His eyes turn to slits. "Trust me? Tell me you didn't ask me that."

Tension fills the air. Neither of us flinches as we stare the other one down. I finally admit, "She did try to kill you."

He grunts.

"She's also pregnant."

His eyes widen. "It's yours?"

"Of course it's mine, you dumbass," I growl.

He puts his hands in the air. "Easy. I was just asking."

"Don't ask stupid questions."

He yanks open the back door. "Go. I've got this covered. Congratulations. I'll make sure I look after your baby mama."

"Don't be disrespectful."

"How am I being disrespectful?"

I shake my head and get in the car. "I don't have time for a discussion on respect. We'll discuss this later."

He grunts. "Or not." He slams the door shut. I almost open it but decide against it. Tiernan's not been himself since our cousin Fergal died. His ego's a bit hurt from Simona stabbing him, too. I decide it's better if I just let it go for now. Plus, it was dumb of me to ask if I can trust him. I already know he'd jump in front of a bullet if needed to protect any O'Malley or our women, including Simona.

I'm halfway to the warehouse when it starts to snow. It makes the journey longer than usual. The entire time, I wonder how much the dean knows about Maria Rossi. Can she lead us to her? Does she know the real reason Maria chose Simona? Or did Maria only tell her to select an intelligent student?

There are too many variables, and my only hope is we find useful information and quickly. When the car pulls inside the warehouse, I get out and go down to the basement.

Liam's outside the fourth cell, talking to my brothers.

"Why aren't you inside?" I ask.

"We're debating," Liam replies.

"About what?"

"Putting Professor Milliken in the same room as the dean."

The sound of dripping water fills the air. We've kept the professor fed, given him a bed to sleep on, and let him shower. It's the nicest treatment we've ever offered any of our prisoners. From what he told us, he's an innocent victim in this charade and just as much the dean's pawn as Simona. We'll allow him to return to his everyday life once this is all figured out, if he truly is innocent. Of course, it'll include a severe threat, a paper trail showing he was sick with a horrible version of some virus Doc will pick out, and monitoring for at least a year to make sure he doesn't go to the police. Liam has the captain under his thumb, but the fewer issues we have, the better.

"I think it's a bad idea. If he's going to reenter society, the less he witnesses, the better," I state.

"I agree," Liam says.

Killian shifts on his feet. "She might sing more if he's in the room."

"No. We leave him and deal with her. We'll keep that on the back burner," I state.

"If he—"

"It's my woman. The mother of my child. I get to make the first call," I remind him.

Killian scrubs his face. "Fine. Arianna has her first event tomorrow night. I don't want to miss it, so let's work quickly."

We go into the cell. The dean sits in the chair, her mouth covered with duct tape, restrained, just like how we had the professor. My stomach flips. I've never interrogated or tortured a woman before—if you don't count what I did to Simona. The expressions on my brothers' and Liam's faces, while intimidating, aren't the same as usual. We're all in unfamiliar territory.

She put my angel in danger.

She's in cahoots with Maria Rossi.

The devil in me claws his way out of my gut until I only see my angel's face, our unborn baby, and red. I stand in front of the dean for several minutes, watching her face scrunch with anxiety.

I crouch down, so I'm eye to eye with her, and yank off the duct tape, then pull out the gag. I toss it to Nolan. "Add some gasoline to this. If she doesn't answer each of my questions honestly, I'm sticking it back in her mouth."

Her lips tremble, eyes dart between all of us, and a tear drips down her cheek.

I drag my finger up until it's right underneath her eye. "You knew who I was when I met with you, didn't you?"

She blinks hard and doesn't answer me.

Liam hands me black leather gloves, and I put them on. I hold my palm out, and Nolan places the gasoline-doused rag in my hand. I move it in front of her nose, and she gags, turning her head.

I yank her chin in front of me. I bellow, "You think you can avoid me?"

More tears fall, and she continues coughing. I intentionally smear the rag on the bottom of her nose and jump back.

She throws up, and Killian claps, shouting, "Bravo. So dramatic. Now fucking speak, or I'll move my brother out of the way and ram it down your throat."

She sobs out, "Why am I here?"

Liam pats her head. "Shhh. You know why you're here. Stop playing stupid. She can't save you. The only one who can is you."

"Sh-sh-she'll kill me."

I laugh. It's a crazed, out-of-control snicker that incorporates all the rage I'm feeling. "She'll kill you? What do you think we'll do? Now, tell me why you selected Simona, or I promise you, what we do to you will make Maria's threats of death look like a cakewalk."

She hesitates, and I pinch her cheeks so her mouth opens, bringing the rag toward it.

A muffled noise fills the room, and I freeze. "You ready to talk?"

She nods and cries more.

I release her but keep the rag in her eyesight. "Tell me now. Why Simona?"

"M-M-Maria chose her."

My chest tightens so much, I can barely breathe. Fear crawls over my skin. "Why? How does she even know about her?"

The dean's eyes glass over, and I realize I'm holding the rag too close. I step back and nod to Nolan. He brings a bottle of water and has her drink some.

"Tell me," I demand.

Her short breaths make it hard to decipher her words, but I strain my ears to listen. She stumbles over her words as she says, "Sh-she d-didn't say."

"Liar!" I roar.

The dean shakes her head hard and hyperventilates more. My gut sinks as I watch, wondering if she's telling the truth.

I switch gears for a moment. "How did you meet Maria?"

"I-I met her at a party. She scheduled a meeting to make a donation."

"You put my angel at risk for money?" I growl.

A river falls down her face, but it only makes me angrier. Her job is to protect students, not put them in harm's way. All she cares about is her precious library wing.

She blurts out, "I asked her what the site was and why she wanted me to do it, and she said if I didn't, she would kill me. She even has someone following me."

"Of course she does. You took money from her. She's a Rossi. What the fuck did you think would happen?" Killian belts out.

"Why Simona?" I repeat in a snarl.

"I don't—"

I fist her hair and jerk her head back. "Tell me now!"

She cries out, "She didn't tell me! I asked, but she didn't tell!"

"What did she say when you asked her? Be very clear, and don't leave out anything." My face is so close to hers, I smell the gasoline I smeared on her nose. Her stale breath hits mine, churning my stomach, so I swallow the bile down.

"Sh-she said 'that isn't your business, but let's just say I have a personal interest in what's mine.'"

I stare at the dean's face, attempting to interpret what Maria could mean. Why would she claim Simona was hers? I demand, "What else?"

"N-nothing. I swear! Please don't kill me!"

The unleashed devil in me stirs with a vengeance so intense, I'm suddenly afraid I no longer have any boundaries. I tug her head back farther. "What else?"

"Nothing!" she screams.

"Declan!" Liam shouts.

I release the dean and spin, striding out of the cell as quickly as possible, needing to get away from her before I do something too early.

The door slams behind me, and Liam opens his mouth, but my phone rings.

A new terror rushes through my cells. It's the ringtone I have for the guards watching my house. They know I'm here and not to interrupt. So why are they calling?

I answer, "What?"

"There's a problem. Tiernan followed Shay into the house and hasn't come back out. We tried to go inside, but the bolts are thrown on every door. Something isn't right."

"Why was Shay inside?" I ask, rushing toward the elevator, my heart squeezing with trepidation. There's no reason for one of our drivers to be in the house. He wasn't even on duty today.

"That's what Tiernan was going to find out."

"I'm on my way. Bust a window if you have to." I hang up and run to my car the moment the elevator door opens.

I try to call Simona, but it rings and goes to voicemail. I attempt Shay and Tiernan, but the same thing happens.

"Fuck!" I scream, not knowing what's going on but feeling like my entire world is about to implode. The only thing I know is that Shay has no reason to be inside my house right now.

31

Simona

An Hour Earlier

WITHIN MINUTES OF DECLAN LEAVING, THE SOUND OF THE garage door opening then shutting rings in my ears. I just got my laptop set up on the desk so I can study. I rise and walk down the hall. "Did you forget—" I freeze.

Maria Rossi stands in the room. Her long black hair is in curls and her cheekbones are high. Confidence radiates from her shining blue eyes. But there's a coldness in her expression. Goose bumps pop out on my skin as she studies me, her mouth curling on both sides.

My stomach flips, and I put my hand on it as I lean against the wall. I attempt to steady myself from the wave of nausea hitting me. My voice breaks as I try to figure out what I can use to protect myself. "What are you doing here?"

She steps closer, but I'm cornered. There's nowhere to go. Her voice is silk cascading through the air. "I've waited all these years."

"For what?" I ask in confusion, dread rolling through me as I ponder how she even knows who I am, much less how she's known me for years.

She reaches for my face, and I recoil. A sarcastic laugh flies out of her mouth, but it's short. She strokes my hair, peering at me closer. "It's amazing how much of our genes you have."

"Wh-what?"

Her floral perfume flares in my nostrils, spinning my stomach faster. "Oh, poor, poor little girl. Tell me. What is it about him that made you run into his arms after he kidnapped you?"

I gape at her, my mouth turning dry.

She slides her hand over mine, and I realize I'm still holding my stomach. "Is it the absence of your father that makes you stay? Does he fill some need you think you have? I have to admit, I'm rather shocked. I thought you were a fighter, but the first signs of a man with some money, and you can't even say no when he took away your freedom."

I push her hand off mine, which only makes her step closer, the toe of her heels butting up against to my shoeless feet. "This distraction is now over."

I square my shoulders, tilting my chin to look her in the eyes. "What do you want from me?"

She strokes my cheek, as if she somehow cares about me.

Repulsion cracks through my strength, giving away my need to get sick. My hand flies to my lips, and I turn and swallow down bile.

"Morning sickness?" she asks.

My heart hammers in my chest. *How does she know I'm pregnant?*

She steps back. "Go."

I run to the bathroom and heave into the toilet. She follows me, holds my hair, rubs my back, and acts like she's my best friend.

To say I'm bewildered would be an understatement. I'm so perplexed about what is happening, I'm unsure if I should be afraid of her or not.

She's a Rossi. I can't let her fool me.

After I wash my mouth out and find my balance, I spin, somehow finding strength. In a cold tone, I ask, "Why are you here?"

She tsks me, shaking her head, her eyes morphing into sympathetic craziness. It's almost hypnotic to watch, but the warning bells ring louder in my head.

She's a psychopath.

"Maria—"

"Aunt Maria would be more appropriate."

Blood drains from my face. More puzzle pieces appear. I try to put them together, but the edges aren't right, and nothing fits.

Her laugh echoes against the tile. "I see I've confused you."

"What. Do. You. Want?" I hurl at her again.

"I see you have a bit of fire in you. You get that from me, definitely not that junkie of a mother you had or your father." She winks.

My heart tightens, skipping too many beats, hearing her mention my parents. Against my will, I play right into her hand. "What do you know about them?"

She licks her lips, studying me. "Everything."

"How?"

A sadistic smile forms on her face, and a chill digs into my bones. "Your father was my brother."

I gasp. *No. It can't be. She's lying.*

"Aww. Tsk, tsk, tsk. You don't believe me?" she taunts.

My entire body quivers. I struggle to keep on my feet. "Who is your brother?"

"Was. Who *was* my brother."

I close my eyes and take a few breaths, cradling my stomach again, as if I could protect my baby from whatever this twisted scenario is.

She continues, "My brother Lorenzo. He's dead, just like the tramp of a mother who delivered you."

Pain slices quickly through my heart. Except for a brief moment in time, I never knew my mother. My father's always been a mystery. My birth certificate says *unknown* in the box for father's name. I can't speak or move. A lump grows in my throat, almost choking me.

Maria keeps speaking like she's waited forever for this moment. Maybe she has. She says, "My brother knocked your mother up at a party. Lorenzo knew our father wouldn't allow a woman like your mother into our family."

Against my will, tears slide down my cheeks. "Why? What was so wrong with her?"

Maria tilts her head, assessing me. "She was a shitty mother. She couldn't keep you longer than a few days, yet you still show emotion for her?"

I turn, wiping my face, wishing I knew what all this was about and how to get past Maria. I shouldn't play into her game, but she seems to have the answers to the questions I've had my entire life. "How long have you known about me?"

Her blue eyes turn to ice. "Forever. Every home you've ever been in, I've kept tabs on. Each move you've made to try and escape it all, I've watched. You've done well. That's the Rossi in you. But now, you're getting off track."

It's a reminder she's dangerous and I need to find a weapon. I rack my brain about what's in the bathroom, but nothing deadly comes to mind. "Off track?"

She nods. "You're smart. I'll take the credit for that. Thank your lucky stars you didn't get my brother or your mother's brains. You got mine. Every test I gave you, you passed with flying colors. But then you tried to fuck me, didn't you?"

I open my mouth but shut it, swallowing hard. Time seems to stand still with her pointed gaze pressing into me. I finally repeat, "What do you want?"

"You're getting back on track."

I shake my head. "I don't know what you're talking about."

She steps closer, her perfume strengthening with each inch, making me queasy again. Her voice is hail raining down on me, pounding into my skin until it's raw. "You work for me. Not him."

"I don't—"

Men's voices reach my ear. I think one of them is Tiernan. The other's sounds familiar, but I can't put my finger on it.

Maria's eyes widen and she spins, leaving the room.

I follow her, but my eye catches on my pink razor.

That's it.

I open the drawer and pull out a new, straight razor blade. I've only seen Declan use it a few times, but I take it and leave as the shouting gets louder.

Gunfire rings through the air.

I change my mind, run into the bedroom, lock the door, then push the dresser across the wood floor until it's against the door.

My entire body is shaking as more gunfire blasts in my ears. I sink against the dresser, put my shaking hands over my ears, and try to think about how to get out of here alive.

Time seems to stand still. There's a pound on the door, and Tiernan's voice shouts, "Simona!"

I don't respond, not sure if it's safe to open it or not.

"Simona! Are you okay? Tell me she didn't hurt you!" he calls out, pounding on the door when I refuse to answer.

My pulse races, and I pull my knees to my chest, wishing I had my phone or some way to contact Declan.

More muffled men's voices, some familiar, some not, leak through the door. I can't make out what they're saying.

Tiernan yells, "Simona! Please tell me if you're okay!"

When I don't answer, the sound of an electric screwdriver buzzes. The metal handle clinks, and one of the guys says, "Shit. Something is against the door."

So much fear fills me, I lose control of my emotions. I start to sob, praying Declan will come home but knowing he's possibly gone for several days.

I'm unsure how much time passes. I'm still hysterical, drowning out all their voices and pleas, when Declan's voice booms, "Simona! Angel, tell me you're in there?"

I pick my head up.

"Simona!" he roars.

"Declan?" I cry out, rising.

"Angel! Are you okay?"

"Yes. I-I...what's going on?"

"Open the door for me, angel."

"Is she gone?"

"Yes. Open the door, angel," he orders again.

I rise and push the dresser out of the way. The handle crashes to the floor as the door swings open.

Declan flies into the room, his face colorless, and pulls me into his arms. His heart pounds against my head. "Did she hurt you?"

"No. I'm okay."

"Thank God!" He holds me tighter.

I cry all over again. "Is-is she dead?"

He holds his palm against my head, kissing my hair. "Yes. So is Shay."

Surprised, I glance up. "Shay? Why is Shay dead?"

Declan's face hardens. "He must have been working for her. He drove into the garage and shut the door. She had to have been in the back seat."

More chills run through my body.

"Did Tiernan—"

"Yes. He shot them both."

I inhale deeply, feeling like I can breathe again. Then everything Maria said comes rushing back. "Where is she?"

"The guys are taking care of the bodies."

I shake my head. "Go cut a handful of her hair."

Declan's eyes widen. "Why would I do that?"

Tears fall again. "She said her brother is my father and he's dead. I want a DNA test."

32

Declan

Several Weeks Later

"HERE'S WHAT'S GOING TO HAPPEN. YOU'RE GOING TO TALK TO all the professors. They'll give Simona the final exams. If she passes, she gets her degree now," I tell Dean Whitehouse, sitting back in the chair and nursing a glass of whiskey.

She closes her eyes briefly, which only angers me.

"There's no choice. If you want to live, you make this happen. If Simona doesn't pass the tests with flying colors, she takes the courses next semester as if this never happened." I take two mouthfuls of whiskey, relishing the burn as it travels to my gut.

"The professors all have their own requirements for students. It's not as easy as—"

"I don't give a damn. You'll make it happen, or you're going back to the cell. Only this time, I'll stretch out your life for years." I down the rest of my drink and rise. "Consider this your penance."

Hatred fills her face, but she also wears the expression of a woman trapped. It's appropriate since she is. After what she subjected my angel to, she's lucky to be back in her luxury home with her cushy job.

"Tonight. I want Simona to get the email before her head hits the pillow."

"That's impossible!"

I open the door and pin my gaze on her, watching her crumple underneath it. When she winces, I smile. "Do you need a reminder of how long gasoline stays in your nostrils, flaring at all hours, curdling your stomach?"

She puts her hand over her gut and scrunches her face.

"I didn't think so. Tonight, or you return to the cell." I leave and get in my car.

Simona finished all her classes and passed. There's only a week until Christmas. The other night, Simona said she wished she could take her exams for the final four courses she's enrolled in for next semester, claiming she would pass them. So, I decided to pay the dean a visit, who was only released from the cell four days ago.

I drive to the house and go inside. "Simona!"

"In the bedroom."

My panic decreases. Ever since Maria got to her, I struggle to leave her even though the threat is over. I go into the bedroom.

Simona's putting her knee-high boots on. She zips them, rises, and beams. "I'm all ready!"

I wrap her in my arms and kiss her. "You look gorgeous, as always."

She bats her eyelashes. "It's all the new clothes."

"Nope. It's just you."

Blue twinkles in her orbs. She pecks me on the lips. "Okay! I'm ready!"

I chuckle. "So you said. Let's go, angel."

We spend the evening picking out a tree and Simona's first ornament. It's an angel. The moment I saw it, I had to buy it for her. Only one of the foster homes Simona lived in had a tree. I'm determined to give her an amazing Christmas, mixing my family traditions with some new ones of our own.

When we return to the house, I bring up the box of lights and ornaments from the basement. I put holiday music on, and we spend several hours decorating the Scotch pine Simona chose.

After the last ornament goes on, I turn off all the lights, leaving the ones on the tree lit.

"It's so pretty," she softly states and curls into my side.

I kiss her head, stroking her cheek. "You picked the right one." I slide my hand under her shirt, caressing my thumb over her stomach.

She tilts her head and opens her mouth, but her phone dings. "Ugh. I'm turning that off."

I reach for the cell on the table and hand it to her. "Nope. Read your email."

She pins her eyebrows together. "Why?"

I chuckle. "Just do it."

She reluctantly takes the phone, swipes the glass, then reads it. Several moments pass until she looks at me, but I don't see the excitement I expected. Blue slits glare at me. She sits up. "What did you do?"

"Why aren't you happy?"

"Answer my question."

"I told the dean to allow you to take the final exams. If you pass with flying colors, you get to graduate. If you don't, you take the courses next semester as if it never happened."

She shakes her head. "I don't want a degree I didn't earn."

"Don't be ridiculous. You've earned it. If you already know the material, then why waste your time? Take the exams," I say.

"It's not right."

"Why? If you pass the exams on your own, then there's no point making you take the classes."

She rises and paces the room, tugging at her hair.

"Simona, this is an opportunity. What's the real problem?" I ask.

She spins. "I don't want to be a cheater."

"You aren't cheating. They aren't giving you the answers."

Red crawls up her neck and into her porcelain cheeks. She scrunches her face. "I'm trying to be a good person so our child is one."

I slide my hands on her hot face. "You are a good person. Our child will be as well."

She squeezes her eyes shut.

"Angel, what's going on?"

She wipes at a tear, whispering, "I got the results. It's true. I have their blood."

My heart almost stops. "Why didn't you tell me?"

"I didn't want it to ruin our night."

I sigh. "You should have told me, angel."

Her lips tremble. "I don't want it to be real. I hoped she was lying."

I tug her into me. "It doesn't change who you are."

She retreats. "Doesn't it?"

"No. You're my angel. The mother of my child. The woman I'm crazy about, who's so damn smart, she's going to pass her final courses without even attending class."

She tilts her head, and an exasperated glow erupts on her features.

"Don't look at me like that. It's true."

Her lips twitch. "You're impossible."

"You still love me."

Her eyes glisten. "Yeah, I do."

I kiss her, deep and hungry, as if it's the last kiss I'll ever give her. When I end it, I murmur, "Take the exams."

She stares at me.

"When you pass, we can talk about your new job with O'Malley Cybersecurity."

She laughs. "I haven't told you what I want to do yet."

"Pass your exams, and we'll create whatever position you want."

"Just like that?"

"Yep. Besides, don't you want to secure your role before someone else slides into it?"

Her eyes widen. "You better not give my position away!"

"We've got a business to grow. I can't wait forever," I tease, but I'll wait as long as I need to for her.

A heavy exhale falls from her lips.

"Simona, take the exams," I sternly order.

She bites on her lip then replies, "It would be nice not to have to go through the motions."

"That's my girl!"

"Don't get too excited. I didn't say I would do it."

I lean into her ear. "If you say yes, Daddy will reward you tonight."

Her face flushes, and her chest rises slowly. She bites on her lip again, and my testosterone flares.

"Daddy's ready to throw some holiday spirit on you."

"Holiday spirit?"

"Yep. But not unless you tell me you'll take the tests." I arch my eyebrows, waiting for her to give in.

She stays quiet.

I drag my knuckles down her cheek, neck, and through her cleavage, not stopping until I'm on her mound. "Daddy's ready to play. Tell me you'll do it."

"Okay. Fine. I'll do it. Are you happy now?"

I smirk. "Nope. I'll be happy when you get naked. Now get your sexy ass in the bedroom."

She wiggles her bottom and glances back at me, her lips pursed. As soon as she gets into the bedroom, she strips. In a breathy voice, she asks, "What now, Daddy?"

"Stand right there." I reach under the bed and pull out red and green chains, then wrap them around her body, my cock swelling. She's a work of art, the only gift I'll ever need. I've never seen anyone more beautiful than her, and the heavy look in her eyes drives me insane.

I kiss her gently on the lips, rubbing a chain link on her pebbled nipple while murmuring, "Should I restrain you?"

She whimpers. "Please."

"Merry Christmas, angel."

"Merry Christmas, Daddy."

And that's all it takes for me to get her exactly where I want her—naked, at my mercy, begging me to make her so high, she can't see straight.

All night, I'm a greedy man, unsure who's more insatiable. I ravish her with tidal waves of orgasms, letting her sleep before waking her up again, only to take and give some more.

Several days later, on the 23rd, she takes her final exams. The same day, the professors grade them. When her results come through the portal, an email comes with it.

Dear Ms. Carter,

Congratulations. It's my pleasure to inform you that based on your GPA, you are the valedictorian for this school year. Graduation will occur on January 25th. I invite you to give a speech during this wondrous occasion. My office will send more information when we resume sessions in the new year.

Have a wonderful holiday.

Dean Whitehouse

I read the letter and pick her up, spinning her around. "You did it!"

She laughs. "This is crazy!"

"No, it isn't! You earned it. I'm so proud of you, angel." I kiss her then set her feet on the floor.

Her expression lights up. "Can we talk about my position now?"

"Not yet. Put on a dress. I'm taking you to dinner to celebrate. We can talk there."

"Mmm...is this another dinner HR won't approve of?" she teases.

I squeeze her ass. "It's *definitely* a dinner HR won't approve of."

"Great! I'm in," she chirps, spins, and leaves the room.

I make a reservation at the same place we had our first date, noting she's pregnant, and to have non-alcoholic champagne in the room.

When we get to dinner, we spend several hours talking about what she wants to do. Once again, she surprises me, telling me about all the programs she already created that should be patented.

"Tomorrow, we're finding the best patent attorney there is," I insist.

"Really?"

"Yes. Angel, I've never lied about your brain. You're the smartest woman I know. If this is what you want, I think you should head up new technology with Nolan. He'll be ecstatic to hear about what you're into."

She puts her hand on her stomach. It's something she often does, and every time she touches it, my heart soars thinking about our little one growing in her belly. "You're serious?"

"Yes. Of course I am."

"Just like that?"

I swallow a mouthful of whiskey. "Yep." I trail the back of my nails down her arm. "Now, let's talk about extracurriculars."

She laughs. "Is this where we have crazy office sex during your lunch break?"

I shrug. "I'm good for coffee breaks, too."

She elbows me, laughing.

We dance for a while then go home. When we get in bed, she snuggles into my chest, tracing my compass tattoo. "The stores are probably going to be crazy tomorrow, aren't they?"

Since we've had so much going on, we haven't gone Christmas shopping. Everyone is getting together and exchanging gifts tomorrow night at Boris and Nora's.

"Yep. We'll be spending the day fighting the crowds."

I expect her to groan, but she yawns and says, "Sounds fun." She snuggles in closer to me.

I kiss her head. "Go to sleep, angel. Tomorrow will be an exciting day."

She kisses my chest and, within minutes, is asleep.

Butterflies spread their wings and furiously flutter as I open the drawer next to my bed and take out the velvet box. I open it, staring at the brilliant sparkle of the three-carat pear-shaped diamond set over the crisscross split shank, which has more diamonds over it. I have a closet full of presents I'm putting under the tree for Christmas morning, but I want her to have this today.

My gaze slides to Simona, sleeping peacefully with a tiny smile on her lips. My heart swells, and nothing has ever felt so perfect in my life.

I don't sleep much, replaying too many times what I want to say, worrying I won't relay everything I want her to know about how I feel about her.

When the darkness of night turns into morning, she stirs and sleepily glances up, her smile still on her lips. "Hey."

I close my fist with the ring in it and kiss her. "Morning, angel."

"Have you been awake long?"

"Little while. Guess what?"

"What?"

"It's Christmas."

Her grin explodes. "Isn't that tomorrow?"

"Nope. Celebrations begin today."

She climbs on top of me and cups my cheeks. "I see why everyone loves the holidays now."

"Yeah?"

She nods. "What time do we need to leave for shopping?"

"Not until later. I have something for you now though."

She raises her eyebrows and bites her lip. "Oh?"

My nerves spin. I tuck a lock of her hair behind her ear, suddenly tongue-tied and not remembering a word I recited all night. I very ineloquently blurt out, "I love you."

"I love you, too."

"No. I love you. More than anything or anyone on Earth, I love you."

Her eyes glisten. "I feel the same about you."

My pulse shoots through the roof. "Does that mean you'll marry me?"

Her mouth hangs open as my heart races. She finally says, "Are you asking me?"

I briefly close my eyes. "Shit. Sorry. Jeez. I'm not very good at this. Yes. Will you marry me?"

Tears fall, and she caresses my cheek. Then she speaks, and nothing has ever sounded so sweet. "Yes. I want you forever, Declan."

I blink hard, wondering how I managed to keep her through all the craziness of our beginning.

She scoots up and kisses me until I'm so hard, I groan.

I mutter against her lips, "Do you want to see your ring?"

She sniffles while laughing and nods.

"Give me your hand, angel."

She holds it out, and I slide it on. It's a perfect fit, and I do a mental high five. I wasn't sure what size her ring finger was and had to guess.

She gapes at it, and her warm tears fall on my chest. "I love it. It's perfect."

"Yeah?"

She nods, staring at it, then kisses me again, wrapping me in all her love.

I might be the devil who stole the angel, but somehow the tables turned.

The angel robbed every piece of me, including the things I thought no longer existed.

She has my heart and soul. And until the day I die, I'll spend every moment loving her hard.

EPILOGUE

Simona

One Month Later

THE GLARE FROM THE STAGE IS BLINDING, BUT I FOCUS ON Declan the entire time. All the O'Malleys showed up, and so did the Ivanovs, who I've gotten to know well over the last month. Every graduate got four tickets, but Declan secured the first set of rows, in the middle, directly in front of the stage.

I can only imagine what he did to get them.

He winks at me, and I take another deep breath. I've never given a speech before. It's one of the most nerve-racking things I've ever done. But Declan reminded me I've done much more complex things in my life and always succeeded. So I reread the email stating I was to give the graduating class "practical advice" and spent days writing it. Then, for weeks, I kicked Declan out of the house and practiced it. Now, here I am, in the middle of my speech, talking to all these students who have never spoken to me.

I clear my throat and continue. "Sometimes, you aren't sure why things happen or what the purpose is. But in every bad situation, there's always light somewhere. You may not know what it is right away, but eventually, if you look hard enough for it, it always shines."

I blink hard then stand straighter. "I used to be afraid of the dark then I learned how to lean into it and gain strength from it. So my only advice to you is, during tough times, eliminate the darkness and find the light. Sometimes that light might feel just as confusing as the darkness. Sometimes others won't understand either, but if you do everything you can to embrace it, all it does is grow brighter. Thank you."

The room rises in applause, and I continue focusing on Declan, the one person in the room who truly understands my words. It was supposed to be a speech for my class, but I now realize I wrote it for him as a way to express who we are.

We had darkness, and now we have light. I'm not naive enough to think there isn't more darkness residing in Declan, waiting to pop out at a moment's notice. Yet, for every situation it crawls out of him, there's always a light waiting to shine through. Maybe my speech was my way of telling him I firmly believe that.

Pride beams off Declan, serving as another reminder of how lucky I am to have him. He supports everything I do and all that I want to be. I never imagined I would find anyone who loves me how he does. If we hadn't had our dark times, I'm not sure we would have gotten here. Every mistake we made led us to this moment, creating vital references about who we are and what we want. And the one consistent thing we want is each other. The good, bad, and even ugly are better than living apart.

The ceremony ends a few minutes after that, and Declan's quickly at my side. He picks me up, twirls me, and kisses me. "Great speech, angel. I'm so proud of you," he tells me for the millionth time.

Still, my heart soars just like it does all day around him.

The next hour is full of hugs and congratulations from the O'Malleys and Ivanovs. We all go to the club for a celebration dinner. Declan reserved the largest room they have, and we eat and dance until it gets late.

At the end of the night, my heart is overflowing with love. I glance around the room, feeling grateful for everyone surrounding me. I may not have had a family growing up, but I do now. And I couldn't ask for better people. They're all fierce, loyal, and full of kindness I never knew existed.

When the party ends, we get in the car, and Declan pulls me onto his lap. "Did I tell you how proud of you I am?"

I laugh. "Only a hundred times."

He kisses my neck and sucks on my lobe. His hand slides between my thighs.

My phone rings, and Declan groans. "Which of your friends is that tone for?"

I freeze then reach for my purse and pull it out, my heart racing. "It's an alarm I set."

"Alarm? For what?"

I read the message, and my gut drops.

"Angel, what is it? You're turning pale."

I lock eyes with his confused orbs. "I umm..." I blow out a breath of air. *Shit. Why didn't I tell him about this?*

This is what happens when I eavesdrop.

"Angel?"

"I overheard Finn and you all talking." I bite on my lip.

"About what?"

I admit, "Bridget and Brenna."

Declan's eyes harden. "Why didn't you say anything?"

I cringe. "I don't know. Blame it on pregnancy brain?"

Declan tilts his head. "Really?"

I sigh. "I know. I should have. But...well...okay. So you told Finn to get off Bridget's back."

"So it didn't cause issues with us seeing the kids," he claims.

I shift on his lap. "Yes. I know. But...well..."

"Well, what?" Declan asks, his eyes narrowing in on me.

"I think Bridget is hiding stuff," I blurt out, my pulse beating so hard in my neck, I think it might pop through my skin.

Declan licks his lips then firmly asks, "What did you do, Simona?"

Wincing, I hand him the cell. "I hacked into Bridget's phone and email. She's been sending vague messages to this person, and now she wants to meet in two days." Blood pounds between my ears, and the air turns stale in my lungs. "I'm convinced it's Brenna."

Are you ready for the grand finale of Mafia Wars? Relentless Hunter is going to blow your mind! Get ready for twists and turns! Find out the mystery behind Finn and Brenna! Click and grab it now or flip the page to read the blurb and prologue!

One moment in time changed the course of our lives...

For over two decades, I vow to find her.

I'm locked up.

Full of rage.

Obsessed with remembering every detail about her.

When I get out, I scour the Earth.

Relentlessly.

Mercilessly.

I know she's out there.

I can still feel her, my firefly glowing in the dark.

I'll never stop until she's back in my arms.

READ RELENTLESS HUNTER - FREE ON KINDLE UNLIMITED

FINN O'MALLEY
RELENTLESS HUNTER PROLOGUE

Finn O'Malley

DARCEY ARCHES HER EYEBROWS. "SURE YOU WANT ANOTHER?"

The twenty years I spent in prison didn't cause her to stop butting into my business. I've known the woman since we were kids. Our mothers were cousins. My father passed away when I was under the age of five. Darcey never knew her sperm donor. So to save money and help each other out, our mothers moved in together. She's the closest thing I have to a sister, but she seems to have taken on a nagging role since my mother passed.

Not that I got to say goodbye or even attend her funeral. I was locked up in the pit of Hell and didn't learn about it until my Uncle Darragh informed me during the monthly visitation.

I sniff hard and scowl at Darcey, putting all the rage I'm feeling into it.

Unintimidated and giving me her death glare, she grabs the fifth, refills my crystal tumbler with whiskey, and studies me. Her brown eyes pin onto mine, turning into golden flames.

Not flinching, I down half the liquid, numb to the burn since I've already drunk too much. I'm pissed off and slowly crumbling. There's nothing I can do about it. It's been a year since I got out of prison. Every lead to find Brenna might as well be ashes scattered in Lake Michigan. The few people who know the truth about what happened to her are all dead. I can't even blame it on anyone else. I murdered them. One of them, Judge Peterson, I killed too soon. My anger and frustration spun out of control with every answer he gave me. I'm pretty sure they were all lies. Unable to stop my wrath, I snapped his neck when I yanked his head backward too hard.

Obrecht ended Jack Christian's life either a moment before or after I stole the Judge's last breath. We were both caught up in our personal vendettas, barely able to see straight. Jack was so far gone at that point there was nothing left for me to get out of him. I spent months interrogating him at the Ivanov garage, under Maksim's supervision. Obrecht nor I should have been near Jack until Liam gave us the go-ahead. Neither of us could stay away. We both had our reasons, albeit different. Maksim understood it and controlled us from pissing off Liam.

Darcey's opinion on how much I'm drinking isn't helping the black hole I'm going down. She should know by now it only makes me knock it back faster.

If I were an ordinary man, I'd be happier than anyone on Earth. The plan Liam and I concocted in prison to drive Jack's company to the ground worked. The clan has billions, which means I've got more money than I'll ever spend.

But I've never cared much about money. The O'Malleys spent years earning a living off drugs and gambling. So far, Killian was right. Our windfall only created new problems.

It hasn't been a black and white transition out of the illegal activities rooted in our clan. We have men who only know that life. They aren't corporate and will never be. Plus, they aren't willing to change. Yet, the real struggle is what to do with the territory. Even if we stopped it all tomorrow, it's welcoming another crime family to take control. Unless we have an alliance with them, it's dangerous.

Several months have passed since our bank accounts got fat. I'm more miserable than I've ever been. In prison, I could only obsess about getting out and finding Brenna. Engrained memories of how she felt in my arms or lit me up when she just looked at me, haunted me for those twenty, dark years.

Everything is different now. I'm not a prisoner, living in a world of someday, unable to move forward with my search. I'm in the present, and it's much worse. I have my freedom, yet nothing has led to her.

In prison, the lack of knowledge about where she was and what could be happening to her made my skin crawl. Now that I'm free, the agitation intensifies daily, itching every inch of my flesh.

"Drinking isn't going to get her back," Darcey reprimands.

"Fuck this." I rise, down my drink, then slam it on the bar.

"Easy," Declan orders.

I spin, ready to lose every ounce of control I have left.

Snow covers his head, shoulders, and coat. He holds his hands out. "Sit down."

"I'm done here." I shove past him, storming through the pub and into the back alley. A wet blanket of snow reigns down over me.

"Finn! Stop! I think I know where she is," Declan calls out.

I turn so fast I almost slip, growling, "What are you talking about?"

White flakes thicken in his hair and coat. He squints and holds his hand above his eyes. "Simona hacked into Bridget's electronic communication. She's tracked her since we returned from New York. I looked at the messages. I think it's Brenna."

My mouth turns dry. All the alcohol I drank suddenly is nonexistent. I'm sober as a baby, and every beat my heart takes pounds in my ears. I step closer. "Where is she?"

Declan lowers his voice, then glances behind him. The wind whips fiercer, slapping the cold snow against my cheeks, but I barely feel the sting. His vein near his eye twitches. "She's in New York. Bridget's meeting her at an underground club in two days."

"That lying bitch," I seethe. Over Thanksgiving weekend, I grilled Bridget face to face. She swore she didn't know where Brenna was and only ran into her once by accident. The next night, I saw Bridget again and interrogated her some more, but she kept to her story. She claimed Brenna wouldn't tell her what was going on and begged her not to tell anyone she saw her, then left within minutes. I snarl, "I'm going to kill her."

Declan's eyes widen. "You don't know her reasoning. Don't do something you'll regret."

His brother Sean may have loved Bridget, and Brenna and her might have been close, but I'm past the point of giving anyone mercy. A sarcastic laugh flies out of my mouth and fills the alley. "Don't talk to me about regret. It's all I've known for twenty-one years."

READ RELENTLESS HUNTER - FREE ON KINDLE UNLIMITED

ALL IN BOXSET

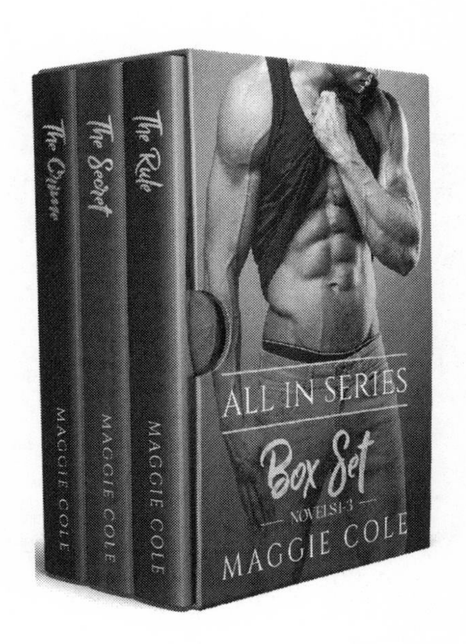

Three page-turning, interconnected stand-alone romance novels with HEA's!! Get ready to fall in love with the characters. Billionaires. Professional athletes. New York City. Twist, turns, and danger lurking everywhere. The only option for these couples is to go ALL IN...with a little help from their friends. EXTRA STEAM INCLUDED!

Grab it now! READ FREE IN KINDLE UNLIMITED!

CAN I ASK YOU A HUGE FAVOR?

Would you be willing to leave me a review?

I would be forever grateful as one positive review on Amazon is like buying the book a hundred times! Reader support is the lifeblood for Indie authors and provides us the feedback we need to give readers what they want in future stories!

Your positive review means the world to me! So thank you from the bottom of my heart!

CLICK TO REVIEW

MORE BY MAGGIE COLE

Mafia Wars - A Dark Mafia Series (Series Five)

Ruthless Stranger (Maksim's Story) - Book One

Broken Fighter (Boris's Story) - Book Two

Cruel Enforcer (Sergey's Story) - Book Three

Vicious Protector (Adrian's Story) - Book Four

Savage Tracker (Obrecht's Story) - Book Five

Unchosen Ruler (Liam's Story) - Book Six

Perfect Sinner (Nolan's Story) - Book Seven

Brutal Defender (Killian's Story) - Book Eight

Deviant Hacker (Declan's Story) - Book Nine

Relentless Hunter (Finn's Story) - Book Ten

Behind Closed Doors (Series Four - Former Military Now International Rescue Alpha Studs)

Depths of Destruction - Book One

Marks of Rebellion - Book Two

Haze of Obedience - Book Three

Cavern of Silence - Book Four

Stains of Desire - Book Five

Risks of Temptation - Book Six

Together We Stand Series (Series Three - Family Saga)

Kiss of Redemption- Book One

Sins of Justice - Book Two

Acts of Manipulation - Book Three

Web of Betrayal - Book Four

Masks of Devotion - Book Five

Roots of Vengeance - Book Six

It's Complicated Series (Series Two - Chicago Billionaires)

Crossing the Line - Book One

Don't Forget Me - Book Two

Committed to You - Book Three

More Than Paper - Book Four

Sins of the Father - Book Five

Wrapped In Perfection - Book Six

All In Series (Series One - New York Billionaires)

The Rule - Book One

The Secret - Book Two

The Crime - Book Three

The Lie - Book Four

The Trap - Book Five

The Gamble - Book Six

STAND ALONE NOVELLA

JUDGE ME NOT - A Billionaire Single Mom Christmas Novella

ABOUT THE AUTHOR

Amazon Bestselling Author

Maggie Cole is committed to bringing her readers alphalicious book boyfriends. She's been called the "literary master of steamy romance." Her books are full of raw emotion, suspense, and will always keep you wanting more. She is a masterful storyteller of contemporary romance and loves writing about broken people who rise above the ashes.

She lives in Florida near the Gulf of Mexico with her husband, son, and dog. She loves sunshine, wine, and hanging out with friends.

Her current series were written in the order below:

- All In (Stand alones with entwined characters)
- It's Complicated (Stand alones with entwined characters)
- Together We Stand (Brooks Family Saga - read in order)
- Behind Closed Doors (Read in order)
- Mafia Wars (Coming April 1st 2021)

Maggie Cole's Newsletter
Sign up here!

Hang Out with Maggie in Her Reader Group
Maggie Cole's Romance Addicts

Follow for Giveaways
Facebook Maggie Cole

Instagram
@maggiecoleauthor

Tik Tok
https://www.tiktok.com/@authormaggiecole?

Complete Works on Amazon
Follow Maggie's Amazon Author Page

Book Trailers
Follow Maggie on YouTube

Are you a Blogger and want to join my ARC team?
Signup now!

Feedback or suggestions?

Email: authormaggiecole@gmail.com

twitter.com/MaggieColeAuth
instagram.com/maggiecoleauthor
bookbub.com/profile/maggie-cole
amazon.com/Maggie-Cole/e/B07Z2CB4HG

Made in the USA
Columbia, SC
09 July 2024

38410620R00286